W 34

Professor Boardman:
   with appreciation,
and sincere regards,
        Jitka
        4/94.

Liston Pope Jr

REDEMPTION
A Novel of War in Lebanon

N.A. GILBERT & SONS, PUBLISHERS

Copyright © 1994 by Liston Pope Jr.

All Rights Reserved

Library of Congress Cataloging in Publication Data:

Pope, Liston Jr. 1943–
Redemption: A Novel of War in Lebanon
1. Lebanese Conflict, 1975-   Fiction
   Palestinians, Phalangists, Israel, U. S.
   Mideast relations   I. Title

93-91788
ISBN 0-9638900-0-X

Distributed to the trade in the United States
and Canada by N. A. Gilbert & Sons, 126 West 73rd Street,
Suite 11A, New York, N.Y. 10023-3030

FIRST EDITION

REDEMPTION

PART ONE

I

The radio erupted: the war. Burst of static, like a distant salvo. It seemed to blast the core of Elie's being, as a male voice spoke in code, with an urgency. Jessie gave a groping motion, upward, pushing away his caresses. With a brusque movement she swept her pencil and compass to the floor.

She gave a cry; but in an instant her fingers came alive; she began to locate her materials and execute.

—Get the compass, she hissed: pick it up!

Elie went limp, breathing deeply. He reached beneath the table for the instrument. On one knee, his cheek brushed the hem of her skirt; he leaned further, kissing Jessie's thigh.

—Hurry! she whispered. Stop it!

With all his soul he wanted to cry out in fear and anguish. Just cling there, to her womanly legs, and dissolve. He cringed at her feet underneath the table.

But she reached down and cuffed him hard, meaning business. He heard her ordering him to get up, and give back the compass. When she reached down for it he kissed her hand convulsively; but with a force she clutched his wrist, and jabbed his cheek with the needle.

Then, stunned, he withdrew from her. He stood up, unsteadily, as she went on with her range finding. From this ground floor apartment in East Beirut she was aiming the Phalangist big guns. She spoke into the transmitter, like a solemn prayer, and then stood by for corrections from an emplacement high in the hills overlooking the city.

Jessica lived in the rear apartment of a rez-de-chaussée on Rue St. Louis in the Christian neighborhoods. A half hour earlier her boyfriend, Elie Madi, had brought his jeep to a skidding halt and hopped down, as the dust flew up. The bright late morning sunlight lent shadows of an eerie depth to the scene of shorn trees, a calcified Mercedes-Benz, a rail dangling from a third-floor balcony.

Shelling ebbed and flowed across the city, as the Phalangists tightened their death grip around one of the refugee camps, which fought on alone toward the bitter end. Elie had paused an instant, and looked around: it was a sunlit, subtropical war fought amid elegant buildings. There was an elegy of the old epicurean Lebanon in the air, in the festive sky and aqueous breeze, in the view of snow peaked mountains bathed in a bluish haze. Depending on the wind he had a whiff of burning oil, marine and seaweed smells, an odor of rotten meat.

No front door; no glass remained in any window. The upper storeys had caught a mortar through the roof. The facade showed a hole two meters wide, charred casements, windows like a vacant stare: the rocket was a Syrian calling card.

For the moment the Syrians were playing both sides. They would keep the Phalangists in place, if possible, while helping them crush any threat posed by Palestinian forces to Syrian designs on the country. On Jessie's building were graffiti in a florid Arabic script:

To be free: now is that so much to ask?

He was feeling anxious, and approached her door, past the stairwell, with a timidity. He knocked, leaning to listen.
—Jess?
—Who is it?
—Me, Elie.
Then she opened. She sat in her wheelchair before him, a hand held out in vague welcome. Her pale blue eyes stared through him, distantly, as he stepped inside.

He bowed, taking her hand to his lips. He kissed her head and pressed it to him. For the space of a deep breath, she acquiesced.

Like him, she was so tired: the temptation of love, between them, was something immense.

—Your shirt is torn, she said, feeling his chest. It's stained, and you smell bad. Why are you here?

She drew back and stared up at him, but opaquely, as if unsure.

Elie stood looking down at her. Should he tell the truth? Did he dare? If not to Jessie, then who? Her head was tilted up, with the thick glasses enlarging her eyes.

Now she swung away, as from the inner space of the apartment a radio erupted. A voice was relaying a message in code. Jessie wheeled herself back to her work table.

II

Her fingers began to dance among the materials there: compass, protractor, a clinometer, as if relocating not them so much as herself among them. Elie Madi frowned at a model in papier-maché of Beirut and environs. It showed Bourj Hammoud and the strategic bridges on around through Sinn Il-Fill, Jisr Il-Wati, Chiyah-Ein Rummaneh front, the Hippodrome and Museum area, Tayouneh, the airport, "belt of misery" camps; an isolated marking for Damour fifteen kilometers south of the capital, on the far edge of the table.

The strategic Camp was ringed and set off by a band of shimmering tinfoil.

There were pointers on small movable swivels to represent conning lines: from Dbayyeh and Beit Mery, Broumanna and other Phalangist emplacements. It was all to-scale, reproducing every side street and building of any prominence on the Beirut landscape. It was the dream-toy of an eccentric child.

There were charts and terrain maps; also tools, a t-square, a battery-lit reading glass for the nearly blind administrator of such a domain. Jessie's world. She spoke low into the transmitter, then listened and began to verify her reading. The effort at precision seemed in contrast to the rest of her being: to the cow-eyed and gentle cast of her features. It was a fierce, mute contest in which she would prove her skill despite everything.

In code she gave the requested data. Her fingers had a life of their own, manipulating the instruments.

Elie was unfamiliar with the code she used. There were reference marks for the city divided in quadrants. There were angles and adjustments of angles, rectifying artillery lines.

While she made her calculations, he paced and fidgeted. He felt breathlessly tender, watching her concentrate over a second problem. In the light of a desk lamp her movements were self-assured. She was strictly business, though with the air of a little girl. She had the quasi-angelic aura of the youthful blind.

More than ever her manner wrung Elie's heart and made him feel protective. She took her reading and turned to transmit in a low, careful tone.

Cellophane crackled as he devoured a packet of melba toast two by two. It tasted like nothing on earth after a day of fasting. On the counter stood a half bottle of soda.

He went to wash in the bathroom, forgetting there was no tap water. Also, her ration in a 5-gallon container was nearly finished. He stood staring in the mirror; and his own image, unkempt and red-eyed, blood on his shoulder, made him turn away in disgust.

Jessie stared toward him. He began,

—It's happened.

—What?

—Sakr — Abu Joseph sent an order to snipe the Camp spigot at all hours. Women have been dying there for days, trying to get water. So I let them do it, a few hours, and then left my post.

—You . . . ?

Elie said quietly,

—Think about it. Who isn't trying to destroy that Camp, including major powers? They provide the means, Jessie, we take care of the details.

He gestured toward her table, and the intricate terrain of war.

She lowered her gaze, seeming to shrink in the wheelchair. There was a burst of static; a voice began quoting figures over the radio, like faroff detonations. She responded with eagerness.

III

Elie took a chair and settled in beside her. He worked his fingers, as if kneading his anguish with a small rocking motion.

She sat forward, electrified. The war with its forces and targets was laid in her lap like a bouquet of flowers. Jessie's fingers strode along the hotel front and then leapt away toward the ridges of Mount Lebanon, Jbeil El-Knisseh. They arched the green distance in 7-league boots. She made a rectification and spoke in the transmitter: range, azimuth.

Now she interposed that same eagle's gaze between herself and Elie. She shied from any further revelations. A traitor? So her lover was a coward?

They had known one another since childhood and been sweethearts for six years. Their relationship was a source of shared experience, of passion and strength amid trials. They were part of each other's family. They drew their faith and belief in life from a same Maronite Catholic community: the famous Maronite Christians of Lebanon, known as right-wing to the wide world,—with their Phalangist paramilitary, also called Kataëb,—when all they wanted was to hang on to what was theirs.

With panic he sensed what awaited him: once he left her dim apartment. He felt drained of his manhood, staring at her across the miniature city, her domain of geometry and death, with a respect as deep as his yearning.

After her near fatal wound he spent a season by her bedside at the Hôtel-Dieu. Then as now, his gaze entreated Jessie's for a hopeful response. For hours he held her hand, stroking her. She let him nuzzle her breasts and kiss her, night after night, as if his caresses were the cure. She clung to him like a hope of walking again. Soon they would be married; soon as the savage war ended. They would have children together despite everything: soon as there was peace.

Be married. The phrase had a magic ring, as if the world could change its aspect. Be married, walk and even dance again, with Elie's help. His way of loving always aroused the highest expectations. Yet a little while, and then joy, together. His kindness would survive the Syrian snipers, crisscrossing Ashrafiyeh.

But then, gradually, she had changed. It seemed no amount of love could drive away her despair at being crippled. With her vision severely impaired, the world had lost its brightness and contour; except this tiny part of it, here before her. Crippled, forever. Never stand on her own two feet again. Marriage for a paraplegic? Joy, motherhood for such a person? It was a joke, and she began hearing the sound of demonic laughter. As if organ-notes could mock someone in prayer.

The political situation worsened. The Maronite community felt trapped and insecure in the extreme; as well as badly treated by world opinion. In those days there was anger everywhere in the Christian sectors. Jessie's people emigrated to France; they fled to the waiting arms of *Umm al-Hannouneh,* the nursing mother. But she was determined to stay, and defeat the evil on its own terrain.

Elie, at that juncture, would have been glad to leave the country. But his mother, already a widow, with her simple and conservative ways, had no intention of moving from the parental house in Hazmieh.

Then the second of Jessie's brothers was killed. On intelligence assignment in West Beirut, he was kidnapped by a Muslim group and never returned. Jessie hadn't been to the other side since receiving her degree in electrical engineering from the American University, in June '75. Elie Madi hadn't crossed Rue Damas since April 13, 1975, when a bus massacre in Ein Rummaneh triggered civil war. He was a veteran, ranking Phalangist and well known for it.

She began withdrawing from him emotionally; although her mind showed every sign of regaining its former vigor. The long despair was depriving her of capacity to love, and say yes to him. As if locked in a dark closet with the garments of a former self, in which she had lived to the fullest: now Jessie knew the sad pastime of trying them on, feeling herself a mature woman in them, only to measure the change. Old outfits of first love and devotion were altered for the purpose of sorrow, vigil; then hatred as a prime means of survival. From month to month she withdrew from Elie's own deep need, his silent entreaty. She was losing the ability to respond. Also, her body seemed odious to her, a burden. Being crippled meant she was always in the way. In company, what means to smooth over the situation? What plausible excuse?

Never slender, now with inactivity she lost her firmness and grew bovine; though her appetite was sporadic. She took his more fervent, extravagant lovemaking either for lust or an aroused pity, a kind of perversion. Touching one another, sex was becoming a negative field between them. Besides, she felt sated. She needed time, months or years maybe to get a grip on this new situation. Nothing felt certain anymore. Love wasn't essential, it dawned on Jessica, but in fact secondary. In its place had come a chronic hatred, had begun a kind of corrosive action. Love started to fade along with the old peacetime ideas, wage earning and rearing of children, the good things of home and family relations.

At present the effects of a shard of shrapnel beneath her cranium were paralyzation from the waist down, and near total myopia. Her plans for living happily ever after and marrying her childhood sweetheart, Elie Madi, were being postponed. She felt a cringing in herself, a sort of dirtiness; as a wound to her selfhood, which festered.

What a need she had to retaliate! It was an obsession during most of her waking hours: to punish the perpetrators of such... an abomination.

Revulsed by her helplessness; exposed to the view of others; she went along groping, unseeing, helpless. More and more she retreated from Elie's intimacy, but was unable to break with him. After all, she wore his ring on her finger. He had worked and saved for months to buy it. She all but squirmed beneath his caresses, thinking of when they would end.

Of late a different sentiment had worked its way to the forefront of Jessie's mind, no less impassioned, and voluptuous. Another idea was beginning to repay her for the utter inadequacy, the feeling of filth deep in a maimed being.

That idea was patriotism.

IV

He sat by the table and waited. It was no small matter to sit still, as he watched her girlish solemnity, her agility within fixed limits. Elie had noticed her growing confidence and felt twinges of jealousy; his thoughts tended to start out hopeful, when he looked at her, when the past came back to him, but then plummeted to where all seemed lost, all absent. Was he intruding?

From one message to the next he tried to grasp a code word or an indication. She was targetting for a battery of field artillery high above Zalke, and tucked in a distant sky ridge. He knew the place: far below, in one of the forested valleys, there was a quarry gouged out of the mountainside.

Now she relaxed, slumping back in the wheelchair. She sighed when a lull finally came; she was cast back on his moody silence. Her slightly bowed head had an obstinate air. Her forehead was overlarge, but beautiful to him.

He felt cut off by her pale blue gaze from emotions lurking in the dilated night behind them.

She said,

—So you're a deserter.

—I sat there in my vantage point, waiting for them to come. Women in ragged black robes, one by one, approaching the spigot half bent-over... I thought of you.

She raised her head like an exclamation:

—You'd do better thinking of your superior, and doing what Abu Joseph orders. In the larger scheme he knows what counts. It isn't a few ignorant peasant women.

—Sakr the sadist? said Elie, though hesitant to contradict her. He knows quite a lot; maybe that's why he drank champagne after the Karantina massacre, with international press looking on.

—Be careful, said Jessie. Careful what you say.

—You think I'm a traitor? Listen, I'll say what I like... if it's true.

—Different truths, she said, for different eyes.

—But there are facts.

—You have yours, I have mine.

She turned her head like an object. She gazed past him toward the front of the apartment: was she expecting someone? Her left hand flitted over the model in papier-maché, her thumb and index describing slow arcs between the Rizk and Murr skyscrapers, which had become opposing emplacements across East and West Beirut.

He frowned, shaking his head:

—Jess, I'm sorry. Sakr sees nothing in the larger scheme.

—My scheme yes, she murmured, he does. But yours has changed.

V

There was another radio call. He stood and paced while she worked as if he wasn't there. When she finished Elie stood behind her, rubbing her shoulders, bowing to kiss the back of her neck.

—I love you, he whispered. I love you more than ever: I'd do anything for you.

—Then, then you'll have to go back—

—I want you, he leaned round to kiss her forehead, his fingers playing in the light-brown hair on her temple.

He burrowed his lips in her neck while his hand went down on her breasts.

He knelt beside her, nuzzling.

But then, suddenly, the radio erupted again with a burst of static. And that was when, fending him, intent on doing her duty, she jabbed his cheek with her compass needle. And Elie's blood began to spurt.

VI

—We went through it before, Elie. You're disturbing me, and not only me that means. Think what you like, with your new "beliefs"— my work is important.

—Were can I go? he said.

—Ask forgiveness of Abu Joseph. Maybe he'll reinstate you, with a demotion. But first go wash yourself, you smell bad.

—No water.

—You said you loved me; that you'd do as I asked. I thought you meant it . . . And I am asking you, no I'm telling you to go back and find your proper place in all this. There's no other way, Elie, you have to be what you are! And please, in future don't expect me to play this mother role anymore, I don't like it. Now leave me alone, this is no time for—

She gave a gesture.

His cheek was bleeding, a rill in the dark stubble of his jaw. He put his thumb to the puncture and stared glumly at her. After a moment he let the blood trickle on his collar and neck as if to say: what's the use? It flowed and he felt it sticky along his neck. He shook his bowed head; shook it back and forth, stirring up the frustration, and then said:

—Like others, you've been hurt. You want revenge. You say, that if I love you I must join in and do the same; but this is something I can't do, Jessica, hate others because I love you. Perhaps it's the only thing. You make me love others. You have that effect on me, like it or not! I say this isn't my fault, and I'll feel the same no matter what happens. Even if you, like Sakr, decide to hold me in contempt. And let me tell you something, let me tell you one more thing: there will never be an end, to this. No end! Not until the hatred has cancelled out everything including itself, the way you're asking me to do. And then nothing is left to love.

—That isn't true, she said, vehemently. Your reasoning is off. We all have to pull together and fight, for now. And you also, it's your destiny, your struggle. And we must die, if need be, for the honor of our country, so that our descendants can be free. If this isn't love on our part, love of the highest kind, then what is it?

—Oh honor of Lebanon! Elie's voice rose, in anger. The same old refrain! Will someone please inform me what is Lebanon? The old way is dying all around us, can't you see? But which Lebanon do you mean? You say the name like it was our prize possession. And woe to anyone who thinks he can be more than a guest here. But what of the others? What about those on the other side, those widows at the spigot? Are they less entitled? Did God create them to live in a camp? What makes us so special?

He broke off, breathless. His words lingered in the small apartment. Jessie said, in a girlish tone:

—They ruined me.

—No, Elie raised his voice, and gaze. It's you, then, if anyone, who should see the truth. You told me, my destiny is to kill them. But I say, yours is to forgive.

—Never.

—And then?

—We'll win, instead.

—Win? With Sakr leading us? You think his kind will ever win anything? His honor is like diapers, stained every hour.

—Especially with Sakr leading us! Listen, those savages came here, we never invited them. They stirred up this trouble, justifying it all with lies.

The radio burst forth again.

—No! Elie snarled, jumping forward and grabbing the receiver. He placed it on the counter beyond her grasp.

—Give that to me.

She looked around, groping.

—Not until I'm finished. We're the ones, Jess, who started. We crowded them in filthy camps, paying them low wages to work in our factories. I'm tired of denying it. And no citizenship for them, lowly Palestinians. Never, as you say. We paid lip service to their cause, many of us, while showing them no mercy. Admit it! We were hindering their struggle in every way. And then, after two decades the camps broke free and we had less to say in the matter. And all the while our "honor" was the old Lebanese opportunism, the Phoenician way of enslaving. Brother, can you get ahead of others? But unlike the great Phoenicians, those slave masters we claim as our ancestors, we did it right here at home. My father did it, in his time; your father the same. Only more efficiently. Better a banker than a teacher. All the older generation, Jessie: we're paying for their mistakes. And now, finally, I admit it.

She said coolly:

—Give me the radio.

Her tone was an implicit threat. But the speaker emitted more static; it spluttered like a wounded thing on the counter.

—When I'm finished, he said. I was addressing our "honor".

But the radio wouldn't give up. Her hand stayed out, like a precondition.

He nodded, and his body seemed to slacken. He turned, transferring the apparatus back to its place.

For a few minutes he sat and waited. Once he erupted like the radio, talking to himself:

—Don't criticize ... you're a traitor!

—Shut up! Jessie threw down her compass. You think we haven't suffered? What about *our* suffering? A quarter million Maronites driven from their homes. Twenty-five thousand orphans in Lebanon, and maybe you think none are ours? And what about 1860! You've forgotten that too?

But she broke off and relocated her instruments, which had a vicarious life to them. There was a certainty when she plied them, a kind of second personality.

—What I do, she said, glaring at him, I have a right.

—We hate ourselves, he said, nodding. And the thing is clear to me, so clear it's blinding. Don't criticize, oh never break ranks. Not from childhood! All those goddamned lectures, all the "entertainment" we had to sit through. Train the body, school the mind. Always ready for your call, my Lebanon. Lebanon is six thousand years old, Phalangist. Being sacred, it is also eternal. It rejects Islam, Arabism! For subservient, *dhimmi* we will never be, and you'll see to it, O Knights of the Virgin! O Wood of the Cross! O Youth of Saint Maroun! God, Fatherland and Family—and down with all those others, the unclean ones, who would kill us if we relaxed our guard a single instant. Phoenicians not Arabs, do you hear? On us depends the survival of Lebanon, the democratic heartland. Who invented the alphabet, if not us? Who wrote the Bible? Who evolved the *polis* if not us, our ancestors? And so we say it, all together: them! them! We chant it proudly: *them* we must exterminate! And then the place will be clean again, it will shine like a goddamned paradise. Oh Jessie it's so terribly clear to me. Black Saturday was a tea party! It was a means of therapy; it freed us, for a day, from the guilt of centuries... See how the guilty, using any pretext, lash out at their victims.

VII

He lingered. He persisted in staying, and after awhile his eyelids began to droop. Elie appeared to doze when the static and urgent voices tuned off for a spell. Whether from concern after all or a kind of courtesy, fear of his anger perhaps, Jessie had not insisted she wanted him to leave. Of course she resented his words; she rejected his critique of the Party. This was written on her features, a part of her personality. She opposed him now with her silence, but no longer seemed as confounded by the change in him. She showed no regret that two people essential to her life had undergone a serious, if not irreparable, falling out; instead, she appeared to retrench for the sake of her beliefs under attack.

Her first reaction had been to defend these, using any means to keep her faith from tarnish. And no matter what the cost to her relationship! Wasn't she beset upon by all sides? Her work was frantic in these hours,—and then in he stomped, looking for apron strings in his own time of crisis. Chaos was at the gates of Ashrafiyeh. She had no surplus of strength.

She only knew what she had experienced, what her education taught her. This was no time for a lover's quarrel; this was a time for rallying to the aid of the Party, and the Maronite Catholics of Lebanon.

He sat dreading departure, deeply exhausted. Need dictated that he curl up alongside her, and refuse to budge. Beyond her doorway there was a scene in progress, a reality he felt unready to face. A day of sunlight and horror. He shied away from any further role.

From the window facing west he saw wide stubblefield: an abandoned construction site, its frame like the gray contours of a truncated future. Combs of construction rods twisting at odd angles, like frazzled gestures. After his night of sniping the spigot, one of the Camp's few water sources, he felt shaken and vulnerable for some reason.

Now he had lost her, estranged his beloved and for the sake of what? Now he must pay the price in loneliness. In a moment he would go outside, and say hello to a world of hatred.

Love wasn't something you found lying around, even in normal times. Why jeopardize it? Why oblige the person you cherished to fight your battles? Let her do things in her own way . . . But too late now! She held him in suspicion like the others, considering him little less than an enemy spy. No love for Elie Madi—not out there, and not in here, anymore.

His own voice embarrassed him when he asked her something; its tone was fear in the essence. Like a small boy tugging at his mother.

—I'll get a boat. There must be a launch somewhere, in the port, or Jounieh Bay.

—And then what? she said, wearily, as if praying God the radio would leave her alone for a few minutes.

—We'll go to Cyprus. We could be happy, Jess, a normal life with kids. I'll be the housewife; you can go to the office.

—Normal life! Jessie laughed. First we couldn't make it anywhere, not to the end of my street, with this wheelchair. In a hundred years we couldn't reach Jounieh because of snipers at the bridges. Or down to the port either. But say we did, and just happened to find a rowboat lying around. I can see us floating offshore together: they'd use us for targetting, our own people from the hills.

He said softly:

—I meant we could go at night.

But her words were like a slap.

She took another call. For a moment he stared at her, his eyebrows raised in a kind of pleading. Then his head fell on his chest.

Outside, there was a barrage of shelling. A file of tanks bucked down a street in the neighborhood; he heard their caterpillars, massive, prodding. Missiles screeched off from a field in the sector: down from the heights of Ashrafiyeh toward the tumbledown morass of the Camp under siege.

She turned toward him:

—There's no Cyprus, Elie. Go where you belong.

—If it's no good anymore? If it isn't right?

—It is more than right. Survival...

—Too late, Jessie. Survival instinct isn't enough, to survive. Too late for us.

—Never! Not in the ninth century A.D., and not now: as long as a Maronite is left here.

—And the million and a half living abroad? Maybe they're of the same opinion.

—They don't count.

—Except when it comes to justifying our privileges.

—We earned them!

—Enforced them, you mean, starting with what we inherited from France.

—Is this some kind of debate?

—Dammit, why are you all so blind?

At this she blushed crimson. She raised the pale orbits of her gaze more or less toward him. It was her turn for a slap, as if this last insult capped all the others. First her beliefs, then her profession and way of life; now her chosen people—maligned by Elie. It was the first time really her attention forsook the miniature city, its intricate suburbs and landscape of a gun-layer. But she rose to the height of her pride. She had never been pretty, alluring mainly to Elie Madi.

She stared at him:
—Right, I'm blind. And you see.
—I'm sorry!

He crossed over and fell to his knees before her. He tried to take her hand, but she held back and said, coldly:
—Don't be.

He was weeping suddenly and pressed his forehead on her knee.
—Forgive me, Jess. I want to stay here with you, I'm so afraid!

Her hand was poised over his dark, shaggy head which rocked and gasped for air amid tears. She hung on the brink of her love for him, and their past. But his emotion was a warning.
—Elie.
—I don't want, he sobbed, to go back out there. You should see them . . . in the Camp.

He was all but writhing on the floor beneath her, with his arms a death-grip on her knees.
—You have to get up.
—Love me! he entreated, from a wrenching emptiness. He grabbed her fingers and tried to fix them to his head.

But she withdrew her hand, and the gesture had a new note to it. In a moment he hung limp by her motionless legs.

VIII

—I'm going. I don't know when I'll see you again.
—Do your work, and then come back.

He leaned forward, pressing his cheek to her forehead.
—Since we were children: as soon as I found you, I always loved you.

He gave a long lover's kiss on her eyes, then her lips, and she seemed on the verge of submitting. Jessie was opening like petals, offering herself to his virile light. For a long moment he caressed her, and it seemed her will was beginning to fuse, once more, with his.

But this time he drew away. She stared up at him with her lips parted, in a sudden fulness, an astonishment.

The tide of his life had been ebbing, for months by now; and it held her from him in what seemed the retraction of a last emotional wave. And then she was beyond his reach, a marking on the beach where she'd decided to make her stand.

The wide world's hatred had come to visit East Beirut. Jessica held out her hand toward Elie, as if to receive something. He bowed his head, kissing her fingers.

—Take care of yourself.

He wiped his tears with her hand, jabbing his lips with her figertips.

—I still care for you, she said.

At sight of her his heart seemed to contract. He turned away, crying for himself, and for her, and all the abandoned people, the orphans.

—I know.

He hugged her briefly and then went out.

IX

Bright slides were projected along the back wall at Ydlibbi's, a nightclub hidden away like a maggot in the carcass of downtown Beirut. People and smiles, breaking in waves of color over the smoke filled bar and gaming tables. Slides of revellers in Raousche, former nightlife district on the seafront Corniche; they lounged, the men portly, the women in décolletage, amid a spread of hommos dishes. There were the Upside-Down Girls of the renowned Kitkat Club, twirling their legs like batons. The old, timeless Lebanon, a sensuous paradise, where money grew lush on the tree of knowledge.

Elie entered, as a new slide flicked on: tanned, beaming gourmets gazed from Bahri's Restaurant, on stilts above the emerald Mediterranean. Waves washed a sun-flecked hem of kelp along the strange rock shelf encircling Beirut.

He paused, once in the door. His mission: find a British journalist named Ligury and bring him across to the Christian sectors. In the port area, Ydlibbi's was frequented by Phalangist officers as well as Syrian regulars; leaders of the Palestinian Resistance, and, no doubt, an Israeli spy or three mulling the elegant, late night crowd. Just being here Elie Madi risked his life; such were the new orders: he was seconded to the Phalangist press liaison Fadi Krem, for special projects. They were testing him. But no more sniping widows at the Camp spigot; and Sakr had sat silently irate at the War Council meeting.

In civilian clothes, Elie knew the scene. At the long bar stood a Western woman on the arm of an urbane, graying Italian: when in Beirut the man could be found down here womanizing, a millionaire pappagallo whose line was anyone's guess. The woman laughed low with a slight toss of the head: not that she was fancy; she was more than that, as her blond hair picked up a warm glow from the slides. Then she spoke seriously; but her smile, raising an eyebrow at the Italian, held a promise of sensual power. Politics, sex. At sight of her the militiamen along Hamra came to attention. A weary businessman, alerted, in the amber haze of Ydlibbi's, had a sense of exotic adolescence.

At a table near the bar Kim Ligury, Mideast correspondent for a British weekly, sat listening to the timbre of her voice when Elie Madi approached and, introducing himself, took a chair. Alongside them a German photographer emitted sighs of appreciative lust.

—We want you to tour.
—Why?

The woman leaned back: she turned halfway and faced the Italian with her eyes only, making conversation now. She wore a business suit, tailored with a hemline beneath the knees. She was tallish, statuesque. A strand of pearls set off her neck to the third button of a beige, silken blouse, her cleavage.

—Tour Ashrafiyeh. See what's happening to the Lebanese Christians.
—And security?

She might have been displaying herself for the journalist's sake, or the club in general; but she seemed, for a moment, so deadly serious, so complete unto herself.

—Two weeks ago, said Ligury, turning to the German, I spent a night with her.
—What's her name?
—It wasn't fun. She seemed... less than thrilled with me, distant.

Elie sat there, feeling ignored, his proposal hanging in the air. That afternoon the press officer told him: human relations are an art. You show no emotion: only the positive. Don't trust what you feel. And finesse your questions: know who you're talking to. If possible, establish trust: be attentive, look for your openings.

In here, the casual talk at midnight, with a keen eye for a sexual partner. Out there, in the contested sectors, people dying. A rocket through the roof of Jessica's building.

—Maybe I was too eager, said the correspondent, with a grin.

Elie waited, listening to the chatter.

Ligury turned back to him, raising an eyebrow, and laughed.

Meanwhile the woman ecompassed the club with a kind of sneer, a je-ne-sais-quoi, demonic,—not without charm, like an intellectual approach to action. It left little hope for Ligury or the others. In the next instant she gave a gesture: of irritation, casual dismissal as her worldly escort said the wrong sort of thing: something male, or too political, and she responded: Oh such matters are not for me, really; I came along for the ride, maybe a little adventure. Serious, gorgeous, the more glittery for her conservative suit, she was the center ring. But who was she?

The photographer rose.

—I'm acquainted with the gentleman. I'll invite them.

X

—So you think the Camp will fall?

A PLO official turned his chair round from an adjacent table. He met the blond woman's eye: he too was a friend of hers? Then a glimpse at Elie.

—You'd think the developed world might intervene. But tell me, why such brutality? And when in history has a ruling class sought to extend revolution?

The official was in his late thirties, well spoken, handsome. He led a double life as a socialite.

The photographer sipped his bourbon with a morbid, salacious air. Now and again his eye, like a flashbulb, lit up her beige blouse.

—Marie Antoinette urged civil war, Ligury remarked, with a smug over-educated glint, for her lone benefit.

The PLO man spoke intently:

—Certain Maronite leaders were pro-Arab in the old days, but they realized that without Washington their power could only wane, as the Lebanese masses grew impatient. Listen,—he glanced at

Elie,—the Phalangists are provoking us. It is their plan to draw in outside forces. While, for months, we have kept out of the war.

—The U.S. may intervene, said the woman, if people in the Camp begin starving.

—But they are! said the leader. And the U.S. will not, unless we submit, unless we accept what's decided for us.

Elie listened. The Western woman seemed a trifle petulant at the official's smooth self-assurance. She nodded when the German photographer finally erupted, after anguished minutes of a stifled pedantry, taking another line. The Palestinian waited him out, and then turned to Ligury:

—Fifty percent of the people here are dirt poor. Four percent of the families, mainly Maronite and a few Sunni, were rich before the war . . . with thirty-two percent of the GNP.

While he poured forth statistics Elie Madi looked at the fashionable woman for whose attention they were vying. His mental reflex was to contrast her with Jessie; though she too wasn't coquettish: a smile of sensual irony played on her lips. Was she mocking all of them? She avoided Ligury's eye, preferring the debate or facile talk with her Italian. Elie imagined her in bed with the correspondent: a sort of subtle brutality, a bit of perfunctory eroticism as the fighting raged across Beirut. Like something she took, that night, against the insomnia of war zones, the blahs of high priced, international prostitution?

XI

Kim Ligury rose, somewhat brusquely, and went to the bar. A moment later Elie followed him, with a question:

—Are you free tomorrow? We'll get you across.

But Ligury blurted, almost comically:

—Have you ever felt that intimate . . . jabbing sense of a woman's freedom?

A lover's confession. Elie Madi frowned, at first. Clearly she had been too much for him, and now the jealousy made itself felt.

—Insidious, said Ligury, the way it sneaks up on you, like a spasm.

So sex wasn't always intimacy; so sex, for the female, might even be flight, avoidance. A hard lesson for a little man. And just now, catching Morgan's eye, Morgan was her name, in a fleeting glimpse

Ligury sensed all the excitement of their encounter a fortnight ago. After chatting an hour she drove him to his apartment where they unwrapped one another like packages. A dangerous toy. But to this moment he didn't know her last name, or where she was stopping, or what she was up to.

—Was I taken in? said the journalist; and Elie nodded, with something calmly tragic in his own eye, remembering the scene at Jessie's apartment. There was a ripeness about her, that night...

And the earth moved beneath them with a grave, with a sumptuous passion: so be it, so be it.

—But I was mistaken. I thought we would see each other often, that once implied a series. No; she disappeared from the scene. I thought she was gone; though from day to day my sense of her grew. Do you know that feeling? It gives me a pained sort of thrill, seeing her again: in public that is, never alone, she'll make certain of that.

From the bar they gazed at her: she let her eye rove the candlelit tables. The Kuwaiti owner, Ydlibbi, paid a fortune to all sides so he could maintain this business like the foreplay of an orgy. Here in no-man's-land, in the shadow of the Ring of Death, between East and West.

Ligury paused over his arak, easing in. The Arab music was a desert pantheism.

—Pant-theism..., he mused. What are we all doing here? Lebanon, and space, and time.

He thought of her secrets.

A child appeared, selling roses. Young features, but a hard brightness to them, the mature midget. And the roses: fake or real? It would cost the Italian less than change, a small fortune for the hawker, to find out.

XII

Faces gleamed in the amber light, reflecting the flashing slides. There was a pleasure in deep fatigue.

Morgan and the Palestinian, Mamdoueh, were back at the gambling tables. The German photographer sat nodding and talked over the geopolitical situation with himself.

Elie felt like leaving; he wanted to get up and say goodbye. As for Ligury, the feminine or virile force of Morgan had relegated his will. There would be no plans made this night.

The Phalangist had an impulse to roam out into the night of war without pausing to duck, without breaking his stride. Not in his jeep but walking, down along Wadi Abu Jamil and under the concrete ramp of the Ring of Death. What if he strolled straight through Burj, the Place des Martyrs, in the moonlight? Moving like an apparition across to Ashrafiyeh, with its tragic Maronites suffering their agony of *libanisme*?

—Hey, said Ligury, growing drunk.

—Hm?

—Man, it's absurd! Just tell me: why are there snipers? An ontological problem. Why a Civil War in the first place, why a Green Line? So history can get to the other side. A joke. Say, this phenomenon of other people, it's a lark really. Who is Morgan? How are they feeling at this moment in the Camp? What's it like to die trying to get water: as our own Kohler, sitting right here, has shown the world in a prize winning photo?

Ligury was drunk.

There were European whores in the crowd; they frequented the pool at St. George Hotel by day. Another prize shot: bikini'd woman toting an AK. Oh, the pompous Kohler knew how to make hay in Lebanon. Elie gazed at the slides: bright and breezy, they click-click'd on a dozen mini-screens. People laughing together or in pensive portraiture, swimming and skiing on the same day, like prewar tourist brochures still in circulation. There were elegant men and women who dined and danced, touching the pleasure points. As if a smile could never fade, and joy was a four course menu.

Now Morgan stood alongside Mamdoueh across the chic nightclub. A hand on his shoulder, breast to his elbow she looked over the roulette table and assortment of players.

XIII

Ligury pushed back his chair and stood up.

—Think I'm going.

The weariness lent a sense of shame, as if one's subconscious were exposed. There were serious words mingled with laughter, a calm effrontery as people leered from the bar. They parodied the slides.

—I'll leave as well, said the German. We can get a cab together.

—I have a car, said Morgan, returning. Why not let me drop you?

Elie watched as the Palestinian took Ligury to one side. The two had hardly exchanged a word all evening. He listened?

—I could get you inside the Camp. Interested?

—Why me?

—So the story is told. I'll call you if it is possible.

They exchanged cards. Then Mamdoueh turned away for a word with Morgan. Heads together, in conference, the matter at hand was important. Tayyeb. Alright. She nodded.

The journalist stood watching them. An invitation to the Camp was strange since earlier, during the discussion Ligury's one remark was termed by the grave Mamdoueh "liberal wishing." Was he being set up? How would they get in and out through the Phalangist siege? Another instant the leader and the gorgeous Western woman spoke at close range.

The rich Italian was staying behind. For him it would be another white night. Elie Madi heard a gambling dispute at the rear of the club: bring on the assorted light arms, fire a klashin in the air. He turned and glimpsed the German, but then noticed Morgan with her hand raised. She nodded: at the magnate? the leftist Mamdoueh?

Elie Madi felt his heart beating faster. Something had just happened. What? His heart was thumping like troop movement, patapa, across the Israeli-held strip in the South, across the mine-infested, the blood-irrigated, the hotly contested zones.

XIV

—Where's your car?

Morgan beckoned with a toss of her head. But she stopped to stare at a group of Syrians who malingered, bantering in the darkness. It was the soldier's oasis called Port Egypt, and there stood a huge henna haired woman, holding her own in their midst. She threw up her hands like a dancer. A ripple went through her enormous body; the arm movement seemed to inflate her breasts like water wings. Morgan looked on a moment before moving away with impatience.

—What, said the German, have you planned for tomorrow?

Ligury considered. Should he bring the photographer along? The man was in such a hurry, lacking good will if he did get stupendous shots.

—Going home. Sleep.

—Make the most of this. You could win a prize.

Ligury gave a spitting laughter, which felt good so he tried it again. That afternoon, touring embattled Chiyah with a Muslim group, he began laughing at something till it got out of control, coming in spasms, contorting his features. He stood convulsed with a laughter that didn't seem funny to the Mourabitoun fighters.

—Sleep is good, but the best would be...

—Come-come, said the other. Together we'll go to Sidon: I have a priest friend there, you must hear him speak of the camps. There is also a woman; she is of war and earth, and they call her Katyusha.

Morgan's VW stood parked in the shadow of the burnt-out Beirut Hilton. The hotel had been on the eve of its gala opening, in '75, when civil war broke out. Now it was stripped bare, strategic, hive-like: the dream of a military planner. The quarter was under control of Fatah which provided minimum services. Camille Ydlibbi's protection fees included this side street for patron parking.

Across the dark harbor waters, up the coast past Antelias shells hit and flared on targets in the Christian hinterland. Each new volley was like kindling, as every rightist gun across the city boomed in unison.

What would morning bring? Horrendous dawn of the defeated. What would Beirut resemble by the first gray light?

A flare lit a river of incandescent smoke from the burst crude oil depot in Dowra. Ligury thought of the young Phalangist who had left them, wandering into the night on his own.

XV

—Hawajiz!

Roadblock. Get out your passport, press card. Syrians controlled traffic into the port area.

It was a touchy checkpoint even in lull periods. People were detained until daybreak on a whim. Submitted to questioning, forbidden water; harassed by soldiers or military intelligence.

—From where you come?

—Mustachioed, glum, he peered in at them.

—Ydlibbi's, said Morgan. Avenue des Français.

—You do what, there?

—Insomnia, she gestured at the sky. Too much noise.

—Journalists? Amerkiyyeh?

He glanced from the driver to their papers. Another waited, klashin poised, a step or two behind.

But it was all up to the first; his decision, for a few seconds, as he kept his flashlight low by the door. Western embassies had been advising their nationals to depart, and offering to provide transportation.

—We just left Mamdoueh, said Morgan, in perfect Arabic. He is our friend.

—You are not with him.

—He had business. But I will see him tomorrow, with your kindness.

The other made a humming sound. Then asked:

—You have eaten kanafi in Damascus?

—Akiid, the world's best.

—You taste kanafi with me sometime. Meshi', you go.

—Thanks, she whispered, without a smile.

Lights off, they drove along the dark Corniche.

She dropped off Ligury. He stepped from the VW and grinned sheepishly. The two of them, therefore: the German, Kohler, and

Morgan. Ah, Sanitation should provide places for it, like sidewalk urinals. But in Beirut there was no Sanitation.

—I'll call you tomorrow, she said. I need a small favor.

As they drove off Ligury felt bad-childish, vulnerable, snide. He dug for his keys and went shuffling toward the door of his apartment building. His superintendent had been beaten up badly by one of the local militias.

PART TWO

I

From hour to hour, in the blazing sunlight, there was no movement across the sector. The bridge lay deserted of traffic, as silence seemed to rise in liquid fumes from its limestone surface. Past a bone-dry Beirut River sprawled the steaming Palestinian camp in its sixth week of siege. Methodical, with the grim rhythm of a collective dementia, artillery exchanges prolonged toward late-morning between Camp gunners and Phalange emplacements along the hills northward. There were rumors of a Red Cross caravan entering the Camp, where cholera and death from dehydration had already been reported; but at present talks were stalled, and no very positive signs were being given by the Kataëb* War Council.

Elie Madi knelt with a half dozen others, in an outpost on Ashrafiyeh side. He took Kuzayli's field glasses, focusing on the forms of two fighters stranded halfway across Bourj Hammoud Bridge. The one called "Little Hani" was seated upright against the low parapet. His eyes were closed—was he wounded? Now and again he raised an arm to his forehead, so he hadn't yet died of thirst.

The second Phalangist did look dead where he reclined, in a rigid posture, a few meters from an overturned jeep. In the powerful binoculars Elie saw flies whirling round his head, while the fighter's gaze merged with his own stark shadow.

Little Hani raised an arm again. He licked his parched lips, and his head seemed to loll with the effort. Two days without water.

Kuzayli said:

—If he makes a move, they shoot alongside.
—From where? Elie asked.
—Abattoirs.
—Shameless beasts, said another. Syrian filth.

---
*Phalangist

Elie lowered the field glasses. He turned and saw Little Hani's brother, who sat murmuring a litany of insults, squinting into the glare.

Noon passed. From hour to hour nothing stirred. Not on the white-hot bridge, which spanned dustbeds and debris along the concrete, man-made riverbed of Nahr Beyrouth; and not on the tragic hill beyond, with its putrid mist, and invisible mass agony,—as if just up there, thought Elie, Pandora's Box had been opened. He said,

—Later, we'll go out. We can rescue him.

—No, said Kuzayli. We can't.

—On whose orders?

Of those present at this outpost in the deep ravine bordering Ashrafiyeh, Elie still ranked highest.

—Abu Joseph's.

Little Hani's brother met Elie's gaze.

—For what reason?

—Only the obvious, said Kuzayli. Little Hani would be long gone, except he makes good bait. The beasts are just waiting for us to come out. They'll snipe any rescue party, and pinpoint our recon position in the process.

—What subtle reasoning, said Elie. Typical of a loser, like Sakr... Why are men like him promoted, when it only cretinizes them?

—Watch what you're saying, said Kuzayli, about Abu Joseph.

—When night falls, then we'll see.

—They have flares.

—It takes more than flares, said Elie, for a Syrian to hit anything moving.

—You'll be killed if you go out there.

—No, I used to come play down here, as a boy. We can save him.

—You're still a boy, said Kuzayli. I'm radioing the War Council.

—No you're not! said Elie, like a challenge.

—I don't think it's possible, said Little Hani's brother.

—Two are needed. Will you go?

Elie remembered fishing down here, as a teenager, when Beirut River was in spate. He thought of Jessica and nights they had spent together, with a stinging sort of nostalgia, and yearning,—all the more determined to risk himself.

PART TWO

II

Smoke from a hundred fires trailed skyward, infusing a premature twilight over the teeming Beirut neighborhoods. There were no stable lights, but a few stars flickered in the drift of fumes. Rival artillery worked at frenzied intervals across the city; the gods were playing pingpong. Shells sped in bristling, orange-hued rows; they were spit with puffs of smoke from upper storeys of skyscrapers, gouged and pockmarked, which seemed to stalk the skyline as night came on. The long roar of mortars echoed and compounded:—shock of detonation merged with barrelling crunch of impact in the downtown ruins.

Elie waited at the lookout post. Their moment was approaching; the renewed shelling would serve as cover. The fate of Little Hani had become less than a sideshow; though he served as amusement, for the enemy, through the long afternoon of lull.

Behind them the radio spluttered. With care Kuzayli set a slice of cheeze on the rim of his thermos. He spoke with Phalange headquarters and announced, in a whisper:

—Madi, your call.

Elie turned from the opening, a jagged loophole facing the river and beleaguered Camp beyond. A silver crucifix leapt from his sunburnt neck as he bowed to respond.

Abu Joseph said:

—Get in here now. We need you in Burj.

—Little Hani is alive. He can be saved.

—Go around through Sinn Il-Fill, in your jeep, and fast.

—Little Hani's brother is here. He'll help me.

—Again you disobey? Waste time... risk lives.. Over.

Elie hesitated. Crackle... silence. He caught the brother's eye.

—No, I save them: one.

—They'll snipe you, and learn the position of Kuzayli's patrol. Over.

—We're waiting for darkness. I know the terrain.

Elie's eyes were dewlapped with fatigue. All last night the assault rifles had ranted; the air was filled with propellor sounds, brief sirens. The Syrians were contesting Kataëb positions—historic enemies in the battle for Lebanon, and yet allied in one theater: that of rooting out Camp Palestinians who fought on alone.

III

Elie touched Little Hani's brother on the shoulder.
—Ready?
—Let's go.
—Bala'shaak? You're sure?
—It's my family. We thank you.
But Kuzayli said,
—You'll both be put on trial.
—Think so? Maybe the War Council will try me, for saving a combatant.
—It's no time for games. Just obey.
—Akiid! But obey Little Hani, who needs our help? Or Abu Joseph who will need Satan's?
—You think too much. That's your problem.
—And Sakr thinks too little, when he starts making threats.

Across the glooming no-man's-land of Beirut River nothing budged. Little Hani sat in rigid profile, his head back against the stone parapet, beard pointing outward. Was he still alive? No chest movement could be seen with the strong glasses, which trembled slightly. Lamplights arched on the far side, like feelers of some huge scavenger about to devour the decomposing Camp.

Would the Syrians, suspecting a rescue attempt in the darkness, give the order to finish him off? One sniper bullet, and the gambit was useless . . . Through the long afternoon they had played cat and mouse with the agonizing fighter; they shot by his side, raising little puffs with the ricochet. Now the bridge had an eerie clarity in the Beirut twilight.

Impatient, the brother hefted his M-16 by Elie's side.
—No guns! said Elie. We need our hands.

Elie fingered the key to his jeep, thinking: Get Little Hani to Hôtel-Dieu.
—Jesus Christ was a medic, right Madi?

Kuzayli had a piqued tone.

IV

They found the jeep where he left it parked, half-up on the curb by a gutted storefront. He took a coil of rope from the floor in back.

PART TWO

—Yallah! Let's move.

The brother of Little Hani, named René, followed the veteran Elie who began running the length of the street and down toward the river across a stubblefield. Elie was a touch under medium height and slender, while the other was taller and ran along with fewer strides. The neighborhood, Sioufi, had been torn up by Syrian long-gunners perched in the distant hills eastward.

A sniper zone extended to the river with its low stone wall. Behind them, and high above Corniche Gemayel, the buildings were luminous like a décor. A smoldering cloud, its underside reflecting the light of detonations, hovered over East Beirut.

—I'll go out first, and signal you.

Elie lurched forward. He ran crouching in a straight line: on a rooftop far across town a sniper might have picked him off.

He made it and slumped with his back to the cement rim. In a moment René was by his side.

—Hold the rope. Hard, against the stone.

—I know.

—I'll climb down and have a look. If it's clear we can reach the bridge.

René caught his breath and frowned back at the intersection. They were working on their own, without cover, as if plunged in an alien element.

Elie remembered seeing René along with his older brother at football matches in Chamoun Stadium. René was a kid then, with sandy hair and a squinting smile. Elie was already dating Jessica, and his father was still alive. He was just starting at St. Joseph's but academically lazy, finding fun in a daring exploit, filling his jeep with friends on the way to a party. But he was moody as well, sometimes, and reluctant to choose a career.

René fought back the fear, trying to quell tremors in his chest. He loved his brother; this was the only reason he would disobey Abu Joseph, and headquarters. He was devoutly religious, a loyal Maronite. He would do anything on earth for his family; and now love for Little Hani was coming in conflict with his pledge to the Kataëb. It was as if, unconsciously, he had asked God to decide. And God told him: go with Elie Madi, rescue your brother from the beasts. René resented the international press for calling his people "rightists" and saying Sheikh Pierre was a "Nazi epigone".

Across the tunnel-like river a siren went crying among the lambasted apartment houses, distant, pathetic, receding in the thunder of cannons.

V

There was a smell of rot and sewage along the riverbed. Elie made out the darker contours of the bridge up ahead. In normal times there were rats in the cement crevices, feeding on trails of debris thrown down here by refugees.

He went forward, stepping slowly while his eyes grew accustomed. At any moment they might trip over unexploded ordnance, or a corpse.

The roar was deafening; the city-wide din of artillery seemed to amplify in the confined space, echoing. The two Phalangists broke into a jog, hands to their ears.

—Another fifty meters, Elie whispered. Stay calm.

There was an animal ferocity in his eyes, as he stopped to strategize. René crouched by his side, and the controlling presence of the older Phalangist tended to give him hope. Everyone knew Elie Madi; they knew he was crazy but brave, a beacon to others. His picture had appeared in *Le Réveil,* when he fought in Ein Rummaneh, and then down in Burj for many months, on the frontline.

Suddenly a volley of AK fire rang out behind them. Six shots, then a full clip from a FAL. Then many more: a tremendous ranting in the stark accoustics of the canal.

They dove head first down in the muck and sewage. But the skirmish only seemed close at hand. There was probing back toward Sinn Il-Fill; the shots reverberated down the long stone corridor like a pitched battle at their heals.

VI

For 72 hours the Bourj Hammoud and Karantina bridges had been closed off by checkpoints on either side, with only a rare car venturing out into the vacant sunlit expanse in full view of opposing factions. Kuzayli had said they were making a run with blood plasma from Jounieh, but Elie had his suspicions. Possibly the two were set up as a probe by Phalangist tactical operations in the area. Otherwise, why such a risk?

For weeks there had been increasing provocations along the Green Line from Burj to the suburbs and beyond. With such kindling a fire had to flare up sooner or later. René's brother was an early victim in what loomed as yet another complicated phase of fighting. The Israelis were poised and waiting in the South, across Haddad-land. Another major invasion could occur, and this was what the War Council wanted: a final solution for civil strife in Lebanon, a definitive imposition of order with Washington as the source. But would it work?

Elie and René neared the bridge. The latter was at pains to stifle a kind of St. Vitas dance each time they paused. Bourj Hammoud Bridge made a low massive arch of shadow; while beyond, in the clear sky above the Mediterranean, a rocket series sped northward along the coast. Two more dark forms sprawled with abandon alongside the pillars. There could be no emplacement down here, but a fire-fight had occurred leaving corpses in its wake.

—Hoist me up.
—Up where? said René.
—I'm going for your brother: no use risking two.
—I stay down here?
—Just wait . . . Cup your hands.

Holding the other's head Elie climbed onto his broad shoulders, tottering a moment. Slowly he straightened and ran a hand along the stone wall. René was strong; he lifted him by the boot soles until Elie got a grip and hefted himself over.

He could just see the overturned jeep: the fighter's form lying on his side now. Any flare east of the city would make his movement clear as day to enemy snipers. Beirut skyline was a yellowish aura interspersed with fumes, almost light enough even without a flare. The very air seemed dizzy with danger, as he poked his head for a glimpse.

Then he started, cat-like, running out toward the center. He sprinted bent over, parallel to the ground, hugging the parapet.

In an instant he was by the side of Little Hani who lay unconscious, if still alive.

A flare went off high in the violet darkness. It lit up the bridge and Bourj Hammoud front like a lurid canopy of lightning. Elie started out for the jeep but then coiled backward; he tried to merge his form with the wounded man.

From somewhere a sniper hit the flare, which extinguished.

—Psst! You with me?

He shook the wounded Phalangist. Had they shot him? Had they finished him off as night fell?

He tapped his cheek:

—You awake?

The other gave a feeble moan. He looked terribly emaciated; his eyes opened a slit, and Elie whispered beneath the din of bombardment:

—René's waiting. I'll hoist you. But don't say a word, don't even move.

He nodded slightly, as Elie took the rope from his belt and passed it under his arms.

Then they were ready, but waited a moment as shelling over the Camp reached a new paroxysm. Of the two Little Hani was heavier; the trick was to get him started, dangling him down; in mid-air as Elie jammed his boots on the parapet, and lowered the rope slow.

But he couldn't let him fall.

VII

René was clutching the rope before his brother landed, groaning. Elie took off a boot and tied his end of the rope to it like an anchor. He crawled out toward the jeep for a look at the other Phalangist. An unnatural bulk, and contorted posture—finished. He lay there as if fused with the concrete; the flesh was cold, fingers stiff and resistant. The features looked crimped at the corners, gnawed by death. Elie remembered a puppy he saw once along the roadside, its fur and small body assuming the form of mud and ruts from passing cars; but its face still intact and staring up, hideous, from the puddle.

Suddenly—ping! ping! A bullet bounced off the jeep. Another scratched the stone by his knee, and Elie recoiled, leaping toward the low wall of the bridge. Angle of fire? In a moment it would be too late: there were shots from all sides. Kuzayli should be aware of what was happening; they were watching the scene with binoculars. Elie scampered back round the jeep on the lee side.

A flare went off, ballooning bluish above the canal. Ah! they were onto the game... At any instant they would RPG the overturned jeep, and it would be the end. Then Elie would be a flare as well, while inhuman darkness closed over. Ping! ping! on the jeep fender, coming from Abattoirs. Time to move, Elie Madi—but the flare? Make his run while the sky was a photographer's studio? Kuzayli, you imbecile, how about some cover. Get the flare.

Elie felt more angry than afraid. Sakr, you stooge—Why not stand up for your men instead of playing bureaucrat at the War Council? Now René would panic in the chaos, weeping over his brother instead of reacting. If only he didn't expose the three of them... Then Elie would die a laughingstock.

The flare extinguished. He knelt like a runner. One end of the rope was attached to Little Hani down below: didn't René have the presence of mind to untie him? The other end bobbed up and down with his boot by the parapet. It rose up ready to go over the top, and Elie dove for his lifeline.

He tugged, yanking as he crouched there, and the rope came free. In an instant he attached one end to the jeep, tying the other round his waist. Bullets clawed the cement as he knelt another second, uncoiling the rope it would take to get him over the side.

Then he lunged outward in the shadows. He dove from the bridge and caught himself, jolted in mid-air and dangling. Looped with the rope, his hands were on fire and his right wrist twisted. Lowering himself down, notch by notch, was an agony.

—Help me! he whispered fiercely, but René stood transfixed.

Just above, the bullets were whizzing.

Now he reached the end of the rope and realized it was four, five meters short and tightening painfully on his chest.

He heard René calling up:

—Can't make it?

He tried to raise himself and loosen the cord from his armpits, widen the loop and let himself fall.

But his hands were exploding, their strength drained completely.

He hung there, turning slowly like a hanged man beneath the bridge. The noose tightened.

IX

Then he lost consciousness—jerked sideways by a blast. He was tossed wildly about, as the bridge seemed to quake at its foundations. Was this *it*? Shockwaves poured over his mind, giving way to a depersonalized sort of dread.

Then he was falling sideways, out of control and given over to the space like a rapids all around. He struck and slumped down, crying out. Somehow René was there to break his fall. The length of rope came lassoing after, flicking the two of them as they sank under the dead weight.

Little Hani was conscious now, blear-eyed. He had revived with the first sips of water. Up above a fire crackled—the jeep was blown up, thought Elie regaining his senses. The rope snapped, releasing him. Now the fallen Phalangist was burning alongside, his two eyes still open as if watching his own cremation.

The long cement waterway was roaring with submachineguns and artillery. Grad missiles; a "Stalin's Organ" rolled its thunder across the wide night of Lebanon. Elie caught his breath; Little Hani lay groaning for more water, while René went scampering from one to the other with a whimper. The spectral Beirut River was an echo-chamber, as far down its course, toward Sinn Il-Fill, there was more skirmishing.

Midnight had passed by the time they made their way in Elie's jeep through the outskirts of Beirut, and back around into Ashrafiyeh. Little Hani wasn't wounded, so they took him to their mother's apartment in Rue Chehade, avoiding the desperate mob scene of Hôtel-Dieu.

Next day the story spread through East Beirut of how Elie defied Abu Joseph and went out for Little Hani. It was added and compared to others, slightly crazy and suspicious, attached to his name since the Civil War began. For the moment Eli Madi was more than rehabilitated: he was the hero of the day.

X

Morgan knocked twice, then once, and stood listening. There was a sough of slippers across the uncarpeted floor inside.

The corridor was pitch dark; she heard no sound except the war downtown. Neighbors were all crouched in the cellar waiting for this latest onslaught to end. That's good, she thought: stay down there another week. Morgan thanked the Phalangists for leaving their calling card in this quiet sector, late that afternoon, in the form of a phosphorous bomb on Rue Souraty.

She had just dropped off her lover, Kohler, and was giving his enrapt caresses the fag-end of a thought when she heard:

—Who calls at midnight?

—A crusader.

The latch scraped.

Dishevelled, sleepy face above a pocket light: Risha. But no face, thought Morgan, could be more deceptive: you would need a makeup artist to look any less made-up. But beneath the frowziness the brain was programmed; it gathered, it processed.

—So?

Risha awaited a reply.

—There's a meeting Sunday.

—And? Do you know where?

—Not yet. Probably the War Council.

—The time? said Risha, in her slight accent.

—We'll know soon enough.

Always asking, was Risha, what she didn't really need to know. With each new liaison-op Morgan told herself it would be the last. In some neurotic way she craved the risk, and romantic assignments;

plus she was becoming an in-company legend. In one evening she could gather more crucial information just by spreading her legs, than the entire male contingent in a month.

Risha said:

—If the accords are signed? If the Camp is evacuated?

—It won't be.

Morgan yawned.

—The Red Cross caravan could happen.

—It won't.

—We must get ourselves in place.

—Listen, said Morgan. I'm going across to Ashrafiyeh tomorrow. If I don't get access and make it happen, who will? You and Peretz?

Risha stared at her in the darkness: a master at her specialty, but too jittery.

IX

The assignment of Khalil, the support agent, had been to rent them a safe and centrally located apartment. Together, upon arrival, they searched high and low for any sign of an audio installation, like a hot-mike in the dead telephone, or equipment so tiny it fit in a pinhole. Even now she and Risha were speaking too loud. There was no imagining all the ways a place could be bugged.

Thus a world had depended on Khalil at the outset. He was guaranteed by the station: by the case officer, Strickland. Khalil was paid dollars and told to count the money before their eyes. It was no quit-claim; he hadn't been terminated. He could be reached anytime with his wife, three children and two brothers, father still living . . .

Every foot of wall space, floor and ceiling had to be gone over for signs of drilling, plaster patching, or matched paint. They looked for hours, especially Peretz since it formed part of his expertise: his religion. Peretz had been trained at an early age, a child prodigy. A grain of sand in new paint might betray a most unwelcome visitor. An infrared beam could be used for eavesdropping. There were subminiature microphones able to overhear secrets as sensitive as a government's survival.

—Right, said Risha, turning her back on Morgan. We'll be patient . . . yet awhile.

She went in the bedroom.

Morgan cursed under her breath. She heard Risha's indolent shuffling: to the dresser, to the window—gazing out on the dark street, Rue Jeanne d'Arc. She heard the mattress sigh as Risha lay back.

—Stuffy in here, said Morgan, startling the silence.
—I opened the kitchen window a crack.
—Where's Peretz?
—Here, beside me.
—Did he go to Ydlibbi's?

Risha paused.

—No.

Morgan undressed in the silence. It would go poorly if Peretz fell into the hands of Mourabitoun along Hamra. His nickname was "The Fanatic" because of his tradecraft. But the game was over for all three of them, if he stumbled into an enemy somewhat officious when it came to strangers.

She rummaged among toiletries in her travel bag. Morgan's hands were abnormally large: the hands of a Titan woman. She went in the bathroom and busied herself there without light. The tap was dry, but she took palmfuls of 3-day old ration from a basin. After a moment she felt less of the stickiness, and intimate layer of fatigue on her skin, in her pores. Less of Kohler, like an apparatus strapped on mechanically.

Leaving the bathroom she said:

—Peretz doesn't leave here tomorrow.
—Fine, you tell him.
—If he leaves, Strickland will know about it. I've asked nicely; I've tried to keep things just between us. But now I'm telling you both: Ydlibbi's is off-limits, and Hamra, and everywhere.
—Fine, said Risha. But remember this: you're out there playing Mata Hari, while we stay cooped up for days. Sometimes I think you'd make a good double-agent, the way you manipulate.
—You two have your moments.
—Moments? I came here to work for my country. For its security.
—At what cost? said Morgan, smirking.
—Any cost. But you wouldn't know about that.
—Patriots don't make the best spies. I'm warning you not to leave this apartment. If Peretz goes out of here again, then as the principal officer—

—Then what?
Risha grinned in the darkness: accepting any challenge?

XI

For a long time Morgan lay unable to sleep, listening to detonations a mile distant on several fronts. So far PLO leadership was holding firm, refusing surrender: the Camp in its seventh week of siege was the "honor of the Arab world." Like Tel ez-Zaater; like Sabra and Chatila, Burja-Brajneh among the "belt of misery" camps; and teeming Ein el-Helweh in Sidon, Rachidiyyeh in the South: it would undergo mass torture for the sake of an Arab world which offered no viable support. How many more weeks? thought Morgan. How many days? In life everything was timing—skill and timing, as they told her years before, during her courses at Camp Peary.

Before this she spent nearly a decade at stations in South America, but never found one so unpredictable as here. Alliances which shifted weekly, constant threat of abduction, political anarchy—Lebanon was like treacherous ice: you might fall through any instant trying to spot, gain access, isolate a target. And nowhere else such an absence of helping hands, since Khalil had about as much cover as a June bride. And Strickland, easily identifiable, virtually never set foot outside the U.S. Embassy.

Tomorrow she had a date with Ligury to visit Ashrafiyeh. Attempts at bugging, telephone tapping, photography, mail-interception which was hopeless anyway due to the state of the post office:—all proved a failure in their efforts to zero in. And yet nine, ten weeks marked the absolute limit of endurance for the Camp under siege: the pieces had to be in place before its inevitable fall.

They knew where the famous leader lived; Risha had been over there, and watched him come and go. They knew his car, at least one of them—a sable blue Mercedes. By sight Risha knew his chauffeur, and several in the entourage—Selim, member of the Politburo; Fadi Krem, press agent.

Tomorrow Morgan had a rendez-vous with Ligury and one of his Phalangist friends. Besides dallying with the spy network, she would start from the ground up, on her own. In the past that had proved her best, natural tack, relying on her extraordinary instincts;

and letting history, her one commensurate lover, determine the time and place.

XII

That morning Elie ushered his two Western guests into the basement shelter where his family was staying. They entered a six-storey building of modern construction: plaster chips littered the rez-de-chaussée, a railing dripped from an amputated staircase. At once, as the three started downstairs, the smell was infernal.

It was a human porridge, exuding its acrid mist in the close darkness. A dozen expensive colognes couldn't dispel the odor of sweat and excrement. Like a vast sickroom, but instead of Betadine solution the pungent tang of cordite... Constantly unlidded by the back wall a vat served as communal toilet.

The neighborhood shelter was filled with Maronites, fleeing and incessantly discussing the latest Syrian aggression; since in this particular aspect of the conflict Syria was a hated enemy. While just up the hill, within eyeshot, Syrian "friendship" was no less clear: vis-à-vis the Camp in its 48th day of siege. For if the Phalange grew too strong, beginning to dominate, then Syria would see its plans for Lebanon threatened, along with credibility as a progressive (Arab nationalist) force in the region. But if the Phalange went under, and Israel sensed a "frontline state" in formation to the north: then a repeat of '82 could occur, and maybe worse.

Haram! Such was Lebanon: play of international forces, aerial bombardment seeming to drift with the geopolitical winds; anarchy in the neighborhoods, car-bombings, killings daily, spate of kidnapping and vogue of Western hostage-taking. *Haram!* said people slumped along the walls, lounging in vaguely hostile postures, decanter in hand. Some had established their own space with throw-rugs and assorted gear. Most had bedding, radios, liquor.

XIII

Elie took Morgan's arm.

—I want you to meet my mother. And here is my younger brother.

Tcharaffna—we are honored. Mrs. Madi had an insecure laughter when she spoke.

—Welcome. I'm sorry it must be here.

—Maman, they're reporters. They are used to this.

Elie's family held a good position along the wall. A woolen blanket lay spread over cane matting; there were cushions, a thermos, nonperishable food, cigarettes. Other people entered, or hazarded a trip outside. One man prowled from corner to corner, chafing at the endless wait.

Mrs. Madi was a petite woman, dark-eyed and wan, with graying hair. Like the other faces hers glimmered in candlelight, with a couch of fatigue. She smiled and frowned.

—Maman, he is English, and she American. They are interested in our cause.

—Then you'll write the truth? Ay! You see what we are made to suffer. And why?

Ligury stared down at her. He knew the story of neo-Nazi Pierre Gemayel, Phalangist founder. And now they were allied to Israel. But people in shelters, thought Ligury, seemed to lack a sense of history's ironies.

—The Syrians are throwing more infantry and as-Saiqa units into Burj, said Elie. Two of our positions are encircled by them: it is a harvest.

—Why are you here? Mrs. Madi said to her son. Why aren't you with the others?

Elie looked down.

—Abu Joseph seconded me to Fadi: I'm press liaison for now.

But he had brought water. People approached him for it, holding forward cups and containers.

A shell hit close by, making the shelter vibrate. The water reflected in amber wrinkles on the wall. More plaster dust came down, vexing tired eyes. The foundation seemed flimsy against a tumult of heavy Syrian artillery.

There was a groundswell of panic, but the onslaught appeared to subside. Morgan appeared to notice a dark-haired girl with the strangest air about her. She sat alone: a crossfire of candlelight gave hints of her features. She wore a pair of frayed battle-fatigues unbuttoned to her breasts, and her feet were bare. Her hair looked greasy and framed her pretty face. The bizarreness of her pose struck Morgan, like a deranged idol.

—Ah! that one, said Mrs. Madi, lips pursed. She has gone crazy. Folle, eh oui. Sylvie, she is called, and mumbles to herself about the Virgin Mary. I never met her parents, but my husband used to mention them.

—She needs help, said Elie. I knew her before—she was a Phalangist. I used to see her in Ein Rummaneh, not a bad fighter, but erratic. She spent a lot of ammunition.

—She gets violent, said Mrs. Madi, if you try to move her. She doesn't like being touched.

Now Sylvie handled an M-16 in a kind of pantomime. Her face was a blank, void of emotion, pose rigid. Her eyebrows arched over fine, deepset pupils.

—Mejnuun! said Elie's younger brother, Emile, with a chuckle of contempt. Completely crazy.

XIV

Further along the wall a middle-aged, graying man labored to his feet as if this act should interest everyone. Glancing here and there, he gathered up his flabby bulk. He wore pinstriped trousers whose threadbare shine seemed to reflect his baldness. Obese, perspiring, breathing with a rasp he emerged from the shadows, and he was angry.

—So! Shu haida? he stammered at a composed Morgan. And does Washington know about this? Does Moscow care?

Both Ligury and Morgan waited for more. But the man's hilarious silence lasted several seconds. His face was cast from a mold of joviality, wide canine cheeks, sparse curly hair like a clown. Yet his features were haggard, and acutely aggravated—thick lips, slits of eyes formed a smile without content.

He awaited a response; but the bombardment kept on unabated. Syrian emplacements along the slopes of Mount Lebanon formed a semi-circle above the rightist-Christian sectors. There was a screeching in the air, like lorries down no earthly highway. Shock of detonation, crunch of impact. Here in Sioufi the upper storeys were gouged, gutted; they collapsed in a cascade of girders, plaster, concrete and jagged glass.

The obese man grumbled to himself on one side while the girl also began growing agitated. She pointed her imaginary gun waist-high, shooting off rounds with a tremor.

—Reenacting Black Saturday, said Mrs. Madi, with her sad chuckle.

—We are respectable! said the fat man. From the old families, Phoenicians or Mardaites. Don't call us Arabs, sir. But our leaders speak to us on the radio. Honor and endurance, they say. La! Will you look at her, the crazy bitch seeking attention . . . she's unclean!

He turned on Sylvie, but in his heart of hearts he seemed to fear, and perhaps crave, the worst.

XV

Her panic was infectious. Sylvie shot off a silent volley and her body quivered, slyly sexual. She jerked backward with the recoil; her teeth and tongue emitted a hissing sound.

A line of people waited for water. Hourly news updates came and went amid static, in several languages, from tinny speakers. Morgan scanned the groups of women, children and old people: this fouled human well from which treacherous shadows seemed to emerge. It was a caravanserai of candles, in a valley of fear. Masaccio's *Baptism*, she thought, remembering some belletristic remark of the Italian's. Human waste and perfume, liquor and perspiration, cordite and gunpowder fumes seeping in through the crevices.

Terrific explosion, like a huge wave breaking over the shelter. A shudder passed over the neighborhood. Things fell, mothers reached for their children. There was a second wave of screams as the flame of an upset candle licked someone's belongings. Shadows hovered and converged; there was a sense of unlevelling, a world out of kilter. Insults were hurled by two women; children cried with abandon.

—God protect us! whispered Mrs. Madi, crossing herself.

Then Sylvie emerged from her cloister of shadow and self, a few steps from Elie's family. She exuded madness, giving vent in her way to the unspeakable.

Before the big explosion she had been posturing, craning her neck like a figure in an ikon. She made it crack like a knuckle.

She trembled and drooled. The obese man gave a gesture of disgust:

—We left her room for six people.

Scowl on his bulbous face, wading into the darkness of sufferers.

—They're burning tires, she muttered. Burning them. Marouf Saad is dead.

Emile cast smug glances at Sylvie. He was too young, maybe, to go fight in Burj; but he was old enough to be brave. Plenty younger than he were down there this minute, but his mother held him back.

A column of Land Rovers clattered over the macadam of Sioufi just above.

Sylvie slobbered and postured. She picked out Ligury and let out a peal of laughter point-blank in his face. The journalist was taller by a head, with broad if rather drooping shoulders. He stared down at her dreadful, beautiful eyes like two patches of folly.

—Ça va pas? he said.

She grunted.

—Yallah! said Elie. Time to move: we'll take her along to the hospital.

XVI

Terrified, she drew back as Ligury tried to plant himself behind her. She tried to kick him; but Elie said something in Arabic, like a command, and she went limp for removal to the bottom of the stairs.

But there she revived and began kicking, elbowing the self-conscious Ligury. She jumped up three steps with an insane laughter; she stoked down at them with her feet and seemed to convulse with another outburst of the M-16.

—Drive her up! said Elie.

Morgan kept her distance from the mêlée, while Kim Ligury was already being scratched and bitten.

It was dark outside. Overhead the lights darted like reflections on a windshield. The smoke-filled sky seemed a traffic of demons, with flares over the embattled sectors, screeching departure of Grad missiles. Long beams of light probed the zones. Here and there a furtive shadow moved amid the rubble, on recon or looting, foraging provisions. There was a pitter-patter of glass and falling plaster from a building nearby. A missile launcher repeated its shriek on the foothills northeastward.

It was hot on the heights of Kahaleh, on slopes above Aintoura, Alay and Kfarchima. The tunnage of 240 mm. guns, of 23-DCA in use horizontally, of tank and RPG fire all combined to pulverize the downtown sectors.

Each plunging mortar dug a wide crater. A mortar killed anything, Morgan knew, within fifteen yards; a missile sent shrapnel to a 300-meter radius.

Elie Madi drove at top-end and Ligury held the girl by her waist. Care for a dance? Head lolled, limbs jutting, she sprawled across him dazed. Elie's driving was such that Morgan held on for dear life in the rear.

A great ranting enveloped the street. Passing trees seemed to pulsate, as Elie drove without headlights over a wake of debris in Rue Sioufi. His jeep spanked like a skiff past the Ecole St.-Coeur. He fishtailed; the tires whined and crunched on the littered surface.

Impact of shells, cascade from the upper storeys as if a building could bleed. Ligury feared for his eardrums. He clung to the girl as she began flailing.

Sylvie tore open her elbow on the dashboard. She struggled over the side, while the journalist with a warm bland taste felt a sickening thrill at the idea he was hit.

She dug her fingers into his neck. She jolted Elie and the jeep went veering, careening on two wheels.

—Shit! said Morgan, holding on.
—Keep her down! said Elie, straight-arming them away.
Whap! on Ligury's mouth, as Sylvie showered him with spittle.

Nearing the hospital they descended toward the sea. They passed a row of burnt-out boutiques reft of showcasing, cemetery of commerce. Further on there were caved roofs, long awnings of concrete over more gutted structures. Patches of building in a drift of smoke.

Past the Lazarieh orphanage, Elie turned breakneck down toward the water: they glimpsed the white gossamer facade of the Greek Orthodox Hospital.

XVII

Along the corridor: another scene of helter-skelter. Entryways to the basement were crowded, as a gang of three Phalangists stormed in with a wounded fighter. Word was spreading of a terrible scene down in Burj. From the other side an offensive had begun which threatened Ashrafiyeh and the eastern suburbs. Hôtel-Dieu had been shelled, and now on all roads to this hospital—sirens and shouting militia. At the far end of the basement tunnel there were makeshift operating rooms.

Corpses in camouflage overflowed the morgue, lined up side by side in the garden. Radios played: *Voix du Liban,* a warped military march.

—Time to go, said Elie. They're waiting for me at the War Council.

Ligury slow-danced with a groggy Sylvie; she had kicked him on the shelter stairway, and his face was swelling.

—And us? he asked, glimpsing Morgan.

—No reason to stay here. Come with me: I'll introduce you, said Elie with an ironic note, to my superior.

—The girl?

She hung at his side.

—At least she's out of harm's way. But decide now, we've got to hurry.

—Let's go, said Morgan.

—Why not take her? Ligury hesitated. At the American Hospital—

—She's gone, my friend. Foutue!

—Come on, said Morgan, imperious.

He let Sylvie down gently, trying to prop her. The girl slumped with a small groan, eyes two slits, mouth open.

More combatants rushed past. They cursed and tripped.

Knees to her chest, Sylvie was a picture of psychotic regression.

Ligury turned away, following Elie and Morgan who moved past people in no uncertain terms. Elie was a Phalangist, heading downtown for combat. Something in his gait made others draw back.

Inside: a blend of isoprophyl alcohol, vomit, a musty scent like fear incarnate. Outside, abruptly, they sniffed a horrendous incense. Sparks, on a building off to their right, like an itinerant hive.

XVIII

An instant after slumping across the aisle she was nudged by a boot, then jolted by a little boy. He wrinkled his nose as liquid oozed from the seat of her fatigues, forming a pool. Was it blood? Sylvie blinked, cringing at a cry down the corridor:

—Injured officer!

—Move it!

They jostled, shoving past. One applied pressure to the officer's torn abdomen and sopping bundle of uniform. Blood dripped from his back like a spigot not shut tightly. Eyes half closed, he submitted.

Sylvie felt numb. Senses enveloped, like a gauze, by her alien body. She spoke random words into the frenzy, and resorbed them, in silence. There was a cushiony sensation as if the world had no limits, one with her being. All things sank in a fearful whorl, contours dissolved. The meaning of things was morbid, untrustworthy like her nausea.

Slowly, she edged upward, getting her balance on a steep soft mattress. She strode along Mount Sannine, with a lethargic giggle. Luckily she had her M-16 but the trigger (she caressed it) was numb. She had to stimulate the trigger, rouse it to action. But the cushiony feeling meant she was invulnerable; the world had no sharp points, no *things*. All the projectiles fit in perfectly.

Arms forward for balance she moved toward the exit, and glided, glided into the night air.

O Phalangist girl, she hummed, apple of your parents' eye. O Sylvie Helou: you lead the procession in triumph through the streets of Ashrafiyeh. From the bumpers of Mercedes they dragged the enemy, O Queen of Tel ez-Zaater.

She walked toward the Casernes, and the air was good to breathe, a crackling fire. She smelled fish, like spring of '75 when war came, and her parents tossed lobster tails in the trash barrels to rot. Marouf Saad is dead! Nobody on earth could resuscitate Lebanon. Rot... To her right spread the outworks of Beirut Port, with a toss of lights up the coast toward Jbeil. A curtain of smoke drew over the east end of the Ring of Death, and pathetic stars.

Sylvie arrived at a park: no lights in the Bishopric. She knocked on a treetrunk:

—May I come in?

Then, for a long time Sylvie saw images of her childhood, in years before the war.

XIX

Hana'a was there: Hana'a Chahrour, the Palestinian kid who came sometimes with her mother to clean and dust. Her doll talked funny, playing a silly game. Laila the doll had a lifeless expression. Dumb Palestinians—at least this was what Sylvie's mama said sometimes, referring to Sitt Chahrour who was only their maid and lazy and overpaid.

Laila sounded sinister when Hana'a pulled the string, whining and spoiled:

—Mama, tuck me in.

What a selfish doll, really. Crush it under a car for staying all day with its mother.

Beneath the trees, by the Bishopric Sylvie lay down in the cushiony night, and heard ancient voices. Over and over Hana'a pulled the string.

—Mama, I wanna drink.

—Na na! singsonged Sylvie, because those two made her angry. They were selfish, always together. So contented.

—Sitt Chahrour will be upset: she doesn't like people who play all day while she does the housework.

—Laila needs me now, said Hana'a, tending to the faded doll.

—It's only a stupid piece of junk.

—So . . . It isn't.

—Well—my mama won't like it when she gets home tonight. Sitt Chahrour is lazy, and won't finish her work.

—She will.

—Not all alone, Sylvie whined.

The doll was mostly forehead with a puff of reddish hair beyond any comb. Sylvie frowned:

—You better go in the pantry, or I'll tell.

—I think Laila is wetting, said Hana'a. Wait while I change her.

Hana'a spoke in a plastic tone like her doll. The diaper was a crumpled piece of wax paper. After pulling the string she had to double Laila over before the small voice could be heard.

—Mama, tuck me in.

Sylvie gazed down at the two of them and felt a need for tenderness like something evil-tasting. Fairly panting with emotion, she felt a raging jealousy of her playmate. Hana'a, who was just a Palestinian, didn't deserve to be lucky like that, with a grandmother at her beck and call, all day long.

That was in their house in Furn ech-Chubaak, in years before the war. Sylvie was twelve then, Hana'a only nine.

—I'm telling. You asked for it, and you're getting it.

—Think I care? Tell.

She got up brusquely. And not Hana'a but Laila gave a sudden look of repentance. Hana'a pulled the string; the small, prissy whimper was garbled. Sylvie gave a superior smile but it seemed to grate on her features; she yearned to snatch away the doll and crush its pink face and tear its hair. Hana'a tended and petted, making a savvy little game of Laila's few words, stirring up Sylvie's anger with each pull of the string.

PART TWO

XX

A rocket tore across the top of the park with a flash and tambourining of leaves. The huge whoosh took Sylvie from her visions for an instant and restored the awareness, the hurt. Like a festering tooth, all full of pus and sick nerve.

It was impossible and she had to get out of there, go tattletale. Then Hana'a would suffer because whose house was it anyway, in Furn ech-Chubaak? If only she wasn't left alone all day with these two refugees. Why didn't they go home? Why didn't they go on back to Tel ez-Zaater? She could do the housework herself, and then her mother would be so proud of her.

—I'm going to tell Sitt. In a minute you'll get whipped!

—No, I won't.

Sylvie's parents left the house on weekdays. They were an active couple, hardworking and prosperous. They ran an import-export business from an office in Antelias, and frequently spent a week in Cyprus, Athens, even Paris. Sitt Chahrour came to stay; and now she responded to Sylvie's lament with a hopelessly kind look, chuckling to herself.

—That's okay. Hana'a knows all about caring for babies, even real ones. She won't hurt Laila; but whatever put such an idea in your head? Better stay with me awhile.

—No, I won't.

She ran from the room and she hated Sitt's sad smile with all her might. Anyway it was good for her, being such a tub of lard, to get down on the floor and scrub. Maybe that would wipe the stupid refugee smile off her face. Then it would be Sylvie's turn to smile, and Hana'a could burn with envy and be left alone all afternoon and sometimes in the evening, too. Anyway Sitt was only a maid in their house and she should never forget it. She lived in one of the zoos, in that filthy slum of Tel ez-Zaater and she would never be a real Lebanese. She was lucky they paid her for her work—Sylvie's parents even said so.

XXI

She ran upstairs to her mother's bedroom. She sat at the cosmetics table with its perfume and rouge, nail-polish remover, mascara, like a miniature city. She took lipstick and twisted it way out and began smearing herself, smearing her dress, neck and nose. That was good, that made her laugh. She could paint on a smile, a frown. But the mirror (hopeless!) made her panicky since her face, with its red lines, had become a puzzle. Her expression was like terror with the features all askew, aggravating her. Sections of Sylvie's face smudged when she tried to adjust them. She erased the lipstick with a powder-puff.

Now Sylvie tried on a smile but this was a mistake. The pieces of her rouged face hurt like a dozen toothaches; she flew into a rage and began throwing a great tantrum. She convulsed and sobbed. She cried hot tears like first drops of a summer storm, and in one motion her arm swept the small bottles, compacts, powder and brushes from her mother's tiny city of make-up on the glass top.

—Girl! Sitt Chahrour frowned from the threshold, shaking her head. What are you doing to yourself?

Hana'a peeped wide-eyed from a fold in her grandmother's long black dress, dusty as the roadside, rather faded; the garb of a widow and refugee.

—Oh, no! My parents will not punish me. This is your fault, not mine.

She broke down sobbing.

Sitt blinked. She felt like showing the poor, lonely girl some affection; she wanted to cross over and soothe her, but a dark sense, between them, barred the way.

XXII

Why stay in the Furn ech-Chubaak house any longer? It was a bad apple, and her father was the worm. She could find herself a garden at night and lay down beneath the trees.

Voices! Businesslike tone of her parents, scolding her. Cash registers with a little ring when they laughed, making change. Sylvie was their transaction. Be nice! Be nice in our way, then we won't scold. Too much. Oh how she longed for her mother sometimes.

Voices inside her: they taunted and dared her to shoot them. Her gun was black and well oiled, cool as a snake along her sweaty body. She hugged it and fondled the trigger, maneuvering the M-16 sensually and thinking, It's good to be punished.

Those were real voices. Real people. Sylvie had dealt with at least three of them, along the Chiyah-Ein Rummaneh front in fall of '75. Then, in August '76, she was present at the cleansing of Nabaa Camp when she impressed her patrol by opening fire on a family, minus the husband, as it fled between rows of shanties. She whimpered with joy; her M-16 strung its death-beads between her sites and a Muslim woman who flung out her arms, wailed and tripped. A few checkered keffiyehs flapped wildly.

Sylvie remembered the day when Tel ez-Zaater was reduced to rubble after months of siege by the Phalangists and Chamoun's Tigers. She left her post and hopped a joyride on one of the bulldozers descending from Monsouriyyeh like creatures from a horror movie. Fedayeen were fleeing through the woods toward friendly villages near Alay. There was a massive manhunt.

On that day Sylvie had recalled, for an instant, as she passed the twisted lifeless bodies of refugees, playing an eternal ring-around-the-rosey before the central mosque, the doll Laila with its unhinged air, and orange tress.

There was the terrible exhilaration she had known before—drunkenness of survival. All else was eclipsed for awhile, even her loneliness.

XXIII

Evidence mounted at Phalangist War Council that the situation was not improving. Through the gray dusk of artillery barrage, Syrian troops stayed in their sandbagged positions a hundred yards across Burj square. There were others, as-Saiqa units among them, in M-113s, Panhard APCs cloaked in shadow along Riad Solh. Soldiers sat palming cigarettes; they murmured with anticipation, and thought of home. A great test, an appalling harvest of rightist Christians was in the offing.

Already an array of 75 mm. and 122 mm. field guns, Soviet-purveyed B-10 (82 mm.), B-11 (107 mm.) and RPAK recoilless rifles along with B-14 and -21 Super-Katyushas, 105 and 155 howitzers, 60, 80, 120 mm. mortars—all combined to labor and furrow the residential neighborhoods.

At Phalangist emplacements there were mortars of every calibre, including a Soviet-made 160 mm. and a U.S. supplied 106 "reckless" rifle. Plus field artillery: USM 101s, the AL 105 mm., French M-50 155 mm., some SS-11 surface to air missiles.

At twilight a few regular infantry and urban guerrillas began risking movement from their deep front of sandbags, overturned and riddled buses, machinegun nests, casemates overlooking Burj in the downtown center.

Now fire from automatic rifles, standard Ak-47 and M-16, FN FAL (NATO assault weapon) was interspersed with FN MAG machineguns, browning 1919 A4s; 12.7 and Degturyev which were jeep-mounted, called Dushkas or "the little queen".

There were anti-tank guns, M40A2s, multiple-barrelled Hispano-Suiza 20 mm. AA; also anti-tank rockets RPG-2 and -7 which were hand-held launchers firing an 82 or 100 mm. shaped charge on a 40 mm. booster, nicknamed the "bamboo bazooka".

RPGs did double-duty as men sprinted among the shadows, the enfiladed doorways, exploding at tanks or at one another. Ranks broke, and many began to fall as night spread over the Lebanese capital.

Several rightist enclaves had been cut off and surrounded. Buildings shook in the hail of grenades, then mopping-up action, floor to floor.

Karantina and Bourj Hammoud Bridges (where Elie went out for Little Hani) were closed to traffic by a lethal sniper fire. The highway north to Jounieh had become a no-man's-land. Rightist supply lines were under blockade. The Nth siege of Ashrafiyeh, in how many phases of an endless civil war, was underway.

XXIV

When Elie Madi, Morgan and Ligury arrived at War Council they were told by Abu Joseph to stay in a room on the harbor side. There was no electricity. Bare furnishings; the light from detonations flickered, silhouetted themselves and another Phalangist.

The roar of submachineguns was a hundred jack-hammers tearing into Burj.

They waited together, hesitant to talk. But the other, who wore one of the ghoulish hoods more popular in early years of the war, when Phalangists still frequented the Muslim sectors for daily business and nightlife, spoke first.

—Why so nervous? he said to Elie.

The small room was like a cage, in the intense flicker.
—Sakr told us to wait.
—He has his reason.
—Eh, Elie grumbled, pondering the hood. But is it a good one?
Madi glanced at the Western guests; he felt a knot forming in his stomach, as if an ordeal were about to begin. The two journalists sat waiting for an escort; they would take their chances at Sodeco crossing, back into West Beirut.
—All of us don't always agree, said the other. We lack the overview, and judgment of our leaders. But the cause is sacred.
—As Virgin Mary, said Elie.
—You doubt it? Morgan asked
—Someone might.
—Is your father here? she said.
—No, he is a Kataëb martyr who never doubted anything. My older brother died in action as well. As for my mother, and Emile, you have seen them: I'd make them go to France if we had money. But they're loyal; they will follow the Party.
For a moment it was a duel of eyes between Elie and the hooded one, who, a hand to his heart, salaamed in the darkness. The mask seemed to mute his smile, as he asked:
—Are you fighting tonight in Burj?

XXV

Elie raised his eyes to the figure of his immediate superior. Greetings were formal, as Abu Joseph spoke in his usual clipped tone. To the point of caricature he had the mien and demeanor of a warrior— dark beard framing his face like ancient armor, indenting oddly beneath the temples. From the bridge of his nose a delta of wrinkles ran off on his broad forehead like a source in desert sands. He was large in stature, big featured, with shoulders meant to heft a cannon. The bulk of him expressed a stern authority; there was a terseness even in his breathing, in a brusque gesture.
—Welcome to the War Council, said Abu Joseph, appreciating Morgan with a glimpse, but addressing Ligury. Sorry I don't have more time for you.
He nodded at Elie Madi who rose at once, stepping toward the doorway. Ligury showed a mild irritation, joining his guide on the threshold, when Morgan asked the Phalangist captain for a moment

alone, and stood speaking with him in whispers for what became ten minutes. Was she after a scoop? thought Ligury, who had wondered about Morgan's press credentials, and felt his own investigative instinct aroused. The walls came alight with the wild spurt of a flare. For an instant they glimpsed a ghostlike port area, the gateway to the Orient being reduced to cinders.

She rejoined them, as Abu Joseph stared at Elie a moment, like a lesson. There was something unresolved in the air, Ligury sensed; like the fate of Lebanon, in the sharp tragic cadence of their boots along the corridor.

The two correspondents stood waiting for a driver who would deliver them to Sodeco. There they must take their chances in a taxi, paying an exorbitant fee for the rollercoaster ride through stretches of sniper-zone.

In silence the eerie, hooded fighter followed them, watching Morgan light her own cigarette.

XXVI

Elie had a sense of being ushered down a flight of stairs, into an underground space. He saw a row of folding chairs. There were several dim figures in a greenish light from phosphorescent tubes. Movement seemed unnatural in the macabre glow, the play of shadows. There was a dank basement smell.

In the center of the room a prisoner sat facing his interrogator: Kuzayli from the recon patrol at Beirut River. Kuzayli pointed a handgun at the other's midriff; he cocked playfully, uncocked by interposing his little finger. In the green aura his smile was a leer which faded with the entry of Abu Joseph.

The prisoner had been beaten. His cheeks and forehead bulged, shining red. He bled from the nostrils; mucus sagged along his parted lips, his mustache gleamed. The man had a kinky orangish head of hair, and freckles dotted his features—a Palestinian.

Then Abu Joseph took a stance to one side of the captive, peering down with an exaggerated irony. His silence seemed so severe, it was mystical. He bowed, slowly, until his face was six inches from the other's, and then gave a low animal snarl.

At sight of Abu Joseph the man assumed a pose of utter submission. By contrast, the look on Elie's face was of unfeigned disgust.

During the civil war he had watched Abu Joseph at work getting information. He had seen him take his cigarette lighter to a man's genitals. Slap a man's ears with his flat gloved hand until the screams of pain subsided. Take a club to someone's feet with steadily increasing force, for an hour. Airplane; mock drownings, "shock therapy", the technique known as "amorous embrace"—Sakr knew the latest methods, like a sadist's banquet.

XXVII

Now he posed questions about the man's unit and intentions down in Burj when he was captured.

—You're as-Saiqa. Admit it, scum. If you lie I'll have Madi here snip out your tongue.

Subdued, desperate, the prisoner could only repeat the obvious. He was part of a unit attacking the Byblos building, with orders to storm and penetrate... How many were there? They had come down Hamra in late afternoon, billeted in Horj Tabet, a column of personnel carriers and other armored cars. How many? He didn't know. The line extended up the avenue out of sight.

—Son of a pimp! Tell me, why tonight? With what exact objective? If you don't talk I'll cut off your ears, and Madi will fry them in breadcrumbs, like an eggplant.

The man's teeth chattered.

—I'm a foot soldier. Would they tell me?

—Scum. Rabies and mange. Thing of the gutter.

—To defend B'B'Burj! and bolster positions in B'Bab Edriss!

He whined. He knew as well as anyone that a full-scale offensive was in progress. Saifi, Ashrafiyeh, Bikfaya—Maronite Lebanon was the objective. At this minute Syrian armor was rumbling southward through Tripoli and friendly Zghorta in the North. Anyone could hear about it on the radio.

Such, at least, was Abu Joseph's idea. But to agree openly, and talk about troop movement in Burj an hour before, when the captive was cut off from his comrades: to concur with the torturer would only provoke him. From minute to minute as-Saiqa was going under, drowning in his own pinkish drool. He said:

—We at'tacked on Saifi side. The B'Byblos was surrounded.

—How many tanks? How many will they throw at us?

—How c'could I know? A hundred, two city b'blocks!

—Don't sneeze on me, wretch. I'll skin you, and make condoms. Where are they waiting? In what street off Riad Solh? You have TOW anti-tank down here, no? Where, to the hundred meters, are they positioned?

Abu Joseph's barrage of questions went well beyond the infantryman's capacity to respond. He worked his mouth and seemed to ruminate answers he would hazard once given a chance. He would gladly tell all. Every last detail he knew. But then the menacing silence returned, and he said:

—You think they t'tell me anything? They say run there, st'tay in line, d'dog.

The others chuckled, except Abu Joseph—and Elie Madi.

XXVIII

For an instant the tension seemed to lessen. But at once the Phalangist officer imposed his silence. He appeared to coil, and maneuver for leverage. The moment of reckoning was near at hand; it lurked in each pause between strategic questions, which in fact were little more than a pretext. In truth, said Abu Joseph, all leftists, Palestinians, and so-called pan-Arabists formed a breed beneath the rest of humanity. They were a cesspool to be dealt with before the Middle East, the world entire started stinking with contamination.

Still the prisoner tried to answer. The stress and exhaustion kept him spluttering incoherently; but far better efforts would have proven inadequate. As each reply grew weaker, more forlorn, the silence of the torturer seemed to menace, impending.

Elie sat in a cold sweat. At instants he shivered with the tension, knowing the climax was at hand, and more or less what form it would take.

As-Saiqa gurgled and tried to swallow. His teeth chattered like a stampede.

—I t'told you I'm with a c'commando unit. I am ordered one thing, only, t'to do it. I'm not lying!

He caught his breath. He was beside himself with terror, shaking his head back and forth, gasping for air. Where are the positions on that side? Where the reserves? Numbers, man! On what street are the tanks?

He gave childish fending expressions at which Abu Joseph leered, postured—growled.

XXIX

The torturer wore dark gloves which picked up glints from the phosphorescent tubes. He prodded the fingers; he stretched them tighter between questions, glaring at the captive. He said sweetly:

—Talk to me. We're both men of the world. We understand each other without a lot of fuss. I repeat: where were you going, and how many were you?

The taut leather of his gloves shone.

The voice of the victim trembled.

—I t'told you. We were six, on that side of the B'Byb'b—

—Never tell me what I know, filth. Litter of bitches. It is too typical of your kind: the way you fawn, and whine, and always lie. How does it feel, asshole, to have your world be a lie? How often I've seen you strutting along Hamra, brainless refugees. You intimidate the true Lebanese: all the willless ones who say you have a cause. But it seems the revolution has gone on welfare.

Abu Joseph swayed gently from side to side. He stamped his foot to the rhythm of his rage, in a kind of rapturous prelude to torture:

—If you had any courage you'd have fought like men, not puppies, and stayed at home. But instead you came here; you came like dogs wanting to eat at the master's table. You saw the beauty of Lebanon, and tried out your half-baked Marxist ideas on the weak-willed Muslim brothers. Truly, they will believe anything; so you sought to enlist them, and grab our riches for yourselves, scum. It seems your humiliation in Jordan taught you that tactic at least. But there's just no teaching you, it seems, that anyone who doesn't love Lebanon the way she is better get out now. Put your tail between your legs, and scram: go try it somewhere else. Or else learn to die without honor, in that putrid Camp of yours—as it was at Tel ez-Zaater, Sabra and Chatila, your great victories. Leave, man, go find yourself a hole and die in it. Since you were too cowardly, unlike us, to defend God, family and fatherland.

For an instant as-Saiqa appeared to revive. He wanted nothing more than to accept such an offer. But the sight of the Phalangist so menacing, supremely aggravated, on the verge of the worst: this snuffed out his spirit, and he slumped back into himself. His head drooped.

Yet some impulse, inability to sustain the tension any longer, respire such an atmosphere: something made him murmur, a mere liquid whisper in the silence:

—Whose L'Lebanon . . . ?

He hiccoughed. The feeble words surprised everyone.

Abu Joseph was too irate to reply.

—Dog, he said calmly, fatally, and seized the man's head in his big hands.

He cradled it a moment on his pelvis while beginning to apply pressure with thumb and index to the eyes. Beneath the action of this human vise the other started to squirm and writhe in his bonds. The deeply futile note of his responses became an astonished whimper. With a last gasp of will he tried to bite the torturer's meathand, snapping upward. That was ill-advised. More pressure was applied, yet more, more as the Phalangist tested the resilience of his captive's eye-socket and optic nerve.

Suddenly he wailed:

—*I will tell you! I'll give you everything, I'm a friend of Khaddam! No! Please!—I will stop them for you, I will—aaaaangh!*

—Too late! Lying filth! You know nothing except how to butt in your nose where you're not wanted. Even the vermin will be disgusted with you, in your grave, which will be unmarked!

Now the upper body of Abu Joseph was tremorous, bending forward; though his fury seemed almost controlled. Jaw set, he grinned with an intentness.

Elie watched with the others. He felt a kind of grisly fascination as the soldier gave outraged cries, trying to turn his head to one side. As-Saiqa looked crazed by the sight of what was about to happen. His face! *His* head, locked in a vise-grip the size of history. He panted hoarsely and then howled as the two convulsed together, in a jerking rhythm, like a sexual act, with muffled screams and groans.

Then they were quiet, except for an intimate crunch, a hiss of breathing, a sigh. Both went limp together. They subsided, as the horrific music played a few more toneless bars, with a finality.

Abu Joseph took his gloved, bloodied hands away and held them up like a doctor for rinsing. The victim's eyes were a red mucid gristle with a single patch of sclera still visible, staring off at the angle of a dashed entreaty.

Now his gaze seemed hung up above the human, grotesque, vacant, plucked of its personality. It was glazed over, like the carcass of a vision.

In the silence a trickle of fluid formed a pool beneath his chair. He gave a small, unconditional sigh and sat half-slumped, as if his mainspring were broken.

As-Saiqa was reduced to the mere physical, the neutral.

XXX

On a gray towel Abu Joseph wiped his gloves. He gave a gesture palm upward:

—Swine.

The soldier moved his mouth slowly, like a gill, and tried to breathe with a small suction. Abu Joseph turned away in disgust. He had defiled himself. He peered at the Phalangists on hand; and for a moment the delta of wrinkles over his nose appeared to smooth and blend with the greenish, perspiring surface of his forehead. He pondered, listened. The rumble of guns, cannons shared one long vibration from Saifi to the War Council.

—You there, he said. Your turn to try. I'm putting you, Madi, in charge of questioning this prisoner. I want to study your "methods". Come, get to it.

Elie stared in disbelief at his superior. The idea of going even further with this broken soul was too repulsive. Hearing his name he half stood up, but another impulse made him pause. He stared blankly an instant, and then said:

—You speak my name in front of the enemy?

—Na, Abu Joseph shook his head. It has no importance, you will see to that before you're finished. Stop delaying.

Elie approached as-Saiqa. His legs were stiff from sitting through the performance. His stare changed to a look almost of defiance; but he approached and straddled the pool of urine. The man had shit himself as well; the underground space began to stink like a mass grave.

All eyes were on Elie Madi as he cradled the submissive head in his bare hand.

The vacant features streamed blood. It was a tragic mask, minus the revolt and dramatic tension.

Elie repeated the same questions in a drone. For a few minutes he varied them, and tried to coax some sort of adequate response. He spoke softly as if to a child, cajoling, even stroking the man's brow once or twice.

Quickly Abu Joseph grew restless. He crossed, uncrossed his legs in the camouflage he wore so voguishly, tight-fitted above his boots like a riding outfit.

Madi managed to extract a hazy story from the captive of how he stumbled over a dying comrade beside the statue in Burj; how he lost heart when that happened because he never thought he would abandon a friend but he had no choice, there were orders. He had to leave those cries for help, and upraised arms.—

As-Saiqa was groggy, pathetic as he muttered. Madi's style invited his confidence.

And now, said the soldier, swooning, beginning to drift into shock perhaps: now he himself was cut off and fallen into enemy hands; though his enemy had never been the Kataëb... He was never an extremist, and knew little of politics, but was only a peasant *by the Prophet;* more peasant always than militiaman.

He stammered and wept. A tremor came over him, a sob or brief convulsion. He spoke in starts, gurgling. Elie held up his head, hoping the prisoner might faint as blood flowed copiously on his own fingers.

XXXI

Also his mother needed him very much at home since all but one of his brothers had been killed in the siege of Tel ez-Zaater while the other, the youngest was in jail in the Occupied Territories and you didn't know what it was to be a refugee, you didn't know the sorrow... But he had not been in Lebanon when Tel ez-Zaater fell, having come of age and enlisted in Saiqa a year later.

He spoke more for himself now, in low tones, like a testament. Abu Joseph heaved a crushing sigh from where he sat by Kuzayli.

And it wasn't true, not true that he had followed the Syrian treachery and turned his gun on countrymen at the siege in summer '76. No, he was the son of an illiterate peasant and his one desire in life was to go back and help his father, alas, *ya haram!* sharecropping near Mari.

All this mumbling and moaning was not what Elie Madi wished to hear. Faint, dammit, he thought. Look at you: how could anyone . . . ? At first he had tried to coach the prisoner; he hinted at a possible answer.

But now Abu Joseph bore down on them both with his grim stare. As-Saiqa verged on a seizure. As he told his life story in jerky tones, the liquid oozed from his eyes and mouth.

—Not good enough.

Elie glimpsed his superior at the table opposite. A smirk played on the lips of the servile Kuzayli.

All this while the hooded one had sat there, also at the table, like a judge in session. He joined the festive proceedings once Morgan and Ligury left for Sodeco.

But Elie's gaze rolled off theirs, with a futile gesture. The prisoner slumped in his bonds, going into shock finally. The room and its lurid shadows trembled with each echo of a detonation.

Then, with a tight-lipped air, as one pushed to the brink, Elie turned to face his audience. And the lines on Sakr's wide brow were incisive, accusatory, taking note of Elie's hand, supportive, on as-Saiqa's head where it sagged and twitched.

And the unidentified Phalangist, whose eyes and lips protruded from the black hood with an amphibious air, no longer trained his gaze on the curly orangish head of the Palestinian but now, rather, on Elie Madi.

—It won't suffice, said Abu Joseph.

XXXII

He felt the force of their eyes on him—slanderous in their envy of his renown as a fighter; quick to seize on this pretext. And he felt his own anger, welling up. But he let the head fall. He took away his supportive hand, as it slackened to one side.

—You see he knows nothing of importance. Why persist?

—Won't suffice.
—This is time wasted, said Elie.
—Punish him.
—Tell me, who is it you're testing?
—I said punish him.
Elie paused, on the verge. He snapped back:
—When he can't feel it anymore?
—I command here, and you do it.
He rose, standing. Elie frowned, glimpsing the horrendous crumpled features, mask of slime in the ghoulish light.
—No, Sakr, you must be sick.
—What did you say?
—No.
He turned to face his superior. In his last word was a note of protest, slightly atremble like the walls, from some unknown depth in him. The small word seemed to arrive on his lips from a distance.
And the Phalangist captain, his voice shearing the sudden silence:
—Imbecile, you disobey?
—And then? With such obedience we'll all end up in ashes.

No reply: again the silence, seeming to reassert its rights. It erased the huge whistling din outside, the roar across Ashrafiyeh.
The blinded fighter rallied, and made wheezing attempts to breathe. Blood dripped from his mustache to his shirt and soaked in. His boot plashed randomly in the puddle around his chair.
When Abu Joseph spoke again, his tone was detached:
—Leave it, Madi. I've watched you a long time, talented but stupid. Always the nonconformist: I think you need a little lesson.
Elie's eyes went wide.
—Are you crazy?
—I'm putting you on the frontline, up the hill. You're not to leave the Camp, Madi, for the duration of the siege. Kuzayli, you can take him up there.
—As you say.
—One small infraction, the slightest sign of any further deviation on your part—you'll be court-martialed.

Abu Joseph turned away; he moved toward the prisoner. But he spun back around, pointing:

—Madi, never say *Sakr*. You never say my family name in front of the enemy. Do you know what that means, for a prisoner?

—Too human of you . . . Sakr.

Elie mumbled. His face had gone ashen.

—What?

But Kuzayli was already escorting his charge, up the steps leading from the bunker.

PART THREE

I

The Camp was a low mass of corrugated tin or pasteboard, zinco roofs, old doors used for siding along with scraps of wood, plaited cane. People lived six and more to a room in normal times; when the wind rose, tarpaulin flapped, siding knocked about—the entire Camp swayed like a field of weeds. If a gale blew in off the Mediterranean, everyone had to stay outside: the adults tried to hold up flimsy structures supposed to shelter them in precisely such times. Children sniffled with the onset of colds, pneumonia. In general it was twenty thousand refugees living in an eyesore.

Before the siege, a fourth of the people went off to work each morning, earning a daily salary of three to ten Lebanese Lira. No benefits; they were regarded as imported labor. Some five percent of the children overflowed schools directed by the U.N. The United Nations paid a high rent to the Order of Maronite Monks who owned the land; an average of 50 Lira monthly per family. The tenants were hired per diem by Beirut industrialists. The Camp was a sweltering, restless maze in summer, and a massive ditch during the winter rains, with a hundred endemic diseases.

But in 1968–'69 came the rise of Palestinian Resistance. After the Battle of Karameh in '68, Beirut's "belt of misery" camps began to grow in political awareness. They armed themselves, constituting a virtual state within a state which was sanctioned by the Arab world, in the form of the Cairo Accords.

II

Hana'a Chahrour paused on mud steps leading to the underground children's clinic. On the heights overlooking Ashrafiyeh, a tall cyprus stood between blue sky and lush subtropical landscape.

The red-tiled roofing of villas lay interspersed with the deep green of shrubbery. Offshore there were whitecaps and several low-flying clouds. After a night of unstinting artillery the distant rumbling had subsided for awhile. Hana'a gazed toward the foothills looking stark and denuded in the early afternoon light.

She was 17 years old, and a nurse. Dr. Kamel, the Camp pediatrician, was a balding but handsome man whose eye met things clearly, with a frequent smile despite everything. Neatly dressed, but never clean-shaven. She thought of the agile kindness in Dr. Kamel's expression: forever tested by reality, as if its cause must be taken up by his sharp eye, his creased brow. He had trained in France before working two decades among refugees.

The underground clinic was cooler and more spacious than anything above ground. Inside, she stood by the front desk and picked up a list of medicines:

—Nystatin drops, ten units. Twelve units Ferlexir . . .

She glanced through a half-open door into the second room. And there she saw them: the small figures twisting, raising an arm or leg like a stick along the row of beds. She heard a thin, plaintive music in a minor mode; it came from the inner sanctum of pain, though only a segment was visible.

Not the bawling of normal children, when they're hurt (one voice did rise in a strange sluggish kind of hysteria); but rather a mournful tone, a feeble puling. Like a dirge of insects.

Children hummed in a dissonance of pain, but the song was almost sweet anyway, and very eerie. Odors of sickness, of bodies suffering chronic malnutrition, dehydration and cloying in the dank fermented air. They seemed to achieve their full effect despite the unripeness, or innate optimism of childhood.

Hana'a looked over a requisition signed by Dr. Kamel, wondering if even one of the patients didn't have scabies. It was like a leper colony; and then they scratched and broke them open in their sleep, which led to vicious staph infections.

Inside, it was a scene of puppets in mild chaos. They made small sounds and movements, as if their strings were in the hands of a bad-tempered puppeteer. It was a kind of primitive brink.

She found Dr. Kamel by a girl's bedside, and asked:
—What about the lentils?

He smiled grimly. Four teachers, advocates of Islamic Renaissance, had refused to participate in the defense of the Camp. They went about calling people to prayer, forever leading the ritual washings (with water a precious substance), prostrations, praying at prescribed hours while a battle raged. One of the four, Moustafa, showed great courage as he scurried here and there mustering the faithful. When the Camp mosque was shelled, Moustafa became the only muezzin left intact.

And then, with one of the others, he came upon a warehouse filled with sacks of lentils, chickpeas and starch. With little food, no bread or milk for the children, the women began baking bread from lentils and a little water. They brewed lentil tea whenever someone came back from risking their life at the sniped spigot. Hana'a joined in with the children when they sang the "Lentils Song":

We eat lentil bread
    And say okay!
We drink tea drawn from martyrs' blood—
    The only way!

Without shame we eat the lentils,
    Little brown ones.
O Tel ez-Zaater, Sabra and Chatila!
    You are our eyes
        And our honor.

The only problem was that Moustafa and his friends, as the siege progressed into its fourth and fifth week, had begun trafficking in the stock of provisions they kept back for themselves. The four were making capital, lentil by lentil, of the other refugees' misery.

III

One girl in the clinic had emerald eyes. She was pretty, eight years old, but her body looked shrunken like a child mummy. Also, her eyes were sick, and unable to rest on Hana'a or the doctor. Her attempt to smile was opposed by the unending hurt, so she forgot him, and moaned a kind of puerile dirge.

—Salwa, Hana'a cooed. Salwa.

Dr. Kamel put a hand on her hot forehead. He raised the sheet from her amputated right leg, and her gaze drifted from them. The bandage was wet and no longer clean. Blood and pus made a hem along its border.

—Hana'a, redo this.
—Yes, Hakim.

It was gristle rolled in strips of skin, beneath the inflamed sutures.

Salwa had been at the U.N. school on the third of last month: the day the siege began, when Phalangist guns opened up suddenly. Often they shelled just to terrify, but this time projectiles poured down on the playground where Salwa was running.

Suddenly the Camp was surrounded. She and the others could not be evacuated; though a Red Crescent team did manage to come in haste, and operated, with their elaborate mobile unit.

Other patients whined along with Salwa. Or they gagged. There was continuous coughing, like a percussion section to the feeble whimper of sufferers. All were prone to respiratory ailments and infections, bronchitis, since their lives had been spent sleeping on the cold earth of camps, or in air-raid shelters. Often there was no water, electricity, no warm clothes and covers. With the women and old people they had made long treks in the darkness during the season of rains. They had fled enemy attacks, and constant troop incursions in the South.

Tarek was a small wide-eyed boy, a victim of chronic malnutrition and presently hepatitis. Dr. Kamel kept him in a small partitioned space by himself. Sudki, frail, his hair a mass of cowlicks on the gray pillow, had an arm gangrened to the elbow. To be amputated shortly; although there was no more anaesthetic, or proper supply of antibiotics. Dr. Kamel had tried without success to save Sudki's hand which was smashed, also during the onset of siege, like a moth on a windshield.

Hana'a and the doctor made their noonday rounds. Much of their method lay in touching, and also tickling. Dr. Kamel put his hairy hand to the swelter of their foreheads; he burrowed his thumb beneath their chins, which made them smile and squirm with pleasure. The young nurse touched their dwindled and tense little bodies in an effort to cajole the pain, so they wouldn't feel completely abandoned, for the time of a vaguely consoling thought or memory of a parent who hadn't been as fortunate.

By one bed she fingered the bruised flesh, like rotten meat, of a boy's shoulder.

Other children seemed to be fading slowly; they receded into the sheets which were off-white with washing, rinsing and pounding when there was no clean water. They shrunk back as if trying to deprive the torment of its full extension.

All looked brain-dulled, and most had sick eyes with conjunctivitis or strabism. They squinted at light. They shied from human contact. The attention seemed to focus them on the wrong done their minds and bodies, and the long morbidity. But Hana'a tickled and cuddled them anyway. Sooner or later they would open up again, and the thwarted trust would sprout a tiny stem, a leaf, a small gauze of root in the earth of their stubborn selfhood.

IV

In the Camp it was a deluge of shelling, day after day, as rockets came slamming in from the overlooking hills. Rightist snipers lay in wait for every sector, but the refugee population lived underground in a system of bunkers, trenches and also Dr. Kamel's three clinics. In the heat of midday nothing moved. There were mortar and anti-aircraft barrages from Dekwaneh and Monsouriyyeh. The Phalangists had tons of captured weaponry, bought on the open market and donated, from past Middle East wars: M-50 Sherman tanks as well as Soviet T-54 tanks, 20 mm. cannons, Spanish 7.62 machineguns. They had anti-tank weapons, ENTACS courtesy of the CIA:—all these and more were used on a mass of crumbling hutments like a garbage dump extending to the Camp dwellers' horizon.

They were also used on a teeming population of rats, stray cats and dogs, huge cockroaches drawn there by the bodies decomposing along muddy roads and pathways. Dr. Kamel had never seen such clouds of flies, like cinders of a dying sun.

The refugees had moved en masse to a second Camp beneath the ground, occupying certain stronger buildings and factory basements. Still, Sheikh Moustafa was eager for his calling, and led prayers routinely. But soon he was forbidden to gather and transport worshipers because of the snipers, at which he protested, and cried it was religious persecution. But the Phalange had started taking pot-shots at corpses from sheer impatience; at scurrying rats for target practice. Ammunition was not what they lacked.

—He would take such risks for Allah, said Dr. Kamel to Hana'a. But would he go out for water?

In the Camp a cup of water was worth a cup of blood. Shelling caused gaps in the piping, which began sucking in impurities. This combined with the heaping garbage, open sewage drains and stench of decay. Now there was no fit drinking water, so sewage was boiled, along with rainwater from cement shelter-holes. But this was infected by the hundreds of living and dead animals as well.

When a five year-old boy died of rabies, Dr. Kamel gave an order to shoot all the carrion-eating cats and dogs. Deep trenches were dug for the dead fighters, also a dozen children per day dying of thirst during the past two weeks. But a mortar had plunged in on a communal gravesite the day before; now there were limbs and pieces of hewn corpses everywhere.

The Camp had become a muddy soup, with immense bloodstains on the pitiful facades still left standing. It was raining death, thought Dr. Kamel, on a people who once owned orchards, living in closeknit villages with a long tradition of peasant life, folkways, yearly festivals.

V

A small boy named Khalifeh gave Hana'a a smile all askew, since his left eye glanced away at its own angle. Poor Khalifeh's smile, he thought, laden with the nobility of childhood pain, like a greeting between equals.

They all had difficulty in keeping food down. The intravenous equipment was running out also, so staff had to administer nourishment in a long drawn-out way, by hand. Hana'a Chahrour was good at it because she was so attentive.

A girl named Fadia, aged seven, showed a mild vague panic when the nurse leaned down and pressed her head to Fadia's small and cringing warmth. Hana'a tried to pace herself, and remember as Dr. Kamel instructed not to impose her own stress-ridden war tempo on the children. She had to take her time; or not her time, but theirs.

Another girl flailed an arm to and fro across her body, and this caused further bleeding beneath the bandage on her neck and shoulder. Hana'a enfolded her face in a caress, and whispered gentle nonsensical words in her ear, while barring the restless movement with an arm. When they fastened her wrist to the bedstead, this girl, whose name was Jihad, began to cry in a shrill small voice that rose in a solo above the chorus of moaning, coughing, whimpering. And now the blood came in little rills, dripping from her ribs and hospital gown onto Hana'a where she sat, arms full, alongside her.

She called Dr. Kamel for a look.

—Just apply pressure, he said, until it stops. The dressing must be changed, but later, and very carefully. This way.

Jihad writhed. She was determined to flail, back and forth.

—She needs sedation, Hakim. Look at her.

—Eh, she does. And you are it.

In the next bed sat Mayser: the mystery case. Unlike the others Mayser kept silent except for a kind of chipmunk twitter. Also, he was sitting up. He sat in the small beige mess of his diaper.

His emaciated torso swung on itself with the steady rocking motion often seen in retarded children. But Mayser was not retarded, at least not from birth. Toward one end of his semicircle he threw out a crooked baton of an arm, pointing at something fearful in the extreme.

Mayser's hair was sandy-hued and unusually sparse. His large forehead was wrinkled like an octogenarian; his eyes showed the wear and tear of an ongoing bout with anorexia. Nearly three years old, he had refused to utter an articulate sound for over six months. He would eat nothing unless with great patience, coaxing by Hana'a or one of the other nurses. Of course, he was a sponge for attention in his way; he was the mascot of the clinic.

But what was wrong with him?

VI

Each day more people went out for water and offered easy targets to snipers using telescopic sites, tripods—at their leisure. After dark a spotlight was trained on the spigot, and Phalangist loudspeakers cried out through the night:

—Don't make any noise! We are trying to sleep!
—If we kill you, your bodies are going to stink!
—Surrender, two-legged animals!
—Look what you do to your loved ones, O selfish pigs!
—Surrender, and we'll give you Coca-Cola!

Often there were children around the water tap. It was like a magnet, and they too were hit by the avid snipers.

Dr. Kamel was supervising the three main clinics; though when the Camp hospital had to be evacuated, a number of other rudimentary treatment centers were set up. It was hard to move people. Cases of contagious gangrene had developed, and these were kept in one of the underground facilities, which had an operating theater, air-conditioning, its own well. But by this time there was a shortage of mazout oil to run the generator.

Thus much of the equipment was more or less useless, and soon Dr. Kamel had no materials for bandaging open wounds. Nurses resorted to tearing up clothes or any cloth at hand, not always sanitary. A corps of fifteen men and women served as nurses, and some were hit by snipers as they moved between centers. Hana'a was rivalling the Camp defenders, including Selman, the leader, in her reputation for reckless courage.

On the south side there were four- and five-storey buildings: the fighters made them bulge with sandbags. There were barricades of overturned cars, kitchen appliances, junk in barrels: all rusted out, which caused tetanus from minor cuts, especially among the children. With the dried-up sewer system, plus trenches and channels being extended everyday, it amounted to a fortified network all underground.

As if hypnotized by Mayser, his pendulum effect, Hana'a stayed by his bedside in a revery. Hour after hour, the child would turn back and forth, pointing at something tremendously fearful.

—Mays-Mayser! she whispered. Little ritual man.

His eye met hers like two molecules. But not for an instant did he break his rhythm, as long as someone sat alongside and watched.

Was it wrong to reinforce such a bizarre symptom? Would leaving him alone be any better? Mayser swung, pointed. He fixed the nurse's kindly gaze and gave a profound grimace. He trembled a little, like fear incarnate, a harrowing soundless shriek.

Then, pursing his lips, very sage once again, he pivoted on his bloated belly. Pointed his arm like a stick. Swung round, with a mask of fright, to report on his vision of terror—proving, once again, unable.

—Hana'a, said Dr. Kamel, I'm going now. You know Nabila is here.

He stooped by Mayser. He kissed him, imprinting a mock-anger on his pale, oldish cheek and forehead. But Mayser turned away from him, very serious.

VII

When the doctor was gone Hana'a grabbed Mayser's head and jutting arm and held him to her. The little boy resisted but she planted a kiss on his temple and smack on the nose, forehead. She brushed away a shock of sparse sandy hair and then warbled and laughed a moment, an unusual thing for Hana'a Chahrour.

Despite his resistance she overwhelmed him with kindness for the sheer sake of it, an almost irresponsible tenderness. He gave a startled sound and let himself settle on her breast for a few seconds, before trying to wriggle away.

—Later we'll play! she whispered, laughing low. Later I'll bring you something, a toy for Mayser!

She rose from the bed. She looked stern suddenly; her goldish-brown hair was darker in this shadowy corner of the underground clinic; it fell in a soft cascade on one shoulder.

All the children loved Hana'a. A few watched the rhythm of her girlish figure as she went from the room.

In the bed by the exit an older child was vomiting, with a frog-like sound over the bedpan; retching almost quietly, lips covered with sputum.

A small bar of noonday sun had crept round the east-facing exit, as if emulating a mole. A dreadful stink mingled with gusts of sea spray, and springtime wafted from foliage of long plantations on the coastal plains south of Beirut. Rotting corpses were tinged with the sunlit Mediterranean, and the year's first jasmines, making inroads on the gruesome odors of a country in its death throes.

Behind her, Hana'a still heard the lament of sick and languishing children, the passive doleful chorus of their protests. At times she caught a most exasperated, hurt wonder in their eyes: as if not being spoiled like lively normal children from morning till night were only the first grave infringement of their rights.

Their bodies were stunted and ill-prepared, she thought, for the pain which wouldn't compromise. From the lips of the children came a lifeless, hoarse elegy for what seemed a bereaved future.

VIII

Risha, framed in the doorway between their rooms, seemed to act as Peretz' go-between with reality. He hung back, brooding, self-absorbed as ever in the rear bedroom. Risha waited in the silence which was stuffy, like a bi-product of their daylong being together. The quiet was an entity to itself, amid a grumbling of distant guns toward the Camp.

She looked prim. Usually she was sharp and talkative, a youngish career woman misclad at the moment in bluejeans and a t-shirt.

She waited on the principal, Morgan, who sat legs crossed and head bowed, writing something in a small black notebook on her bed.

A portion of Peretz was visible beyond Risha's figure in the doorway. He sat naked from the waist, a patch of sunlight on his neck and shoulders. Peretz stared straight ahead, as if transfixed by the wonder of something beyond science.

—We are considering the need to—

Morgan looked up from her jotting. Risha's ability to irritate was more important than anything she might have to say.

—You claim you're on the right track. But it's dragging on too long.

—Not on the "track"—I said soon we move across the city.

—So you did. Is the VW running smoothly at least? Is it ready?

—Ask Peretz; that's his department.

—Fine, but we aren't satisfied. As you know, I'm not speaking merely for the two of us.

—Why so nervous, Risha? I respect you for sticking it out this long, and keeping your head. We knew there were no angels here; Khalil has done what he can.

—That's not the point. The assignment was clear before we arrived. You—

—Aren't you up to the stress? I wish it was easy, too. But this one is big.

—The thing should be set up by now.

—It takes time to get access in East Beirut. Now I do have the contact.

—Too much time. It becomes necessary, I'm afraid, to decide.

Past Risha, past the doorjamb Peretz sat engaged in some slow, intricate activity. He was tinkering with the electrical gear; but in the way of a snake charmer, an Old Testament seer. It was nuanced, terribly involved, as he handled the wiring. Once and again Morgan sensed his dark eyes like sparks along the pattern of black coil, as he tried to ignite her as well, perhaps, and share the mystery. And Risha sensed it also, as if her jealousy, in these six weeks of fond togetherness, had grown an eye in the back of her quick-witted head.

In that instant Morgan understood Risha's impatience, staring right through her at the quirky Peretz. And it seemed to her, trying to defuse the situation, that one of them would be sacrificed before this was over. One would be martyred to the cause—on the altar, no doubt, of her lover's high mystery.

She recalled how, when Risha was out spotting, once, he involved her in his ritual. He had sat on her bed and explained, in the tone of some hallowed office, the complicated mechanism. He showed her his modified transmitter/receiver, then the relay, which he tested several times. Then the detonator—mystical element in the process—

which couldn't be tested without proceeding to the ultimate step. And Morgan sat alongside him, head bent down in a grave appreciation. She was being led by a secretive Peretz to the altar of what high sacrifice, what immolation which could make a Job of nations? Afterward he wanted to make love but she said: wait till we succeed.

IX

Lately she realized that although her partners might sleep together, it was she and not Risha who counted Peretz for an ally. Probably... And why? Because Peretz was dying of hunger for the impossible. Risha was just too exclusive in her tastes. As if being patriotic meant she should have her way, in little things, at all costs. Everyone was duty-bound to cater to her, because of her total dedication. But this was all too routine: too well-trodden a path for the great explorer who was Peretz, with his technological passport into unknown realms.

Before long Risha's charms would declare no contest, in a contest with Morgan. It was a fine thing, she thought, how much brute force resided in a woman's palm. She could radiate like a goddess by merely thwarting his male will.

—You go out there. You enjoy yourself on company time, meeting new people, sleeping with them. You call that "access"?

Morgan gave a low laughter. She closed the small notebook in her hand. Go on, bitch, snap. I have you now.

—I hear your frustration. I know your concern, and I agree. But the time is almost ripe; we must stick to the plan.

—You run off to Ydlibbi's, and the glamor. Is that serious? Is it working for the cause, or even earning your salary?

—Don't oversimplify.

—I thought we shared ideals. But it's no wonder. Did your parents, your grandparents die in Hitler's gas chamber?

—Listen, Risha. I care, and I'm trying. What's more we have every chance of... carrying this through. But you can't push people beyond their limit.

—Uh-huh.

There was a twinkle in Morgan's eye. She caught another fleeting glance from Peretz. She peered past Risha and said:

—Will his lordship leave the apartment today?

—Probably, he said, calmly, I will not. Tell me not to, dear Principal Officer, and I won't.

Risha waited to hear the reaction. He was being seductive. Morgan evaded:

—Is the gear in order.

He didn't answer. He wanted her to play along.

—At any moment I may come bursting in here, and say: now's the time. Are you ready?

—I may go out later on: for a newspaper.

Risha cast a glimpse at her lover. Her large mouth was petulant and very expressive, contradicting the tight control of her eyes. It seemed prehensile.

Morgan looked from one to the other:

—You jeopardize the mission, and our lives, each time you lack discipline and walk through that door.

—Don't tell us about discipline, said Risha. We've stayed in here for weeks.

In the other room Peretz smirked. But he had a dangerous habit of strolling along Hamra, buying the Tribune and reading it over an aperitif while ogling the local version of yeh-yehs, future bourgeoisie of Islam. And with the first false move, arousing the interest of a shop owner, or passerby, there would be trouble. All had contacts with the local strongman; they were sensitive to the comings and goings of their dense quarter.

For every Arab ruined due to politics there was another intent on profiting from the wave of xenophobia, kidnappings, fabulous ransoms.

Now Morgan suppressed an urge to let it all out, and have done with her own six-week arrears of irritation.

Peretz still smirked, waiting for his answer.

I have to go, said Morgan. There's a lot to do. But please, you two, hold on a bit longer.

—We resent your attitude, said Risha, solemnly.

—That's fair. Just stick to the plan. And let me tell you something. The *Memuneh* chose me—do you even know his name? He said: one fiasco was enough for us. Bouchiki was enough, we'll not be scandalized... So listen, Peretz, you will not leave this apartment. It's a command.

She made to depart in a flourish. But as she closed the door behind her, Risha played a trump.

—You remember what I said, as well. We've decided on something, and that is: your time is limited. If not "soon", like you say, we close up shop. Botched mission. When you return, Miss Principal Officer, please have the details in your pocket.

X

In the Sioufi shelter the obese man, named Saleem Il-Hrawey, was staging a losing battle against himself. He went over the same old story; but this time he spoke for the benefit of Mrs. Madi and another housewife seated alongside her. Elie's younger brother, Emile, considered it beneath his dignity to listen.

Il-Hrawey punctuated his sentences with small gasps for breath.

—And I had the foolishness to think one may trust a Musulman. Ben-sharmouta! (He spat.) And a landlord as well... But he was waiting; the s.o.b. waited to see how it would be, in Kantari, when the battle was over. I was obliged to stay with a friend at the time, on Hamra. My own apartment was fifth-floor, the downtown side, and exposed. So this *ben* he called in a few of his Kurdish friends; they were just flocking into Burj and Bab Edriss about that time—refugees, with nothing on earth, you see. The whole thing was prearranged with the *zaim,* our local boss, since that coward of a landlord would never do anything on his own. The ones controlling the quarter: they had their eyes on me a good while before this time. And then those sullen Kurds came with no truck or wheelbarrow, just some men from down in Wadi Abu Jamil. First one thing, now another, and with what eagerness they moved me out. No need for stealth either: they transferred me gratis into the land of refugees. Tables, lamps, a family heirloom in their filthy hands, stained with the grime of markets. And so my life of forty-five years was dispersed in a matter of seconds. They ruined me piece by piece. *Iani...*I am an only child, sole surviving heir. And now my family tradition, from Beit Mery on my father's side, found its way into the hands of thieves—in a snuffbox, a landscape painting; rocking chair my mother had loved.

The fat man fairly panted between phrases. There was a kind of hissing in his front teeth, on the verge of tears.

—I almost felt the grandparents were on hand to watch, their spirits preserved in those keepsakes. I was a bachelor, on my own for twenty years. My life took its meaning from the Kantari apartment. But that was before *they* arrived. And before *they* began pissing in our ciboria, poking out the eyes of our saints with their Klashnikovs, desecrating the cemeteries. Didn't they ransack and plunder St. Elias? For decades the cry of their muezzins, like a man with a bellyache, has drowned out our chiming belfries. And then the sound of dying was a thousand muezzins, calling the world to prayer. But who ever heard?

"So I happened to come walking from Rue Spears in the sunshine, and there was my oakwood bedstead, bumping along. Every bump was a bruise on my soul. There goes my mahogany secretary, and my father's old armchair which needs reupholstering. All of it went down a side street toward Bab Edriss, in the clutches of Kurds. It was my own life passing by me in a cortege. It was like going to my own funeral, performed by infidels.

"So I turned and went along the other way. No word spoken, motus. My mother's dresser, its mirror in the ornate frame. Even a fur covering for my toilet seat, and genuine too. I'll probably see it on tv some night: the wife of a Chi'ite v.i.p. wearing my toilet cover."

The obese man broke off, sighing. He swallowed. Mrs. Madi and Emile heard him gritting his teeth in the darkness.

—So I had to say something. I said, Heu! These are my things you're hauling off that way. Alright, they said, you pay us for delivery. It was the *zaim* who sent us, we work on his orders. Pay up right now or the worse for you. You know, I laughed at them. The tears started, and I spit at the man's feet, saying: I am a Christian.

"But he took a pistol from his shirt like a bandido and touched my nose with it, back and forth, saying: Empty your pockets on the ground. And then they discussed taking my clothes as well, all but my underdrawers, so I wouldn't insult any women passing by. That done, as I stood shivering, one kicked me and I fell on the sidewalk. I cut my forehead, see the scar? And the other said, Get out of here, and never come back. Go find your Christian brothers in East Beirut: die with them like a pile of dogs.

"My life was nothing to those men. Less than the price of a cartridge. If this was during one of the hot times, when they need hostages... But the thing happened between rounds of fighting; and I was one of the innocents, I wasn't involved.

"So I stayed there flat on the ground, groaning like a pig. A dresser, a Persian rug... my suits and trousers on hangers. Family portraits in the hands of a lice-ridden child. I lay there, taking a last look at my past filing by.

"One of those rascals nudged me further into the gutter. But I didn't resist."

Across the shelter the candles flickered. A pocket flashlight glowed in someone's palm. The green phosphorescent tubes lent a sinister glow.

Upstairs, the door swung open. It was dramatic, as an envoy of the bright lacerated afternoon came down the steps. In the odor of human closeness, the scent of liquor and sharp perfume, a whiff of fresh air came in to taunt the languid gathering.

XI

One by one, stepping down, three figures eclipsed the sunlight in the entry.

—Allô! Careful ma soeur.

—A bit of light for us on these steps!

It was Père Zaki in his white robe. There were stirrings among the crowd. Everybody knew Père Zaki; he brought hope like Christ's sword.

At his mother's bidding, flashlight in hand, Emile Madi took the stairs two at a time.

But the obese man kept up his narrative, still cursing the Kantari landlord. Mrs. Madi tried to pay attention, as Salem told of relations prior to the eviction. It seems they were on the best of terms, salaaming with a grin. One paid homage to President Nasser, with a topical remark, while the other made a pedantic reference to Western progress. Now and again they sipped coffee together, and shared the newspapers they read. Oh! it was a sly Judas, confound his soul.

Clad in a splendid white robe Père Zaki minced no words as he told everyone what was happening.

—Ein Rummaneh, mais quel désastre! The bombardment is beyond description! This time they are going all the way... But we must be very steadfast; our heroic leaders are telling the story, loud and clear, for all the world to hear. They are bearing witness to the truth. But just listen to your radios; you are better updated than I am, running from shelter to shelter. I assure you we have great cause for pride.

A child was crying, feebly. Saleem Il-Hrawey was obliged to pause at the entry of visitors. Soeur Davida and their driver went stepping among groups of family and friends in search of the children. She brought two 5-gallon containers of water.

Soeur Davida was tried and true in this difficult work; she was an old hand at succoring the needy even in peacetime. Also, she knew how to dodge and make her way among the outstretched hands. One man asked her for a wee bit, a teaspoonful; he pleaded for a spot of the precious liquid, but she refused, aware from his bleary eyes that he wanted to stretch his gin a bit further. Why wasn't he at the barricades? Why wasn't he down sniping in Burj?

XII

All this time Elie had been sitting by himself to one side. He came straight from another abortive meeting with Jessica, after spending 72 hours in his position overlooking the Camp. Now he badly needed a place to hole up and think things through.

At first his mother's reception was a fretful one. She sensed something was wrong, and Emile also wondered why he didn't want to talk, or discuss the siege. Elie sat arms crossed over his drawn-up knees; he appeared to doze with his head bowed to one side. Ordinarily, he would have told the fat man to shut up and stop worrying people with his rancorous spiel. But now his own position, among them, seemed vulnerable and open to question. He was a Phalangist whose resolve had been shaken, as if he shied from combat. Gone therefore, in his own mind, was the fighter's privilege of imposing his will on others.

But he sat trying to understand his own feelings. Hadn't he seen more than his share of frontline action? And rendered unquestionable service to the Party? Were these people, in the shelter, grateful? Had they been out there? No, they had no right to judge him a coward if, in the depths of his being, he felt tired and spent as a combatant.

For awhile he sensed they were giving him sidelong glances, pinning a label on him. But let them go have a look at Abu Joseph in action; let them be under Sakr's command. Elie felt in his marrow how they wanted him to go away, and even his brother. He almost welcomed the chatter of the undisciplined Hrawey, diverting their attention, and his anguish.

He felt a dire inexplicable need to be near his mother. Other fighters were out there perishing, as combined Left forces stepped up attacks to relieve pressure from the Camp under siege. But where could he go from here? There was certainly no safe place for him until nightfall.

Elie remembered Sylvie Helou and somehow felt a keen sympathy for her. She had no place to go either; she too was estranged from everyone, including her own family. No longer able to grab hold; away from her people's cause, she went drifting without a lifeline. And then? Where to now? The earth entire was given over to war and hatred.

In his fearful shame, Elie Madi saw the name of SAKR over all the exits leading from Ashrafiyeh.

XIII

Père Zaki shook his head, denouncing the opportunist Syrians, aggressor Palestinians, wayward leftists of the Lebanese National Movement. A major Phalangist counter-attack was on the way, just as surely as he stood there. Yet a little while, and it was coming. Père Zaki spoke of what for a civilized being was the best offering to God, and true sign of election, namely defending one's homeland against the pagan hordes.

Hrawey murmured,

—Jesus, it's the same refrain.

He was piqued at being so rudely removed by Zaki from center stage. Even though he spent much of his time in this same Père Zaki's *Centre Catholique*. On weekdays he had lunch there for a pittance, and was permitted to display his new collection of shell fragments, grenade pins and other such objets d'art in a glass case.

—What nonsense is this, Saleem?

—I said a fifth of scotch would be more to the purpose.
He muttered.
—"Your suffering is equal to your courage," Père Zaki quoted Kataëb radio.

Elie raised his head a little. His dark eyes gleamed in the shadows, like some wild thing. Candlelight lent the father's smudged robe a luster.

—What? You here?
—Never mind, I'm resting.
—Never mind? And what of the others? What of those covering your absence, and dying in Burj?
—You're not my keeper.

Père Zaki's face was stern, sere. Mrs. Madi looked stunned, and there was a murmur among the others. But just then the fat man broke in, storming the podium:

—I would ask the father, he panted, to define a concept! It is "honor of Lebanon"—define it, please, and prove Socrates was no Catholic!

—Mon cher, said Père Zaki, you're quite an intellectual.

Emile Madi gave a chortle, enjoying the circus. But Elie bowed slightly, staring straight ahead; he thought: soon I'll have to leave.

The priest smiled, unctuous:

—Then I will tell you, Saleem, about "honor of Lebanon". I will say what you know already; though you seem to have fallen back into childhood, and become worthless to us.

The father's pale face detached like a mask from the darkness. His wrinkles were dense yet precise, incised by a burin of survival.

—Père, you and I know this concept can't be made clear. We talk about it constantly, but why?

—It is, said the father rocking a little, taking a stance. It is to be a torch, in a region like the valley of the shadow. We, Maronites, are a cultural haven. Look at our towns, our streets. See the order there— and then, Saleem, go to Mazra, even Hamra. And don't mention places like Sidon and Tyre, those dens of iniquity. Go take a look, my friend, and then return if you're able. Can they match our mail delivery, sanitation, bus service, our parking lots? Do you think there are buses in West Beirut? No, only rusted illegible signs, marking stops in a world defunct. Alas, our Muslim neighbors are confused; and their daily lives, regulated by the Koran, make an easy prey for the irrational. Ah, they dare to call us fascists; but I say their holy Koran is the real slave-maker. Whereas we uphold individual freedom, a free-spirited glory in a climate of intolerance. Please run the "concept" of Islamic Bomb through your mind, mon cher, think of it. A world-destroyer in the hands of fanatics.

—*Merde,* said Hrawey, sighing to get a word in edgewise. Our leaders resemble theirs—politicians capable of anything to preserve their little power. They don't care about us: we get massacred, while they manipulate.

Hrawey's eyes rolled toward the ceiling. Père Zaki countered:

—You, of all people, can say such things? And to me? They expelled you: they ruined you. And you think that happened by accident? I took you in, Saleem, when you were homeless.

—Eh, Père, it's not so simple.

Suddenly the father turned on Elie Madi, whose eyes seemed aglow with interest.

—What are you staring at?

—I'm waiting.

—Oh? And for what? Till it's too late?

—Hm.

—You have no business here. You belong at the Camp, where you're needed.

Elie met Père Zaki's stare.

Hrawey grumbled.

—Shit on "our honor."

—Saleem, said Elie's mother, shaking her head. Is this suitable?

Her voice was mild, but deeply disheartened.

—He's finished, said the priest, a finger to his temple. The stress has broken down many of us; but one must be so proud of our people. We will win against all odds; we have hurled our gauntlet at the uncaring world.

—Nonsense.

—"To be Lebanese," Père Zaki recited, "is to fight for one's liberty at the cost of one's blood."

XIV

Père was well-known in the Maronite community, a figure of great influence. People greeted him in shops and along the streets of Ashrafiyeh. They showed him a casual reverence, exchanging a few words on the Lord's blessings, or current state of political affairs. He had held forth in the discreet splendor of Mrs. Charles Malek's salon; he was adept at debriefing any liberal Westerners who might be on hand. Also, he knew as well as the next Maronite shepherd, Charbel Kassis for instance, how to dismantle an M-16 and service it after use.

Outside, there was a high whistle; a sound of creasing air, explosion, fissuring concrete. The priest never flinched, but Hrawey was gulping his saliva by this time, breathing audibly like someone with angina pains. Elie sat folded on himself in the darkness, in a posture hinting of regression.

Soeur Davida returned; she moved through a group of women pleading in subdued tones, about to clutch a piece of her as she passed. They pulled Soeur Davida back like an undertow, as one knelt to kiss the soiled hem of her robe.

—Sister, where can we go?

—Have they overrun Burj as Radio Liban reported?

—Ay, think of it. Will there be an evacuation?

Their driver was a feisty and humorous old man; he went in front trying to calm their anguish with his two hands. At the same time he gestured people back from the black-robed nun, whose plastic water containers were long empty.

A circle formed, on chairs and crates in the bay of semi-darkness at the foot of the stairs. Others crowded round. On a hot plate Mrs. Madi prepared a dense pungent coffee.

—I have witnessed so much heroism, said the sister. Many of the children, who instead of playing and going to school, must learn to endure down here—they are the first to understand. We must all pull together; it takes only an instant for the snake, the sin of doubting, to enter in.

—God tempers us in His fire, said the priest.

—I remember, said Soeur Davida, I will not soon forget a week I spent in the vicinity of Chekka. Not one of us was safe. It was two o'clock on a certain afternoon; you sensed anything was possible, and life had lost its sacredness in the eyes of our enemy. A group of armed Muslims arrived in the village. They took over the police station, and demanded that one of our leaders go with a group of their people to a place ten kilometers distant, and help resolve a tense situation. Had the Kataëb staged a reprisal for Muslim acts of aggression in the area? Had a chain reaction of terror been set off in these mountain communities? Mystère! But the man, named Dr. Paul Rizk, was obliged to get in the car.

"Meanwhile, they tore down the Lebanese flag and seized arms in the village gendarmerie. A number of local Muslims began setting up checkpoints, controlling the roads. They seized the communications offices, and prevented any contact with the outside.

"By evening there were cars arriving with more armed men. They wore keffiyehs and carried Klashnikovs. I ventured outside, thinking they wouldn't harm a nun. But Blessed Savior, what a feeling of suspicion in the air, what tension in the crowd of men at the central square.

"Still, nothing came of it that evening. We lived through those hours in a state of anguish, feeling we were just on the brink. All of you have known such hours, and sleepless nights.

"Then I arrived at the Merhabi home and found them gathered in the living room with very long, not to say tragic faces. They told me their son Georges had gone out around five the previous evening, saying he would return in two hours. Was he kidnapped? Quite possibly, and they whispered the dreadful word in a way which evoked my deepest pity. But what was the motive? Why him, since he wasn't a member of the militias? And why had hundreds of armed men chosen this village, nearly half Muslim as it was, for their base of operations? Why cut off access routes? Why encircle this modest group of homes, striking fear in every inhabitant?

"Roads in the area were unsafe in the extreme, but we couldn't just sit by, hour after hour, imagining the worst. We managed to find Muslim friends willing to drive out with us in search of young Georges Merhabi. Before long two cars were arranged, manned with both Christians and Muslims. I think, sincerely, the latter were as worried about the situation as ourselves.

"But then a goatherd appeared. He told us of a corpse lying a mile distant on land he had used for pasturage. At once we all grew silent, recalling the secluded spot on a certain back road. Otherwise, why did the goatherd come directly to us, as if on someone's instructions?

"That obscure site was always dangerous for Christians. But I went there at once with the boy's parents, who insisted on coming, though badly shaken, and a Muslim who volunteered to drive."

Soeur Davida paused a moment, clearing her throat, sipping coffee. No one else spoke.

—Then we found that boy of seventeen lying there, alone, among the wildflowers. His mother gasped, but her scream was stifled, at first, by recognition of the green jacket he wore. One of his eyes was open. The other half of his face was bluish, swollen like a tumor. On his chest there was a hole, and this cross I'm wearing could have fit through it. There was a frayed border of flesh, like a ballbearing... but I can't describe it.

"Later, I was allowed to wash him. He looked more at peace with his Maker, and very handsome. Together, that night, we kept a vigil by his body. And the next morning, in a radiant sunlight making tiny rainbows in the dew of the village cemetery, we buried Georges after a touching eulogy. Many Muslim townspeople were present, and even they said he must have been a saint.

"But the menace continued. It hovered over the village like a pall upon the living. We learned a few days later that Georges had been taken, at a certain intersection, on the outskirts of Chekka. A mobile checkpoint pulled him from the car and ordered his two friends:

"—Douse your lights. Beware, if you turn back to look!

"But why just to Georges then? His parents said he had been to a retreat center in Dhour ech-Choueir some months before. You see, he was devoutly religious. He was one of God's select young men. But his murderers probably accused him of attending a Kataëb training center. And then, it hadn't been a month, at the time, since Black Saturday."

XV

Soeur Davida held her audience in suspense a while longer. Here and there Père Zaki inserted a few words:

—No more everydays, no ascent to daylight for yet a little while. But who could predict the ways of the Almighty? Instead of living and laughing, there must be steadfast courage. The future of a historic people was at stake: the only autonomous Christians in the Middle East.

Père Zaki sipped the grounds of his second demitasse. His eyes were blue; they were steeled with Party fervor, like his pronouncements. He nodded at Soeur Davida, who resumed her story.

—Troops came and went in the night along roads surrounding the village. I remember even the stars seemed hostile, to us, and there was no moon. We slept in fits and starts, still fearing the worst. A leftist Muslim offensive was in the offing.

"The third night there were skirmishes to the south. I knelt peering over the windowsill, and it was clear that heavy guns were in action. Along the slopes between mountain villages, rockets hit and flared up like a hand crumpling paper. At dawn there were reports of a dozen killed, among us, and many more injured. I mean both Christian and Muslim, in the initial toll. There were rumors of kidnapping and torture, with three other families grieved by loved ones missing."

Soeur Davida broke off with emotion.

But Père Zaki took up the cause, raising his voice like an orator.

—A counter-attack is not far off. And believe me, it will be sustained. For we are not alone; nor will we ever divide, among ourselves. Never. The world's greatest nation is on our side. And woe to any individual, moreover, who doubts the Party and its sacred objectives."

XVI

The three visitors rose to leave, promising to return soon. Their exit was dramatic, as a few came forward and knelt before the father. Mrs. Madi embraced Soeur Davida and thanked her effusively. Then, the old driver led the way with his gruff voice. When the shelter door opened, a ray of sunlight pierced the darkness; there came a pause, a catching in the throat. The three envoys of hope and Kataëb unity went away.

Minutes of a thoughtful silence followed, in the Sioufi basement, as people groped among their things. In the pause a mother called her child, though within arm's length, and her voice had a note of fear. Someone knocked over a container, with a gasp.

—Be careful!
—Did it spill?
No radio went on. Scarcely a voice was heard.

Outside, the relentless shelling of Ashrafiyeh continued. Russia and America had made a deal to divvy up what remained of Lebanon! It was an international conspiracy.

XVII

Elie sat alone. He dozed a moment, sitting in shadow by the wall; but he kept a sense of those nearest him. Though his eyes were closed, he could feel their keen disapproval. They were digesting the apocalyptic words of Père Zaki; they were glancing at this Phalangist shirking his patriotic duty. In a moment, he thought, they would accuse him of being a spy, planted among them. But what difference did it make if he sat there a few more minutes, near his mother? Not even next to her, since the good family name might be tainted, and Emile's macho self-image offended. But I'm the one, he thought, I fought your battles for you—now don't cross me.

Still he could feel them: they were worked up by Zaki's exhortations. Don't try to thwart me, thought Elie Madi, and not if you're my own brother. Who is my mother, and who my brethren?

He stretched his limbs, changing position along the wall. Now I'll leave them, he thought, I'll go away for good. And Jessie . . . Here I come: a Phalangist at the Museum crossing, for starters castration. That for hors-d'oeuvres. Be my guest, use my face for an ashtray. He had dreamed, at night, of ten enemy corpses laid in a row, castrated, in Dbayyeh Camp. Where to, Phalangist?

Feet first from a back fender, through Sabra. Or at a friendly checkpoint, alerted by now: stop the traitor, shoot him, the worst of the worst.

Emile ventured into the no-man's-land surrounding his older brother.

—Hey.

His mood was less brash. He shook Elie's shoulder gently.

Others noticed, looking over. There was a silence, as Elie opened his eyes.

—What?

—When are you going back?

—Why?

—It hurts mother, seeing you here.

—Then I'll move away. She won't have to see me.

—No, in the shelter . . . You know, Emile gestured, these people.
—Father died, didn't he?
—Yes.
—Was he a hero?
—Yes.
—What if he wasn't?
—Huh?
—What if he just . . . saw no way out?
—That's crazy.
—Poor fool, who died in a ditch. What do you think he would say to his posthumous decorations?
—I think—
—No, you don't.
—Elie, I know—
—You don't know shit. Sit over here, where I'm sitting: then maybe you'll know. A few people know what's best for us to do, all geniuses no doubt.
—Won't you leave?
—When I'm ready. In the meantime you can drop the fraternal tone.

He closed his eyes.

Emile backed away, returning to his mother. They whispered, heads together.

XVIII

Saleem Il-Hrawey reappeared. His mood was calmer, less exalted after locking horns with Père Zaki. But hardly deflated as, noticing the failure of Emile's mission, he seemed to express what was in the air:

—Madi, we all think you should leave. Go back to the siege, it's where you belong. We all think so.
—Did you say "all"?
—I did.
—And why is that, brother?
—Because you . . . lend dishonor.
—Ah. And you, in this darkness—you've done nothing "dishonorable"?
—Don't joke, Madi. We're not playing with you, we can feel it.

Elie gave a sort of laughter.

—All you heroes, masturbating your honor. Has Père Zaki roused you to a wet dream?

He closed his eyes, ignoring them. On the other hand, he thought, I was looking for a lover. But she told me: make believe.

Hrawey retreated among the others. Elie heard their murmurs:

—... a breakdown... like Sylvie.

—Insulting us.

—... puts himself above.

Hrawey was intent on making amends:

—He can't stay here, in any case. Let's call in—

—Need help? Elie chuckled. I know the code.

—It lowers morale, said an older woman.

—Madi, said the persistent Saleem, you better leave.

Elie gave a toss of his brow, refusing. But he said, more gently:

—And you, Maman? Am I an embarrassment—never mind, it's unfair to ask.

By now there were a number of people staring at the outcast. They approached, but still didn't stand over him, keeping a certain distance. When one took the notion to shine a pocketlight on him, he snarled:

—Turn that off.

—Then leave.

—We know you don't have a gun.

—You're a fighter. You don't belong here.

—What if the enemy comes? They'll kill us all!

—Leave, said Hrawey. Just leave.

Murmurings extended back among the crowd. It was becoming a small uprising.

—Or we'll throw you out!

—No, said Elie, you won't.

He wished he had brought in his gun.

—You think we're afraid of you? With fifty thousand Arabs pounding on the door?

—You're afraid of me, he nodded. I'm surprised you haven't gone howling up those steps, despite the war. Why don't *you* leave? I was out there: why not take your turn awhile? Go defend the fatherland.

He heard his mother weeping. Yes, it was her, like a leak in someone's soul. While the others stirred themselves up toward a decisive act, Mrs. Madi wept. She had tried to keep her family whole and alive; but they were dying anyway, one by one.

—I'll go, he said, rising slowly, very tense.

Emile was also on the verge of crying. He reached forward awkwardly.

Elie shrugged his shoulders, taking the tender hand.

Then he broke through the barrier and kissed his mother's forehead; his lips brushed hers.

—I'm sorry, he said, if I hurt you.

Her features worked. Tears streamed down.

—No.

—You could be proud of me, he said, if you understood.

But he broke away from her. He seemed to tear the last threads. What's the use? he thought, glancing around.

He went slowly up the stairs, step by step, making them wait a little.

And then, as he turned a final time, in the instant he opened the door of the Sioufi shelter—Elie was impaled, squinting with pain, by a ray of sunlight.

XIX

The grandmother of Hana'a, Sitt Chahrour, was also called Ashatra, "the clever one" in Arabic. For years she was a servant in Maronite homes such as Sylvie Helou's in Furn ech-Chubaak. She worked on a per diem basis, a few lira plus a meal in return for doing the household chores, cooking, laundering. Many women of the old Tel ez-Zaater camp had earned their living, more or less, in this way.

Sitt Chahrour's husband died during the 1948 exodus from Palestine and left her to raise four children. Among her grandsons, now involved in defense of the Camp, were Saleh, Ismail (whose wife was Kamileh), Khaled in his mid-twenties and working for Fatah; Ahmed; and the youngest, Mansur. Zeina, the eldest granddaughter, had died at Sabra in '82. Three of Sitt Chahrour's own children were still alive, residing in other Arab countries.

Long ago her neighbors had nicknamed her Ashatra because she did so well, despite heavy odds, for her family. Besides menial housekeeping she used to walk along Sidon Highway gathering snails in a wicker basket. Sylvie's affluent parents liked all things French, including the consumption of escargots in a fancy sauce; and Sitt Chahrour was able to find plenty of them among the Damour orchards. In fact, she began finding so many, she took her surplus to the Museum area in Beirut to sell.

It was during the sixth week of siege that Ashatra decided she was going out to the deadly spigot and fetch back a can of water for two of her great grandchildren who looked in a bad way.

—Don't go, Sitt! said the youngest, bringing tears to the old woman's eyes.

Everyday for decades she had worn the same dusty widow's robe, repeatedly hemmed and patched. She sniffled, dried her eyes on her sleeve, and took up the rusty can.

—Please! said the other child, tugging at her.

But she disengaged his small hand, and raised the plank which served as a door.

It was one thing suffering herself, in resigned silence these many years, buffeted about Lebanon—Rashidiyyeh Camp in the South to Wavell in the North, to Tel ez-Zaater; and now the worst of the lot . . . That was one thing; but when she saw Ahmed's two children dying of thirst before her eyes, Sitt simply lost control and decided to venture out, like so many others the past two weeks, on a death mission. At any time the Phalangists could have invalidated the Camp's one remaining tap, but they left it perniciously as bait for their snipers at various vantage points.

Day after day the Camp held out, while the world's weaponry sent down an infernal barrage on this shambles of a shambles. Camp defense resided, militarily, in TOW anti-tank to forestall Phalangist blitzing. Over 150,000 heavy shells had been expended so far by Lebanese Forces during the long weeks of siege.

Camp fighters lay on mattresses. Sitt Chahrour saw them, making her way through secret passageways of gutted buildings, where they catnapped by a jagged loophole in a wall dripping plaster. Night after night, she knew, the bodies of refugees were dumped in a ditch a quarter mile from the Montemar Hotel. She heard rumors of how Phalangists took their prisoners there and pushed them over the side.

—Enjoy your "night journey", Mohammed!

They sprayed bullets on the captive losing his grip, falling headlong among the corpses.

Each morning there were cars parked alongside the dumping place: journalists, Lebanese on their way to business as usual insofar as conditions permitted.

XX

She approached the Camp's lone functioning spigot, and her probably fatal gambit into a stretch of open area controlled by how many snipers? Emerging from underground for the first time in days, she couldn't believe her eyes. Mud roads like garbage dumps, with bodies putrifying along the shoulders. In the midday heat she heard an isolated shot, a dog squealing. At first the bark was louder than any siren; but then softer, as if someone turned down the volume... and off. Both the church steeple and minaret of the mosque had been hit until they crumbled. In the twisting alleyways, between huts and shacks, whole families whom she recognized lay disembowelled to the flies, beside the poor remains of their refugee quarters. They lay still like a photograph. The Camp had proved the last stage of their journey through a hostile land. At Tel ez-Zaater, at Sabra and Chatila—and now here, the blood of her people flowed alluvial. From the scorching sun, from the heat of fires these bodies were merging in a viscous mass. How long could it continue? she wondered.

Buildings had collapsed. People were resorting more and more to sewage in their desperate need for water. They were subsisting on a few lentils; and meanwhile their bodies looked like lepers, with horrendous rashes. Disease in the Camp, despite Dr. Kamel's heroic efforts, had already reached epidemic proportions.

Many came apart mentally. At times even the fighters, the Camp protectors went crazy and surrendered individually. They went out into the street screaming, AK blazing away.

As Sitt Chahrour went along she felt over her head in death, ready for the worst—which she would have sought out actively, except for the terrible reminder of Ahmed's two children, their immediate need of water.

Even the leader Selman's rhetoric was flagging the past few days—even the people's belief in the Return, it seemed, was being put to an inhuman test. Sitt Chahrour's spirit was drunk with dying, with respiring the stench of it in most sacred thoughts of her martyred husband.

—Sitt, take this.

A fighter handed her a piece of siding as she paused before the final door.

PART FOUR

I

Morgan paused in the shadows outside Brasserie de la Paix. Behind her a tree, stark in the gloaming, showed its white wound from a rocket. The sun was a crimson carpet on the dark waters of Jounieh Bay, as Morgan paused, waiting for the Arab.

The glass doors had been cracked from the sonic boom of Phantoms. They were taped profusely; and looked grotesque to her, refracting a smudged sunset. From trees lining the Ashrafiyeh boulevard, pink and sheer, the glow hung like a negligee.

She thought of Halloween; but a memory of childhood, to Morgan, was a kind of abyss . . . Where was the man? It was after six. Or he had come on time, and declined to wait? His oriental pride, she reasoned; he was uncouth and insensitive despite his degree in engineering, high position in the Party. No doubt he lacked savoir vivre.

In a moment the oglers would gather if she stayed outside. Off-duty Phalangists, a legion of men all eyeballs, fixated on the oversized fetish—oh primitive society. In college she had immersed herself in *Beyond the Pleasure Principle*.

The streets were unpredictable, and given over to militiamen.

She went inside. A waiter met her, bowing with ceremony, a hand to his heart. His smile is flypaper, she thought, with a smirk. He is devout, and my breasts are his holy places.

Nodding, grinning, he gestured her on before him.

And Morgan mused, Kiss my... obsequious—with your subtle mind. She had read, recently, in Tel Aviv while awaiting an assignment, a book called *The Arab Mind* and found it highly interesting. But in ways only half-glimpsed by its author.

The first waiter called over a colleague to assist in serving her. Couldn't handle it alone? Such a virile pose.

The two of them stood over her, white-vested in the flickering light. Two wounded trees, smiling where the branches parted.

—Welcome.

—Such a pleasure. Bin't jamili ktiir, ma'hek? Such a lovely girl, you are.

—Do you come from America?

It was, to her, the most tiresome litany.

—Bring me an espresso.

—An espresso!

—One espresso!

The word rang out in a relay toward the kitchen.

They asked more indiscreet questions in their halting English. They gave what seemed to Morgan puerile looks and gestures. She answered their importunate flirtation in a clipped tone, if at all.

But the two waiters began to relax, as one drifted away still beaming. Look, thought Morgan, at what you will never touch. Though another of your sort shall, in a moment, and we'll see if he enjoys it.

II

Along one wall there were booths. Toward the rear a group of three gathered round a coffee table. Lanterns danced to detonations a kilometer in the distance. The waiters came and went primly. They bowed over the few patrons who sat pitting their leisure against the military onslaught.

She lingered ten minutes, reminding herself why she was there. Be calm, thought Morgan; stay above. They brought her coffee and watched as she stirred, then blew gently on the surface, sipped. They salaamed, confirming her pleasure. But Morgan felt a sinking in her stomach; she was on the verge of bolting, and only remembrance of Risha's ultimatum held her in place. She put a cigarette to her lips and lit it, in one crisp movement, sucking the smoke as if in a trance. The movement was so nimble; her first waiter jumped in too late with his match.

She heard steps, decisive, hard on the polished floor, and realized all eyes were focussed on the entry to her back. She leaned to sip the espresso as Abu Joseph's dark, bellicose figure appeared by her side. As usual he seemed in a great hurry; it was his style. The Phalangist captain pranced forward on his narcissistic steed; he would waft her away and make her first among concubines: the one he truly loved.

They left the Brasserie with a flurry. Wherever Abu Joseph alighted in Ashrafiyeh, these days, it was a cameo appearance. Even in wartime the Beirut weeklies had an about-town section with glossy photos; and the playboy Phalangist might be featured, Miss Universe Georgina Rizk or some society woman on his arm, in a trend-setting duet.

Night was falling. They sped through a deserted Ashrafiyeh in his spacious Mercedes. Armageddon landscape of Rue Sursock.

—Since our first meeting, said Abu Joseph, in French, I've looked forward to this special evening. It has intense significance, for me. If you wish we can dine together; I know a place with the finest cuisine, better than Bahri.

—Sorry, but I—there isn't time.

He looked away and said, more formally:

—I too am sorry.

He brooded a moment, but then began speaking of the escalation, and his people in the shelters, feeling desperate but steadfast. He spoke of their dedication to the Maronite cause, as if that should concern her. Abu Joseph was irrepressible, a different man in his leisure hours; though wearing his dress fatigues. He looked precious, somehow, and even kinky, thought Morgan, the way his well-trimmed beard framed his features.

She responded with a certain warmth and began stalking, in her attentiveness, a slightest invitation to confidences. She nodded, and then gazed out the window on her side. At moments she showed a calculated impatience.

Morgan smiled at him, and his words began to flow with a verve, a kind of sensuous patriotism. Original "line", she thought smiling noncommittally. Here was a romantic who paid the highest prices, from the pocket of his people no doubt, to satisfy a sexual whim. Business is business, said her silence. Few things could interest me less than who you are, and what you believe; unless, of course, you knew something fascinating... There had been a moment at the War Council, as she and Ligury waited there with Elie Madi, when the Phalangist captain fairly begged her to find him useful.

—This is it, he said.

The driver, Abu Joseph's bodyguard, pulled in with a violence, lurching on the curb. That one was something ferocious, nearly attractive to her, he was so supremely repugnant. His skin was rich silt borrowed through with vermin. He wore a leather jacket, with a .38 clipped to his belt. His dark face looked runneled with a gust of desert sand.

III

They entered an apartment set up for just such trysts. It was neat but impersonal; there were posters of the Eiffel Tower, a church in Compiègne—alongside the Gemayels. A neat cozy interior: the inevitable chairs round a glass-top coffee table.

—My man will prepare...

—I haven't time. And I drank one, waiting for you.

He gave the bodyguard a glimpse of displeasure. The other nodded, impassive, a trifle contemptuous as usual.

Abu Joseph opened the door to an adjoining room, and salaamed with a gracious irony.

She stood before the mirror like a statue. He closed the door and turned to her; his eyes seemed to project a kind of obscurity, inviting abandon. His brow had a stubborn cast, as he paused to admire what in a moment would be his to enjoy. Sakr stared at her face, her beautiful neck with a virile tenderness.

She endured the force of his gaze like a cold shower; she felt suddenly undressed, objectified, reduced to a role in this all-male perfunctory decor. She had been put there in order to serve his ugly self-deceptions. And no doubt this discreet pause of his, this momentary appreciation of her charms was Sakr's way of being spiritual. He was a big child, staring at the wrapper while smudging his lips with the candy.

And yet she might have done herself a favor by sinking to his level. A portion of Morgan yearned to become a thing, and a function of some anonymous masculine desire, like a bludgeon which manipulated. Gaudenti, Ligury, Mamdoueh, Kohler, who's next? The bodyguard, with his face like gravel? Just lay back and let it happen. Be a leak in the universal flow, thought Morgan; a repository of male ecstasy, in other words a sewer. She heard his breathing a few steps away, like a bull trying to be courteous: this took its toll on the illusion.

He stepped forward and put a hand, trembling slightly, to her shoulder. And then Morgan was restored to herself. She sensed his touch as alien, repulsive. There was the usual problem of eyes, a kind of Medusa effect. As a rule she felt out of place, and *de trop* when being touched by a man: ever since the first, Willartig. Trust was a farce once you knew what was really happening.

—You are, he murmured, so very wonderful.

His voice had a note of clownish eagerness, and a pathos. His fingers moved on her neck, toward the delta of her breasts where the silk blouse parted. He bowed and pressed his lips to the fabric. He kissed her long fingers which were limp, engaged in a distracted caress along his hairline.

Morgan decided to feign a swoon. She veiled the alertness of her gaze, remembering moments when she aroused herself in sly little ways. Sex is mental, said Willartig, one of her college professors. She thought of Risha and Peretz, the musty after-odor in those bare rooms off Hamra, where the cabin fever was an orgy in itself. Emission . . . mission, thought Morgan, gazing into space, as Sakr made ready to assault the citadel.

A palm to the back of her neck, he began rubbing her breasts with the other; he kissed them as if to extract their essence. He murmured something, childlike and forlorn, while she ran a hand through his curly scented hair and rocked gently, in a prelude to mechanical passion. Sakr freed his lust from a button, then another, on the verge.

—I love the woman in you, he whimpered in Arabic.

But she thought: you love pawing my whore's body. Now she hung forward, sprung loose and triumphant from the moiré blouse. He worked his bristly face over her; his cheek scratched her brassiere.

His desire was almost frightening, like another's; but she kept her distance mentally. She knew just what he wanted; she would rub his face in it, and then rely on his gratitude. His hunger was vulgar, and universal; it was in her, as well, a form of hatred. But not here, not now, for Morgan. She resented his self-abasement, and detested this role he made her play. Like a child, he insisted on getting his own way, and would gladly pay.

He seemed to drift alongside her. His lust was a kind of worship, while she stood enduring the foreplay and readying herself to take advantage. She was a stage prop to his male greatness.

She fondled his locks as if, at any moment, she might snip them with her shears: cut them at the root. In a small dosage she would give him what he wanted, like a hint of new regions. Exotic whiff of oases lost beneath a torrential sun. She beckoned her lover on a dangerous journey. She would give him what he wanted and then he, amazed, would repay her in kind. And he would say with his silence: Do it again, and, please stay with me.

To herself she was ugly. She felt silly standing there: the cow goddess nourishing the prince. She flicked down her straps; and he groaned, as if clubbed. She leaned stiffly above him, as he sank to her feet and started moaning.

But Morgan stared past him, intent on seeing nothing. It was no time to laugh as he knelt before her, in a vortex of nature. She tried not to breathe. Between them, there was a thin line of emotion. He persisted in groaning; he stroked her and with a fervor caressed her knees. Thus a little boy seeks attention from a cold guilt-ridden mother. Thus a leader of Christian soldiers, a crusader knelt grovelling before a whore. And Morgan's tall opulent body was given over to goosebumps as well, at the thought of its own power. She had what he wanted.

IV

Then it was all him, him. It was disgusting—and the more so the better, for him. She lay back amid pillows, atangle in her clothes, a suction of blouse and brassiere, blond hair, stockings, skirt shoved up on her midriff. The strategic parts were all drawn and bunched toward the middle. But the extremities hung forth, lewd as voyeurs. She lay back against the creaking bedstead while he panted, sighed like a sitar. Gawking barnyard movements, action and reaction, physics, the stars.

Oh, there was no end to the nastiness of human functions. She tried to contract her nostrils against his scent. In public, among people one might pass by such things like a sordid alluring sideshow; but in reality they were the three rings of life, where it all happened. And now this guy, at the magnetic center down there—him.

—Ah! he entered her, and it stung. Ah! In this she would never acquiesce. All were terrorists; one fake diplomacy was worth another... Their stomachs slapped like bars of a raucous music. Morgan thought, Wait: only hold on now, and him, him. This is the hard part.

A shrill sensation, like a fountain in her nerves, spewing. She clasped his shoulders, impassive.

Then she reacted, straining upward, as if to rein him in. The physical pain meant nothing to her; she scorned it just as she did death. Of pain it was only the implications which counted. No one cared; no more than this Arab chasing his treadmill pleasure on top of her. Nothing to lose, except one's illusions. She could have enjoyed the hurt, almost, except for its relationship to him, and him. Have fun, she thought, urging him with her rhythm: you're going to pay for it.

He reached his orgasm, grunting. Ecce homo. A bit flabby though; too much good life and hommos for this Phalangist hero. She cuffed his temple, but Sakr kept on gurgling, with a floundering note to his passion. He seemed to have a fetish for chewing on her face. No marks, sir. I need my looks. Isn't this romantic? she thought, as he drove home his pleasure.

His body flew in an intimate rage for a few seconds as she lay there, beneath him, contracting. She stared at the ceiling. Motes, in the air, by the low light of a kerosene lamp. Troop of gnats. He came to a slow halt and his passion cooed. His desire abated, and became a gentle persistence.

—Fuck, thought Morgan.

V

—Never twice.

She stood in the doorway to an adjoining bathroom. Abu Joseph lay propped on two pillows, like a basking satyr. He was very imposing, with his demonic something, rugged features telling a woman he might be hers—shameless liar. Why were opportunists so attractive? The bodyguard's face was shot through with centipedes, but this one had skin like parched vellum. Probably he concluded, from his rapt lovemaking, that he was a mystery of strength and tenderness.

Now Morgan stood in the dull lamplight from the lavatory, awaiting her chance.

—Never? he said.

She smoothed her stockings and skirt. She eyed him with an anger because he'd gotten what he wanted and nothing could be further from his mind, at this point, than to blab.

—Just once, sorry.

He seemed incredulous. He was in love with his Party, yes, but used to getting his way. For a moment she watched him; she thought women were hardly an issue for him, the way he filled up any room with his ego. Better to hire a woman's services for an hour; then send her back where she came from, into what viscous night . . . ? Take a break. Then get on with the business of leftists.

After the session she had moved to her side of the bed. With no show of tact she reached for her watch on the night table, and for a cigarette. At first he followed along and touched her hair, putting his lips to the nape of her neck. Again he tried to fasten on; then with a sigh she propped to a sitting position, and he lay back with a little snort.

She sensed his dark eyes, watching her from the sensual mass of his body. She moved from his side, and Abu Joseph countered with a low chuckle.

VI

Morgan returned from the bathroom and stood posing in the blond aura of her hair. Her figure beneath the lintel had the tension of a caryatid; it was imprinted with the stamp of her task, cool, ever arrogant. She waited. Sakr rose also, slowly, toward getting dressed—the return to reality. They eyed one another in their bout of silence.

—I'll escort you. Where are you going?

—I'd rather walk. I can use the air.

—It is dangerous.

He nodded, a bit perturbed by her small discourtesies. But Morgan crossed the room; and leaning above him, seductive, she ran her fingers through his hair and kissed his forehead. He tried to reengage her, but she drew back gently.

—It was good. For me as well... I'd love to see you again, if you feel the same. But not tonight, this isn't the time. Tomorrow afternoon I'm free.

He gazed up at her, charming in his ogrish need, his disappointment.

—In the afternoon I have a meeting.

—When?

—It begins at four. I don't know when we'll end.

—That cuts across my free time, said Morgan. We wouldn't have long together.

He nodded. A hand to her hip, he pressed his temple to her wrist and gave a sort of basso coo. Morgan felt a dark power; she murmured, her breast on his cheek:

—I could meet you there. We'd have a few moments at least. Show me off to Elie and the others: I like them. (She gave a warm wondrous laughter.) I want to be their friend, learn about your life. Tell me where it is...

—At the War Council, a weekly affair. But—he hesitated; he caught himself up, eyeing her—this could be changed. Why not at six: would that be too late? In the Brasserie?

Morgan smiled. Suddenly she was girlish and happy with him. She kissed him on the forehead:

—It's okay. I'll cancel something.

—But wait for me, he said, if I'm a little late.

Her voice was soft now, and giving. She made an effort to pet him and play the mother. Erase it, she thought, teasing; erase the slip from his mind. She showed her gratitude.

Morgan laughed softly as they kissed, and seemed to stoke one another's fire. He was aroused. He started up again. Make him forget it, she thought. She went along for awhile. But at the bit with the straps, and groaning, she pulled back with a whisper:

—Tomorrow.

—Alright, he murmured, subsiding.

Her victory seemed definitive; the great captain was in love with a prostitute. He would jeopardize his cause, and how much more, for an hour with her.

She leaned above him with a smile. She was quite taken with his charms, and sorry she couldn't stay any longer.

They rose to leave together. As a pair of the species, their vitality and physical prowess were impressive.

The bodyguard stood waiting. He smiled, but seriously. Morgan's mood reverted on sight of him; she was alerted.

—I'll walk you downstairs, said Abu Joseph.

She nodded at the other in passing; he watched her, taking a brief order in Arabic, which she understood. Going down the steps her escort thanked her:

—This has been . . . intensely special.

—You embarrass me, she said, a hand on his shoulder.

On the threshold he kissed her with tenderness.

She grinned then, turning away into the darkness.

But he said:

—Aren't you forgetting something?

He held out a thousand-Lira note.

The Phalangist smiled; he seemed pleased.

—I knew, he said, from our first meeting, you were not what you claimed.

—Prove it, she said, smiling as well, and left him there.

VII

The streets of West Beirut were forbidding: dark and empty. There were glimmers like St. Elmo's fire on the upper storeys. Stars seemed to blink in the smoke of a hundred fires.

In Burj the shelling was in a listless phase. A cannon in Ein Mreisse exploded punctually, thirty seconds, then thirty. Morgan walked along briskly after her breakneck taxi ride through Sodeco crossing. Unlike in Ashrafiyeh, here the heaps of garbage were beginning to vye with Egypt's pyramids; the stench blended with emanations from Burj. She imagined the rats at her ankles; their filth and little squeals, like a lover's kiss. The rats, the rats of the world—think of them all, making babies.

She approached the glow of Hotel Bristol; there was a dim light in the entrance. Her blond figure emerged from the darkness toward two astonished employees, courteous young men in waistcoats and white shirts to match their gleaming teeth. They met her with strained smiles.

—Welcome.

—Miss, said the other, it isn't safe.

He gave a gesture of disapproval, pointing at the Bristol facade. And Morgan, seeing the charred gouge of a rocket gave a peal of laughter that scandalized them.

—You should not laugh. Two died.

—Does your phone work?

—Perhaps there is a line.

They were serious, polite. Students probably.

A young doorman showed her a deference; she smiled at him and chuckled. Her spirits soared.

Inside the booth she got a dialtone.

Risha's voice sounded distant.

—Got it? Ready to move.

At the next phone a woman was weeping. It was still possible to call across the city, which made for macabre conversations.

—Call Khalil.

She hung up the receiver.

She sat alone in the Bristol coffee shop, wondering how they stayed in operation from week to week: who tipped the waiters?

A graying majordomo brought her a steak and glass of burgundy.

—Sahteen.

Sipping the glass of wine she said:

—Bring me a demi.

He bowed and went off. The food looked vulgar, a thick sauce drowning the parsley. By candlelight it reminded her of something decomposing.

Morgan quaffed the red wine; her eyes fell away from the food a moment. She gazed off in a revery, as if resting the reality-muscles:

after the "intensely special" hour with a brave Phalangist, and then risky return passage. Which is the better orgasm, she thought, AK or M-16? Both will inundate you with . . .

VIII

She spent her idyllic childhood in a Boston suburb, and was trotted out by her mother, almost from the crib, to a circuit of concerts and vernissages. Her father was a lawyer transmuted to banking, who seemed to park his locomotive will for business on the family threshold. He became gentle and demure the instant he entered, knowing his wife to be capable of anything, and afraid of her calculated tantrums. She would tolerate no interference from him; she wanted carte blanche with her personal life and children, as well as in the stores. Her plans were elaborate, a product of considerable neurotic anxiety. Thus Morgan's father went limp in his financial section, or on rare occasions tried to join in his children's games in the nursery.

Back in his office overlooking Boston he came alive; he was all grit and millionaire, scourge of lower executives while doing pitched battle with a tax bracket, or finding oil by long-distance telephone. In the office he made money.

Again at home he stodged about, a man relegated nowhere special by his wife. Seeking refuge with his children, the paternal presence seemed to alienate them too. The minute he appeared their games would pall. Also, there were servants. Sometimes he tried hanging out with them in the kitchen and garden. The cook's name was Clurman; there was a handyman named Bill. They were Negroes. They lived with their families in an outbuilding on the sprawling grounds of the Brookline mansion.

Everything was prearranged. An odor of cologne or some long untasted food, eggnog at Thanksgiving, peanut brittle at Christmas, might cause her to remember, and nearly vomit. That was rare. She had tried to dredge it up in therapy; but after such mistrust . . . Morgan's childhood lay far back across a gray level plain like the two doomed cities. Life there had seemed rather frantic and unfair, occurring above her range of vision. Her parents moved about in a realm of their own, with polite but frightening strides. There was some kind of struggle going on, up there, and she spent much of her energy trying to avoid the shocks and collisions. As a child she was always in the way.

Then came puberty. It felt like a demon showed up to inhabit her. This was a demon of tenderness, and anguished need to cling, like precocious maternity. The urge was terrible to hug someone to her: hug them for a long time until they suffocated. Oh! she yearned to give and receive kindness, so her life would be more predictable. As Morgan developed physically her father shied away. Her mother seemed to lie in wait, emotionally, at every turn. The smallest daily affair could become a scene fraught with guilt. Life with her mother devolved, during that period of ferment, and difficult puberty, into a desperate game of improvised rules.

Her feelings took a grandiose turn when, as a teenager, she devised a plan of travelling from town to town giving kindness to anyone who was truly in need. She would set a saintly example by acting on her finest impulse of the moment. Also, she was having her first crushes on boys; these were ardent and hard to dissemble. She was obliged to recognize male coarseness, and nullity—as her mother said, adding that such terms were used "by the great Goethe to describe his contemporaries." But Morgan felt more and more vulnerable, and rather distracted. When she compared certain boys with her brother Michael, it made her retreat from the mission of love, and bestowing kindness.

As she grew older and filled out physically the demon adapted, and changed its nature. The family mood darkened: her older sister went off one night for an abortion and nearly died in days which followed. Then the mother went on a rampage; though often silent, seething inwardly. In a look, in a word she condemned, and the verdict was final.

The father proved unwilling or unable to lend support to his favorite daughter during the weeks of her convalescence. He seemed to write off the whole thing, like a deductible loss. To his wife he stated, firmly: It's illegal. And all the committee meetings, wide office overlooking Boston, chauffeur-driven limousine, were like insulation against the shock of family emotions.

He resented it vehemently. Weeknights he began sleeping at the bank instead of returning to Brookline. He was a past master at inventing pretexts, which his wife hardly bothered to question. He took up golf and played with business associates on courses across the U.S. and abroad. All the while his wife was an Erinye, with a repertoire of reproaches for her children, even the angel Michael.

Morgan cowered. She was deeply embarrassed and reluctant to bring home any school friend for dinner. More than ever she felt confused and needed guidance, seeking any slightest kindness in her direction. But her parents were both too implicated, estranged forever, playing their torturous comedy. She was cast on her own resources, growing ever more intimate with the demon.

How sadly she felt cut off from the outside. Her friends were still schoolgirls, stifling the giggles and acting coy, carrying their own books as yet. Some were more advanced; but it seemed, to Morgan, like a game of pre-adult copycat, trying to bluff their way. As for her: she hid her emergent beauty, and a sort of dark astonishment she felt in herself, a jubilance, a nastiness. Her body did in fact contain a balm for the world's misery;—but everywhere she turned there was the demon, leering and obscene.

Then *they* began to surface—on street corners, in the stores, anywhere in public: the gapers. They stared with an unfeigned vengeance at what they would never understand. Young and old, short and tall: they were men. They tried to fob off their own dark wonder, and asked her, in silence as a rule, not always, to play a game of catch with the sun or moon. And the effect was vulgar; moreover, it was hopeless, like a scene in public.

IX

Depression set in. With the energy required by her guilt, a certain teenage sense of shame and failure, there was little left over for living. She began to face the academic pressures of college, and felt tremendously lonely, into her emotional reserves. She had no close friends.

In desperation she began dating, but there were unwanted kisses; intimate grappling; the inevitable refusal to bring her back on time. Fun and games in the front seat, struggles to say goodbye. Once a senior grabbed her to him while driving. He kissed her and "felt her up" but then crushed his front fender against a tree. Then he blamed her; he swore and shouted until a group of spectators gathered to watch.

At last she faced a choice between staying in her room, signing up for a carrel in the library (even more dangerous, back there among the stacks) or investing in a chest protector. Also, she knew so much more than her suitors, about life, aesthetics, human emotion. She was conversant with the great world, and receptive to beauty.

Somehow, she got through her junior year as an undergrad. Despite everything she worked hard and made the dean's list, mastering her subjects without much interest. But she was always depressed. She tried to cry and couldn't, dry-eyed with her loneliness.

At times she suppressed a feeling of insanity, and kept the corrosive tension in. And while life, people, college seemed to grow gray and recede in a buffer zone of lethargic depression,—all the time her demon grew stronger. He made a meal of her enthusiasm and capacity to live. He said awful things in her ear, until she actually thought someone might overhear. At any moment her enemies, who were many, might be eavesdropping. Her teachers would be scandalized and give her a C for the course. The illusion of reality threatened to burst like a soap bubble, as the demon forced her to ever nastier concessions.

X

Fall semester of her senior year she enrolled in a course given by a rather well-known literary critic of that time, since forgotten. His syllabus appealed to her, since there would be no final exam at the end: less pressure, and eleventh-hour cramming. After making high grades for three years, she detested the process like a sort of chronic indigestion; and at sight of a "blue book" had a nervous reaction. For a long time after college Morgan underwent a recurrent nightmare; she missed too many classes, she would fail and be forced to return another year, and another, at a school she hated.

Secretly, she was in therapy: three sessions per week. She took out a loan, but not from her father's bank. A sympathetic roommate, Lou, proved a great help to her that year. Lou was adept at taking calls when Morgan failed to show up for a rendez-vous; she was gently ironic with the male egos, yet protective of her friend's privacy. With disbelief at times, with humor and pathos she told of her day on the telephone.

But word got around. Before long Morgan was looked on as a deadly tease: as a being with some sort of basic malfunction. This didn't stop the flow of incoming calls, timid or convoluted invitations, muffled obscenities. On occasion she was embarrassed in public. Her space was violated. A group of athletes might pass by shaking their heads and sniggering. One student even tried to sneak, on his knees, beneath her desk in study hall.

In her distress she began dating again; she went out with a Harvard senior, Phi Beta Kappa, future lawyer. At least he wasn't a hockey star. On her part there was a ripeness, if only he didn't make the usual untimely advances. On the third date she consented to petting, which led to an all-out brawl: a fight for the right to go home.

It was thoroughly upsetting, and abnormal. Perhaps she was attracted, in her guilt and needy perversity, to men of that kind? Again her love was replaced by an insurmountable disgust, and withdrawal. She spent the night crying, pouring out her heart in Lou's arms. Lou was frightened by delirous ramblings about "the golden age of the demon"—as by the messy convulsions; but Morgan would not allow her to call in a doctor.

—Just be another man! she said, coughing. Everywhere you look, the roaches.

—So I'll get a woman, said Lou.

—Even worse.

Morgan doubled over with a cramp.

—But this isn't helping.

—Wait. It'll pass.

And Lou put her arm around Morgan, hugging her, admiring her lonely courage. They slept that night in one another's embrace. The taste of Morgan's sickness didn't deter the devoted Lou from kissing her face and lips, when she finally drifted off.

XI

All hope was not lost however. A crisis had occurred; campus life continued. Yet another in a long line of dates was distinguished by his humorous approach. He had a Brooklyn accent and liked to make cracks. His father, importer-exporter, owned warehouses in two boroughs; but this son of the mercantile class felt no inclination to take over the reins of Dad's business. No, his dreams comprised travelling, looking good and feeling free. His major was still business, but only to "keep 'em cool on the homefront."

He explained to Morgan the charm of hitchhiking, some "spring night when the moon was full," down to Tampico for a swim. He asked her to "stick out her thumb" with him, and gave a loud guffaw with nasal breathing. He launched into his imitation of fish reacting to a scuba diver; or struck a boxer's pose and jabbed her, "noogied" her arm:

—C'mon! he sniffed, right here! Gimme a good one.

She laughed. It was a relief from attempted rape. But she told Lou it was all over with him, and refused to talk when he called. Time and again he phoned, saying:

—H'lo? This is me on the line, you know, Mr. Lonesome?

Every two or three days for a fortnight he made Lou cackle with laughter; until it seemed she was falling for his antics.

Then Morgan consented to see him once more on condition he "desist with the slapstick." When at last, after a month of light-hearted persistence he found himself in her presence, infused with the sheer feminine aura of her, the animal opulence, he had grown decidedly less bold. He still cavorted, but more discreetly, a trifle sadly.

She began thinking about him in moments before sleep. She remembered the faded lace and girlish delicacy of her long-ago doll's world; its tenderness, and sense of mission. In vain she tried to construe her present relationship as a first grown-up reliance on someone.

She knew he wasn't harmless, not yet at least. Anyway, what challenge in a eunuch, like her father? She hoped, at least, that he had no intention of degrading her; and thus Morgan's spirit seemed to sigh with relief, and take a deep breath of air.

XII

After class one afternoon in early December, the fashionable critic invited Morgan to his campus apartment for the goûter, as he called it. He did so with such urbanity, making the invitation a kind of veiled homage to her "special situation," that she went along. He was very much published: a tenured professor in his mid-forties. His name was John Willartig.

She thought there could hardly be cause for alarm. Also, she hoped to be noticed by the side of Professor Willartig; she might begin to prove herself, and get back some of her own, in this long dark night of callow undergrads. She fell in with his stride, walking across campus. He seemed rather bookish, bespectacled but handsome: a bachelor who attracted no few coeds with his self-absorbed, intellectual mien.

Willartig's warm apartment was filled with bookshelves. There were hard and softbound volumes in a few different languages.

—What civilization has produced, in the humanities, worth keeping.

He glimpsed the Loeb edition of Homer; French volumes in *Pléiade*, German classics in Insel, Hanser, etc.; Spanish leatherbound Aguilar... Original titles, great names in gilt on the bindings thrilled her, as she took up a thousand-page tome and fingered its Bible paper. She flicked the silk marker from the page, and murmured a few words of *Dichtung und Wahrheit* which to her were incomprehensible. What a genius. And the critic stood by with his spiritual grin. The hair in his nostrils twittered like a flea when he exhaled.

This scholar was even-tempered. He made a style of everyday conversation, like Eckermann. He was a critic in his prime, represented by agents in New York and abroad. He had a Midas touch with the things of high culture, and liked to speak of "orgiastic intellect" with a chuckle that made Morgan blush.

At first Willartig liked to evoke the great enduring writers for her. He described the role of loneliness, sickness and death in this or that long creative effort.

—"Utility of despair" said Baudelaire... and what didn't Proust see in the phrase?

Death was prevalent in Valéry, yet what mind more refulgent with sunlight, and life's reflective brilliance? He asked Morgan her opinion and then listened attentively to the response. Head slightly bowed, he knelt to one side of the divan, applying a bellows to an incipient fire. She sat facing him in a wonderful old armchair which smelled of pipes and leather, of his cocker spaniel snoozing on the rug.

Years later, in the office of a psychiatrist, Bergland, in Tel Aviv, Morgan would remember the first interview with Willartig. It was like a rite of passage; or, in a sense, like her first polygraph test. The exquisite books, the warm conversation lent a superior intimacy... A dusking frosty light bathed the windowpanes; the tea he served had a smokey oriental taste. Yes, this was a place of calm privilege, away from the strife of families, mediocrity of college. It was a refuge, thought Morgan, yet still a part of adult reality. Here were no costly scenes, enforced petting, elaborate maneuvers to be taken home.

Where her mother failed miserably trying to invoke such things in her Brookline salon, her "Wednesdays" which were a glorified bookclub: this man succeeded with a casual flair. Literature, its lofty themes were a daily leaven to Willartig, dazzling his classes, writing superb articles for New York magazines.

In this place Morgan's demon would be shut out, and its nastiness have no access. Or so she thought. There was such a steady stream of words, ideas, visions. There were the complex redemptive schemes of a Mallarmé, a Hölderlin. Just say those eternal names: say them like a rosary, and you felt new trust in the universe. Stefan George's circle, Rilke—Willartig's brandy was an ichor, infusing her with a godlike glow.

XIII

After class the following week he renewed his offer, and she accepted. And then regularly. They talked until dinnertime, and then he walked her home. He ended with a brisk handshake and thanked her for the intellectual companionship. On the windswept front walk of her dormitory he remarked, with a smile:

—It doesn't seem to... fail.

They had spent another afternoon speaking of literary method, human relations and sexuality. A colleague, a group of gaping students passed by, but he appeared uncaring.

Gradually, the teacher's words fused with Morgan's silences, engaging her loneliness on a new terrain. At night she had strange lingering dreams; her body was made whole again through some elaborate ritual. She was afraid, but there was a sense of joyous self-sacrifice. Sweetest craving for a kind of sexual suicide, mirrored on the blackboard. Most haunting and beneficial of nightmares.

Thus Morgan's intimate thoughts became a dialogue with John Willartig. Meanwhile her persistent suitor, Mr. Lonesome with his "Bronx-itis" and import-export father, had been placed in the inactive file. The last time they were together he sulked and asked indiscreet questions.

—The whole campus knows. You're aware of that?
—Knows what?

He gave a snigger:
—In the Biblical sense—get me?

Patent absurd grin, but askew now with jealousy. He threatened to leave her and go to Tampico.
—Don't let me stop you.
—But will you come?
—I'm busy.
—Yeah, seeing him.
—What?

For Morgan it was like other scenes, less unpleasant. Of late he had grown so intimidated, young and hurting, she almost felt pity for him. The nicer people were, the easier to get one's way with them. Besides, this time Willartig was a key factor; he gave her strength to withstand, and stay above: she felt less compromised by her own need.

—Don't call me again, she said. Alright?
—It's a free country.
—But we're not right for each other. Our destinies—
—Say what? he gave her a sidelong glance. You mean you're too good for me, la-di-da.
—No, but different.

He sat nodding over the steering wheel, questioning his world as Morgan stepped from the car. She leaned back in:
—Bye, and thanks.
—Hey wait. Will you marry me? My Dad's money.

He gazed at her blond hair, crimson scarf in the cold wind. She walked away, buoyant across the frosty grass. The laughter died down inside him; he stared from the driver's seat a moment. There was a happiness to her gait, a meaning in each step forbidden him to understand, much less share.

He didn't call again. Morgan's roommate phoned him once; but his apathy with regard to Lou was pronounced, and almost coarse.

XIV

Sessions with the refined teacher proceeded. She stayed for dinner; he cooked steaks on his hearth. Many a world historic figure was on hand, Goethe rescued from his fate in Brookline, Nietzsche lending aphoristic inspiration to this special relationship between teacher and student. A new note of enthusiasm played like a flute in Morgan's conversation, lending fioritura when she posed a question, or gave her latest thoughts on some symbolic passage. Rarely did they revert to "everyday banality" and notes on campus life.

Willartig showed a real patience with her. No doubt he sensed her anxiety at times, being there with him for hours. Was she implying she had little to offer?

He knew the art of enjoying nuances, the small side issues of sexuality described so well by that old rascal, Balzac. He glimpsed her beautiful large hands when she reached for her teacup on the table between them. Blond, strong: the hands of a Viking woman who also showed signs of a lovable neurasthenia. Perceptive aesthete, he enjoyed her hesitations, her flush of appreciation when he translated some prosodic figure into simple English for her. Despite Morgan's attempt to dress casually, and conceal the obvious, he only sensed her charms the more fully. What passion lurked beneath her modest plaids. What promise beneath a loose-fitting blouse, a prim and vested suit. Once she wore an old schoolgirl costume, with necktie and saddleshoes. To such lengths she would go, and even further, for the sake of her ideal relationship.

But her restraint merely served to sharpen the edge of his anticipation. In fact, she was occupying his thoughts when he least suspected; when he had a lesson to prepare, or writing deadline to meet. Willartig was reaching a stage in life where being thwarted could give a man pleasure, where waiting gave savor to the stew. Also, she was hardly the only fish on his line, though certainly the most playful.

With Morgan there was a new finesse. There was a sense of verbal stalking, a lingual tension unknown to his experience. Sex had become philological, as the hunt went on. They talked endlessly about literature: Kleist, Lautréamont, Trakl, no writer was too obscure. They passed through a vivid landscape of image and symbol, hand in hand, alluding quite consistently to the role of genitalia in Shakespeare, erogenous punishment in Dante. Altogether it was a pedantic relationship. She seemed ravenous, thought Willartig, for the literary.

Morgan felt deeply grateful to him. Thanks to her mentor the long depression seemed finally lifted. Senior year was a personal renaissance due to her weekly tête-à-tête in John's apartment.

But despite any number of subtle confidences, and quiet renunciations, she still found herself doubting his sincerity. There was something keenly real about him and yet ever distant: as if vaguely resentful of a parsimonious mother, or some other factor deep in his past. To date he had never once telephoned; strayed in any way from their set routine. He never betrayed his true feelings, not with a word, not with a gentle harmless gesture. Who indeed was he? A computer of sublime ideas? He simply nodded and caught her eye after class: after a rousing lecture filled with great citations, fascinating tidbits of biography, and then they went for their meeting.

Once, as spring finally approached, he was detained by a student and Morgan lingered along the corridor. She went downstairs and waited outside, before an expanse of campus and gray denuded trees. There was still a thin layer of snow with deep green earth peeping through like a groundhog. For a moment she heard poetry in the chapel bells, which rang out in the crisp late afternoon. She knew ecstasy in the flight of two crows, their alternate cawing.

One week she was feverish with flu and had to miss class. But he didn't telephone or send a card. And what was she to do: call him at home? Why should he, a close friend by now, be so reluctant? True, they were student and teacher; but didn't a love like theirs transcend the taboos? Weren't they "equals" after all?

No doubt he preferred his books and articles by a cozy fire. He was using the time to catch up on latest trends; for Willartig followed the reviews quite closely, and could be a technocrat at times, in his approach to literary form. He had a book review to draft, and his publishable correspondence to maintain. Probably he had access to the most enticing women of his time; so why should he care about a Radcliffe undergrad, one among hundreds who smiled at him each time he passed?

XV

In April they sat side by side on his divan before a crackling fire. Willartig had beckoned Morgan from her usual place in the armchair; as they shared a macabre and moving passage in the last chapters of *The Possessed*. It was when the decadent writer, Stephane Trophimovitch, went stumbling along a road of charred apocalypse. Behind him all was smoke and ashes, flame-licked with black contorted structures. He had been to witness death in a miserable suburb put to the torch by his son's group of self-styled revolutionists. According to Willartig this was a kind of *Hochzeit* in literature: one of the rare moments when writing achieved an amplitude of opera, while remaining true to its own fictile requirements.

—Here, he said, this is what I mean.

—Yes, said Morgan, breathless, I see.

—A character mocked by its author, scorned through the course of the novel... Then Stephane frees himself. He tears away from Dostoyevsky, assuming his own raison d'être. He enters into the sublime—and sublime, for me, occurs when forgiveness in life, redemption of death are the presiding questions, embodied in form. Then, haggard and dying, that incendiary light in his eyes, he goes out along the terrible road. A bit later he meets his patroness and lover, Darya Pavlovna. And she, despite her self-indulgence, all her encroaching pettiness, is transfigured as well. She becomes what I will call: immanence of beauty. Oh, this is the epitome of Dostoyevsky, who was malicious in his fiction, who enjoyed writing in a crude style for instance, writing a hundred boring pages on purpose, and slandering his own characters. He goes looking amid inanity, amid utter selfishness for the stuff of the sublime. What a thing it can be, to live on this earth! His genius shows us precisely that...

Willartig read from the text a moment. Then he paused, as if overcome by the power of the passage.

—Thus... thus the author—

Morgan gave a start, a sob perhaps. Their shoulders were touching. Their hair brushed; it was a merest graze on the exposed nerve of passion, sending a tingle through her unknown body, causing a dreadful sweetness to course through her. Could one's nerves throw up the reins, and lose control? He watched her hands, like two big exotic birds on the verge of flight.

—The author... let them go, so to speak. He gave up his hold.

—Exactly! said Willartig, turning toward her with a transport caused by the novel. Morgan, I—he grunted: I wish—

—No, she bowed her head.

He kissed her hair, temples, slumping a little to kiss her cheek and lips. He had bad breath, she noticed, from studying so much.

—You too are immanence of beauty. You are new life to me, vita nuova. Ah you, you—

He was caressing her breasts, and she gave a sob. There was a tremendous feeling of release, like giving birth to a new idea. But perhaps something ugly, some dead thing would emerge from her depths at any moment. She felt a small convulsion which threatened to embarrass her. Suddenly she had a melting sensation, like taut silk about to be ripped. In a minute she would be offered up to the big sensual force in herself, raging for sacrifice.

His lips, his prickly cheek grew insistent while his hands moved over her. He was tense and sensual, like the others; he provoked her resistance. She pushed at him and began to whimper; he too was a kind of wild beast, like the future corporate lawyer, like Tampico, and the sniggering athletes. Ah! he did pose a grave threat to her, this would be worse than murder.

Then the doctoral Willartig was a dread uncompromising force, as he went pawing all over her, maneuvering to possess her. His hands pressed on toward new regions, gaining dominion over her intimate self. It was unfair, degrading, inevitable.

Morgan lay back stunned at first. She was unable to trust her own reactions. Her five senses seemed in mutiny against her mind. Sexual desire was about to burst from her in gueysers. And then, losing the battle on two fronts, she gave it up; she relented, and went limp beneath his clutches. And at that instant, sensing his victory, he dragged her to the floor, undoing her, pulling her out, ripping the buttons of her blouse:—then gasping with wonder when he flung open the doors of the feminine sanctum. He seemed to gaze, on such an abundance, as one hypnotized.

The next phase began as he bore down on top of her. She opened her mouth, and legs, because such was his desire and inflexible will, like a final solution. Morgan was mortally afraid of him, and of herself. The highly esteemed critic had become a savage beast in mating season; or an envoy of her old demon? His prodding brow, his spouting gasps for breath reminded her of the white whale. But was he this antisocial?

In a moment he seared into her, and she tried to stay in control, weeping in little jolts. She went rigid and it stung worse than any injection. Then she tried to relax by instinct, holding herself up like a chalice. All open, spread there beneath his will as he drove it home. Blinking through tears, she stared up at a blurred new world.

But the second it ended, and he was panting for air on top of her, Morgan knew the thing was not what she had thought. Somehow she was the one who felt victorious, as if the enemy just delivered his main weapon into her hands. And by the time he spoke a word into that eerie, dawning silence, her tears were already dried.

Afterward, he was elated and very gentle. He was timid, loving as they had dinner together, cooking steaks over the fire as he concocted a certain garlic sauce with mayonnaise, *ailloli,* a vestige of his student days at the Sorbonne. They drank a bottle of red wine between them; and later he put his finger on the Paolo and Francesca passage in the *Inferno.* This he translated for her with the usual wit and charm. Laughing he said Dostoyevsky had been their Lancelot. Morgan gave a thought to Lou, back in the dormitory, and felt a little sad. By now her roommate had guessed that "it" was happening.

Later, they went back to bed despite Morgan's protests. She went before him as if in a haze, feeling drunk and, as he expressed it, subconsciously whole again. Before the night was over she had startled him, at the height of his somber pleasure, with a sonorous, velvet, wet peal of laughter into the wee hours.

XVI

For a few weeks she felt truly alive. It must have been love. She could hardly conceal her jubilant mood whether in class, in conversation. She paid little heed to the oglers and replied with ironic banter to the psst! psst! of some workers dealing with a cesspool outside the main administration building. An enlivening springtime seemed to drape its images across a series of most satisfying rhymes.

The long suppressed childhood in Morgan was aroused. She and Willartig walked arm in arm across campus, making no attempt to avoid the gossip. They were a famous couple, constant source of debate and a kind of cause célèbre. A less successful man (he was one of the faculty drawing cards) could not have avoided censure and perhaps dismissal by the trustees. But for Willartig this was no mere case of professional fondness. It wasn't a casual affair, literary fling à la Ibsen; or else love of love's renewal, as in the aged Goethe's case with a teenaged Marianne von Willemer. He and Morgan seemed dead set on one another. They wanted the relationship, and the literary allusions kept flowing.

Quickly Morgan gained in confidence. In May she felt a kind of ascendancy over her lover, and he appeared rather less formidable. Indeed his vows, proposals of marriage became a constant refrain between them; but she demurred. He grew somewhat obsessive about sex, and she lay back impassive night after night. In that strange act she was taking a kind of revenge on her past. And then daytimes—in the woman's faculty toilet once, and then, fantastically, in the last row of a movie theater. Whenever their study hours coincided, wherever their desire happened to find them, she lay back voluptuous or else propped there above him, stroking his dark hair maternally, feeling a distracted hilarity in the absurd pose. But sometimes she had to force herself; it was like loving a puppy. She cheered him on, she laughed out loud and said:

—Do it for Grushenka.

Her noncommittal distance seemed to increase his lust, and she wondered why he loved to humiliate himself that way. Did such a posture exist in literature? Such base needs were amazing in a man of Willartig's stature. Apparently, thought Morgan, you could work wonders merely by holding back, staying above, using your charms as bait for the biggest fish. Nietzsche was right, most people feared the heights; they sought out a herd with its pitiful illusion of knowing where things were leading. And this, she thought in accordance with a pet view of Willartig's, was the flaw running all through communism.

Stay on top! It was the only sure method. Be ruthless, since the natural order implied such an attitude. The tenured professor, author of books and a few hundred articles, gave a more profound and tragic accent to his sensual moans and groans. She felt like a figurehead forging onward toward new worlds. She was ocean-conquering; she was capable of some fabulous violence like Columbus, who set an example and precedent for the mastery of continents.

Their ship rocked with love, with love. It seemed to contest the magisterial waves, on this her maiden voyage.

XVII

In late May she sensed a gradual cooling of affection toward her ardent first lover. She felt confined by him at times. Final exams were not far off; she had much catching up and review work to do (except in one course) if she wanted to make her grades.

To Willartig this seemed almost like an overthrow of nature's domain. After all their intimacy Morgan was still quite self-possessed, even indifferent—uninterested? To be sure, she glowed inwardly with a full complement of future. In her smile there was a new strength; but when turned on him it was the smile of a sphinx, and he didn't know the correct response. Had first love left her blasé? How could she be a young adult and yet so totally in control? It seemed fairly monstrous.

Once she said in passing that she felt ready for the "next phase". This stunned Willartig. Him? Famous person, competent in his field—and a "phase"?

He went about distracted and ineffectual when away from her; his career even suffered. But he was beatific, and unable to conceal it, by her side. He lived that unique springtime with incredible intensity. "Youth would and age could" for Willartig, briefly, in his affair with Morgan *la fée*. He was bestowing his prime upon her: a flower all the more enchanting, its season was so short.

At times he wanted to sit down and write something dramatic, turbulently creative: a novel *à longue haleine* to rival Dostoyevsky. But he was headed in quite another direction; rather out of breath when it came to literature. Besides, he was unable to sit down and begin with the concrete work. Form eluded him. Any idea could be inspiring, any material alive and pregnant with significance:—but living came first for Willartig. If his ambition had been substantial, his "greatness" was certainly a mirage.

—After commencement, she said, I'll go to New York and start out on my own. A woman needs to join in the work force, at least a few years. Yes, I must do that. You did.

She gave a gesture, and laughed. Always a move ahead, at this stage of the game.

—You have a way, said Willartig, of holding up my experience to me. Are we in some kind of loving competition?

—In a sense. How could we help it? But I also have this strange way of rejecting double-standards.

—You think our love is one?

—Sooner or later, life shows its true face.

—Life, said Willartig feeling his world start to spin the wrong way—life is what people make it.

—Amen. I think I'll try my wings.

—And then?

—Who knows. But there's nothing for me in this... zoo of academia.

—Ha! Meaning—?

—My parents: they said it all about zoos, and did it, too. I won't be like them.

—Even if I let you be the zoo-keeper?

—Mon ami, that was the wrong answer. And it would be your idea, not mine—but not very literary. If you could just let things happen, if you were strong enough there might still be a way. Like Rilke and Lou Andreas-Salomé, not often together, but tremendously so on occasion. I know I could keep you warm intellectually.

She laughed at him.

—I'm not Rilke. Anyway, geniuses go through withdrawal; they get lonely like anyone else, which debilitates.

—Then what were all our good talks about, our intimacy?

—To make the rest tolerable, I suppose.

—Ah! she paused. But... that makes it a little like lying.

—You will see me with other eyes, saith Zarathustra. Wait till you've struggled out there awhile. When you've learned to see, come find me.

—Zarathustra meant something rather different.

—Hm... Talking back to your teacher?

She chuckled and stroked his head. He submitted and burrowed into her, enslaved by her extraordinary freedom, but deeply in the mood.

In truth Morgan was sated. His love had enabled her to look back and to exorcize (a kind of ego-loan from the patient Willartig) the demon of her past. She felt liberated and exuberantly strong.

She could hardly wait to finish her exams, graduate and go off to joust with reality. Once she said to Lou, during her last days at the college:

—Someday, I'll really get my way. All I have to do is dream up the goal, and then go about actualizing my power.

—Huh?

Lou shook her head under the barrage of high-flown pronouncements.

XVIII

She completed her senior thesis on Russian poet Alexander Blok, quoting a Soviet critic (which made Willartig jealous) thus:

"It was not the physical vitality of which we have already spoken, but an exaggerated sensuality only partly connected with natural energy and, in essence, pathological, which drove him to seek experience in the underworld of tavern night life. Here, beyond doubt, was the source of inspiration for the second and longest period of Blok's poetry with its burning evocative power, its all-pervading eroticism, its despair, its mystic aspiration... For Blok, the very vortex of excess, the burning of the flesh in the sweet torments of sensuality were, in some sort, a source of mystic experience. Drunken debauchery, spicy infatuations, wild affairs..."

On their last night together they celebrated her stunning victory, Phi Beta Kappa, in a downtown hotel. They ate lobster and drank a lot before taking a room. Toward dawn they lay clutching one another, but the professor pulled away staring at her with drawn features:

—You really mean to, no bullshit now!

—What?

She yawned.

—You could really just... off into the sunset with her? Brunhilde rides again.

He mumbled something.

—John, dearest... *the* John.

—You can't do it. You aren't really serious.

She gave a childish laugh, and slapped him.

—I thought you were so great, a man of the world. Inured to... the human.

—Nobody is, but it's a secret. Only manured.
—Liar, said you were inured. Liar liar pants on fire.
—Secret . . . known by all.

He withdrew into a silent pouting, heedless of her caresses and mutterings. He frowned up at the first gray light on an alien sill. In the past few weeks he had hardly mentioned (except when sparring with her about "freedom") the undying works which lined the shelves of his apartment.

Morgan took it for granted that she loved him; she expected to correspond, and then get together most weekends. They would spend time together from month to month, and still have their quota of fun and sharing; but she needed some distance. She wanted a year or two on her own before thinking of marriage.

Now she couldn't understand his tragic air, lying there naked beside her in the fancily nondescript hotel room. She enjoyed such a neutral decor, like a prelude to adult life. Willartig was clownish and pitiful when he brooded.

XIX

Later that day he was not to be found at his apartment or office. He left no note for her. She spend the evening packing, chatting one last time with the faithful Lou, who even cried a little.

Next morning she said goodbye to her roommate, and to Radcliffe, without a glimpse backward. She went for a brief visit to the paternal home in Brookline, expecting to collect her graduation present and hoping it would be a generous sum of money.

In the dozen years between college and her activity in Lebanon, she never saw Willartig again or returned to the Radcliffe campus.

Depression set in. It was cyclical from week to week but it reached unprecedented depths, shocking her. Morgan's life was a sunless polar region in the midst of a Manhattan summer. Her acute moods scared her because unrelated to any personal drive, or apparent objective factor. In her first days there she found and furnished an East

Side apartment. Any number of times she dialled Willartig's number in Cambridge. Had he gone off to Europe? Was he taking a love-cure in Baden-Baden, like the hero of *Smoke*? Her letters received no response either; and soon one came back marked "return to sender."

Then in late July his telephone was disconnected. What had happened? One day she came upon a book review with his by-line. She read through the insipid thing with distaste, but then tried to reach him via the editor's desk, to no avail.

Morgan settled into her new surroundings. She spent the graduation gift of two thousand to pay security, first month's rent and living expenses, plus modest furnishings. She found New York menacing, tensely indifferent,—not so much the crime and filth as a sense of mediocrity, lostness which was pervasive. It was like a detraction from nature, and her Zarathustrian spirit, whenever she ventured outside.

Everyone else had a job, attachments, nine to five routine, pleasures on schedule. But she was idle all day and felt less than human. She read much of the time, whether trash or the classics, until the mere act made her nauseous. She haunted the museums as incognito as possible; then sat shyly hostile in a singles bar. All the while she longed for distant places, travel, European cities and cafe society; or else the tropics, beaches, piña colada and dancing beneath the stars. Love of a revolutionary, guerrilla warfare—anywhere out of this world.

Toward the end of August she had no job, almost no more money, no friends she could fall back on. She mused over wild schemes such as calling Mr. Lonesome's rich father in the Bronx, or summoning Lou to the rescue as of yore. She was dragged down by depression, bereft of initiative what with the steady run-off of her energy. She had no tolerance for the classified ads, and felt a strong urge to stay in bed all day. By now she couldn't read anything, at most a magazine. Of course, her parents would always bail her out financially, but the idea of asking them for anything seemed worse than taboo.

XX

She walked to a midtown hotel one evening and sat at the long oak bar with a martini. She waited alone, frowning, running a hand through her blond hair, like a confused goddess. Almost at once a man appeared, a businessman in from Houston. They conversed. He led the dance.

—Spend the night with me?

—Alright, but I need money.

—Sure, how much?

—Well, there's my rent, and ...

She thought about it while he seemed to grow taut and more eager. The idea of paying for it excited him. This was a "beautiful gal" and the big one which might get away. With his quickened breath, the familiar little signs,—Morgan felt whole again, and on the offensive for the first time in two months. She straightened in her chair and felt like laughing.

—We'll make it a hundred.

—Fine, I have a travellers check.

—You get it cashed. But, you know, I mean a hundred per hour.

—Will do, he said, more meekly, meeting her smile. We'll make a night of it.

Coarse in comparison to her first lover, he also proved gentler and more humane in his way: more contained.

—Shall I tell you a secret? she said, afterward. You won't believe it.

—Shoot! he said, happy now.

—You're the first one, I mean this way. All tolled you're only the second.

A concerned look came over his face. An hour later, as they sipped cognac together he asked her to marry him. He would get a divorce "pronto" and the whole "sheebang for his topsy-turvy l'il gal." Successful sales representative, on a whopping expense account, he became her first regular client and phoned her each time a few days in advance. He brought her flowers. He dreamed up new ventures to justify his visits in New York City; and he didn't mind taking a loss.

On her first try as a prostitute she earned six hundred tax-exempt, and her views on the human condition seemed to expand. She deemed even her sorriest paying customers a rung above normalcy, if only for their sly sense of rebellion, and the way they said yes to instinct, in the end.

No more anxiety due to inaction. Risk was a sure cure. City days were for resting, now that she had actualized her power. But she did have to be careful.

Before long she commanded five hundred per night from a few select customers. She carried a small handgun, wondering when a local pimp or perhaps organized crime would try to step in, becoming troublesome. In the latter case she would leave; she was saving up her money; she already had a "full service planner" tending to her portfolio—on the advice of a customer, and through his contacts.

Morgan didn't mind catering to the kinky tastes of her clientele; she wasn't squeamish, within limits. They reminded her, many of them, of Willartig without the months of foreplay and rococo. On a given night there was this or that new twist: some brilliant production number dreamt up by a male subconscious. She played the heroine in any number of bathroom tragi-comedies; but she made them pay for it beforehand. And she was preparing herself for violence, taking lessons in self-defense, which excited her. She was a courteous and at times innovative quasi-sadist; but never ironic, never sneering. She performed for them with a certain seriousness, like an ancient courtesan she imagined. The moment drugs were introduced she sought an exit; if there was any problem she knew when not to insist.

Thus Morgan lived a world in those few months. She survived a few scrapes and close calls. She was a beautiful risky call girl, more gorgeous than a Manhattan autumn.

In her first year as a whore she had three offers of matrimony, including the salesman from Texas who decided to divorce his wife of eighteen years regardless. By chance the successful Radcliffe grad appeared on the front cover of a fashion magazine; its sixty year-old publisher being a grateful customer. But you can't fool the female public: yet another attempt to introduce the "big look" met with stiff resistance.

Morgan lied no more than necessary, and arrived on time for her appointments. She inspired many different men without making them wish particularly to hurt her. Also, she never accepted abuse nor did she have to: she could hardly lend herself to the masochist's role, or feel comfortable in its demands. But she didn't understand it then. Morgan didn't push things; she performed, like a genius of phantasms.

And the demon in her? That something monstrous which had made a meal of her adolescence, and bright college years? As Faustian adventuress she might keep the evil off balance for awhile; even make it serve in her behalf. In fact she learned how to let it feed on others, love's cannon fodder, consuming the most devoted.

But whoredom, for Morgan, was a phase. By the following spring she had grown, once again, inhumanly lonely. Whereas Willartig's love had been a constant high, now the weekly hunt proved a morbid sort of drain. As a prostitute she began needing a hundred eyes, sleeping in haggard shifts, to keep watch on the age-old demon trying to enlist her heart in the ranks of what destructive ideal? The evil kept reappearing, as Willartig might have said, "like contradictions in an ever higher form..."

XXI

For hours Elie holed up in the long corridor of the Greek Orthodox Hospital. Toward late afternoon he had parked his jeep in the rez-de-chaussée of a gutted apartment house. Snatching his black hood he looked under the seat for his M-16, but it was gone. He raced to a side entrance.

Approaching, he put on the black hood, the cagoule. Masked Phalangists were a common sight in the streets of Ashrafiyeh, and they were all running. But without the assault rifle Elie felt naked and vulnerable.

—You can't come in here.
—What?
He peered at a tired hospital administrator.
—Only the wounded. It's dangerous, much too crowded.
—You move—
He grabbed his lapel and shook him; though the poor man was bigger than this skinny fighter. For a moment Elie stared into the

burnt-out passive eyes. He shoved him backward and outside, slamming the door.

—Ya Sakr! he raged inwardly. You bastard, you would tow your own grandmother—or anyone who tried to reason with you. Ya *ar's*, pimp for your own sister, you forget my performance in Kantari when it all started and you, Sakr, were needing a change of underwear. Who kept his head, me or you? Oh Jessica, I loved you...

He went along the dark aisle with a reckless air. The ghoulish hood caused people to draw back and let him pass.

There was lamplight in a congested foyer—heads, shoulders in stark outline. He began his descent into a region lit, here and there, by candle or penlight only. Women and crying children; old people doddering, a tangle of limbs and souls.

Elie went along the corridor. The others seemed to close behind him like a wake. He heard their murmurings, as they gave vent in small ways to the great fear. The way was all but impassible. Only a blood-soaked stretcher and hysteria could make the crowd shrink back, creating room.

—But you forget my steadfastness in Burj, ten long months, O hypocrite. Pay me fifty lira and 7-Ups for a night of fighting, while you preen yourselves before a camera. Since I was seventeen you ducked my head in shit of your own making, and it was wrong. Now you'd court-martial me for refusing to torture a peasant as ignorant as yourself ya Sakr, *manyuk* Sakr.

He went down a flight of stairs. He threaded passage on the long subterranean space, glancing here and there. Along the line of faces he paused, glaring at a chatty woman, jolting her with his gaze—two tiny glints, animal-eyes in the shadows. The woman's stream of words trailed off; her listener gathered in a child who was playing with pathetic little sounds.

—You forget my supply run into Ashrafiyeh in October '78 which you thought was impossible. And you hush up other things as well, being so self-righteous. But you would never overlook to have someone tortured, and by God you'll be obeyed. Horror-monger, please ask yourself what is Madi's reason; just what is his problem? Why didn't he join us for champagne and caviar, in front of the correspondents, after the fall of Tel ez-Zaater? One of us has a clam's brain, and that is the problem.

Elie stopped, sniffing. There was a strange tart perfume, as if a flower were being raped. It overrode a scent of burning lacquer, and the oozing from human pores of arak and fear. Beneath the shrill perfume there was malodor like an unremitting ache.

Elie stopped and found a place in the darkness. He sat with his knees drawn up as in the Sioufi shelter. It was stifling but he kept on the black hood, and didn't move. He waited, sharing the dreadful inertia.

A military march throbbed on a tinny radio.

—Have you been at Burj?

A bolder woman poked him on the shoulder.

—No.

—Are you wounded?

—Tell us! said a second. How does it look down there?

—I know the situation's bad. My husband fell—

Elie, in a toneless voice, interrupted:

—I was on the other front.

—In Sinn Il-Fill?

He shook his head, ominous. Another comment died in the teeming silence.

Where was Sylvie Helou by now? He knew exactly where Jessie was... His mother as well, in Sioufi; and his father in a hero's grave. But what next for Elie Madi? Alone. It seemed he had been going and going and now he stopped, here—but for how long? Someone kicked his boot. He looked up and saw them passing like a cortege in Hades.

No purpose for his life anymore. But these others kept moving by, stumbling over stretched legs. One tripped, groaned, bickered over his right to a little niche on earth.

XXII

For an hour, and another, Elie sat unmoving. The women asked themselves if he was hurt, or just gone mental. There was a humus of sound in the underground area: tense rustlings, radios with willful announcements contorted by static, news reports of events in the neighborhood. Six, seven o'clock—by now it was dark outside. But something was drawing nearer, hour by hour, and it too would happen in the darkness.

He was detaching himself, disowning reality. He thought of Kuzayli and Sakr, Little Hani and his brother. He had been with them as a child and stood by while the fathers played trictrac on crates, smoking the narguileh outside their shops. The fathers dandled the children on their knees between customers; they juggled a bright future from knee to knee, patting it on the head. One extended family, and Maronite.

Then with the war their world sliced in two: on one side *them*, the beasts—on the other *us*, a sacred community. And then there was Sakr everywhere you looked, calling himself Abu Joseph. From April 1975, from the Ein Rummaneh bus massacre through the early rounds, battles in Kantari and militia actions around the big hotels; then on Black Saturday in December of that year, when a few hundred Muslims were slaughtered in Burj; and into '76 with the trade-off in Karantina and Damour, making January the bloodiest month so far; and the combined-Left offensive beginning in March, battles in the mountains, when a host of young cadets and Maronite montagnards, of the Metn-Kesrouan, departed for Zaarour, Sannin, Qanat-Bakische, Fakra, Ouyoun-Siman, pledging their lives;—and then on and on, the Syrian turn-around, first incursion of Syrian brigades fighting with Elie's people now, assisting in the siege and fall of Tel ez-Zaater where he himself was vitally present; and even after Riyadh where, in what was thought to be the end, the issue was "decided" by half a dozen Arab heads of state, plus the PLO leader, minus Phalangist leadership; but not ending there, either, not at Riyadh but flowing into a long aftermath through the tenure of Arab Peace-Keeping Forces, and the Ehden Massacre, and so-called Summer or 100-Day War of 1978 when Ashrafiyeh took its turn for a thorough lambasting; and then during the merciless merger of Lebanese Forces, bloodbath of Chamounists in spring of '80 when many of these took their chances across the Green Line, risking clemency among leftists whose families they helped to butcher, rather than sit to judgment by their Kataëb allies:—all this time the Phalangist Party's grip was tightening, closing with a force of sacred conformism on the minds of its thousands of members. All good is here, all evil over there. So let's be done with them! And through those months and years the good and evil, for Elie Madi, imperceptibly, were growing harder to tell apart. In 1980 during the merger, Kataëb gunners sent rockets onto quiet East Beirut beaches. They opened fire on their own people, rightist Christians along strands in Maronite sectors near Jounieh. Then, in '82, the Israelis invaded with a huge inhuman impact seeming to break the Lebanese scale, and send everything in splinters.

Gradually, he lost his belief in the official explanation. It took a long time, too long.

XXIII

He began drifting off to sleep. He had a soaring, panicky feeling—of sudden elevation. Once he jolted from sleep and adjusted the black hood on his sweating features. The women turned away from him. He sat alone with his fear and a cushiony disoriented sense. Like a figure in a pantomime Jessie retreated, shaking her beautiful lobed forehead in sad disapproval. Suddenly Abu Joseph slapped her, hard, but with a sly cunning since she liked it. There was no sound when he whacked her and stood back like a painter from his easel, as mutely she implored for more. Jessie's cheeks were two live coals: Elie wanted to place his lips to them.

—How much longer? said a woman.

Surgical operations were underway in a room at the far end. Groans, screams came undulating like waves beneath a pier.

—I'll go mad if they make me stay here. I swear to Christ, what a life! They killed my Georges, but on his way to heaven he dropped off a few at the other place.

Harsh, familiar tone of voice: a virago. But weak compared to the steely gentleness of Soeur Davida.

Outside, there was a howling across Ashrafiyeh, like a factory hooter. Jessie offered her bare breast, smiling coyly, to a debonaire Abu Joseph . . . Madi's case was the talk of headquarters; they were using it to raise morale. If they found him they would shoot him without discussion. He whimpered as bricks and plaster came gushing through the wall; he glimpsed the action of the rocket. He screamed but his voice was a gnat's in the shock of explosions clapping his ears with an inhuman hand. Like a giant peering over the horizon, he opened his eyes: Kuzayli sat in Buddhist posture, but shrapnel had scythed off his face cleanly. A mask of tragic features hung to one side, exposing red gristle, a greenish squib and contours of a skull, emerging.

—Georges was decorated, you know, the week before his death. And then afterward they made him captain.

Elie awoke to the woman's words. She sounded ever so angry at Georges for getting himself killed. Others knew how to play it safe, and live to kiss their wives another day. Nobody would have dreamt of making poor Georges a captain while still alive, and giving him any advantage. Not her, his beloved wife, and above all not the leadership:—until his moment of glory keep him sternly in the ranks, no deviations.

On and on, the battle raged. Outside, a mortar plunged in with a crunch, cascade of building framework.

Rattle of M-16s, from another world. Tank movement, Elie guessed, toward Place Debbas. The single-action firing of a sniper punctuated a rocket series whooshing, creasing the air. Across Burj the leftists were using old anti-aircraft guns horizontally.

On and on, the widow insisted about her Georges. The other nodded, but less to her words than the olives and flatcakes she ate from her lap.

XXIV

Through the night of war news reports, rumors passed in whispers along the hospital corridor.

Elie felt a soaring effect when he closed his eyes. Shrieking reawoke him an instant. Then he strolled in a strange landscape where trees symbolized loss of honor. There was Sylvie Helou, white and tattered, trotting on the horizon. She called to him, and her low sobbing was like a nightingale.

—I'm coming! he blurted.

—Ah, he speaks, said the widow glancing over her shoulder. Monsieur, take off your hood—aren't you hot?

—Why are you here? said the other.

—Messenger, he said, pulling off the cagoule.

—I know you! You're Elie Madi: I remember your picture in *Le Réveil*.

Once that one had been gorgeous, forestial, like one of the cedars. Now she had two deep lines of anger slanting from her eyes... Elie stood, turning away from them. He listened to a sudden shrill wailing. It was a long treble peal of outrage; but it snapped and broke off croaking. The voice seemed to swallow, and took flight again over the buzzing corridor. It squealed; it hissed a note beyond the human range—but was near submission now, fading out.

A slovenly woman, a hag by the door to the operating room launched into a wild laughter, seeing the crazed Phalangist approach:

—We're losing! she cried, but stopped as if overhearing herself. Nobody wins all the time, it's okay to lose once!

Elie burst past her into the operating room. Hood back on, authoritative though his voice trembled:

—What's going on?

—No! said a doctor, or med-student stamping his white shoe dashed with red. Look at you: and you didn't scrub!

His voice was muffled by the surgical mask.

—I'm Elie Madi: you answer—

The doctor spoke tensely a moment beneath the shrieking. He wore bluejeans under his gown like a butcher's apron.

—I'm operating on this girl. She has shards of shrapnel in her abdomen, understand? She has multiple wounds, and while we talk, she bleeds. Will you get out now?

—Why the screaming? There's no anaesthetic? I'll get you some, but put her to sleep.

—There's anaesthetic, he gestured with impatience, gazing from Elie to the nurse. But there isn't time: we're performing these operations cold because *there isn't time*. And now get the hell out of here. This girl will die of hemothorax because of you.

The surgeon maneuvered her chest tube like a stick-shift. She was strapped on the stretcher, and held fast by a male orderly. She wailed, trembled, convulsed.

Elie plunged from the room.

He moved along the corridor, striding wildly, tripping over legs, sowing panic. Violent as Barabbas, he elbowed his passage.

XXV

Outside, cadavers lay side by side in plastic bags. They were Phalangists, and in passing he recognized a woman friend of Jessie's: face glazed, streamlined beneath the plastic wrapper. He felt a twinge of jealousy; she had been Jessie's friend and confidant. He used to envy their phonecalls lasting for hours, giggles and whispers. The body alongside still wore the black hood.

His jeep was waiting. An ascendant moon soared high above the Casino; it showered Mt. Sannine with a lucent mist. Elie turned over the ignition. He felt refreshed by the night air, and unrolled his hood like a sock, pulling it over his eyes with a tickle on his bristly growth of beard.

The jeep lurched from the rez-de-chaussée, its tires grinding glass and gravel, and plunked down from the curb. Elie sped away toward Mar Mitr. He jolted over the ruts and felt elated. For the moment he was back in action; the brief sleep had restored him, despite his nightmare. The jeep went flying along a side street toward the Ring of Death. Up ahead two patrols jogged silently toward Burj, as if marking time while he speeded past. They made an eerie vision on the vacant avenue: school of dolphins in a moonlit sea. Twelve men trotted in unison, M-16 in hand, wearing shiney kneeboots.

The moon rose over the foothills, as Elie raged along Selim Bustros and then swerved right down a side street. Maybe he could find Sylvie and save at least her, escape in a launch from Jounieh Bay. That was one idea. Or he could drive out on the Ring of Death with a megaphone, demanding an immediate end to all hostilities . . . He slowed down, approaching Rue Sursock.

Sa'iqa and PLA units held Burj along with a few buildings on this side. How far had they penetrated? Just what did they control? He heard the bursts of machinegunners down in the square.

Elie hit the brakes skidding, hurdling a curb. He had felt a momentary surge of hope, thinking: lines of fire, positions! But the sudden halt was unendurable: his jubilance turned to anguish the instant he stopped anywhere. Where to? A Katyusha slammed into an upper storey—clicking of tiles, torrent of plaster chips.

He backed off the curb, turned and moved along in the jeep. Moonlight glinted on the stripped and spectral laurel trees of Ashrafiyeh. He knew there was no going back now: Sakr considered him a traitor because they did not agree, they would never agree on the question of torture. Or else Sakr would decide to sacrifice him on a whim, make him go out and challenge an RPG for a decoy, meeting death as a test of loyalty. Aie! The Maronite Christian must fight and his sons must fight, as they came of age, and their own sons after that as the generations revolved. But if you emigrate, coward, then don't bother to return. Love Lebanon or else scram.

XXVI

Where the Phalange had manned a checkpoint on the eastern ramp of the Ring of Death, Elie was shot at. Running by a low cement wall he heard bullets clink harmlessly on the concrete. One hissed by his ear. The long drumroll in Burj was without pause.

Saifi seemed unclear, a checkerboard of unsafe positions, and any further movement involved risk. He heard shooting close by and knelt to watch. Down an alleyway figures clung to a doorway. MG fire clawed a window sill, sending up puffs as a fighter flailed his arm, tossing in a grenade. Were they mopping up?

Elie sprinted forward a few yards; but he darted back, huddling. Just ahead were three men in camouflage with bandoliers slung across their shoulders. They wore webbed belts of ammunition, and grenades like ornaments to their masculinity. What was happening? Had Syria managed to re-coalesce its leftist dupes for a fullscale offensive? Would they overrun Ashrafiyeh, while Israel stood by shaking a finger at its Christian allies: what about our peace treaty now?

He saw sparks on the side of a building. The long-range shelling came in waves. Detonations rotated from Kataëb rocket launchers deeper in Ashrafiyeh near the Rizk Building. There was a *houn* (howitzer) in action by the Sursock Museum.

—Wrong! He ran along bent from the waist, his torn shift flapping at the shoulder. In his mind flashed the memory of a leftist dragged feet-first from a rear bumper. The shredding body left a red wake through the streets of East Beirut before applauding crowds. That was after a great victory. That was the day Tel ez-Zaater fell. Now another camp was on the verge of succumbing: what would happen this time?

He raced through an intersection. The rear position of a squad of five turned and stared as he crossed. From street to street the bees were swarming. A Dushka flew past in the opposite direction toward Burj. The driver wore a wet handkerchief in a bandana against the smoke. Long mounds of sandbags. Dutch dikes of sandbags against a raging sea of Arabs. Fighters crouched or ran along them, klashins held out, RPGs on their shoulders.

A dense ashen-tan cloud hung over Ashrafiyeh like an aura of Massada. Soon the Camp would fall, if this desperate offensive failed to lift the siege. Soon there would be another slaughter, Sakr in his glory.

Tongues of flame mingled with moonlight; they curled on the charred casements of upper storeys, licking their lips after a meal of civilization.

XXVII

Mamdoueh sped through a traffic light blinking red-green-yellow at once.
—Never look back here: you'll cause an accident.
—How is it in Burj? asked Ligury.
—Only souls, evaporating.
—What will happen tonight?
The setting sun cast shadows over rock-shelves lining Beirut Corniche. Refugees lived in shacks down amid the inlets of sand, rippling tarp and fish leavings. A lone vendor sold malban sweets, tea with miramiyeh herb, from the back of an ancient van. There were rumbling reports from the suburbs; a blast offshore, fifty meters beyond the surf, sent up a gueyser with sunset in its crest. As a man hurled cylinders of TNT on the waves, his partner scooped the fish bellying-up in a net.
—We call these fish *muwasta,* said Mamdoueh. We eat them whole, fried in oil.
They passed Bain Militaire with its pilings and surf-tossed breakwater. From here an evacuation of Westerners would occur, Ligury knew, before long. He said:
—Think we'll get through?
—Our people will create a diversion.
Ligury thought: responsibility . . . Of all things on earth, he mistrusted it most. At the Camp they would start an armed action to divert the Kataëb and get him inside. Some might die, therefore, so he could write the story.
Rows of market stalls on the southern outskirts: tents of vendors migrating from Burj in war season. An old man pushed a cart with pistachio nuts, chestnuts, sunflower seeds. A legless boy sat on his roller behind cigarette cartons piled in a pyramid.
Domain of windowless high-rises, stark across a wide mudland.
—See the flag of Fatah? said Mamdoueh.
Laundry fluttered on high sills, emulating the seagulls.

Ramlet Il-Baida, swarming with vultures. Meloy, U.S. Ambassador, was retrieved here in June '76.

XXVIII

Rags, scraps, fringes: the hovels of Auzai. Heaps of concrete and plaster stained by gulls: and across South Lebanon it was the same. In Marjeyoun, Ligury had seen dogs roaming in packs, feeding on furniture stuffing as they reverted to wolves. For weeks, after the '82 invasion, not a bark was heard; then one afternoon they reappeared and kept up a din for days and nights.

Miami Beach! Fabulous Summerland... Resorts still in operation.

They drove down the coast past seaside villas, palmswept boutiques and restaurants left like driftwood where the Mediterranean sidled up with its turquoise murmur on the gray sands. Soon they would turn left, heading up into the Chouf while risk began. Why me? thought Ligury.

Lovers lingered along this strip before the war. Devoutly hedonist; lush blue moods. Pearl of the Middle East! O perfumed garden. Oil princes spent vacations here, unable to say goodbye. Then a fig leaf made Adam and Eve more naked, but they stayed on a day, a week, savoring rancid fruit. They arrived at curious interpretations, excusing the unpropitious season. They said "the events", referring to atrocities. If you pointed out Camp misery to them, there were always stories of rich Sunnis. Kamal Jumblatt had been a feudal lord, a millionaire with the Lenin Prize. There was no real poverty in Lebanon until the Palestinians brought it like bacteria. Once Lebanon was a miracle. And now this whole affair was a conspiracy: U.S. and Russia had a joint plan.

—*Jawez! Shuh, amercani...?*
—*La, ingliis.*
—*Sahafi, ma'hek?*
—Yes, journalist.

The commando recognized the leader Mamdouch.
—*Yallah!*

Citrus and banana plantations spread on a twilit coastal plain, where railroad tracks long out of use curved away toward a glooming strand. Narrow lanes shot off behind rock fences, orchards and villages. The limestone walls were festooned with red Arabic lettering: *Liban Rouge! Yes to the Vietnamization of Lebanon*. Slang for disdain; classical Arabic in praise of the good guys.

Collapsed roofs. Jagged facades, mounds of colorless rubble. But the air had a keen smell of thyme and crude olive oil, so different from Beirut. Ligury's voice trembled when he asked a simple question. At least, for a moment, he wasn't engaged in jealous thoughts of Morgan.

From the Sidon Highway Mamdoueh turned left with a kind of violence. As night fell they made their way into the Chouf foothills.

XXIX

Dr. Kamel paused on the threshold of his clinic, which marked a brink before plunging into the shambles. Would Mamdoueh make it through? How best to impact this story on the journalist's conscience, so he would tell the world? Lately, the children had developed a strange kind of anemia; endemic only, perhaps, to genocide. Dr. Kamel thought it would make a good article in one of the professional journals: "Effects of Extermination: Preventive Care..." There was gangrene in the Camp, as well as tetanus: quite interesting cases. But who was this correspondent—a friend? Or one of the insensitive ones, asking the five questions about a people's misery—then putting us in brackets, justifying with lies. I'll show him a thousand jaundiced specters, eyes glazed over with hunger, moving slowly, using their bodies to a minimum. The flies will be our friends, when they gather about his well-fed "journalist's objectivity".

—Hana'a?
—Yes, Hakim.
The girl's voice came from Mayser's bedside.
—Is Sitt Chahrour well enough to sit up?
—Why?
—Tonight she must make a great effort. She must tell her story.
The mother of Hana'a, whom people liked to call Ashatra, had returned from the Camp spigot with a can of water—but shot in the neck by a Phalangist sniper. By the time she arrived, blood dripping from her neck had turned the water red. Sitt Chahrour refused to be

taken to Dr. Kamel's clinic: she said she wanted to watch her grandchildren drink before she died.

—Hana'a?

—Yes.

Mayser rocked back and forth, pointing out his usual vision of terror despite the girl's efforts to soothe him.

—A reporter is coming—Western.

—When?

—Tonight, if Mamdoueh can get him through.

On the hillside surrounding the Camp were jeep-mounted recoilless rifles—like insects from an infernal hive. They shelled the hospital, preferring targets related to medical care, as well as security. Day and night they fired off rounds from sheer boredom, keeping themselves awake. They hurled down insults over their loudspeakers.

Selman, the Camp administrator, was doing a job which referred back to the time of Titans, confirming all the legends. From day to day the Camp population lived in utter filth; and Dr. Kamel's only remaining antidotes were salt and water. He applied rags to stop bleeding, and used human hair to bandage. Camp dwellers were making cigarettes of grape leaves, and something called *umbuz* which was food for birds and related to opium. Everyone was skeletal: the doctor had dropped to 110 pounds, though his frame was no small one.

Grief. Death on all sides, in the rotten air.

Phalangist loudspeakers cried out:

—Surrender! Your leaders on the outside are laughing at you!

—Never. The world stands in awe of our steadfastness.

—They are eating hommos and tabouli while deceiving you!

At times it was a war of sound systems; at others, of silence. Every niche of the Camp was occupied with the dying, the decomposing. Space had taken on an added dimension, thought Dr. Kamel: horror. Graves everywhere. Near the mosque, in the Camp center, was a monstrous hole containing limbs, faces, swarming flies, birds, rats. The teacher Moustafa, future sheikh, cavorted on its edge in search of the faithful, defying Selman's strict prohibition of gathering at prayer hour.

The doctor thought of taking the journalist there. He would show him the bodies locked in a jumble of bones, like so many links in the chain of a collective destiny. They would remain at their post forever, taking deeper hold, as the Camp became a field of overgrown weeds, with Phalange emplacements on the fringes. Just as no grand finale of death would prevent the thyme from growing, peacefully, in little clusters of lobes, on the hill overlooking the Camp: so the dead heroes would require no loudspeaker to be heard by history. And the thyme would murmur of liberation, whenever a breeze arose, from the sea beyond Ashrafiyeh.

XXX

—This robe (Sitt Chahrour took a pinch of hem, showing the journalist): it is the third . . . I thought it would be my shroud, when I went for water and got sniped. But I may need another two or three, to get me where I'm going.

Ligury appeared uncomfortable. In fact he felt set up, and glanced at Mamdoueh: come on, man, give me the story and let's go.

—I wash it out at night, every week or so. The material is coarse, I can tell you. Also, it must be dyed black from year to year, and what an unpleasant thing, having to re-sew the seams in black thread.

Sitt Chahrour fell silent. Suddenly the impulse seemed to fail; she sipped her few drops of coffee and looked annoyed.

—When did you get the first dress? said Hana'a.

Ligury stared a moment at the striking girl: was she taking all the Camp's problems on her skinny shoulders?

—That was in 1948, the first one. I keep it folded neatly in a box, old rag that it is. The second and third also: despite myself I outlived them. It's a race to see which of us will turn to dust.

—But the first, said Dr. Kamel with a tender irony. Tell us, Sitt.

—You have only heard, *owlaad,* a dozen times. And many can tell this story better than I; or they could have . . . *Tayyeb,* since we are honored by a brave journalist.

Ligury's thoughts wandered, and he thought of the evacuation being planned for Bain Militaire. Would Morgan leave? He and Mamdoueh almost died getting inside this refugee inferno—and why? So he could attend a theatrical performance? Sitt Chahrour reminded him of women in the tragedies, speaking in an earthen tone, with primeval sighs.

XXXI

—Well, it was a day in April. Same time of year as now, but colder I remember. Soldiers came with their Bren guns, and jeep commando columns. They came to the city of Acre where we lived. They had armored cars, tanks; they even had airplanes, and flew over towns and villages strafing. But what did we have? One armored unit arrived from the south dressed in checkered *hattas,* disguised as Arabs you see. Our leaders went out to meet them and were shot dead by way of greeting. Haram!

"The Arab Liberation Army was disorganized, and without communication. Often it was every man for himself in those days. They wore the keffiyeh instead of helmets. Maybe they thought bragging would do for bravery; and because of their performance I'm afraid we made jokes about them. Enemy sappers came in and blew up our houses, one by one. So we began taking to the roads, nearly a million of us, in the springtime of the Disaster.

"I remember it was a bright day: the sun blossomed out amid almond trees and wildflowers, after a rainy winter. But fear was spreading through the villages; the people were panic-stricken, and began gathering up a few belongings. But when I tell you about my man, Hassan, you won't even believe me.

"I remember a leader of the resistance, Abdul-Kader, had just been killed. A funeral was held for him in Jerusalem, and its effect was disheartening. Abdul-Kader, you see, had fought well in what was called the Battle of the Roads, and now he was a martyr. Well, martyrs are good for the in-between times, when the struggle lulls, and one must endure in everyday ways. But in those weeks and months we needed living fighters, whose mere going and coming was a matter of heroism. We didn't need any spectacle of death.

"Then I heard the blare of loudspeakers. You have no chance! Our forces are superior! Take such and such a route: use the road to Ras Nakourah. Or to Safed, that one is still open. Soon you will be killed, run at once! Or they told us something like: Flee for your lives—the enemy is using chemicals, atomic weapons!

"I remember as well as yesterday the attack on Acre. When it began my husband was seated on one of the dining room chairs with an old Turkish musket in his hand. He sat facing the door; but that was foolish, I thought, since the door was closed. Outside, the mortar shells were whining and crashing in on the city of our birth. And the beautiful Arab homes, with facades of polished Jerusalem stone; those old solid-masonry buildings with their gardens and trellises: one by one they were exploding in a cloud of rubble beneath the shells. All around, you see, our world was crumbling. But Hassan sat there and never glanced right or left, as if to say: Just peep your shameful face in here. Just come through that door, and try taking away my home.

"And then we started pleading with him to bring us away, begging to flee and join in with the others. At first we didn't say it outright; but there was silent pressure from myself, my mother, even the children."

—Abu Saleh too? said Hana'a.

—He was young, and confused. It was his way to side with his father, but now Hassan seemed to go against everyone's wishes. It was obvious we were losing the battle, if not the war. But he just sat there and appeared to do nothing. His jaw was set. He hardly gave us a glimpse, immobile as a statue. I think by then he was sort of crazy, because we kept getting more and more worried; and I began talking him down, and doubting him. I thought he would slap me or lash out in some way. And that would have been the first time, for such a thing, in our family. Also, my mother was brooding in silence; she was outraged he could place us in such danger.

"You see, we had all digested the name of *Deir Yaseen* by then. It could happen to us, as well. As if some monster had risen up from its cave somewhere, in the loneliest stretches of the Negev, and begun stalking the land and devouring its inhabitants. It ate land, this monster, and innocent people's homes, and human lives.

"Meanwhile our fighters, I mean the real ones, tried to make a stand with those outmoded weapons. Our men were already decreasing in number. And many in Acre were thrown down a certain well by way of burial. Which may explain why the region still stinks to high heaven, and may prove a center of contagion infecting all the earth. *Haram.*"

Kim Ligury gestured toward Beirut, and said:

—That's possible.

XXXII

—They came like a hurricane into Acre, our beloved city; and there was more thunder and lightning than even the god of Joshua could produce. They were rampaging their way through cities as part of a campaign we later heard of as *Hahshon*. This was the name, they said, of the first man to walk through the Red Sea during their exodus. They were telling us: Your turn now. Go out on the roads, and learn what we have learned for centuries, about exile. And yet we had helped provide a haven for them, from Hitler.

"So it was our turn, now, to wade through a Red Sea, namely the blood of our people. Many, many went rushing out of doors; they could hardly wait for the Disaster. And it still hasn't ended to this day. With each new settlement how many are displaced? How many have to die, Mr. Ligury?

"Then we began ranting at him, shouting at my husband. We obliged him to get up from that chair, and this was the first step for us. I abused him, at one point. I cuffed him across the shoulder as you might a child, a stubborn son. And my mother, she was even more merciless, in her way, than I . . . The children joined in the chorus, Abu Saleh and the others, badgering him. By then the shells were slamming into our very neighborhood, or so it seemed.

"He kept waving one arm for us to stay behind. The intruder might arrive, at any minute.

"Another hour passed. Maybe it was less, or maybe a couple hours. But we were not about to relent. We coaxed, insulted him. Look at the terrified children. How can you do this?

"Hassan stood up from his chair. He had been leaning on the back with his gun in both hands. He seemed to rise in an agony, as if he would never walk straight again. At first I thought he might threaten us; although he had never laid a hand to me. But then I saw there were tears in his eyes, the tears of a man. And the old rifle drooped to one side, its barrel pointing toward the floor. And he submitted.

"—Alright, he said, I'll take you. We will go to Lebanon: to the cousin in Bint Jbeil.

"—Hurry! I said.

"And then, with great relief after the hours of panic we gathered up a few belongings, plus all the money and jewelry on hand. Also bedding, and some quilts, cane matting. An old radio I can show to you; it is here, inside. I've followed the course of how many wars on it, since that day?

"We made ready to go. But I will never forget the look in people's eye that afternoon. You see, we lived on a street leading out toward the road to Ras Nakourah; so I could watch as they came passing by.

"It seemed the old life was dying. Palestine was marching off, or rather stumbling, toward the horizon. Many went on foot. Others in cars bulging to capacity; and they moved in an attitude of grief and fear. Also of shame, I confess, once it was underway—shame at our frantic haste to abandon the place we loved most on earth.

"The men's faces were glum. The women raised their eyes in supplication. Suddenly the whole thing seemed wrong to us: it was all so resigned, and cowardly. And in a certain sense selfish, yes, when you think about it.

"And then we joined that line which led away to a world of endless waiting. To a life of anger which nothing, ever, for me at least, would appease. We nodded to our neighbors in that unending line. And they were only too willing to leave a gap for us, so we might enter. They were quite eager to share their part of the *Nekhba*, the Disaster of 1948.

XXXIII

"I remember the last glimpse of our home; though I hardly believed it would be the last, and still don't. In my own defense, and that of others, we thought the Return would be soon. Tomorrow, or next week, the Arab armies would sweep in and correct this error.

"Our home: the final glimpse. Sunlight on the modest facade, our jasmine trellis in front, the *mustaba*. Already we were being wrenched in two directions—away, but not too far, to safety; and back homewards to our rightful life. The anguish of this has never ended; it hasn't even varied much, to this day.

"In our pocket we carried the title deed to our land, and I have kept it put away securely. Yet a little while, and there would be a force of our own, able to restore justice. For now a last look at Acre; and a world of loving and planning, building a life, suffering together for many generations: all of this vanished. We were thrust on the reality of the long merciless road, of this road curving north and eastward away toward Safed and the Lebanese border. We had family, a first cousin living in Bint Jbeil, so we decided on the longer route. But our plans were thwarted; we never made it to Bint Jbeil. Once security is gone, who can predict?

"That curving road: it rose and fell slowly, among the severe hills. It was like Hassan's state of mind, sinking slowly, and then rallying toward the next vantage point. Thus we took the road of least resistance, *haram*. We let ourselves go the way of deluded hope. Oh, never travel the wrong road, Mr. Ligury. Strength will leave you, and you'll suffer for sure. Despair will be your escort.

"So the sight of Acre, the beloved, gave way to this road as well. It took a last resentful glance at our departure among the curving inclines, the ridges tantalizing us with yet another view. Our people went from ridge to ridge into an alien distance.

"There were others, and no few of them, far worse off. In Lydda, the enemy used Sten guns like brooms to sweep the streets clean of inhabitants. In Ramleh our people were stripped of all belongings and foodstuffs as they fled the city over its bridges. And this was termed: the Redemption.

"All the while, as we were leaving, my husband cursed under his breath. He ranted in whispers: not at me, or my mother in league with me; but the scheme of things, the way fate had us going. Once underway, be it said in my defense (which I decline) I was no longer sure ... For awhile he could see Acre in the rearview mirror as we rolled along, rather slowly, in the midst of that cortege of cars and vans. He muttered:

"—The shame.

"He hissed the word emphasized by our slow departure. The invaders were glad to see us go; it costs time, bullets and risk to kill. But we in our panic had jammed the roads and made our escape, cursing one another, at a snail's pace.

"—We could fight them! he whined, banging the wheel, cursing the would-be Arab leaders, Kawktji and them. We're out-weaponed but we do know the land, there are advantages.

"But he never even mentioned the enemy, that I remember. Along the road to Hmeimeh, then Saffouriyyeh, there were so many others. All sharing the dust, and sweltering sun. On a three-day trek into Lebanon or the Transjordanian Hills. And for many, the very young and old, it proved fatal and they died of thirst.

"Some ate grass or drank sewage. All marched on, as long as they were able, in a daze. Their family possessions, heirlooms and bedding fell from them along the roadside. Many cars were a bundle of arms, legs, heads protruding from the windows; they seemed to grasp some invisible lifeline. We were really all tangled up in one another: have you ever felt the grip of a drowning man, Mr. Ligury?

"At night it grew cold, and there were hundreds who endured exposure where they slept beneath the gnarled trunks of olive trees. I heard the story of a child who went out in the night to relieve herself, and was found frozen to death the next morning.

"—We should be staying! said Hassan.

"Late that night we passed through a Druze village, I believe it was called Yerka. There were people drinking from same pools as the cattle. Children carried smaller ones, pick-a-back. Others cried out at us about family members who had been separated. And everywhere you looked: dehydrated strained faces, frazzled old people, defiant men stomping the earth. Oh, there was degradation. And contempt, my friend.

"Later I realized that there, along the road to Safed and beyond: there before our eyes the Palestinian people were being transformed. In the old days of the Mandate, as in past centuries, each village had its way of welcoming strangers and taking them into its midst. Few hostels, restaurants existed outside the cities. It was all done on trust, with great courtesy; often to the advantage of arriving refugees. But before my eyes, in Yerka and a hundred other places, our people were travelling the road that leads from a fool's paradise. That was our valley of dry bones. And we were scorched by a new reality..."

Sitt Chahrour paused. She sipped the coffee grounds which had grown cool during her story. Ligury listened while she spoke as if time wouldn't hold all the words that were in her. But he still felt impatience, thinking of Morgan and her lover Kohler, and Bain Militaire.

—So we changed along the road to Safed, escorted by the fact of our loss. It seemed to taste, I remember, like *bamieh*, you call it okra. And it is bitter. We had brought a large basket with us, and from stop to stop we fed ourselves and others with the *bamieh*.

XXXIV

"Late at night we came to the border, on our way to Bint Jbeil. We saw the other side, a stretch of road after the restless lights of the checkpoint. Lebanon... The cars and dead-tired pedestrians squeezed through, one by one, and went off into the darkness with their tail between their legs. Word came along the line they were stripping people of valuables. Shots rang out. One man, we were told, was shot through the head by enemy forces controlling the first checkpoint. For insulting them. And when I think we were a growing crowd, they a single unit.

"Awhile later they told a dozen or so to run for their lives. Dash out along that stub of road like a gangplank. The guards fired over their heads and laughed. Go quickly, don't turn around if you know what's good for you—don't even look back. Guns were being confiscated: you had to give up your gun before going through.

"So Hassan sat quietly at the wheel, clutching his old Turkish musket, staring out at darkness. Up front there were more shots, a few screams. Behind us, somewhere down the line a dreadful moaning, a woman giving birth. Or maybe from thirst. I remember there was that eerie tone, far-off yet intimate, of voices in the night sometimes.

"Toward dawn our turn was nearing. I was shaking with nerves: you know, Mr. Ligury, the way your body does sometimes? Without daring to look I sensed Hassan coiled up inside, ready to explode. Once I asked him to give me the gun, and then, a few minutes later I told him to do it, if he still had any love for me. But he turned and stared in my face as if I was the enemy.

"My mother, she was not a help to us then. She said something about how he thought he could take on the whole world. He paid no attention to her, understanding it was the pressure of the moment which made her talk that way. He grew even more furious in the silence, using what self-control he still had to fend me off. I should've told him to wait; he could comply now and then return later, joining the bands of guerrillas that were forming. I should have spoken calmly, letting it depend not on me, but on him, his judgment. Even in disaster there's a wise course of action—so many things I could have told Hassan. But this is not the point about passion, that you can tell it things. After all he would have had to give up the gun, which he clung to like his honor.

"You see, I failed too. All of us except a few, in places like Gaza—all of us were lacking, when it came to the new reality. I gave in to my own emotions, using wrong arguments as we sat there in the middle of the night, on the verge of the worst. Suffer enough, Mr. Ligury, and you'll master your heart perhaps. But by then there won't be too much left of you, either.

"Our children slept fitfully as we waited. They clutched for warmth in the cold April night. I think Hassan would have pulled out and turned the car back toward home, but it was impossible. Once you formed up and made a link in that chain: the road was blocked for miles in both ways. A few did try to cut back across the fields which were soggy with the winter rains. But we had been rounded up, and were being herded away.

XXXV

"A soldier came along the line, making an inspection. Oh, this one was young, and very arrogant. (Sitt Chahrour sighed.) He almost strode past, but then stopped before us. It was sudden, in the darkness; there was no time, then, to pray to Allah. He spotted my husband's musket and stood waiting an instant. And do you know what happened, Mr. Ligury? Seeing that soldier so full of presumptions about life and yet knowing nothing: I tell you there was an earthquake in me, at that moment. Something had been wrong, deep inside. The truth is a universe, Mr. Ligury, and no lie like a geological fault but it must be righted somehow: you can expect violence: As soon as I laid eyes on that brash shocktrooper—I knew, I knew. For the first time I understood life, and my husband. Both at once, you see: this is the point about love, and being together. Your man is like the earth itself; as he goes, so you as well. And all at once I saw how it worked; I knew Hassan as if I was sitting inside him, with a knowledge that was too much to bear. And I was the one, holding onto the old musket, leaning against the wheel, staring into the hostile night. I felt an earthquake of love in me, after so much doubting.

"Hassan looked straight ahead, avoiding the soldier's gaze. For years the anger had been seething, building in us. You see we're from Palestine, the old Canaan, a land of peace and seasonal activity. Our country is dotted with olive groves and vineyards, fig trees, almond and apricot orchards; but many of the villages have since disappeared.

"Hassan the man had never hurt a soul, never laid hand to a human being. But for years they were nudging us, telling us to move over some more, and some more. They rejected our society, and bought up what land they could from the absentee landlords. We knew their intentions—and so what wonder people began losing their heads? What wonder there were riots, and the mutual killings began?

"For years the hatred had been nourished on hearsay, events in other places. But now it was all too sudden, and new: a face-to-face confrontation. One human being against another. Aie! Confront evil sometime, and then come tell me about it.

"The checkpoint soldier said to Hassan:

"—The gun . . . I'll take it before you blow your foot off.

"He smirked. I watched my husband bristle. He began raising the musket, but by then the other held his revolver pointed at Hassan's forehead. He was smiling, and said in Arabic:

"—Slowly . . . Children shouldn't play with guns.

"Killing is easy, I guess, once you get the knack. He realized it was his life or the other man's: why delay the affair?

"My husband was a good man, a human one. Even at the crucial instant he was still pondering. The soldier had provoked him and drummed up a pretext; but Hassan sat thinking of myself, the children, my mother. Ah, you must never play with violence, am I right, Dr. Kamel?

"For Hassan it was not the right moment, so he only bristled. The other cocked: I'll never forget the look in his eyes. And then the handgun exploded, with its snake tongue right in Hassan's face. Death spit at him—and he slumped forward, still bristling, and I screamed. I screamed with horror but it meant nothing. The young soldier gave something like a laugh; he reached in, eyeing the rest of us, and said:

"—Now I know you'll be a good boy.

"But the musket had a mind of its own and wouldn't come loose. So he had to pull him, wrench him out of the car onto the ground. He grunted and kicked Hassan in the bleeding head while I, the woman, sat frozen with terror and watched it all happen. The shot still echoed in the night of murmuring, up and down the line. I don't remember if my children awoke and started crying. Maybe they slept through the death of their father.

"I don't know how long, maybe a minute, the trooper played tug-of-war with a dead man alongside our car. He yanked at the rifle, blood spurting here and there. I thought he would shoot some more. I stayed in the car, as the soldier moved off, half-crouching, no longer so prim and arrogant.

"What did we ever do to him?

XXXVI

"Then I went down; I caught the one man I ever loved in my arms. There was no time after that for any vigil. I looked around and it was already morning; the sun was shining on the wild grasses and flowers. Another day on earth. How many times did I call around for help, but none was forthcoming? And none could have been. The orchards, land and sky of Palestine were reflected in Hassan's eyes. But in mine there was nothing left of this world except rage and hatred. For awhile, I confess, the woman's tears had their way with me..."

There was a pause. Then Sitt Chahrour spoke softly:

—By the time we took him, myself and the children... and carried him, attentive father, tender husband to me, a man who could have become a leader of the Resistance... by the time we crossed the border into Lebanon, my tears were dry. They were shed down to the last one, and my life was changed forever.

"So you see, Mr. Ligury, I was widowed. On that night in April '48 while we waited in line at the Lebanese border, I was left to fend for myself. I changed from my print dress with flowers into the first widow's robe, my costume of suffering.

"That same morning in Lebanon, a villager charged us one Lebanese pound for a bottle of water.

"For myself, I will go on living. And I'll always be talking a lot, like tonight. We must tell the truth about how things were, and just what happened, in those days when we left Palestine. It may take ten of these widow's robes before the truth is finally known—but otherwise, believe me, there will be no peace.

"Even in my grave I don't intend to shut up, if I can help it. No, I don't mean to let it die, not ever. That will be my gift of love to Hassan, my husband. Every word I said to you was in his memory.

"When the *Hajj* occurs, when it's time to return to the Homeland: even the dead will rise up, and go along those ancient dusty roads.

"Many times the last words of our old people are to this effect.—Rebury me, someday soon, in Palestine.

"Thus it is an honor, for us, to have grandchildren"

Quietly, Dr. Kamel said:
—We could love them, the Jewish people. They have been hurt, and they deserve a homeland. Everyone does. But you see, Mr. Ligury, they are living in our homes, while we die here, in a squalid refugee camp. The Western press has covered up the facts; and yet the facts must be known, for peace to have a chance.

PART FIVE

I

Camille Ydlibbi browsed and mingled. He smiled at a whore, who gave him a flirtatious frown as he passed her barstool. Photos flashed, tremulous like the ice in cocktail glasses. People talked, laughed in the glow. Toward the rear they bowed over green tables, placing bets, pawing their winnings.

—Julienne, bien le bonsoir!
—Et à vous, M'sieur Ydlibbi. Après nous le déluge, pas vrai?
Julienne squeaked.
Portly, bland, he grinned:
—We'll make it a deluge of champagne.
—Ah! C'est très charmant.

A waiter hefted a dripping bottle. Julienne's lips pursed, full and moist, two cherries, as he twisted the wire-casing from the cork. She was a French whore with a certain girlish chic; she gazed up at the dark green bottle popping amid cheers, bravo. Champagne flowed tonight like a misty Niagara.

—Eh, les mecs! Bon courage.

Ydlibbi, scandalized by his own imaginings, saw his private stock in the hands of barbarous hordes. He surveyed his table of correspondents, the boorish Kohler and another, a famous one from Paris. Pfui. Didn't like them. Talk with such men was a tournament of egos, no pleasure.

Urbanely, he smiled and bowed:
—Gentlemen, everything as it should be, this evening?

At a table by the far wall sat the woman Ydlibbi thought of as: la belle mystèrieuse. And by her side a Palestinian comandante; also the burly Englishman, shy, slightly clownish, not aggressive as other journalists. What spiced her beauty was the question she raised— American yet fluent in languages, hmm, her Arabic went beyond most Westerners', plus she knew Russian. Very blond, but masculine somehow, from the waist down. A centaur. She carried a press card, but he knew she moonlighted in prostitution—if someone pleased her that way, and could afford the exorbitant rates. Hadn't nature given her everything? Olympian figure, a mind into the bargain. But there was something quite snide, Ydlibbi mused, in bad faith beneath the surface, like a halitosis of the soul. Yes, it was just perceptible to him, a connoisseur, under the gorgeous perfume.

He drew closer. Mamdoueh was preaching as usual. The Britisher with an Italian name sat thoughtful.

—In fine spirits, mes amis?
—Join us, said Ligury, pushing out a chair.
—I'd like to. But I might not get up again.
—I've heard, said Morgan, when you drink with customers it brings them luck.
—Mademoiselle, you heard no such thing.

Ydlibbi's smile was thickly French like his accent.

—Let's pretend, she said.
—How do you mean? said a serious Ligury, slightly inappropriate.
—I mean life is either luck, or a math problem. No doubt both.
—There's no progress? said Mamdoueh. No march of history?
—It's a fiction, like another. But remember that "pretend" has two meanings. If a man wished to marry me (heaven help him) he should "pretend" to be my husband when he's with me.
—Where will it get him? said Ligury.
—In any case we're all bad children, said Morgan, enigmatic.
—What has this to do, said Ydlibbi, with my bringing anyone luck?
—Luck filters down as in Dante's heaven, said Morgan, from the proprietors.
—No, said Mamdoueh, upward from the people. The exploiters' position is untenable, their every act unlucky.
—Progressives have their own teleology, said Morgan.
—If you're arguing pacifism, said Mamdoueh, smiling, I tell you blood will flow like a Mississippi, until—
—There are imperialists, she said, and would-be imperialists.

Ligury looked from one to the other with a kind of awe.

Ydlibbi remarked:

—My club is full but rather quiet, in comparison to other nights. In honor of Miss Morgan's beauty, which is no pretention but a true fortune for all who see it: let me offer you my finest champagne.

He bowed, turning away. Ideological discussions were not in Ydlibbi's line.

II

—Mr. Ligury, will you join the evacuation?
—I don't know.
Mamdoueh gave an ironic grin:
—Have you packed?
—No, but I live in a furnished flat, with few belongings. And you? he glimpsed at Morgan.
—My only plans are to have no plans.
—I'm glad, said Mamdoueh, that you may both come and go as you please. For us, on the other hand—

Suddenly voices were raised. There was a crush of people by the entry. Two men hollered in Arabic, pointing, accusing. A woman's voice cut through theirs; then someone shoved her brutally and she fell with a cry.

—I know the tall one, said Mamdoueh.

Ydlibbi hopped between the tables with surprising agility. He shook an outstretched arm at them, but the exchange grew hotter; they were shouting at one another. Ligury picked up the word Kataëb—then *jazoos* meaning spy. He guessed it was between a pimp and customer refusing to pay, with the girl in between. One demanded the other give him something immediately.

There was an instant of angry silence, then shots:—two, three blasts from a revolver. Women shrieked. People fell from their chairs onto the floor. A man gave a groan.

And then a submachinegun volley, horrendous in the underground space.

Ringing silence. Sigh of someone hit, and falling quiet.

For a moment no one moved. Ligury, still in his chair, glanced back at Morgan. He saw her crouched alertly, facing the outburst with a small pistol in her hand.

A duet began: the soulful moan of the injured, imploring help.

III

In the aftermath Mamdoueh rose, excusing himself politely. He knew one of the wounded, and began arranging, with Ydlibbi, for cars to the American Hospital. Streaks of blood glowed a pale green on the parquet floor. A wizened Arab in a tarboosh came to mop up, while waiters did their best to reassure the crowd. One by one, Ydlibbi's patrons reappeared from beneath the tables.

Some didn't hesitate; they laid out bills with no thought for the change. It was a few minutes past eleven: Ligury and Morgan found themselves alone together.

—Close call, she said.
—You seem in the habit.
—Hardly.
She looked away.
He caught himself staring at her hands, so large and expressive, as if her personality had taken refuge in them.
—Lebanon.
—Sure, she said, or else Daddy and Mommy after a hard day at the office.
—What does that mean?
—Life is violent.
—You don't seem the type, said Ligury, who would play mommy.
—It is rather trite.

Her voice was rich, womanly, but it was in retreat somehow. In the tense atmosphere her bit of laughter had an uncanny sound; and Ligury thought, glancing down: Her laughter separates . . . while I sit here, begging in silence.

Morgan glimpsed her watch. The time makes her nervous, thought Ligury.

When a waiter came by their table it seemed a moment of truth.
—One more?
—One.

She glanced round the nightclub. Peretz and Risha, she thought. No scenes, let them get settled in; our time is nearing.

Ligury was an emotional contortionist the moment silence fell between them. She barely responded to his profound comments, or a question concerning her work. Thinking of Kohler?

For some reason she thought of Willartig, her first lover, comparing them distractedly. It wasn't the same thing at all: this one sat there, well-bred duffer—true gentleman but no scholar.

—You're restless, he said. What ever are you searching for?

She had another start of laughter, nearly spitting forth a sip of cognac. She threw up a hand, grandiose gesture gone limp.

—Years since I asked myself. Holiday, freedom: what's supposed to come, will.
—How so?
—The conductor threw up his hands and said: play.
—But how do you live?
—That whereby I *live,* is . . .

He nodded, while she thought a moment. In general she made him feel insecure, wrong in his approach. She could dally and mystify her own goal in life, but his seemed all too obvious.

IV

When would the F-16s come raging up the coastline?

Elie Madi sat hunched by a cement wall. He peered out at Burj: the tracer bullets, bristling shells spurted up or tore in laterally. A flare burst in a bright canopy over the square. It lingered a few seconds before being hit by a sharp-shooter.

Elie saw arms, torsos. They looked blotched, twisted in the moonlight. A lone guerrilla walked several paces and fell crazily on his face.

The bodies, flattened against the concrete, had a gluant look. In the vortex of Burj: faces lacking contrast, glistening. Colloidal eyes which reflected the falling stars.

—Seen anything?

Startled, Elie turned. He saw himself: the black hood, tiny crucifix beneath it, glinting. Dark eyes, lips like two worms.

—The time is coming, said the other. Our chances on a throw.

—From where, you—

Directly across, the Gold Souk was an avalanche of stone. The martyrs, with Mother Lebanon, writhed on their pedestal: a rape scene in the rusting, rotted center.

—Recon. You?

Elie felt AWOL panic. His own image . . . It was a nightmare of wandering around off-limits. He was truant with nowhere to go, no one to love. And the square, the rows of skeletal buildings there before them, a swirling moonscape.

—Need a chance to—

He gestured.

—What?

—Like you, said Elie. Recon.

The guns were a hundred jack-hammers tearing up Burj. The other put a hand to his ear:

—What?

—Special. Sent down here—

—See? In the Regent Hotel, third floor—

Machinegunning, like a sparkler. The other put his two-way to his lips, speaking code. Elie felt on the verge of ripping it from him.

Rhythmically, across the square, enemy gunners fired 150 mm. over Ashrafiyeh. Elie crouched down and waited, giving the impression he might lurch into a sprint any instant. The black hood stuck on his sweating cheeks and neck.

—It's set, said the other. 2:20!

—What is?

—The end, man. The revelation of truth to the animals.

In Youn Il-Simane, in Baidar, in Keskinta the night of war was filled with whispers. Kataëb *services-d'écoute* were picking up enemy transmissions.

Burj lay in shambles, broken cornices beneath a horrendous moon. The Rivoli marquee showed a pair of lovers embracing, grinning with an elite mystery—bullet-riddled like a decade of orgasms.

One detachment of Syrian armor waited along Riad Solh, another in an alley bordering Souk Sursock, west of the center.

APCs waited on the lee side of burnt-out buildings. Behind the fire support of tanks and artillery, Sa'iqa units were trying to penetrate certain positions in Saifi. The environs of Burj (Bechara Il-Khoury across Place Etoile to Rues Foch and Allenby) were a patchwork of units each with its own perimeter. Rear gunners hung fire or sited a pinprick of light on the side of Tour Rizk, high in the eastern sectors.

When would the planes put an end to futile maneuverings?

V

The time approached. Abu Joseph climbed the stairs in a building on Burj side of St. Joseph's University. He carried a long case with a handle; also a thermos, small portable radio with an earplug. Binoculars hung on a strap round his neck.

A few more steps, trying not to breathe—then he stopped. He paused to listen. Had the vermin got in this building as well? It was strategic, facing Rue Damas on the frontline. He had seen no one near the side door; no watch or patrol in the immediate area.

But they could always be waiting, silently, in their lair, shit-brained leftists. Abu Joseph moved on the landing; he crept forward: make one mistake, you sons of shit, earth's diarrhea—Here was the door, ajar. He heard no sounds except the din outside.

And if they were just within, coiling in readiness? What if they had spotted his approach on the street below?

In a moment he would know.

He paused a few seconds, his ear to the knob. Laying the thermos, guncase, radio to the ground, he unclipped his revolver. Ah scum-brained, you slime. He could almost fit through without budging the door.

But he slammed it open, hurling himself through with a cry.

Empty.

He tripped over a chunk of wall. The room had been broadsided with a 140 mm. and looked ashen, a decor of chaos.

He retrieved his things from the hallway and began settling in by the window. It was a good post: the windows faced west and northward. Beirut lay moonlit and fuming, a sieve of smoke from a thousand rooms on fire. A river of smoke flowed out past the embassies and A.U.B. campus from the burst crude-oil reservoir in Dowra. It went roiling above the sea.

Abu Joseph gazed across the city, its streets and neighborhoods seeming to shrink into themselves. He saw an eerie band of light extending east-west over the capital; this was Chehab Fly-Over, the Ring of Death.

He uncased his rifle, fitting the sites.

There was a second thin strip of light which appeared to veer southward through Mazra. It was the unfinished Autostrade Saida, incandescent with moonglow; it soared across the city like an unearthly highway.

On the Ring of Death two cars were calcified, thrown sideways as if to block traffic. The driver of one leaned dummy-like over the wheel. There were two, three wormish shadows: corpses a few meters from the cars.

Before the war Abu Joseph had been a civil engineer employed by the government. He was a consultant for the Green Plan, a program of land development. He was a man of some culture as well, and had tried his hand at a book of meditations in time of war. His text was bolstered with passages from classical French authors.

Now and again the Party called on him to guide a journalist or visiting church delegation through beleaguered Ashrafiyeh. But this was not his forte. He had little patience, even less than Père Zaki, for people who didn't see the truth when it was plain before them.

Abu Joseph settled in. He waited, raising the binoculars. He knew what would happen shortly, in just a few minutes, and his adrenalin was flowing.

His gaze went from Burj out across Beirut to the western sectors. He saw the two luminous overpasses, Ring of Death and truncated Sidon Highway. With their ghostly stillness they seemed to clamp down on the teeming quarters like a huge cross.

It would happen right on time. The allies to the South kept their appointments. Abu Joseph checked his wristwatch: 17 . . . 18 past two a.m. In just over a minute History would erupt before his eyes. On time, and overwhelming. It would rise up from the perfunctory gunning, and dying, like some monster of the Apocalypse.

He stared through his field glasses and started counting down.

Now he heard them, and had to contain a shout of joy. But weren't they coming from the north? There was a ranting which echoed from Bikfaya and the mountain towns: in seconds he would see them. The high rumble was already terrifying.

He let the glasses hang down and stared at the panorama: trails of smoke, white buildings of Beirut as they waited defenseless, in a mist of death and decomposition. There was a kind of silence; all but the Phantoms seemed to cower like a child waiting to be chastised.

Were there four? Six? O the sacred F-16s! They came roaring closer—but where? He searched the sky and his heart leapt; he saw them from the window facing north, like pellets at incredible speed. They veered down along the mountain face, toward the city: inhuman fingers tearing the heavens. They arched in over the buildings.

Explosions. All the way! he thought. Explosions on all sides, or was it sonic boom? Syrian anti-aircraft was pitiful by comparison; the leftist 23-DCAs responded across the city but they were a joke!

F-16s glinted and swooped in a steep arc down the side of Mount Lebanon. The sonic boom was deafening. Rockets and red darts shot up toward the approaching conquerors.

Guns were roaring from every niche of the front, and from the camps, the hills above Damour. Spurts of heavy machinegun fire, detonations in rapid succession, swarming sounds:—like a child's raging play sometimes, ecstatic in chaos! He waited out the first moments: a flare soared up, subsuming the moonlight.

The planes dipped over Burg, screaming—was it napalm? A blazing curtain dropped for a hundred meters along Riad Solh, and Abu Joseph rejoiced at the scene unfolding before his eyes. 203 mm. fell in clusters; several plummeted down on the old Opera House collapsing like flatcakes.

There was a high wailing like a chorus of outrage from the hive of Syrian and Sa'iqa gunners circling Burj. And Abu Joseph waited, caressing his rifle with the telescopic sites. He waited for the first of them to begin taking their chances in the streets. They wanted to transform Lebanon, but instead of that mission they would come out ragged and caterwauling. They would cry out for death and defeat at the hands of their master's high stalking pride.

F-16s streaked over the sea; and Abu Joseph tried to gauge their course beyond the fuming junkard of downtown Beirut.

The napalm flames retracted; there was nothing combustible in Burj except leftist guerillas. Isolated flames shot up in accusing gestures from the rooftops. Abu Joseph felt the tremendous heat. He knew a Kataëb company was on its way along Saifi side, with orders to search and destroy after the air-raid. Be rid of the brutes forever, O human larvae. Good riddance to you, locusts.

Anti-aircraft roared, drowning out the planes. He scanned with the binoculars. If they dropped toxic gasses on Burj—which way was the wind?

Now the return—they were coming back, a matter of seconds.

But he saw others: Syrian Mirages to the southeast, maneuvering for a counter-raid on the eastern sectors. The beasts. Shoot them down. Make them and their mothers understand what shit it is to be born.

Sonic boom, more bombs. Smoke and squads of ten soldiers, ten and ten along Gouraud and Bechara Il-Khoury. He surveyed them; they were running. Here come the F-16s, he thought—look there, *sacré* cluster bombs. And now these animals will know, for a few seconds, their mistake in leaving those outhouses in the desert they call home. Look at them squirming; see them spin like tops! Ah, you blessed West—tell me, when you put something together is it a darling? Is it a masterpiece *fait pour enculer le monde*? Wait, one of ours is hit. They've hit one, goddamned Russian missiles.

More napalm, a long fire-fall down Bab Edriss to the Rivoli Cinema at the north end of Burj. The bombing continued: the crazed all-out act done as if in passing. Stone buildings stomped on, collapsing. The rear end of an F-16 seemed to glow first like a cigarette and then burst in a circle of red flame beyond the cement breakwater of the port. The Syrian jets had disappeared from Abu Joseph's view, out over the Chouf.

He raised his binoculars, beginning to ferret for victims. He performed the task meticulously, intending to hunt a couple hours before returning to the War Council.

There were more flares. Heavy and light arms made a crescendo of detonations, filling all space, stating their outrage yet jubilant at having survived.

Kataëb patrols advanced with caution along the side streets. On the Green Line tanks rocked forward, turning their long guns. Men with klashins, hand grenades, RPGs on their shoulders grouped behind the tanks before hazarding an intersection. The air-raid had specially targeted enemy anti-tank emplacements.

A nimbus of horror was forming over Burj. Jagged contours were outlined against the waves of flame.

Across the square, stupified by the fire and inhuman heat, a few were showing themselves. Abu Joseph raised his rifle, taking aim. His eye explored the reticle, honing in gently, like a caress.

A dark figure amid the smoke, in the reemerging moonlight: that one, crossing the spider-lines, there—

Hit, one sat down ponderously.
Then another: he went limp, and slid down a doorway.
A third was out there howling, the fool, with his back on fire.

VI

Hôtel-Dieu, in Ashrafiyeh's southernmost corner near the Museum Crossing, resembled a haunted mansion. On the grounds large trees had snapped at mid-trunk, and swung upon themselves with deep groans. There were craters from the mortar shells, and the facade showed two black maws, teethed with crags of torn wall, in an orangish glow. Ripped branches and hedgerow rustled, listless, as Sylvie Helou moved about like an apparition in her white johnny-coat, shivering with cold. She heard the lacerated foliage when she passed, dancing to its rhythmic whisper. She was barefoot; her feet were blistered and there was pus on a gaping cut in her ankle. An hour ago a militiaman grabbed hold of her on an adjacent side street and tried to rape her; but her bizarre gestures, and smell, scared off this fighter with the habit of tanks and guerrilla warfare but not of lunatics. It was a man in his forties, paunchy, with a scraggly beard; Sylvie snorted when she saw two hand grenades hanging from his cartridge belt. He was a former Tiger, one of those who managed to fit in with the "merger" of Kataëb and Noumour, requiring the massacre of so many allies. He was on his way home to sleep awhile and get a wash, a clean uniform; but the front aroused sexual instincts in a man, and Sylvie's figure was quite fetching even though she was psychotic. She squatted to urinate on the grass. She was afraid and very hungry; she could eat grass but it would make her puke. She could go inside Hôtel-Dieu and look for food but her parents might be in there. Her parents liked to climb the grotesque trees like monkeys, or copulate on the cold dewy grass, raping one another. If she saw her parents they would make her bend a knee, stand on her hind legs and twist her wrists forward: Earn a biscuit! Then maybe they would give her one, after counting it first. Her parents went off early each morning and came home late after she was in bed. And Sitt Chahrour, staying on in Ashrafiyeh so she could take an extra dog biscuit back to her refugee's kennel (said Sylvie's parents), Sitt Chahrour put her to bed and stroked her forehead. She hummed a lullaby even though Sylvie was bad, wrangling with Hana'a all afternoon, a little pest who hindered Sitt's work in the pantry. Sylvie, foul Sylvie not worth one biscuit not even an old stale one. Hana'a now, she deserved a present for always being good but not that nasty Sylvie who wouldn't ever learn to behave. Pissing on the sweet grass. Why else would they leave her alone all the time? Why else would Sylvie hate herself (Hana'a didn't hate herself) like a mirror with pimples? She was hungry. She had a rotten foot which made her swirl in her white johnny-coat in the moonlight beneath the amputated trees.

Leaves rustled. Sylvie trembled. She started crying but tried to clear the tears from her eyes by spitting. What if they mauled her? She ran across the lawn, limping toward Hôtel-Dieu arms held wide, about to take flight. Oh, it was dark. She shuddered: what if there was a bunch of rats all in conference, with grave airs? What if the prominent rats sat discussing conditions for a ceasefire; negotiating fifty-five truces and then one of them farted loudly, renewing hostilities? It was awful to smell bad and not have a biscuit or a friend: not even a rat to discuss a peace settlement. She no longer noticed the roaring guns, the plunging stars.

The front door of Hôtel-Dieu was bolted shut. Was there a broken window she could crawl through? Rats in tuxedos were deciding between pâté and marinated herring; a starchy majordomo bowed and took their orders. A hint of muslin moon was saying: bye-bye. Leaves rustled; sparkling guns gave off no light. She stood by the bolted door, shivering. She backed off and slumped down on the dewy grass and whimpered.

VII

Morgan lay on her cot in an East Beirut apartment secured by Khalil, the support agent, via a Canadian liaison living here in the rightist Christian sector. The white VW was in place just this side of the intersection; she could see it from the window. It contained enough plastique explosive to disintegrate a radius of thirty meters.

An hour before dawn Peretz had inserted a radio with an electric detonator, an arming device. Now the security problem was alleviated: the wayward Peretz was no longer such a liability, this side of the Green Line. Across West Beirut the leftists were licking their wounds; the counter-offensive, with air-support from the southern neighbor, had been a complete success.

Morgan knew the time was drawing near.

Before long, if all went as planned, they would cap this mission: as soon as the Red Cross (ICRC) went ahead with its proposal to evacuate the Camp. A first attempt had failed the week before; but negotiations were proceeding, as reports of children dying from dehydration reached the international press.

Risha was outside keeping an eye on the War Council. The target car was a sable blue Mercedes, shiney and unscratched, parked at times on a side street five minutes away. Morgan sighed, thinking how much smoother, predictable, the work went over here, away from chaotic Hamra with its constant threat of kidnapping. The "Canadian" woman was a pearl of a contact; their apartment dominated the key intersection. What remained was to confirm the route and precise time of passage.

And would Abu Joseph be with them—part of the entourage? If he had second thoughts; if he realized her ability to extract information each time they met, might the venue be changed? He was hers—in the moments just after lovemaking, when the first words intruded on a silence sodden with intimacy, and yet distant, inutterably lonely... And she reached for her blouse while he brushed back his hair and lay there breathing heavily. She sensed his subtle clinging; and the energy began flowing her way now—and she made the great warrior lick her palm and beg her to stay. At the moment of orgasm her arm had not gone up and around his broad shoulders; there had been no mystical borne traversed, or attempt on her part to clutch and hold his eternity, as if the moon received dictates, and the tide held fast to its furthest mark up the beach. And Abu Joseph felt stunned in his male prerogative, humbled by a whore, as his moment had passed and he sensed it was too late to dominate her; and the bliss receded quickly. Morgan was the master; she maneuvered in that silence, casually, leaving a little gap for him to fill; and he responded reflexively to her question. But now he must never know, or even, for a second, begin to suppose. Together they would take a step in what great, momentous dance affecting the fate of nations?

On her cot Morgan drifted toward sleep... Someone was there: a hand reached over and touched her, alien and rude. It had nodes, a cluster of floral growths above the thumb... Touching brought her profound remorse; touching was a sin, and irredeemable. Gloved hand, pulling down a blind... Black hand, cause for mourning.

She awoke from her dream flushed with fear, wondering if she had said something ill-advised in her sleep.

VIII

But Peretz still worried her. He was back in their room, either praying or working on the transmitter/receiver which would detonate the VW. He was setting up the transmission circuit used to trigger the bomb. The radio operated a relay, he said; it closed contacts, completing circuits to the detonator. But why wasn't the thing ready?

If you asked him a question about his tradecraft, he grew touchy. He gave reassurance and insisted it was ready minus a few final adjustments. For a half hour she had heard nothing from the adjacent bedroom; he was quite prudish about his religion. As zero-hour approached, he grew more self-absorbed and spooky.

But Peretz came with the highest recommendation; he had scored on difficult assignments in the past. Still Morgan wished she could do the entire bit herself, and not be dependent on such a kook. Risha was capable and dedicated to her country, but Peretz was too much of a genius beneath the yarmulka he wore whenever in the apartment. The idea he would risk the mission by carrying such a thing through B.I.A. customs sent a tremor down Morgan's spine.

She lay on her cot thinking, reluctant to question or push him, but fitfully unsure. An hour before, with Risha already out on her rounds and Morgan deep in thought in the same position, he had managed to creep up behind her and begin fondling her breasts. He snuggled up to her backside a second, before she drew away startled:

—Careful.

—Just this: I wanted to show you this. (He brought forth the transmitter/receiver as if offering to let her hold his baby.) It transmits two circuits in a series; the first arms the bomb. I push the switch to receiver... Receiver picks up the transmission to arm the mechanism, sending back an initial tone. The bomb is armed.

—Why twice?

—This is the safety device. It requires two transmissions; otherwise a stray radio signal might detonate.

He spoke in the most reverent tone. Perhaps he held Sarajevo in the palm of his hand? She was experiencing his mystery, being initiated as he knelt there, subtly attractive to her, his breathing quickened either by the technology or their physical contact.

She drew back.

—Good, Peretz. So long as it works.

—You'll see.

His voice was exalted, strange.

—Get up now. It wouldn't do, if Risha came through that door.

—Afterward, maybe, in Cyprus.

—Your job, Peretz, just do it. We're a ways yet from Cyprus.

IX

Risha appeared, cheeks flushed, very serious. Catching her breath from the stairs she announced:

—No change: car's still there.

—And your lookout?

—I've got several.

—Don't stay here too long. Get back in place.

Risha paused, staring at her. It was no coincidence if she rarely left them alone. But as things came to a head with the mission she was forced to go down into the street while they, as a twosome, worked at close quarters up here together.

—I need to have a bite.

Morgan returned her stare. She could sense the cutting edge of the other's jealousy; she felt a big anger and thought of ripping away all the prim, adultish trimmings from the female package that was Risha. How many times she had come across these straight self-righteous women who were always manipulating. In a crisis their true nature was revealed.

All was set therefore, in order. Thanks to Khalil the location was optimal. VW parked near the corner: it seemed Yahweh provided parking spaces. In a few minutes Risha must take another walk past the target car, past the pied-à-terre apartment of the man they would destroy.

But Risha stood ready to crumble before her eyes, eager at a false word, any mistake on Morgan's part to intrude her emotions and ruin the painstaking enterprise.

—Why can't I stay up here?

Silence.

—What? said Morgan, softly.

—You go. I'll stay up here. You radio the departure, I'll spot for Peretz.

—Wonderful. And you think we've gotten this far without these people knowing me? I can just see myself out there, crouching in the debris with my blond hair.

She nearly called in Peretz for support—mistake. Deal with her, thought Morgan, trying to appear calm where she lay raised on one elbow. She is the key, not Peretz who would rather score with me than defeat his nation's enemy.

So long in the planning, so very complex—and now everything hung on the most foolish of human games.

—You can go. I don't want to.

—We have how many hours? And then it will be over, Risha. The two of you, alone, wherever you like. I'll go my way and you yours. But until then, do as we planned.

—I take the real risks, out there. You two sit up here.

—Oh? And what do you think got us access—pleasant dallying? Listen, this man is known worldwide, an obstacle at present to your country though we thought him friendly. There will be an entourage, and I'm known personally by at least two of those people. We couldn't take the risk. (Morgan spoke lower.) Risha, you've nothing to fear from me: you're my teammate. I want to succeed in this; nothing else matters, I'm as fanatical as yourself. Believe me, I wouldn't jeopardize what we're doing here in any way; and you must see your own part through to the end, as I will mine. And Peretz his.

Silence. She stared up at her, waiting. The other sighed:

—Let me eat something. Don't rush me, that's all.

X

In the end so little could be controlled. She had a sinking feeling about Peretz and the apparatus. Suppose she sat waiting, peering over the sill and meanwhile Risha was detected? Suppose the device malfunctioned? Or the code-word was picked up over one of their radios?

Risha was in the bedroom with Peretz, trying to regain her poise. She must go back out there and give her signals. But Risha was tottering on the brink.

Morgan called in:

—It's probably time.

—Alright!

Peretz was coming on to her nervous energy. She could hear them in the bedroom; he was doing it to spite her, Morgan, plus they were all charged up as the mission moved into its final stage.

For the Nth time she imagined how she would take up her position by the window. Within two minutes of Risha's signal the target car would cross the intersection. Morgan would watch the far corner; while Peretz armed the bomb. One task, one accurate reflex per person. She knew every wrinkle in the victim's face, having studied a close-up film and dozens of file pictures.

They were in there together: love's juggernaut. Morgan, stonefaced, stared out the window at an Ashrafiyeh neighborhood looking almost routine again, after the latest round of "events".

XI

Already there had been ICRC initiatives to evacuate the Camp of women and children who were wounded and quite obviously in the process of dying. But the present conjuncture of forces would not permit it. Red Cross vehicles venturing into the no-man's-land surrounding the refugee camp were shelled from several directions, and turned back after suffering much-publicized casualties.

Then an outlying district of the Camp was surrounded by rightist units, controlling the two entrances of a key building with sniper fire. A few hundred people were stranded in the basement, as the first impulse to flee alerted a Phalangist recon, and support pillars were shelled without pause through the afternoon. The building collapsed. Tons of stone and plaster came through the basement ceiling onto nearly three hundred refugees huddling for shelter. All but some twenty were crushed and killed. A number of children twisted and squirmed toward a chink of daylight, escaping in a cloud of dust and debris.

In broad daylight the cries, the screaming and groaning from underground... International media devoted a paragraph here and there to this Phalangist offensive, in its daily coverage of the war. Kim Ligury was furious when his home bureau put a series of articles regarding the "summer of siege" on indefinite hold, and increasingly rewrote his weekly quota of copy. At Ydlibbi's, Ligury clearly lost an argument to the German photographer, Kohler, after resorting to rather emotional grounds. It seemed the situation was getting to the quiet Britisher, losing his journalistic objectivity: a man named Adnan had lost his entire extended family in a matter of minutes; but this was a "personal consideration".

On the 23rd, in response to international opinion, the Phalange allowed seventy of the worst cases to leave the Camp. They were transported to West Beirut hospitals. By this date there were fourteen hundred dead and countless people wounded among the Camp population. Then, a week later, another two hundred and fifty were carried out in truckloads; but this time there were snipings and instants of panic for the convoy. Remnant elements of Chamoun's *Noumour* forces, remembering their heroic role in the Tel ez-Zaater bloodbath of summer '76, grew edgy and cried foul from moment to moment.

Ligury went among them taking notes. He felt a certain exhilaration, risking his life during the mad minutes.

—What's wrong?

—Their leaders! one cried. They've got 'em dressed up as sick and wounded!

From his vantage point Ligury watched Lebanese Forces gunners spray the Red Cross cars with automatic fire. "In the spirit of killing," he jotted, watching a former Tiger Cup level his M-16, finger the trigger: "like an itch in the genes, an atavistic revenge."

—Stick to facts, said Kohler.

Next day, back in his Hamra apartment after a hair-raising return via the Museum Crossing, Kim Ligury grew exalted over an article. "When the last car passed through the outer checkpoints," he wrote, "there was a rightist bombardment on the flimsy, muddy, death-infected Camp which went beyond anything previous."

Kohler announced himself, looking like an actor in his new battle fatigues, tramping over his colleague's threshold in a pair of combat boots spitshined for a dollar on Rue Sidani. Annoyingly he yanked Ligury's inspired article from the whining platen, and laughed:

—What's this? A rhapsody? "All water, medicines and food were confiscated from those entering the Camp." Who said so? Are you sure? "It is a grim contest in these last days of siege and tragic resistance..." Teufel! What is this, Schiller? "... as a sector of the international community rubs its hands, with a certain satisfaction..." Unglaublich! And you wonder why they don't print your stuff these days.

—Give it here. It's not finished.

Ligury grabbed away his typescript and declaimed:

—"Across the earth they have watched these wretched cartloads, going out slowly from a Camp in shambles. The children, their bodies eaten by gangrene..."

—Hm, Kohler nodded.

—"Features contorted, they glance around frightened. Who did this to me? Why? Glance of hurt wonder."

—Keats the journalist.

—"They whine feebly, eyes closed, in cadence with the ruts in the road."

As afternoon progressed there was a coolness in the air, a sense of September in the offing, and rainy season on the way. The sunlight went deeper, more contrasted, as shadows merged with a dozen years of detonations over Ein Mreisse. Long bands of mauve trailed into the inimitable Mediterranean blue.

The German photographer stared at his struggling friend with a sort of sympathy.

—"While, across the city and up into the hills, *humanity's Philoctetes* sends out a stink like a gauntlet to the peace loving world."

XII

At dawn, on September 7th, Phalangist loudspeakers began announcing an "official evacuation" of the Camp. Confirmation of the ICRC plan had reached Camp administrator Selman by radio from the PLO leadership. Any political gains could no longer justify such prodigious physical and mental suffering... The ICRC *responsable* was indeed a courageous man; but would he be able to guarantee a general ceasefire amid the tremendous tension of the moment?

In early morning Dr. Kamel, with Hana'a at his side, began supervising evacuation of the pediatrics clinic. Little Nadja, with her sandy hair and dark eyes, like two shiney olives; Mayser alert to the new situation and swivelling on himself with greater frenzy: one by one the children were brought out on stretchers. They joined in the tableau of inconceivable horror which presented itself, after months of siege, in the open air.

Dr. Kamel glanced around. Where was Sitt Chahrour? On all sides, in the treacherous silence, the people had begun emerging. They left the fetid inferno of shelters with a stunned glimpse, frowning in the bright light, a hand to their eyes. How many days had it been? How many Phalangist attacks had been repulsed? Where was Zahir, or Saleh, or Dalal—sons and daughters off fighting on the perimeter, who hadn't been seen in weeks? The survivors gazed dully at their Auschwitz, as the tattered muddy cortege began gaining momentum toward the exit points. Many were gathering in a football field, on the edge of the defended area.

Dr. Kamel, Hana'a and twenty others from the clinic moved slowly along one of the side roads, while the sun rose blushing on a massive shambles color of sewage and dried blood. Swiss and Lebanese Red Cross units were setting up zones for the primary treatment of survivors; they sent them off in vans, though the registration process was painfully slow, a kind of madness given the circumstances.

Dr. Kamel moved with the rhythm of a revenant, seeming to gather up his patients who moaned, and gave a doleful chirping with each new step. Up ahead he glimpsed two of the four UNRWA teachers, who had played a contradictory role during the siege: Moustafa the Righteous exposing people's lives as he called them to prayer; a second, whom Dr. Kamel had seen trying to merchandise his store of chickpeas while the masses starved. The four of them refused to take any active part in the Camp organization and defense.

—How much further? said Hana'a.

—Our gathering point is another 200 meters, at the Hotel-Training Center.

—Hakim, I'm worried.

—We'll make it. Keep the stretchers moving.

Hana'a could feel the Phalangist presence: she sensed the Kataëb, the old arch-enemy Chamounist and Tanzime fighters which made up Lebanese Forces holding back ever so tensely, surveying the defenseless processions. There was hatred in the air; they were frowning mightily at this unexpected outcome, and were ready to pounce at the slightest pretext.

Meanwhile the ICRC workers waited with a show of weary calm: pale European faces which made the scene even more alien and grisly to Hana'a Chahrour as she went along. Coughing, clinging to one another's ragged clothing like a gypsy caravan, the people were emerging now on all sides, beginning to make their way toward the edge of the Camp. From a dilapidated shelter to her left Hana'a watched a group of women, filthy, emaciated, come out squinting at the sunrise.

—Ah!

—Just don't look, said the doctor.

But he was devouring the scene with his own eyes. As the line of stretchers and assistants turned into the Camp's main thoroughfare, no less muddy than the others, but wider, leading to the mosque,— they saw the bodies. Along each shoulder was an interlinking chain of bloated arms and legs, faces scavenged until they became a featureless gristle. Along this royal way people doubled over and vomited drily, going to one knee alongside the gore. Once, thought Dr. Kamel, putting an arm around Hana'a's frail shoulder, this was a bustling Beirut suburb, and source of cheap labor for the industrialists.

Corpses of neighbors. Relatives. The rising sun, and the river of mud; and the corpses. In the distance he could see the white buildings of downtown; and beyond these a pale vapid sea of late summer, effacing the horizon. But here, just under his feet as he trudged along, were human bodies.

As six a.m. approached, the evacuation appeared to be going smoothly. The first trickle of refugees (a group of Kurds) arrived at checkpoints on the other side.

Then, as the first Palestinians passed through the outer roadblocks, a cheer rose up for the heroic survivors.

A few shots rang out, destroying the permissive silence. But these sounded like shots of celebration, marking what loomed as a victory for the overall Arab cause. Some rightist cried out:

—It's no wounded man on that stretcher!

But things were smoothed over by the well fed, it seemed inviolable figures of ICRC delegates, who smiled as initial contingents arrived and were given treatment, nourishment, their vital signs checked at once.

At shortly after six the first hundred people through safely were met with bursts of shooting, shouts of joy and a din of automobile horns. They were packed in cars, and a few minutes later welcomed as victors at the usually dangerous Museum Crossing.

Relatives and friends smiling, waving—most of Mazra, along with a sound-system for the occasion, and journalists from across the Arab world, had come out to greet them with cheering.

But back in the Camp, lines at the checkpoints were growing unmanageable. Why the red tape? thought Dr. Kamel. Why hold up a procedure which at best would take up much of the day? Why provide occasion for who could guess what unfortunate incident?

XIII

After a pre-dawn rain there were broader patches of blue across the sky. Rays of sunlight began piercing through with a warmth. There was a quickened respiration of the wind, seeking refuge through the closed window from an intermittent fracas of guns. Wind moaned and tried to creep in between the casements; it meant to snuggle its way, though undeserving, among the perfumed sheets of Morgan's bed.

Then she sat pondering the buildings opposite, the two intersections. Each car turning down the street gave her a start, as she glanced at the man driving, frontseat passengers. On a chair she laid out a business suit, also her beige blouse, stockings, undergarments. She transferred other items to a leather attaché case.

Soon now she would wake up in Larnaka with sun shining in her window, an opaline sea in the changing season. Palmtrees would fan the quay beneath her balcony; and she might linger a few days, eating kebab and drinking wine in the seaside restaurants. This cursed thing would be done with: the Middle East could go under for all she cared. Cyprus—interim of peace before another mission became emotionally necessary.

Risha had gone out finally. She was on her way to the observation post, a burnt-out store. In the end her devout patriotism had triumphed over jealousy. And now, with the Camp being evacuated, their hour had arrived: success or failure, but in any case this was the homestretch.

Some years before, Morgan had spent eighteen months at a certain CIA station in Latin America. Most of the victories, in agitation and intimidation, street counter-demos, surveillance: most of the progress was made in spite of her station chief, a former FBI man who was just too oversexed. She spent days and nights on a sensational, damaging document against one of the key Left leaders; or else drumming up propaganda to dampen a protest march; and then this man began using all his neurosis, male competitiveness, to forestall the proper effect. It took her that one stint as a station officer to see she was unfit for in-house activity. Better contract herself in a liaison capacity.

She remembered her sessions in Tel-Aviv with an expensive, reputed psychiatrist named Bergland. Her months there prior to this assignment were probably the darkest, most depressive period of her life. She had plenty of money and absolutely no interest in making the rounds as a prostitute. Her mood shifted between anxiety and spells of a semi-abulomania, keeping her in bed all day. Her mind suffered noticeably, with thought-disorder involving a grandiose personal mission with implications for world peace. What an arena for action, she daydreamed, if a Third World War should erupt. Then the Nietzschean would be given their chance for freedom, transcendence—in an open contest, and no longer dragged down by bureaucrats, other sneaky *de facto* conspirators.

Morgan began devising her scheme. She mused over sparking off the Apocalypse, and playing a consequential role in universal suicide. She conceived an eclectic doctrine of sado-masochistic revelation, a kind of cosmic orgasm; basing it all on her reading, in college, of Kierkegaard, Von Hartmann, Heidegger,—and Professor Willartig's profound commentaries. Why couldn't she, Morgan, make the Big Boom happen? When she set her hand to something: anytime men were involved she would succeed. The crucial thing was positioning oneself correctly in space and time. Then anything was possible.

To the much-published psychiatrist, Bergland, she began speaking of "immortal longings" and "teleological suicide". All books of a sententious, a serious nature, all further reference to "writers like Dostoyevsky" must be suppressed. Burn them in one great heap: literature above all should be annulled.

—Why? asked Bergland, his dark eyes lingering on her incomparable neck. I'm no intellectual, hmm. (He cleared his throat with a periodic rasp.) But I think Dostoyevsky is tremendous.

—He misleads.

—Misleads? Hmm. How's that?

—Could anything be more wretched than mankind? more worthy of annihilation?

—In what way?

—At the end of Dostoyevsky's road, nothing is sacred. There are no more illusions. Yet he greets you there with a cross. No, doctor, he's a clown like almost all men. And don't think Alyosha marks the last word for him: piety was never his intent. But the worst of it is, that he only wrote his books. What about us? What of the poor fools who took him so seriously? We were left at the end of that one-way street, and our despair wasn't funny anymore. Look where he stands, this miserable jester, this Dostoyevsky with his sickly songs. Thus we kneel down to Satan, imploring our daily dread. Lucky for me, Satan is a man.

—Hmm.

—And look at you, Doctor. You're oversexed; you should write me a check when the hour ends. (He looked down, a mistake. She laughed and said): You can't win, you know. Not even the immortal psychiatrists get their way. Life is a no-win: try as you might, there's no avoiding wretched need, and feelings. No end to their nastiness. But if you want to succeed, then remove all human elements from your team. Do the thing with robots; let a robot plan it, and execute.

In Tel Aviv she endured; but it was life at zero-level, week after week. She waited, waited to be delivered by a mission. Her isolation was a disaster, and a series of less ambitious obsessions came in her mind. She thought her body was producing death, and there was no way to stop it: a kind of metabolic death wish. Often she thought about doing away with herself, but felt keenly vindictive that life would continue without her. Willartig would live. Ligury would live. Even nitwits like Kohler, Abu Joseph, Peretz would persist and procreate. She reread Nietzsche's late works, and felt hopelessly megalomaniacal in her better moments. But then she was saved from going crazy by the Beirut mission, almost commensurate, perhaps, with her daydreams worthy of Cerberus.

Morgan hefted a .38 special. She freed the chamber, revolving it slowly. Into the homestretch now. Soon she would see the car, *that* one. Win or lose, she deserved a monument for tolerating her two chauvinist colleagues.

Peretz seemed quite withdrawn. He was in the bedroom tinkering with his gear. The door was ajar. She could feel all the musty, pent-up anger in him: his spite toward her, now the Risha-dream was expended.

Was he ready? Was it? Were the three of them up to a big one, like this?

Oh! get it done, Peretz. I'll give you a reward you won't forget.

XIV

Elie Madi raised his new M-16 high. He felt jubilant to be reinstated, back in the saddle now at a critical moment in his people's destiny. Gray months of civil war; sunlight in the soft hair of Jessica. Tel ez-Zaater, and the other fallen camps before this one: manly wager of life and death, armed struggle until victory was definitive. The loyal Abu Joseph was right after all.

There was a blaze of light as the sun rose over distant Mt. Sannine. Suddenly the coastal crescent was bathed in morning rays, as if nature couldn't have cared less about the dark affairs of men. Palestinians were waiting on all sides; they gathered at rallying points along the perimeter. The lines were unrealistically long by now: thousands of people as tormented by impatience as they had been by months of hunger and thirst. At present there was still a mere trickle: soon they would flow across en masse to the schoolyards, mosques and churches of the western sectors. If nothing went wrong.

Elie gazed down the long sloping hill toward Corniche Mazra; he could hear the festivities in progress, and thought: You Palestinians always did lack discretion... Once again he thanked his lucky stars for getting him rehabilitated, and placed here—in command at one of the exit-points from the Camp. When the loneliness, when the despair over his fall from grace became too much for any human being to bear, he had gotten in his jeep and driven at breakneck speed back to the War Council. The panorama of death which was Burj; the utter futility of his isolated gambit, namely the idea of suing for peace with a loudspeaker, alone, out on the Ring of Death (so he would be let off the hook): all the fantastic folly of his recent actions struck Elie at once, and he had to make a choice. Was he Sylvie Helou? Was he one of these raving Leftists with a utopian scheme more destructive than any Soviet Union gun-shipment?

Once he reentered Phalangist ranks, and reassumed his proper role, then everything else fell into place as well. The future loomed bright at Jessica's side. His mother no longer suffered the pangs of hell for his sake, while his father's name was not disgraced. Emile, his younger brother, could put him (almost) back up on his pedestal. Incredibly, Abu Joseph became a friend and protector, all at once, and lost the monstrously shameful aspect which Elie Madi had glimpsed in him, like some kind of optical illusion.

By this time a few hundred refugees had been permitted to leave; but the process was painfully slow. Small groups made their way out on foot or in carloads, showing a terrible emaciation. They cast glances back toward their menfolk and loved ones. The level of fear was high; they understood that in reality it was the Phalange, and not the Red Cross, which controlled the gates of their hell and their hope.

—Why this delay? said Elie, shouting up ahead, waving his M-16.

— It has to be fair! shouted a member of his unit, while a close inspection process went on, including body searches, of each refugee in the line.

Elie waited. Nominally he was in charge of this one checkpoint; but he no longer felt as strong and respected. He was not in a hurry to give orders to men (though all younger, less experienced than he) who knew of his unpredictability and AWOL spree.

Meanwhile, inside the Camp, many residents went running about and used the precious first moments of freedom in search of family or friends they hadn't seen for weeks. How long had it been, huddling, cramped and suffering a hundred ways, in what during peaceful times were miserable shacks? Elie gazed across at the panicked scurrying of women, who dragged children and possessions after them. It appeared some didn't want to leave! And others didn't know just what they wanted, obliged to flee their home, such as it was, of ten, in many cases twenty years.

So far the evacuation had gone smoothly, if tense and agonizingly slow.

Without question it was best, thought Elie, to take one's chances in this first hour, instead of running about in a wild-goose chase on the trail of the disappeared. At 7 a.m. all was well, but in Lebanon you never knew what was coming.

—Move along there! Stop dawdling—

—It's you! a woman in sackcloth, covered by flies, pointed with a trembling hostility at Elie sitting on the hood of his jeep. You're the ones, holding us up!

XV

Morgan glimpsed the alarm clock on her mattress. It was perched in the folds of bedding like a small boat. Nearly eight a.m.; it wouldn't be much longer. She glanced over the sill at the sunlit intersection. Since sunrise the shelling and machinegunning had picked up in volume. In the downtown sectors, in Chiyah and Ein Rummaneh there was fighting. A rare taxi cruised beneath the window, causing her heartbeat to race. No one honked; they glided by quietly.

Morgan waited on Risha. No word for the past ten minutes. Risha was poised; she crouched amid the rubble of a dynamited store: unless something was amiss, and they had spotted her. The hostile eyes were everywhere: the hive fascinated by its own activity. Beirut was a cramped city, teeming and dense. An infant crying in the night could be heard for blocks. When the wind was high, the sea murmured through courtyards and salons of the dense limestone quarters.

Risha was out there. She was at her post. Peretz knelt in the corner alongside a remote control; he was worrying her; he made tinkering movements with the wiring, the contact switch, and then looked around perplexed.

—Any problem?

—No, he replied, but in a tone less spiritual than usual. I'm making sure.

—You seem at odds.

—No problem, really.

Every minute or two a car came along. Then none for awhile, or several behind a slower one. She hoped they would arrive on the side street, and then timing would be pat. She might see them with seconds to spare at the far end of the block: the Phalangist leader making his last turn. Risha was to radio-in which way the Mercedes took, whether on Rue Ibr Pacha or before. If before, if they arrived via Rue Charles Malek the job became more difficult if not impossible. Then Morgan should be spotting, as well as operating the transmitter. The crucial time would amount to a few seconds. She knew the car; but Khalil, the support agent, had been unable to find them an apartment in the precise corner building, with windows on both streets. They were one down from the corner, and on the east side, incorrect for their purposes. Her view of the intersection was impaired by the adjacent building.

Still, they might conceivably do it if the Mercedes came that way. Her hand would be raised. In the instant of its passing she must signal Peretz to push the button.

But across the room Peretz gave a sigh. When he touched the tips of his fingers and jiggled the apparatus, the effect was none too convincing. She glanced from the intersection back to her partner. Also the scene down below, a car scurrying by and then nothing, a void, seemed fraught with insecurity.

—Well? she said, an edge to her voice. Is it ready?

—Yes, said Peretz. Coming along.

—Man, we need to be certain.

—Sure, sure, said Peretz in his lisping accent. But then, as an afterthought: Nothing in life is certain.

XVI

Risha waited. She knelt in the rubble of a storefront across from the target house. Before being dynamited this must have been a pharmacy since the chemical scent still lingered. Among the charred debris there were warped tins, dispensors, bits of pestle or syringe and chips of glass tubing. Probably the place was blown up by the Phalange when its owner refused to pay protection. Or a stray shell into the area ignited the pharmaceutical stock.

Risha crouched in the shadows away from the gaping doorway. She peered at the sable blue Mercedes, glinting in sunlight some thirty meters away: it was parked before the target house, a six-storey apartment building on Rue Ibrahim.

She entreated them in a whisper: Will you hurry up! Oh typical Arabs, in there drinking coffee and talking politics ad nauseum... And all the while her trusty partners were waiting in safety; back in the bare apartment with just mattresses, alone together. Intimately—ah! at such a moment would they have the nerve, the sheer arrogant chutzpah to get it on...? She knew from little signals, feminine intuition, that Morgan was favorably disposed... and maybe Peretz too. They were spying after their best opportunity... now...

Risha felt a tremendous spasm of jealousy. It was like a convulsion, a kind of monstrous neglect. She knew what was on Peretz's mind every since they arrived in Beirut together; he was capable, with ease, of an erection in two directions at once.

Risha called them; she spoke in code. By doing so she went against the plan, since any call of theirs could be monitored. Never mind. These Arabs drank their *ahweh,* and talked politics, and their attention span was rather limited when it came to strategic communications.

—Still no sign.
—Uh-huh?
Static. Morgan was annoyed. Why call then—
—Is it ready?
—Yes.
—Is it sure?
—Yes, and out.

She answered right away... But they could be making love just there by the receiver. Morgan was fully capable of passing a polygraph test while seducing in three positions. She had seduced her way this far, in the mission, and why wouldn't she do it now as well?—timing it so Peretz's orgasm coincided with the big blast. Had her voice sounded breathless? Yes. But wasn't that natural? No, they were traveling the rapid transit together... Morgan was propped on pillows with an eye on the intersection, while Peretz got in some practice pushing joy-buttons. Why not? They could afford to relax a moment; their job was almost over. Remained only to throw the switch... No doubt about it: they were inspired by the impending explosion, and immense political fallout it would cause... Ah, the cold woman would probably have her first orgasm, right now—at whose expense? Or else she'd lie there like an iceberg and consider the whole thing as just another tactic, a liaison operation brought successfully to its term. The Brunhilde of a spy would screw her way into Valhalla, and all the while poor Risha was out here kneeling among the rubble, doing the menial work. No doubt about it now: Morgan was getting it on with Risha's man. These Arabs—always think they can solve the world's problems by mouth, and then they cause more! In love with the sound of their own voices. Or maybe Morgan had gotten the wrong info? It was a ridiculous plot to get her out here, so they could be together.

Risha squatted in the burnt-out store, her free hand clinched in a fist. This woman isn't in it with us; she doesn't even know our language. Risha felt a surge of relief; she felt joy, imagining Morgan as the outsider, liaison agent, a tool of her nation. We wanted what she could do for us, her skills. Damn her, she has those. But I was born and I belong in the beloved homeland, I would do anything for my people—even tolerate *his* faithlessness. They already see me as a hero; think, when this mission is over... If the two of them don't make us blow it—once we're done she'll fly off to Canada, and a good riddance. Go on, leave, the whore, the further away the better. And then we, the blessed two of us, will begin vacationing and get a few stamps on our passports.

The street was empty. If they did emerge it would make an unlikely scene. The Kataëb leader in this forbidding place, with rockets flaring on the distant sky, and drums of destruction beating all around? But the Mercedes was there; it at least was no hoax. Morgan claimed this was the car; a rough man in a leather jacket had come outside an hour before and lifted the hood. The mere look of him made her shudder: a face like retribution.

Risha wondered about Morgan's lingual skills; often they spoke their language in front of her, they insulted her in it, enjoying the privacy. She didn't seem to pay any mind, but she did speak a fluent Arabic, as well as Russian. What if she was a double-agent? What if she understood every single word they were saying, some of it quite sensitive? The intelligence coup would be immense. Then Risha might return to the apartment and find Peretz dead, with a similar fate awaiting herself. The revenge of Abu Hassan and other terrorist "martyrs" courtesy of the Russians. Stay calm, Risha. She had a shortness of breath; her pulse was quickened, she felt giddy. I crouch here like a fool but who knows what's happening in that apartment... She wanted to get up and leave; her impulse was to go back there, but she stifled it another moment, she sighed invoking the unshakeable faith, the sacred homeland.

Risha changed positions; there was a small clatter of glass chips, the crunch of a charred dispensor where she knelt in the shadows.

A car drove up. It swerved and screeched to a halt, parking two down from the Mercedes. Audi sedan, tan with what sounded like a modified engine. The doors opened and men got out, first another bodyguard peering round; then a balding, tallish sort who looked too benevolent for politics. A small gentleman remarked at something and smiled like a frog, as the bodyguard made certain all doors were locked, glancing side to side while the leaders made a picture of nonchalance.

Risha whispered on the two way.

—Reporting.

—And?

Clipped tone of Morgan: this better be important.

—Late-model tan Audi, three men gone inside.

—Stand by—out.

Risha was trembling. She coiled like a sprinter awaiting the starter pistol.

The three men approached the building entrance. The bodyguard stepped in front; he peered inside, then cast a glance back out, surveying the surroundings. He gazed an instant straight at Risha.

XVII

Now Peretz was making Morgan very nervous. His fingertips moved over the wiring of the transmitter/receiver mechanism. His features revealed an effort which might prove, after all, inadequate. Where was the flaw? in the detonator?

—Well?

—Well what?

—Just tell me if something is wrong.

He shook his head, not taking time to look up:
—The arming device isn't working.
—Why?
—I transmit a tone by pushing this switch. The receiver should pick up my transmission to arm the bomb, but I'm not getting a tone back. I set up two transmit circuits in a series...

She figured at most ten more minutes. Unless they arrived late at their meeting, which was unlikely. The thing was moments away from happening.

She glanced down along the side street each way to the intersection. The window faced west, and her blond hair mingled with morning sunlight like protective coloring. She stared unblinking and sensed the small, nervous movement of Peretz across the room.
—I have to go down there, he announced. Dammit.
—You're sure?
—An adjustment: it won't take a second. I can bypass the arming device down at the car; it'll be susceptible to any signal.
—So get going.

He rose:
—How much more time?
—Five minutes, maybe.
—That's plenty.

He went calmly out the door.

Morgan felt cold. Her mouth was dry. Her five senses seemed to downshift, as the moment grew near.

XVIII

Risha readied herself. She fumbled to no purpose with the two-way radio. Her hands shook; she hated the wait and her thoughts kept wandering.

Now she was back in Tel Aviv with her family; with her father who was a doctor, her brother and two sisters. At home she was safe; she was part of a vast and powerful team extending over the five continents. Her nation had the greatest ally in history; it could never fail. Wasn't *her* land the one which strove for progress? which brought enlightenment though surrounded on every side by tribal feudalism? Didn't *her* people deserve to win? They were making a desert region fertile; it was a unique experiment in history, taking decades. And she was helping in a major way.

At home she was safe and respected; but here, in this savage city anything might happen. She was doing what the select few, what the most talented must do, if the dream was to last. But it was dangerous, and lonely. Someday the world would be safe again; it would smile peacefully on her grandchildren, the fruit of her love for Peretz. Someday a monument would be erected to them both in a public square: the homeland's greatest espionage couple. Her father would attend the unveiling.

Risha kept her presence of mind; she might crack at any moment, under the strain. Come out of there, damn you. Finish up with the talk already. Maybe Morgan got the wrong information; yes, that would be par for the course, because what did she have at stake? And why, in the first place, bother contracting among outsiders? Were they more capable?

Ah, the father—he would be so proud. Her younger sisters and brother held her in awe. Surely there would be a secret ceremony, with decorations, and the Memuneh would be on hand. As for Morgan, just give her the money—now go away, please. Fly off to Canada; you could care less about what we hold sacred. But what do you care about, in the end? You care about seducing, and more of same, never mind your coyness and posturing. You make a fetish of seducing men who belong to others; so you're just another agent with a specialty. I know you: the way you get a rise from undercover work, but all your life is smut and treachery. So what if we can use you, you're still expendable; whereas I, Risha, am a patriot. And to hell with Peretz also, if he can't tell the lower from the higher. No, he loves me . . . I can elevate him, in the long run—

—They're coming out.

There were five men now: her heart beat wildly as she spotted theirs among them, a face recognized around the world.

Three new ones therefore: victims who didn't know it yet, looking quite unconcerned. Plus the bodyguard. Which car? or both?

No, the Mercedes. The bodyguard opened the doors on one side—duck back, Risha. Did he see?

They pulled out, jerking from the space. She whispered on the two-way:

—Falcon, gray falcon: set for hunting. Wings are flapping—wait . . . Plan number one. I said number one.

—Falconer.
Static.
Risha rose at once. The car had turned now, out of sight. Along Ibr Pacha.

She started running; she crossed over, then down a side street parallel to their own.

—Careful, Risha! She said out loud, laughing, waving her arms.

She raced toward the scene, panting, filled with patriotic adrenalin.

XIX

Morgan crouched by the window, watching Peretz. She counted seconds, imagining the progress of the target car while her partner leaned inside the booby-trapped VW. Should she call down to him? The back door was half open. The seat was wrenched up; he might have been watering the battery. His movements were not visible at that distance, in the morning shadows; but Morgan guessed their meaning. She sensed his desperation. They had come so near, so close to the goal. And now it hinged on a technicality. Still he gave no sign.

She could feel the target car approaching. The problematic ally was exposed, and in their hands, for a moment. And down there Peretz grovelled, after six weeks of promiscuity and playing the mystic; while she went out and risked and finally implemented the plan. There lay the sublime Peretz, tinkering even now while the countdown was in progress. And his gear still not in order. She felt a deep loathing for him; her work, her very life were being jeopardized by a bar-mitzvah candidate; she was sent into the field with children.

Again she glimpsed her watch: nearing a half minute since Risha gave the alert. In seconds they should arrive, and come flying right beneath her window, down the vacant side street exactly as forecast. Unless they detoured, doubling back and charging along Rue Malek which meant a long shot at least, and messier.

Khalil had made his calculations; he knew what he was doing when he indicated this post to the Ashrafiyeh contact. Risha had said: plan number one—coming via Ibr Pacha, and sitting ducks.

Now Peretz lay sprawled over the running board, long legs on the sidewalk. A half dozen steps from Morgan, toward the door, the transmitter/receiver waited helpless on a chair. It lay open, a maze in miniature, skeegaw with wires. To Morgan it was a mystery, resembling a battle of question marks. Seven a.m. well past, the sun had risen above the rooftops of Ras Beirut, its long rays penetrating the clay-hued shadows of Manara, rock shelves and surf along the winding Corniche across the city. Evacuation of the Camp, she knew, was well underway—how many had already been let through to safety? Now was the time; one chance, and for us also. And then no more.

Morgan stared down at Peretz. She waited out the last few seconds.

And if they saw him? Spotted his gangling form stretched out on the pavement, when they turned?

XX

And then there it was: dark and gleaming, the sable blue Mercedes. Having dreamt it for days and weeks, she was certain. Here it came, bathed in a Head of State aura. The car seemed to absorb all the sunlight of the street, gliding toward Morgan's window. But not too fast; she glimpsed a casual elbow. There were three in front. It was them.

She sat by the sill and watched them approach. She cursed silently. Peretz still protruded from the Volkswagen, out of sight from the waist up. She realized they wouldn't see him on the sidewalk side. They came cruising along, unhurried. She saw the driver gesturing; it looked like the ferocious bodyguard from her trysts with Abu Joseph. But she knew the Phalangist captain wasn't with them; he was busy directing tac-op at the Camp evacuation.

Her heart kicked in her throat, as if she might give birth to some supreme curse. Still she stayed in control, considering. And then, propelled across the room by an unknown force, she crouched by the mechanism, utterly calm, trying to make a small, measured movement:—two seconds, one, they were out there at this instant, just beneath the window. They were passing.

Where? Which one? This little switch?

She fingered it, as Peretz had shown her once, when he thought they were flirting.

Slowly, and back—the tiny switch beneath her finger, down and up again. Transmission of a frequency tone.

There was a vacuum of sound, curious, a mote in eternity. And then the building shook.

A huge force rose up and stung Morgan's face, as if clapping her ears with cymbals.

The explosion dwarfed anything she had ever heard or felt. Another followed, but duller, more extended than the first, as one of the cars ignited and went fanning, metal doors, human limbs, strips of frame and asphalt, in every direction.

She was hurled against the wall, gasping. There were more explosions, the equivalent of 150 kilograms of TNT setting off a chain reaction. Another car caught on fire and burst into bits.

And then silence. A pitterpatter of metal and debris. It was gruesome, and comical. Something like a red sponge came splatting the twisted casement, and fell over, inside. Matter rained on the street below; a fire started crackling.

—God.

It was a mini-Hiroshima. The corner was a pond of charred slime. Automobile carcasses and human remains were visible, but of Peretz she recognized nothing. One torso burned alongside the curb, headless, its flesh going brown as it mingled with the flames. Here and there lay the carbonized parts, the twisted blue-gray metal. And no one moving. Other parked cars were battered, the fenders torn, windows gone. One was thrown on the trunk of another like a grotesque copulation.

Flames. A silent seething.

As yet no one appeared. Where was Risha? Without this the Beirutis had their daily fill of terror. But it didn't look good for the getaway; she needed cover, and the presence of other people. In a moment she would be the only person down there, fleeing along the street which still echoed of a local apocalypse.

It had worked. Provided that was the right car, and their target was among its passengers.

She knew it was—and he was. So ended a national leader.

For a moment, between anguished thoughts of escape, Morgan stood gloating. She had written tomorrow's international headlines; she grew exultant, staring at the vision in the street below. Still not a single witness; at the end of the world there would be no witnesses. But someone had to make this fact known back at the Camp. And then a Phalangist massacre of leftists, Palestinians, as planned.

Soon security forces would arrive; but probably no traffic or pedestrians for awhile. Not a car had passed along Ibr Pacha; they were turning back; they detoured with the first whiff. Three, four—she could make out the corpses more or less. One lay in a tangle of gray shreds, half clothed, gashed and disfigured. There lay the illustrious Phalangist, wrestling with flames.

Peretz was disintegrated; he had rejoined the divine efflatus.

—Ah! said Morgan, reaching in her handbag. Here comes Risha.

She watched the young woman darting between doorways. Risha looked panicked. Her movements, as she approached, were like a scared animal.

But where were the fearless Phalangists? The War Council offices were just nearby.

What to say to Risha?

Before long they would cordon off these streets: then she would be trapped. Such an affair was sure to stir tension for weeks. And impossible to lay low: she was much too near the scene. She had to escape somehow, and get across to the West. Do it right now: this was her chance.

And Risha? She was almost here; no way to avoid her.

Morgan gloated another second at the window. She gazed down at her masterpiece, the fuming, crackling fires. No other movement; silence and flayed, dripping tissue.

Then she sprang for the door.

XXI

Nobody on the first landing. Row of closed doors with an air of people inside playing possum, and not a whisper. Some were downstairs in the shelter, while the others weren't likely to budge.

Someone entered. Footsteps in the front hall, moving quickly. It was Risha.

In a moment she would appear, hysterical. Morgan took the handgun from her purse; she unsnapped the hammer-guard. She held it poised in her left hand, the safety off, in a side pocket of her jacket. In the other she had her purse, while the valise hung on a strap from her right shoulder.

She waited a step or two from the dim landing. The other sprang on the first flight; then gasped and drew back, seeing her fixed gaze in the semi-darkness. Morgan said:

—Success, Risha.

—Where's Peretz? she said, wide-eyed, uncomprehending.

—See them down there?

Risha shied; she glanced past her, whispering:

—Peretz?

And Morgan thought: Time . . . it's time. We'll both be taken.

—He's dead too.

Risha stared up at her, with a grunt.

—What?

—Last minute repair. He had to go down there, the Mercedes came . . . No choice, Risha; your man was a hero.

—Then you —?

—I did the necessary. That was our chance, so I took it.

—I know you.

Risha hissed. She was shaking with sudden rage. Morgan thought: Do it now, in a few seconds she'll scream.

—He should've gotten his gear in order. Six weeks here, and all you two did was—

She gestured.

Risha, in her fury of grief, could hardly speak.

—Nazi.

And then her word, Morgan supposed, for devil.

—You'd better calm down.

The word again. And Risha gave a great sob, her eyes bursting with tears. She bent over, giving way to the spasms.

—Peretz!

She stared up the steps and her prim, adult face was glazed with the tears.

—I'm warning you, Risha. Let's go.

Morgan's lips were atremble, and very pale. She spoke so softly, the other, on the verge of hysteria, could hardly have understood.

—Aaangh—

—Shut up.

Time . . . she thought. At any moment they will be there, a Kataëb security patrol with M-16s. Get away from here, now. At least as far as Sodeco, then the Commodore.

She said sharply:

—Peretz was a bungler. Do you know where he went, Risha, each night on his walks?

—What?

—Every night he visited a blousy Arab woman on a side street off Hamra. I saw him go myself; he went to the cheapest whore in town. Varying his diet, no doubt, and giving his mysticism a little rest... Fuck, he asked me enough times for it—he begged me for it.

She laughed, sneering.

Risha looked up, eyes blurred. She was choking with rage; it took her a moment to understand.

She gave a shriek, and shaking her head lunged upward, arms outstretched, toward Morgan's neck.

Morgan staggered backward. She was big and much stronger, but she nearly lost her balance and toppled. The purse and valise were a mistake. They swung wildly, hampering her reaction.

The other grabbed at her neck, screeching:

—You filth! Devil! You killed him!

Despite Risha's hysteria she knew how to fight; she was well trained. She got a firm grip and began squeezing.

But a first shot exploded, jerking her arched body. It rang out on the landing, deafening. The smaller woman hung on; she screamed and clutched, as if all her being were bent on revenge for Peretz.

A second blast; and she fell away, grabbing air, slumping backward. A tiny flame purled on her blouse above the navel. Her blood soaked through at once.

Morgan kicked her. She shoved her on the breast, and Risha fell back helpless. Her head cracked; it bounced on the stone steps.

Morgan's hand trembled. The shots had made a hole in her jacket. She gripped the gun.

—Just me, she said out loud, gasping for breath.

But she collected her wits, straightening the purse and valise. Good for you, little girl. You botched it like your boyfriend.

She kicked her, again, in passing. The shots still rang in her ears. Risha's face was a frozen shriek where it lay bent back on the top step. Blood pooled beneath her breasts. She quivered.

—Only me. Well, that's better... Morgan moved down the stairway like a big cat.

XXII

There were pieces of charred matter, strewn about, fuming. She turned her back on the gray scene, a neighborhood Armageddon. So far no voices. Soon militiamen would converge, in jeeps. Now a cab, she thought. If I can get to Sodeco chances are good. Eyes, eyes—

where am I going? Ten more steps to the first corner: she burst into a run as if lunging for the tape. Goodbye, Ashrafiyeh, and forever. To Ligury's then? No, not there.

En Nahr lay deserted as well. Exposed, here I am walking. Complete the mission, take the consequences. I completed it—in spite of my partners, but they're forgiven. Taxi? She scanned the street for a means of rescue.

The fighting had lulled to a sporadic shelling across the city, as evacuation of the Camp proceeded. She walked along jubilant and desperate to escape. Sense of impending release: stay alive, Morgan, savor Cyprus. The air smelled of sulphur and decay. The sky was free of smoke for a moment, a more radiant blue. Small shops cowered in a row behind their iron gratings. No window showed a sign of life in this teeming quarter. Through a gap in the rooftops she glimpsed the smooth, marble monolith of Gefinor, across the teeming capital; but scored now in places, a fallen idol.

Still not one person, not a car. Only Morgan, walking briskly and thinking of freedom. Ydlibbi's, I can go there awhile. Should be other Westerners; I'll need someone, an escort. Fatah is supervising the Bain Militaire evacuation. Idealists, making things easy for their enemy. Men are dupes. She went along hugging a facade.

Now she glimpsed the dense funnel of smoke which twisted out to sea from the burst oil reservoir in Dowra, on the eastern side of the Ring of Death. The limestone city lay smoldering after its night of war.

—Nam, nam! She saw a cab turning away; she gasped out: Taxi! ah dammit—

But the man heard or else saw her in his rearview mirror. He stopped on a dime, and immediately she grew demure, she didn't run. Life is well-made, she thought; at every street corner someone waits to do my bidding. Presto: salvation for a hundred lira. My work is done here. And it is done.

—Ydlibbi's, Avenue des Français.

—Three hundred.

—Okay, just drive.

—Now, he waited. Pay it now.

—Eh!

She fumbled in her purse. Treat life like a whore, she thought, and it will almost always do your bidding. Then no emotional errors. For a little money life will entrust you with its prize possessions. There will be no more secrets, and no mystery.

The wheels cried out round a corner. The car flew down vacant side streets in a roundabout way toward the port area. The driver reached back his hand for the bills, cursing under his breath, muttering in Arabic:
—Crazy tourists.

XXIII

Suddenly, at a few minutes before nine a.m., the aura of safety and supervision evaporated in the Camp. At the checkpoints people were being seized and lined up not by the Red Cross, but by men in black hoods. They were made to hand over money and watches, jewelry, wedding rings. What had happened? Was the evacuation based on a false promise in the first place? on a letter "officially signed" by the Phalangist leader, stating that an Arab League mediator could supervise transport of civilians by the International Red Cross?

Dr. Kamel had seen to the exodus of his clinic and then returned to lend a hand wherever he was needed. All at once he saw Christian militiamen pouring unresisted past the Camp perimeter, overrunning the mass of pasteboard sheds and shanties. They came storming up the main road from the central mosque with its bodies bloating, decomposing in the sunlight. Now they were hurling insults, shouting out obscenities. They shouted out names of places where Phalangist forces had gone down vowing revenge:
—Chekka!

One hooded figure dragged off a woman by the hair; she flailed wildly, her body writhing beneath his grasp. Where is Hana'a? thought Dr. Kamel.
—Damour!

He saw three rightists in a sea of flattened petrol cans which had served as roofage; collapsed siding, bricks granulated beneath the daily artillery onslaught. The three stood arguing over booty and firing shots past each others' heads. Were they drugged? On every side the horror was on the march.
—Kantari!

Dazed, but sensing his own grave danger, Dr. Kamel began moving back toward the perimeter. There was nothing to be done now; he was unarmed, and he heard the sound of grenades being tossed inside the delapidated shanties, followed by machinegun fire. What had gone wrong? Women were screaming. Groups of males were being gathered at the factory of a man named Matta. Shots, screams. He was trembling as he walked past a long line of bodies, torsos twisted at odd angles, limbs interlocked like a gruesome mass sculpture. There was more submachinegun fire, and shrieking in unison.

Moustafa, one of the four UNRWA teachers who had remained resolutely pacifist through the long weeks of siege, arrived at a checkpoint in Funduqiyyeh sector. Behind him, men in cagoules or wearing surgical masks ran through the streets crying revenge. They waved assault rifles and looted the miserable remains, snarling and disputing the spoils. Tanks and APCs were descending upon the fallen camp: Moustafa knew it was all over for the resistance, and while sharing the sense of tragedy, and utter exhaustion, he also felt justified.

At the checkpoint he was asked for his papers.

—Monsieur, je . . .

—Halla! cried the Phalangist in Arabic.

Beyond the roadblock which had skull and crossbones as its emblem, a Camp fighter was being attached by his ankles to the back fender of a Land Rover.

Moustafa, the Islamic Renaissance and his religious calling notwithstanding, began talking in Broken French about Western progress and the superior culture of Catholicism. Big beads of sweat rolled from his hairline down to his trembling lips; but the hooded face distorted in a sneer:

—By the Prophet! Take this one *water-skiing* too.

They carried him away screaming:

—Sheikh Gemayel is a beacon light! Victor Hugo!

A militiaman gunbutted him down, while another tightened a slip-knot on his ankles. As he lay writhing, gasping incoherent protests of his neutrality, a last few lentils of Moustafa's private stock spilled from the front pocket of his trousers, and were lost in the pitiless dust.

XXIV

Elie Madi had strict orders, from the Politburo member Selim, to release no males aged fourteen to sixty; and to refuse egress to anyone wearing the Red Cross insignia, or otherwise identifiable as medical personnel. Elie had just watched an old man—who had spit on Kuzayli, and proclaimed he was a Palestinian from Acre—being drawn and quartered between two cars. The neck distended; the body fell back and detached... Across the human dumping ground of the Camp a side of building jutted up from the ruins, one-eyed with its tilted window casement.

What time of day was it? Still morning? Elie felt disoriented, as if the mass hysteria on all sides gave him a kind of amnesia. In truth he was hardly playing more than a *pro forma* role, putting his newfound fidelity to the test during these proceedings at a key perimeter checkpoint. Distantly, he heard the automatic weapons' fire, and guttural screams tapering off as more people fell; but it all seemed to occur at random. Kuzayli was the one directing traffic, and implementing decisions handed down by radio from Abu Joseph, who got them in turn from the General Staff.

Like the others Elie had heard the horrendous news, and what was happening now, before his eyes, seemed logical. At one point, sitting on the hood of his jeep, klashin across his lap, he wondered why the leftists would stage a terrorist attack just at the moment when their people were most vulnerable. But his thoughts were swept along in the immense rush of events... With the exception that he kept daydreaming of Jessica, and making love to her that same evening.

Dr. Kamel walked along a narrow path under Phalangist guard. He knew what they were going to do with him, but because of the physical exhaustion, and everything else, it didn't seem to matter. Hana'a was gone; he didn't know where. No doubt Sitt Chahrour was taking her chances like everyone else. Incredibly, the doctor, as he trudged along toward his death, was thinking abstractly about grief, and how even one bereavement represented an almost inhuman task for a survivor. Think of the psychiatrists, how grandiose (or venal) they were, believing they could allay the grief, or anxiety, in X number of lives each year.

—Fuck Palestine!

The shriek of a fighter gamboling over the morass brought Dr. Kamel back to reality.

He moved along passively, glancing at another group who were doing the same, stung numb by the sudden turn of events, like sleepwalkers on a ledge.

But now, trudging in the mid-morning sunlight, he felt his hand being grasped by someone's fingers. Tiny, seeming to clutch him from all sides, somehow: one of the girls from his clinic, a six year-old, had caught up to him and innocently entered the armed escort. The others had gotten across to safety; now what was she doing here?

He was wretchedly thirsty. The women in the other group were moaning, either in sudden mourning though themselves about to die, or from hunger and thirst.

Black-hooded figures went running past, shouting, brandishing M-16s. One yelped and gave a sexual laughter as he leapt between corpses and a maze of splintered barracks. On his gunbarrel was a decal of Christ.

The road was choking with dust; Dr. Kamel's throat was parched. A rightist lingered with a spray-gun, painting over graffitti of a Camp propaganda team organized by Selman. Over the words: *A gun is the sole legal representative . . .* , he wrote:

—MY PRICK FOR THE BIGGEST LEFTIST IN HISTORY.

There were coils of barbed wire, and broken weapons, parts and spent rounds, the glaring sun. Everywhere bullet holes, and red graffitti. *Team of the Return! Remember Tel ez-Zaater!*

Just up ahead the Kataëb checkpoint was a tense meeting ground. People halted. A woman glanced back and her eyes said: what do they want with us? What have I ever done to them?

Another stooped to gather in her children; she was crying. All the men were being pushed to one side, detained.

The sun beat down without mercy, reflecting off the fiery stretch of asphalt which led to freedom just beyond. There were thin shadows along the road; a few were still being let through this particular roadblock. A kilometer in the distance windshields glinted: ICRC transport cars awaiting any stragglers. Nearing the hooded fighters, people grew quiet. The little girl by Dr. Kamel's side moaned with thirst; he remembered she was returned to her mother the day before.

But something was happening up ahead. A woman said:
—Which is it?
—That one: with no hood!

Unlike elsewhere the line was indistinct: evacuees waited in hushed panic before the grim Phalangists. A man was denied passage, and led away. The doctor knew this would be his fate as well; they would do it with pleasure since his name was known. But the girl's small voice, her tender clinging hands held him fast. She also moved, leaning against him, toward the place of decision.

A helicopter flew over. In the background there were constant shots; but the noise seemed slight in comparison to endless weeks of shelling. There was hysteria in the air, with a scent of open sewerage.

But now some kind of argument sprang up among the rightists. Heated words. One shoved another. They were trying to browbeat the militiaman with no hood; but he stood his ground. What was happening? He looked boyish like a student; but he also appeared in charge, maybe the corps leader? There was another thing about him, unlike anyone else in the panicked crowd: he was calm.

The girl of six hugged onto the doctor's side. She whispered:
—Hakim.
—Huh?
—I must drink. Soon I'm going to fall.

She said it again, tugging his trousers.

He stooped and draped her on his shoulder.

The strangely calm rightist had an AK which he pointed, directing the scene before him. There was an instant of silence when he cocked and sighted one of his own, another Phalangist. The latter's hood quivered with irate words he spoke; but he seemed to subside, as the first took control.

At this checkpoint they started letting people through, without questions, even omitting paperwork.

XXV

Now the doctor's thoughts were on the march. He saw the self-possessed rightist overruling protests, expediting things at this critical exit point. He seemed to move in a different element.

—Move along. That's right—hurry up!

Refugees passed by without looking at him, or anyone. A sluice gate had opened; he pointed to the other side, commanding:

—Don't block traffic!

This to an old man with a face like shoe leather, who stopped to thank him. The other Phalangists turned: even the black hoods showed surprise, because this grandpa still looked like a fighter, a veteran of the Arab Rebellion in the late Thirties.

—Get along, you go through.

The one in charge had dark eyes, dark curly hair. He had a soulful elated look, using the M-16 to herd people past:

—Don't look back, either! The bulldozers are coming: you're in the way here.

He took a look at each one going by, but they passed on, unblinking. Dr. Kamel thought the Phalangist had an inappropriate look, given the circumstances. One, almost, of admiration.

There were more flurries of shooting. Sun beat down on the staggering exodus. Almost through, keep moving; but some faltered as the moment approached, and went to the their knees. They were ground down by the summer-long ordeal; their silence implored an unlikely help. A breeze stirred the curly hair on this corps leader's temple; he nodded as the doctor came nearer.

—Go back where you came from, said the Phalangist. Get out of Lebanon.

His mates were casting glances right and left, awaiting reinforcements?

Perhaps twenty had gone through by the time it was Dr. Kamel's turn. He was the most probable victim in this line: a leader of the Resistance.

He approached with the girl on his shoulder, limp and emitting little breaths. A few others had grouped around him. The rightist held up his hand, eyeing the adult male:

—Name?
—Dr. Kamel Rehanna.
The flow stopped.
The other hooded militiamen paused to watch.
—Age?
—Forty-two.
The final checkpoint was a pocket of silence amid the shooting. A helicopter hovered with its methodical whirr. Submachinegun fire interspersed with bells pealing in the West Beirut churches.
—What's wrong with this girl?
—Dehydration, for one thing.
—These people: they're all with you?
—Let them pass, he said. I'll stay if you want.
The other gave a gesture at the field of rubble. His expression, though smiling, was tragic as he said:
—All this ... was it necessary?
He shrugged and asked something else unheard by those watching. The doctor stood tensely, fearing a flare-up on either side. He sniffed their chance and felt impatient with the unpredictable Phalangist who held them there. He paid no heed to acute loneliness noticeable in his enemy's smile; he wanted only for the people to pass, some fifty by now, while it was still in the non-hooded Phalangist's power.
But Elie paused another instant, staring in Dr. Kamel's eyes. There was a kind of question mark and a hopeless plea in his gaze,— referring to the consequences of his action?
What are you stalling for? thought the doctor. Damn you, let them through.
—Go on, said Elie Madi. Come—come ... *Mien halla?*
The little girl lifted her head for a look as they moved past him, slowly. He wore a tiny crucifix round his neck, on a silver chain.
Elie stared at her as well, for an instant; but then turned his gaze back to the Camp and a figure, flanked by two guards, whose angry prodding gait resembled Abu Joseph.

XXVI

Early that afternoon survivors were gathering at various sites in West Beirut. In a schoolyard not far from UNESCO headquarters there were already eight hundred evacuees. But by now the chorus of cheers had turned to a citywide lamentation. In congested Mazra, along Hamra in Xatt area: a dirge for the mass martyrs.

Meanwhile Sitt Chahrour was one of the last to leave the Camp. She was looking for her family. Hana'a had disappeared: no one knew where Hana'a had gone, but perhaps she was safe in Ras Beirut since the last time anyone saw her was early that morning, escorting the convoy from Dr. Kamel's pediatrics clinic. Saleh and Ismail, Sitt's eldest grandsons and frontline defenders of the Camp, were said to have fled when the ICRC evacuation suddenly became a bloodbath.

At mid-afternoon Sitt Chahrour arrived, alone, at the same checkpoint controlled briefly during the height of hysteria by Elie Madi. Once again her world had been burst apart; and she trudged along black-robed, frowning at the dusty ground.

A hooded man called out to her:

—*Ya* Ashatra! Still looking for snails?

There was a group of them: all in hoods. Their movements were jerkily abnormal, and sinister.

—No, leave me alone.

They laughed at her grumbled protest.

—Na, na! We have another kind of job for you, Granma!

Three Phalangists hoisted the old woman off the ground, depositing her in the back seat of a jeep.

—Going to rape me, you bandits?

—Ah ha! Listen to her making suggestions!

—Thinks she's still a pretty sweet piece!

—Ha! ha!

Sitt Chahrour's hope was fading as they drove her at full speed back inside the Camp. Fuming piles of debris; bloated corpses aflame in the bright sunlight... As if hell had annexed this plot of earth; and Satan's legions wore hoods and surgical masks, scampering about the landscape.

—*T'al!* We want to show you something funny!

They took her to a place where some seventy males were waiting to be executed.

They hauled her out, laughing at their prank, and brought Sitt Chahrour face to face with four of her grandsons: Khaled, Ashraf, Ahmed and Mansur.

While one of her escorts stood parleying with the captain in charge, two others held back the old woman beginning to decompose with grief. Her breathing was convulsive, but she didn't scream.

—Now, Granma! the fighter returned, looking more serious. We're going to let you save one of them: choose!

She waved her arms, going on her knees.

—If you make a scene we'll take it back. Stand up!

Ashatra got to her feet, somehow. Her features were working; the tears streamed down her wrinkled, whiskered face. She stared pitifully at her grandsons, pleading silently for their forgiveness.

But the three older ones were nodding at Mansur. They wanted the long ordeal, made worse now by her presence, to be over.

—Take him, Sitt, said Khaled. Take Mansur, and go. Be grateful to our hosts.

—*La la!* She must decide herself, and point to the one ... Then you can all curse one another for ever coming to Lebanon!

Ashatra was beside herself, her face awash with tears. But she nodded, and raised her black-sleeved arm.

What happened next was more than she could comprehend. Khaled, Ashraf and Ahmed were lined up against a chunk of wall striated with bloodstains reflecting a pale sky. The shots rang out and they fell, taking a step or two forward while slumping back.

Mansur was guiding her along, whispering gentle desperate words to his grandmother and urging her to stay afoot. Would she make it? The Phalangists laughed grimly and sent them on their way, after staging what amounted in their eyes to a coup de morale. Ashatra and her youngest grandson walked through the Camp unescorted; now at four p.m. they were the last ones to make their way: Mansur coaxing and glancing about nervously; Sitt Chahrour stumbling amid the rubble, her mourning garment shredding on her calves.

There were automatic shots, an extended burst but neither of them flinched. A bird chirped. A pasteboard wall flapped in the rising seabreeze.

As they reached the perimeter a jeep drove up and braked with a squeal. It was a "flying checkpoint."

—Papers! *Hawajiz!*

Violently they pulled Mansur to one side.

Ashatra began shouting at them, hoarsely:

—We made a deal! Back there—she shook her finger toward the Camp, then at the mobile guards—they said I could take him! They made me choose!

—Ummi! cried Mansur. Now you're the mother of all Fedayeen!

One put a trigger, routinely, to Mansur's temple and pulled the trigger.

They drove off.

XXVII

In the overflowing schoolyard Dr. Kamel began tending to the children. Cases of gangrene, and tetanus infection, were separated while arrangements could be made to have them transported. But there were others who kept themselves apart, and sat beating their heads in a listless rhythm against the cement wall of the school. Where am I? Nobody... Dr. Kamel tried to reorient them, but a few lacked strength to form a response. How many required immediate treatment but were still going unnoticed amid the general hysteria? He watched a teenage girl lay back helpless, succumbing to the nervous reaction in her limbs. Distended, grotesque face: no name, parents unknown. Unless someone in her family was found, she would have to be renamed.

Dr. Kamel came upon Nadja, the little girl from his clinic with sandy hair, and eyes the color of blue sky reflected in two olives.

—Nadja, are you okay?

—Yes.

—Are you hungry? I'll bring you something.

—Where's Mayser?

—He's here too. Don't worry.

In late afternoon the journalist Ligury arrived at the schoolyard. Dr. Kamel was giving him a tour, describing what he had seen of the evacuation.

—No doubt they will write, in London and New York, that this is the *lama sabachthani* of our resistance. You see the West, no offense intended, is very backward. They want it that way.

—In Ashrafiyeh, said Ligury, there's cheering in the streets.

—You were there?

—Covering the assassination story.

—Ah. No doubt it's more important.

—No, but you see . . .

Ligury showed him a telegram: assignment orders, with a lead sentence in quotes to boot.

—I'm worried about Hana'a, said Dr. Kamel.

—She isn't here?

—I haven't seen her since this morning.

—And the old woman, who told me about her life?

—Someone saw her outside the Camp perimeter.

—I hope they're safe.

The two men fell silent. The doctor looked around, distracted; it seemed as if, across West Beirut, an atonal requiem were being sung in the moans, cries, supplications of the survivors.

—If you write an article about this, Mr. Ligury, you may not get it published.

—So a friend of mine, a German photographer, tells me. Write what "they" want, or it's: *Sterbe, Hund!* In a most ethical silence . . .

Dr. Kamel stared at him.

—And?

—I'll give a try.

—You see how we go on aching, limping, grieving. It seems like only we're aware . . .

Kim Ligury nodded. He noticed Nadja who was looking at him calmly from her stretcher. When he met her pretty gaze Nadja managed a smile, somehow, and the demure Ligury felt a sort of intimate convulsion, in his chest, like an air-bubble rising in a water cooler.

PART SIX

I

Elie's hands were on fire. The flames shot down his wrists, engulfing his elbows, purling along his armpits. Like a dragon's breath they spread to his neck and face, and merged with the thirst. Spasms shook him. Gladly he would have surrendered his mind as well.

Meanwhile a guard, longtime Chamounist named Giorgio, stood restless and fidgety in the doorway. Lost in thought he gazed at Elie Madi; then grew bored and called down the hallway of the War Council.

He gave a chuckle:

—Like it, traitor? I'll tighten the noose a little.

Elie's dark eyes were fixed on the wall opposite, showing intense effort. His hands were bound separately and attached to the iron casement of a skylight, from which he half hung, trying to prop himself, while his feet were tied with a length of cord extending across the room. Now and again he worked himself almost upright, slowly, imperceptibly. But the guard noticed and yanked back the rope: once again Elie was sent writhing, dangling by his wrists which were dangerously blue.

There was really no point in resisting; it only invited more torture. But to ignore Giorgio, a well-known sadist, only tended to frustrate him and stir him up even more.

—No chance, Elie groaned, for a sip of water?

The guard leered, shaking his head:

—Water for a cactus?

He shuffled, postured; his gangling form filled up the doorway. He fingered the stock of his M-16 propped by the doorjamb. But Elie's ruse worked: keep your water, jackass.

The guard was restless; he said in a bored tone:

—We're going to take you out and attach your balls to two cars. You'll like it.

Elie Madi held on; he tried with all his might for balance while appearing to hang suspended. But the pain screwed up his features, betraying the great effort.

He could always end it: whenever he wanted. This old Chamounist was so twisted inside, himself so tortured, also vindictive against Phalangists: it would require a few words sprinkled like salt on the open wound that was Giorgio's ego: unless there were orders to the contrary. But Elie held back the word, prolonging his misery; he wouldn't give them the satisfaction. For what seemed hours the flames did their worst to his frazzled nerves; but they hadn't reached his mind as yet, or the thoughts of rescue that were stubbornly entrenched there.

He squirmed inwardly, not daring to budge; he couldn't show any weakness. The trousers slid from his pelvis; a torn shirt, ruffled on his neck, showed his lower ribs and a stomach gnarled with the strain.

Giorgio fidgeted. Without moving he seemed to prowl a psychic cage of his own. He glanced behind him, surveying the empty corridor for someone to engage in conversation. Once he called out to a messenger between offices; but no one was prone to smalltalk now—as just outside, without pause, they heard the thud-thud of tanks stalking through Ashrafiyeh toward Burj, toward Ein Rummaneh. And Giorgio, who had danced to the basso waltz of war, felt roused by it now and grew more impatient guarding this pitiful prisoner. He was left to his own limited devices, facing the archenemy boredom.

Giorgio maneuvered his angular frame, striking a pose in the doorway. With one hand he swept back the curly hair matted with sweat on his forehead, and stepped into the room:

—You should enjoy this. Little children like to swing.

He inserted a bent cigarette in the center of his lips. Taking the cord he jerked it twice, and the prisoner's body flopped like a Raggedy Anne. Atrocious pain seared Elie's wrists; his legs swung out and he gasped for dear life.

—Rockabye baby, on the treetops! Ah, did baby fall? Did he hurt 'isself?

Giorgio swung and yanked, cackling.

For a few minutes Elie had found a way to restore circulation by placing more weight on his toes. Keeping these edgewise, so they appeared limp, he could get a kind of grip on the concrete floor. But then the goon, at a loss for amusement, began using his body once again as a plaything. It was a variation on the method called "Airplane".

—Does he like to swing, hum? Does boobikins swing?

Elie offered no resistance. His face was a drawn and quivering mask; his eyes dark, two viscous slits.

—Ring the bell! Does Père Zaki ring the bell, when a traitor dies? No, he does not; he doesn't give a fuck when the traitor to his people croaks. But I do, Giorgio does. I give a fuck as long as this *khara* has the arrogance to live. Ding-dong, bim-bam, back and forth. Ha ha: how does it feel, you *ben sharmouta* son of a whore? How many friends died so far because of you? This is for them.

Giorgio sweated with the exertion. The ash-tip of his cigarette was ready to drop of its own length, an orange worm edging from his thick lips.

Elie's body flopped and swung. At each end of the pendulum it paused an instant, before wreaking havoc with his chest, and extremities.

The flesh tore. His blood began dripping on the stone.

II

He lost consciousness. He fell into a region of somber stark masses, black icebergs. Then he saw spewing gueysers, like a polar fireworks which crystallized in mid-air, and hung like stars. There was a nauseous odor in the sky; it affected continents. The world was sick to its stomach, as he watched himself fly by on a roller coaster, star to star.

But the big fear brought Elie back. Somehow he was up on his feet, and nobody was on guard; no sniper's eyes watched him beneath tousled greasy hair. So he had left poor Giorgio all alone, and this time the old Chamounist could only blame himself for the horrific malaise. But there was something else: not the bleeding, that was no novelty—not the blood, but the smell. The room stank to high heaven.

Now Elie Madi revived to a blessed relief, standing upright; along with an acrid sense of having shit himself during the ordeal. He bit at the rope on his wrists. The room reeked. He gave short gasps, gnawing like an animal at the cord.

The guard returned. He screwed up his features in disgust, hanging back in the doorway. Elie stared at him and actually smiled, demonic while trying to loosen his bonds. Giorgio sneered mightily, but seemed to realize the consequences of driving his prisoner too far.

—Traitors like you: we shoot them right off. Why play around? It irritates me, now you've got to be cleaned up.

Elie said:

—How long would you last?

—You . . . talk to me?

—I said how long, slob, before you whined for mercy? Come on, I'll trade places with you, then we'll see.

—They told me: don't kill the little shit. Try to be careful—but why? He stinks like nothing I ever smelled, it's a crime when someone like him even speaks to another person. You're going to hell, man: get used to sulphur.

—No, said Elie, eyes filmy. It's you and your kind, Hitler's nephews.

—That's enough. Get back in position.

Elie rubbed his head on the rope. He cried softly and shivered:

—I can't.

—Big talk, said Giorgio, for someone who can't.

He jerked back the rope and brought him sprawling. But Elie kicked out and tried to regain a foothold. The guard yanked away his end; he was finally getting what he wanted, some sport on the end of his line.

Elie struggled and flailed his limbs. A boy appeared behind Giorgio at the door.

—They sent me, he mumbled. Clean up the shit.

—Huh?

—It smells down the hall.

—Oh, fuck. Untie him first, hurry up.

He shoved the boy inside.

III

In his limbs there was a frayed sensation. His feet were free, but this time he couldn't stand and just hung by his bloated wrists. The boy of twelve reached up and grasped Elie's arm, fingering the blood-soaked knot. But the Chamounist snapped:

—Leave that alone.
—But they said...
—Who?
—Command said it's enough, let him down.
—Piss.

There was a square of blue in the small skylight, seeming faded with distance. The sun shone brightly on the other side, but the room where they worked on Elie was gray and bare of furniture. A big disgust showed in Giorgio's eyes, his twisted lips when the task of supporting the prisoner fell to him.

The boy also cursed, working with the stubborn slip-knot. He flicked away Elie's limp hand; the cyanotic fingers, beet-red wrists lit by the opening just above.

—Will you hurry up.
—It's stuck.

The boy gave a grunt. He happened to kick the pail, and a towel toppled onto the filthy floor. But the pail was empty: water was precious in Ashrafiyeh under siege.

—That's one.

Elie's arms fell, causing a great spasm across his chest. The numbness was pierced by a lancinating effect on his released shoulder. In a moment his upper body felt a shrill prickling, which made him whimper with astonishment.

—There—

The other arm fell; Giorgio shoved him at the boy who let Elie drop onto the concrete, and curl up foetally.

The prisoner grabbed up the filthy towel and began sucking on it. Catching the abrupt movement Giorgio spun with his submachine-gun, and seemed to consider firing. Giorgio was no coward when it came to action. But now his forced inactivity made him edgy and mean; he barked at the boy to get on with it, and then cursed them both under his breath. He shifted postures in the doorway, fiddling with his M-16 and sighing. When a shell whistled overhead he appeared to come alive.

The horror always brought Giorgio out of himself, like music; it allowed him to breathe more freely, and he craved a demitasse of sweet pungent coffee. As a rule he was rather easygoing though capable of anything, a skilled mechanic and lover of modified cars. Before the war souped-up engines had been his life, and chasing girls.

But when he was out there, when the enemy gunners pumped on their Stalin's-Organs it seemed to drown out his frustrations. He yearned for the martial music of Kataëb emplacements; he lived for the instant he would leave this degrading post, and take part in a fierce firefight.

Giorgio considered himself a mercenary; he would gladly fight the communists and all such rot across wide unconquered lands, in Africa if necessary, in Latin America. Like some Greek hero he would choose the best of the women when it was over; they would make savage love in the ashes. Then he might hire a ghost writer to be his Homer, and make a million on a book. Yes, Lebanon was really too small for a soul the size of Giorgio's. Someday he would be a kingmaker, once he got himself relieved from this luckless latrine duty.

He fiddled with the cartridge of his weapon. His nerves were abuzz with the renewed onslaught and shelling across the city. To and fro—whoompfff! Pfwizzzt!

The boy grunted softly under the burden of turning Elie. He wrinkled his nose while swabbing him with the towel. The boy's features were lean and spur-like, a crow's expression with the mesh of black hair across his forehead.

—Turn.

Giorgio harassed the boy:

—I know it takes some elbow-grease, cleaning off scum. An amount seldom seen. But get the hell done with it.

He chuckled and gripped his rifle, taking aim from the hip and winking at the Phalangist youth.

IV

The port area was particularly tense, and her cabdriver screeched away the instant Morgan stepped clear, slamming the rear door. High on the pockmarked smudged hotels, rockets whooshed in from the eastern sectors with a barrelling blast. Shells hissed along the waterfront, sending up a towering gueyser, or shower of sparks when they landed. The street resembled a landslide, with three, four corpses at once meeting the eye: dusty, bloated up, as if breeding in the late afternoon shadows. The Mediterranean toward Jounieh was a lush semi-precious blue tending to green in the shallows. There was the usual blond glimmer, on sunny days, lining the mossy rockshelves of Beirut Port and long horseshoe waterfront.

She paused on the verge of entering Ydlibbi's nightclub when a striking figure emerged a few doors down. It was one of the women, outlandishly fat, in a saffron nightgown, from Port Egypt. She seemed to beckon Morgan with her gaze, stretching as she glanced across the harbor, oblivious to sounds of war.

Downstairs, the club was all but vacant with its bar and empty tables; the gambling section rearward in a smoky amber light. The silence grumbled.

Two men sat on bar stools, talking to Ydlibbi: one a businessman, three-pieced and arriviste, the other in his thirties, the kind likely to answer an ad in one of the old-boy soldier magazines. But no journalists on hand, no Kohler, or the decent reserved Ligury whom she wasn't eager to see, and yet wouldn't have minded . . . Nobody she recognized except Camille Ydlibbi, suave and resigned, coming forward to mix her a drink.

—Ze fighteeng eez heavee. C'est fort maintenant, vers le nord.

He spoke with a burr.

—Après?

—Soon, Mad'moiselle, zere well be no après. We will cross ze Rubicon, et puis nucléaire, poof!

—You know of course, said Morgan, it was all prearranged.

—Peut-être: a leetle experiment in dyeeng. Quelque imbécile dit SS-4; but ze othair end, he hears SS-twentee.

—No time to shop for a coffin.

—C'est ça. Eh oui.

Ydlibbi gave a sort of spuming gesture, his invitation to the dance.

—What is happening here eez too unpleasant, he said. Better to be an ant, in a Thibetan treetrunk—a light goes out, et voilà.

Ydlibbi turned away, replacing the bottle.

Around the wide nightclub she missed the blinking pictures. No people laughing, no flesh jumping out at you, daiquiri and subtle lust. No skiing and swimming the same day, loving the bright-lit surface of things, festive pre-war days; European chic, like icing on a moldy cake.

Ydlibbi tossed his brow, and gave the standard champagne gesture: a bit for her, more for himself.

V

Time had begun dragging, with her sudden enforced inactivity. The airport was closed, the country in turmoil after the car-bomb death of its *de facto* leader. Her one option, while an investigation blitz went on in every neighborhood, and stupendous reprisals exploded on the front pages of *l'Orient-le-Jour* and *Réveil,* was to lay low at the Commodore. From day to day the evacuation of foreign nationals from Bain Militaire was postponed. Her mission was completed: a thing of glorious horror which might swallow her up as well in its aftermath. Thank God her partners had both been eliminated.

Morgan's mind wandered. Again she recalled the period of stewing in her own juice, during weeks which preceded her arrival in Lebanon. With no regret she said goodbye to the psychiatrist, Bergland, who was her mainstay in Tel Aviv. She never quite learned to care for men with his alienated caseworker approach. Decidedly he was in it for himself, a kind of sly liberal—open, like a trap, to others' thoughts and feelings. Still he had been there: that was something. He gave support, a measure of perfunctory routine, with her three visits per week. It was a relief in the menacing boredom before she picked up her mission. But how long would it be this time, before moving on ? Her demon was at bay, for the moment, after the catharsis of success; yet she intimated the anguish of its scaley tail ... rising up at some unsuspected moment to enwind her. Or had the kinky creature been exorcized at last, put to rest by this new and qualitatively greater risk, this triumph of death resounding across the region?

How long, before she began risking sensitive phonecalls? When would she go to her next treacherous appointment?

The prospect of idleness was always alluring. She promised herself a few weeks of "abulia" in a plush Montreal hotel room, reading Jacques LaCan's tortuous divagations, and venturing into the wide night of genitalia when the spirit moved her. The vicious cycle spiralled inward, upon itself, and the next task would be yet more grandiose, as she continued her quest of a glorious end.

Morgan stayed in touch with no one; she rarely wrote letters or received them. Her banker was a number in her head, a credit-card dial which tended to the necessary: bills, taxes, a quiet funeral if such was required, even a lobotomy if she so decided: she could implement it with the irrecusable code, plus insertion of her plastic card. Recently it had bought her New York City apartment and handled all the details: negotiations, mortgage, closing, payments. She was never there; she hated that East Side coop with an inexplicable passion.

Now she sat alone in a booth toward the rear of Ydlibbi's, giving free rein to her thoughts. In Tel Aviv they had alighted, she and Bergland, on the subject of a certain childhood doll. From age eleven to thirteen this large elaborate doll held a keen fascination for her. It ate little bits of plastic food. It could wet. And what was the age of the doll? Perhaps pre-menarcheal, or else (with its bright pink cheeks, and long lashes, stylized features) a quite young mother.
—What was its name?
—I don't know.
—What did you call it?
—She . . . her.
—Hm.
Bergland's profound silence, which had its way, tacitly, of degrading. Like sharing soiled sheets, she thought; but this time who was the customer?
—Why were you . . . what was the, uh, attraction?
—I liked taking her for a nap. I held her close, and rocked beside her, a little, so she cried.
—Cried how?
Morgan made a sort of abandoned sound.
—With her little nobody voice. Don't hurt me, she seemed to say; hurt me.
—And then?
—I felt her trickle on my . . .
—Hmm?

—These.

Morgan grabbed her breast roughly and shook it at Bergland. Her laughter seemed to incise the psychiatrist's silence.

—What happened to her?

—I don't know. Years later, the third summer I guess it was after graduation from college, I was touring Italy when a curious thing happened. I had to change to a different pensione everyday, because...

—Why?

—I was enuretic. It was strange, frightening—to wake up in a soiled bed, a grown woman. I couldn't sleep. I could hardly trust myself in public, until I quit the tour and went home, to New York that is, to lick my wounds. But for some reason I recalled the doll; I longed for her in those terrible sleepless nights.

—And then?

—Then... well, I fell in with some jet-setters, after I got back. I started out whoring, but their after-hours playtime seemed to turn me on, for awhile. A few were well-known, shy about their sick pleasures but longing, you know, to do them in front of an audience.

—And?

—They finagled mention in the society columns. They cruised, ate lobster and took laxatives; fucked and flapped up from the ashes like some big tropical bird. One night... I was with some of them... they played a game called "Next Excess". You see cocaine abounded. It was a turn-on, hearing them discuss ground rules as if they did this sort of thing regularly. Ever read *The Bacchae,* Doctor? Neglect the... orgiastic side of things, and you'll surely pay for it in disgusting little ways—even an immortal like yourself. Only, for us, new extremes are necessary.

—Then what?

—They discussed limits imposed by health, or the law. It was a strange convention. I saw a lovely, svelte woman stand up after two hits and announce, "I shall glorify the bodily functions." My, uh, body... had never till then produced an orgasm: not for Willartig, not even for one of your august colleagues I seduced, on his couch. But I felt so tense, watching this woman, kind of like with my doll. So utterly vulgar and lewd she was, beneath the glittery fashions— not like my "demon" with his urbane gestures, a snake in a tuxedo. She made one of the males present (I had thought he was gay) perform an act which to me was a revelation.

—What?

—You know . . . sort of . . . unlimited; the filthiest sort of smut and yet it turned me on, watching them. I held back from their Roman carnival, with its whipping and other "labors of Hercules". Chance was introduced; but I wouldn't allow my name in the hat. It was all voluntary, you see; and that's why, I guess, it was still impossible.
—What was?
—To put myself in position for an orgasm.
—Someone has to put you there? said Bergland.
—I think so. With them it was all free will, but it wasn't free.
—What did the others think, when you held back?
—I don't know. That I was an insatiable voyeur.
—Are you?
—Sure. Want to know what my "thing" is?
— . . .
—I like to watch nosey psychiatrists try to hide their unprofessional instincts.

Bergland laughed, uneasily.
—Touché. All of us at times, uh, find a certain relish.

Morgan remembered how, in Bergland's office, she had seemed to perceive the soulless beauty of her own face, and wear it like a mask. Where was the male capable of ripping it off—her wimp of a father? her pedantic failure of a first love? her endless succession of ineffectual "Johns" who made love as if it was a trip to the toilet? No; it was her mother, long ago, who tore off her real face and replaced it with a mask classically designed to drive men like Bergland wild. To get behind it, ever again, would require an uncaring, gratuituous, perhaps feminine violence.

VI

People began to emerge on the winding, dusty road which led through the village. While the men conferred in low tones, one widow and then another appeared on the steep asphalt bathed in sunset. They moved, Sitt Chahrour among them, against the stark and broken contours of the houses. Who survived? Who was missing? Cries were heard. Whispers drifted down like bits of cinder from the balconies. Sunset spread its long shadows amid the eaves; the sandstone cross of the church was flushed with crimson.

Along the beach, down past the citrus groves, a breeze was stirring as the tide came in. At dusk, Camp survivors lingered along the sweet-scented streets overlooking the sea and westward sky. They spoke in subdued voices.

—And the youngest?
—Shot as well.
—Shh, she is near.
—Where's Hana'a?
—*Haram*.
—I think... she's helping Dr. Kamel.
—And Selman?
—Shot, according to Mahir, in Monteverdi woods.
—Who told Mahir?
—I won't believe it, until...

A few children trotted from one conversation to another, holding up small hands.

—Mamdoueh has brought relief supplies.
—The Red Crescent has asked everyone to report.
—It must be wrong, about Selman.

More people appeared, more survivors: haggard, limping on canes, seeming to gape at their new surroundings. The discussion extended up the street; adults repeating the brutal facts, unable to digest them. The children looked anxious, tugging on a skirt or jacket, unable to play.

VII

Mamdoueh stood in a group with Adnan, Abu Il-Rudub and the journalist Ligury. There was word of new troop infiltration in the South. Infantry and two armored brigades were making their way under air-cover toward Tyre. One massacre had hardly ended when another was in the offing. But would they come this far north? Forces of the Resistance were on full alert.

A man turned away, wanting only to sulk and let his hatred fester; but another grabbed his sleeve. A woman began wailing; she gave a burst of grief and her lips, the lower part of her face contorted. Selman was a good man, a kind one: he had cared so for her child, and all the children. She seemed to snort out her pain, but someone said:

—Do that at home, if you must.

Over a thousand killed at the outer checkpoints, and numerous leaders. Men and women relied upon in the hardest times, able to organize, teach and encourage, serving the rest: now they were gone. For them it was over. The people listened to the details, like first stars in the crimson sky.

—At what time, did you say?
—Aie.
—It will never end, this—this—
—Struggle.

Eastward the Chouf foothills had gone a deep mauve, dotted with shrubs. Hana'a stood by herself to one side of the building being used by the Red Crescent. No one's arm was long enough to reach her. She lingered, listening to the others, but it was all confusing to her. Their talk mingled with the seabreeze and rumbling of distant guns. To her left stood a low tamarisk with twilight in its branches. The leaves murmured and stirred with a grieving motion.

Hana'a Chahrour felt far from everyone, and strange, as she edged toward the rear of the building, and then walked slowly down a path. She thought of going to Dr. Kamel's new clinic and having a chat with Mayser; but then shied from that idea as well. Now the valley behind the town was a pool of darkness; there was a rustling of trees, shrubs, and the guns. She wasn't afraid. Nothing would scare her anymore, not even death. All the anxiety had been burnt out of her, leaving a sense of eternal homelessness, and grief for her brothers.

In the darkness she made out trees, an expanse of orchard on the steep slope. Stars twinkled, but cast no reflection in the deep pool. She heard the falling note of discussions, a male voice raised in anger. She could feel a tense current in the air, a kind of surging among them. In the orchard some bird had a raucous, near human cry: a nightingale. Its grief poured like a great truth over the wide attentive night of the valley.

She had survived because of her courage. The important thing about death was to learn from it, and grow stronger. Her only fear was of dying a little inside, in her breast where her brothers were buried, and the poison threatened to kill her too as they decomposed. She was going off by herself to suffer, which she knew was wrong. Someday she would make the enemy howl with pain and sorrow for having done this to her.

So hopeless, so ashamed, the nightingale. It waited for cover of night to erupt.

VIII

For Ligury, wind rising in the village streets carried a sense of destiny. He felt the emergent life of springtime as, an hour before, he watched the long coastal plantations seem to ruminate sunset beneath a vast amphitheater. He stayed on the edge of Mamdoueh's group with a foreboding. There were Fatah people, living further down, who came to join in the crowd and mull over the momentous details.

Kim Ligury wished he was a doctor: his sense of uselessness came over him as he stood in the restless breeze, by the maze of lanes and stuccoed structures, converted sheds where the Fedayeen slept. Where was a task for him? What was he good for? He felt thankful for the darkness, standing there, summing up his past live, his divorce, journalist assignments, observer status everywhere, with a shrug. If only, he thought, I had something concrete to give. I would stay here, with them. But what do I have?

Ligury remembered the evacuation from Bain Militaire, calculating how much time was left to him. His things were packed; he could run by and fetch them. The roads, the alerted checkpoints would be treacherous. Lebanon, if not the earth entire, was about to fall apart.

Around him people reached out to one another. They responded to the anguish; but Ligury stood self-consciously silent, alongside Mamdoueh.

—Stay with us if you wish. You will be my guest as long as you like.

Mamdoueh's smile began with his eyes, his doleful eyebrows. It took a moment descending to his long curved jawline.

Ligury nodded:

—There's someone I must see. A woman, at the Bain Militaire presently.

—Are you leaving?

—I haven't decided. My luggage is ready.

—One of us will drive you. It's very dangerous: anyone not accompanied will be held.

IX

The walls shook. Clearly the office was too small for such proceedings: cluttered with file cabinets, a gray metal desk and chairs. Five haggard men sat pondering a verdict.

Outside, a parade of tanks and M113s churned along Rue du Fleuve. A moment before, Abu Joseph had paused in his testimony as a squadron of planes came thundering up the coast toward Jbeil.

Giorgio glanced sidelong at Elie Madi and waited: he wore his old-boy grin, ready for anything. They both sat between the door and desk, so their knees nearly touched. Elie had his eye fixed on a jug of water at arm's length from his judges.

A lawyer named Nazo sat beside Abu Joseph: it was his desk routinely. On his right a political officer, Selim, whom Elie knew, seemed to brood over a recent manicure.

From the coastal regions northward there were salvos in tremendous overlapping series.

—You saw this action yourself? said Nazo, rubbing his eyes.

—No, said Abu Joseph. We arrived, and Kuzayli was gone, a bloody pulp.

He gestured. Elie rolled his eyes and said:

—*Akiid!* I threw the rocket at him.

—You wait, said the political officer, sharply. Don't speak unless you're addressed.

—May I have a swallow of water?

—Not now—do it again, you'll be held in contempt.

Elie tossed his head and grinned. He could feel Giorgio gloating to his left.

—About the desertion there can be no question. He was roaming round Ashrafiyeh in a jeep. During that period he was seen in Sioufi where Père Zaki heard him arguing in a shelter. The father radioed in a report, saying Madi's statements were bad for morale, and seditious. All the time he kept to himself, as if angry, and spurned even his mother and younger brother.

The Kataëb official's eyes, the sag of his face seemed like fatigue incarnate. He stared glumly at the prisoner. But the respected attorney, Nazo, punctuated Abu Joseph's words:

—*Sah!* I see.

Elie sat thinking: lash out at them and end this farce? Why not jump at the desk and scare them, make them understand what dogs they are? The good Giorgio might even shoot one of them. He's stupid enough to use his M-16 at this tea party. Then it would be all over.

Abu Joseph continued. His hard eyes and the dark beard which indented, strangely, in the shape of an antique helmet: his expression told the probable outcome of the hearing. He spoke to Selim in a clipped tone:

—As I said, he was spotted later at the hospital, along with a British journalist suspected of leftist leanings. And then he showed up at Burj, we know—on recon I think, probing for the enemy? All this before he fooled us again, playing the repentant sinner, getting himself reinstated. My mistake, I admit it, putting him on one of the Camp checkpoints.

—All false, Elie interrupted. You twist everything around.

—I repeat, said Selim: this isn't your time to speak.

Elie muttered:

—You'd make up any story—to get your way.

—Shut up, said Giorgio, calmly, and cocked.

—Strange plan, said Nazo, fingering his beard.

But he seemed beyond being very interested.

—At four a.m. yesterday, said Abu Joseph, we took him in custody and confiscated the jeep.

—Did he resist? said Nazo.

—No; or, he may have.

—In truth, said Selim, we're dealing with a saboteur.

—No, said Abu Joseph. It's more than that. It's ideological.

X

Thirst was rubbing against his ribs like sandpaper. Each breath was intolerable, and he thought of lunging for the *jarra,* the water pitcher on the desk. But he also felt a need not to humiliate himself, and this seemed to make the thirst even more terrible.

While the doctoral Nazo discussed a point of law with the Party official, annoying him with a quiddity no doubt, Giorgio eyed the water as well. The mercenary fidgeted and made his chair creak alongside the prisoner. Behind the desk were three windows, side by side, and light drifted in above two filing cabinets, from the north. It ringed the drinking pitcher on the way to Elie Madi's face.

Selim said wearily:

—*Tayyeb:* let's hear what he has to say.

Selim paused a moment, phrasing a question.

—Madi, what were you trying to accomplish in that jeep? What were you thinking about when you went AWOL?

—Sir, he croaked, I would tell you but I'm very thirsty.

—The water's for us, said the Politburo member, whose brow was prominent, like an unctuous bull. You don't really seem to realize what's at stake here.

Elie felt a spasm of anger:

—I realize, but I haven't had a drink today, or yesterday. Is it justice, if I'm too weak to plead my case?

Selim:

—Across Ashrafiyeh, in Jounieh, Bikfaya and the mountain towns, our people are enduring. You think you're special? They are heroic; they don't crack under pressure. Loyal, and worth struggling for, worth saving. So you see, we mean to save ourselves together, and the water is for this purpose alone. I wonder if a single drop should be wasted on a traitor.

His voice trembled slightly. Through the windows, beyond the file cabinets Elie saw the writing on a wall: *Arab Equals* . . . a smudge. He half smiled, as if distracted; he pointed a finger past his three judges. Elie's sallow face showed the days of dehydration; his almond eyes were ringed with shadow. Features tense, accentuated with grime and perspiration, he seemed aglow in the daylight from the window.

Abu Joseph glanced back over his shoulder, then said:

—Act self-righteous, petit salaud? Care to condemn yourself? Just say so. We could do without all this bother.

Often mentioned in *Le Réveil,* Selim was in his mid-fifties with a distinguished air. His chest bulged on the silk shirt he wore, beneath an expensive suit; his graying hair was sparse but combed back neatly in a wave. He seemed weary of the esteemed Nazo's pedantic observations, among other things.

—Tell us what you were doing in the jeep.

—I rode around. I brought water.

—And then?

—I saw my girlfriend; also my family in Sioufi, in the shelter. I was looking for something, I don't even know what.

Elie shrugged. Abu Joseph sat in an indignant silence, looking stoical in his patriotism. In this matter, why wasn't his own say enough? Why drag out this bullshit trial? Why let Madi insult both the Party and their integrity? It was rather foolish to consult traitors in the appraising of their own guilt, while other things needed tending.

—What then?

—I stayed in the shelter. Père Zaki was there, as you said; though I didn't do, or say, any of what he claims. Later, I went to the hospital.

—Why?

The one word seemed to cost Selim quite an effort, as if asking a question were like lifting a great weight. Elie stared at the water.

—I don't know. I was tired. We had taken Sylvie Helou there, myself and the journalist, Ligury. You know her: she went crazy. She was carrying on in the shelter, discouraging people. They wanted her out, so we took her. Before that I had brought them water.

—And the reporter?

—I haven't seen him since. He seemed confused, a liberal if anything. I was assigned to him a few weeks ago, so he phoned from the other side, when it started this time. There was a blond woman with him: I think you met her.

Elie grinned at Abu Joseph.

—What did you show him?

—We were at the Press Bureau; I took them around Ashrafiyeh, the shelter in Sioufi. Ask him (pointing at Sakr): he spent some time, I believe, with Ligury's companion.

Nazo and Selim shared a glance. Abu Joseph grimaced, and his silence was like a death-sentence.

—What did you tell him?

—Nothing, just the usual. He heard all he wanted in the shelter.

—What does that mean? Heard what?

Elie sneered at the water: it was futile, a lost cause. He said, meeting Selim's eye:

—That our leaders are glib hypocrites. That they started this whole thing, though denying, in order to provoke an invasion.
—Why would we—?
—To liquidate the Camp, and our enemies; take over West Beirut. But instead, we lost our leader.

XI

Brief conference. The two at the desk whispered, with Nazo showing more zeal, more brio in his arguments. Abu Joseph caught Giorgio's eye as if to say: what is the point of this? Dammit, we've got other work... Past the wall with its graffitti Elie could see, in the distance, a patch of blue beyond a grassy field. Karantina? Beirut Port. There was something dark, obtruding on the left like a barrier: the east wharf of the harbor.
—Who assigned you to this journalist?
—The Press Bureau: call them, they'll tell you.
—So you ushered a leftist all over Ashrafiyeh in your spare time.
—I said a liberal, and more open-minded than some I know.
Elie gave a little jolt; now his anger was on the march. First their insinuations; Abu Joseph's gaze, as if insulted by the mere idea of an inquiry, itching to handle things his own more expeditive way;—then their disregard of the facts began stirring his rage even despite the thirst. He stammered something at them, aware they wanted him to speak his piece, and betray himself. He knew that, but his fury was hard to control:
—What are you saying? I couldn't be trusted no doubt. Listen, you: my father and elder brother are lying in their graves, they died for Lebanon; while you sit here debating. Damn all of you. I curse you, do you hear? I spent six months on the front in Ein Rummaneh; I fought in Burj another ten. I was at Tel ez-Zaater during the siege, but where were you? In your command posts. Oh, sure, I know this bloodaholic here, this *Sakr* was at Tel ez-Zaater as well, making a great spectacle of himself. He was at Dbayyeh, and other places, each time he saw an opportunity—for—
Elie broke off. His voice shot up in a whine before cracking, which made the others smile, except Abu Joseph. Elie glared with hatred at the three men sitting in judgment before him.
They wanted something unstated from this court-martial. What? A confession, some piece of information, an idea of how far the rot

was spreading. Behind a mask of fatigue the Party official, Selim, waited, listening to Madi's words as if stalking an admission.

Abu Joseph had squirmed visibly, a beam in his eye with the allusion to his trysts with Morgan. He sat in silence, returning tenfold the traitor's contempt; at one stage he pointed his finger at him and shook it. But the motives of the two Phalangist *responsables* were less than clear, and not so important to Elie. He knew death was Sakr's hobbyhorse; Sakr could hardly wait to hear the verdict, and have it carried out.

Giorgio seemed to get a kick from the prisoner's sudden outburst. Such a sideshow was balm to Giorgio's gnawing boredom; he was a trooper who just followed orders while keen on any kind of joyride, something to talk and joke about in barracks. With equal gusto he would kill, dance to disco, or work on his modified car.

—This correspondent, he went back across?

Elie nodded.

—Where, exactly?

—Through Sodeco. We found him a cab after reporting to the War Council. But the blond woman stayed on for a chat, didn't she Sakr?

—This Ligury's at the Commodore?

—No, he has his own apartment, in Hamra.

Selim paused in his line of questioning.

XII

Nazo chimed in with a kind of summation:

—A glutton for blood: is this your phrase? You've forgotten a few facts, my friend. Duly recorded ones, and historical. We welcomed the refugees here, we recognized their cause; but they abused the privilege. They were our guests, but they yearned to play host, and began committing many crimes against the Maronites. In early '76 their intentions came out in the open: they went on the offensive. But you conveniently forget such things.

Elie shook his head:

—All my life, since I can remember... Men with minds like yours, telling me stupid things. My father was no different; he discouraged me from questioning, until I felt unworthy. And I was too insecure to learn anything, taking the line of least resistance. But now thanks to this great warrior, this guardian of civilization, Sakr, I've seen through your lies. The reality stands before me, and it hurts to look. You may be brave in battle, but your minds are cowardly—it isn't a sea of Arabs which surrounds you, it's the truth.

Nazo countered, ever pugnacious, his sentences like jabs:

—Your memory is too short. And your intelligence small, so you're unaware of the facts. The Arab cause, the *oumma* which blends their hearts as one: is it unknown to you? They have entered our towns and villages with the cry of *al-Jihad!* on their lips. And apparently you haven't heard, my little friend, that the *Islamic Bomb* is fast becoming a reality.

Elie's face was flushed. For a moment Selim had been looking at him almost with respect, at least a willingness to listen. Elie said:

—And what of us? From here I can see Karantina—you call that a welcome? You call that "our hospitality" which they abused? But who were "they" in this case? They were mostly Lebanese, like ourselves, at Karantina. Since I can remember, our leaders asked us to believe this one thing: every kind of pressure, they will use, getting us to—

Nazo gave a leer; it almost spoiled his composure, like a grease spot on his leisure suit.

—We've no need to force anyone to believe. The choice is simple: be human, or an animal. Horche Barada was sufficient cause to believe; but you've forgotten the desecration of our cemetery there. How they strewed the remains through the town, as if telling us something very specific. No, the Maronite people hardly needs any brainwashing, I tell you. Such realities date from 1860, and before; they're clear enough by now.

Elie:

—Realities which our leaders went at least halfway in provoking! Always claiming we took in the refugees, and espoused their cause. Do you call the Camp espousing their cause? You wouldn't, if you had to live in it! Or the way our business community made sure to kill any reforms—no, man, our greed came first. No citizenship for the refugees! Ah, they posed a threat to Maronite privilege, and the big census lie. So we rounded them up in camps, and denied them any real means to further that cause we were "espousing" with words, only.

Elie bowed his head and coughed. Not Nazo, or Abu Joseph, but the Politburo official seemed to take a certain morose gratification from the debate. Selim:

—The Lebanese government controlled the camps.

—*Akiid!* said Elie, thousands of people in the gutter while we refused to reform our system! We gave them lip-service instead of citizenship.

—They didn't want it.

—Hm, we did everything in our power against them.

—You are naive, said Selim.

—I think, said Nazo, that Madi's still rebelling against his father.

—I'm tired of being lied to. These refugees—what are they to me? I just want the truth for once.

—You suppose they wouldn't trade places with us? Take my home in Jounieh, slob. Oh, I prefer the idealism of camp life.

Elie Madi had been growing more and more agitated.

Now he shouted:

—Stop lying! You want me to hate them so I'll fight them for you! So you can maintain your little power at all costs—ah! the fat man was right after all, Hrawey had it correctly the first time. I've been fed your lies so long I need to vomit them up at long last, if it means my life as well. I killed men because of them. I fought my best for you, and believe me (Elie whined) I was brave. Anyone can tell you whether Madi was courageous, and devoted; even while you, the so-called leaders, made wrong decisions and took another step and another, along with so-called friends who are more powerful and know so well to use us. We let them come in, and now look what they—

—You're raving, said Selim.

—Yes, I've heard how they talked about it, everyone knows this secret. Do you think we're all fools? Their endless schemes were too transparent, coveting their neighbor's river ... Bunch of geniuses, like you—why it was probably *they* who today—

—I think this will suffice, said Selim.

Abu Joseph smirked. Giorgio sat amused as Elie appeared almost out of control, ranting, stuttering:

—Damn you, it won't! Let me finish! For years we provoked—

—Ah but they—

—I never criticized because it was my people; it was the Maronite cause, and together live or die. I believed! I gave myself! And all the while we needed criticism; oh, we were the ones ... It made us evil to be so wrong, so paranoid in defence of our privileges. And everywhere the camps, in front of our eyes, damning; we built a wall to hide them from tourists, we tried to clean them, wipe them out like our guilt! We actually needed a civil war, so we could die as well, some of us, for the sake of our hatred! We were hating one another just like Hrawey said, before Père Zaki came along and broke him down too, shut him up. We detested one another but it was taboo to criticize! So people stopped trying. And that's when I began hating you above all others, more even than the enemy, you hypocrite leaders. You used that hatred, our suffering; you used it to control us. No matter whether it was Arab, Muslim, even Christian—just as long as it was the *other*, someone besides ourselves. Ensuring us, you, from criticism! Oh, that's how you always pin your labels on people.

—Novel ideas, said Selim, ever circumspect.

Nazo whispered something in Abu Joseph's ear, and they grinned together. Elie's speech seemed to fall of its own weight in the small room, and die.

During a brief silence he frowned at his three accusers. Then he said, in a hoarse whisper, to himself:

—Finally.

The room grew quiet a moment. Voices, a command from down the hall. A *houn* anti-tank could be heard from the direction of the bridges. Giorgio changed position, making the chair seem to plead beneath his bulk. Long shadows merged with a milky light across the acres of Karantina campsite.

—In the end, said Selim, with a weary pathos, we can only defend ourselves. Never mind the circumstances. The idealistic, in this world, are doomed to perish. The truth is, that idealism lacks necessity, a basis in social relations; it's a juvenile phase. But let's take five minutes and discuss all this together. Escort the prisoner outside, please.

Giorgio cuffed Elie's head, with a chortle.

—Tayyeb, said Nazo.

—Now I think, said Selim, glimpsing his watch, it is time to reach a decision.

XIII

—The young man claims he has seen combat action. Would he be so good as to say where?

Elie's head lolled to one side; he frowned at the water-pitcher.

—Well?

He threw up a hand:

—I told you already; you weren't listening. Convict me, but no more answers until I get water.

—Our problem, said the astute Nazo, is that you will try to take it all. That could be messy.

—Christ! Just pour some in a cup for me.

—There are no cups. We drink from the same *jarra* or we don't drink. Anyway this one is not for prisoners.

—Stupid! Then shove your questions up your ass.

—It seems you want to die, said Selim, demure. That would follow from your statements.

—I want to tell you, Elie croaked, head on his chest, that you have no right.

—Where did he see combat?

—He's right, said Abu Joseph, Ein Rummaneh, Burj sector.

—Tell them, asshole, did I further the cause?

—Later, at Tel ez-Zaater—

—His performance? said Selim.

—I admit, in the early months of the war he caught on quicker than others. But then he changed; he should have been a medic. I saw him go after two Tanzime fighters, young ones, in that jeep when there was curtain fire. He saved them; but, let us say, after Tel ez-Zaater he wasn't much use anymore. Somehow he kept his rank, as well as our respect, for awhile.

When Abu Joseph spoke to a superior, his tone was muted.

—And then?

—Well, at the Camp evacuation Madi was a scandal. You can believe I wasn't on hand to stop it, I was only told later. Really, the shame prevented me from raising a stink; I had put him there, I was responsible. Plus in the atmosphere of victory . . .

—What happened?

—He gave over an important checkpoint to the enemy. For an hour he allowed dozens, maybe hundreds to pass through unquestioned. Known Fedayeen, leaders including the doctor Kamel Rehanna (who never showed us such mercy)—they all escaped thanks solely to Madi, and are regrouping now of course. It could only have happened in such chaos. Later, after Kuzayli's death he was arrested.

Abu Joseph fixed the accused with his boxer's stare.
Selim:
—Madi, what do you say to that?
—You're not my judge, that's what. You need judging yourselves—get your cherry broken, moral virgins.
Elie gave a bizarre laughter.
—Gentlemen? said Selim, about to rise.
—Vierge folles! But you have to have a strong nose . . . ha! ha! ha!
—Il délire.
—Nothing like you will someday.
With a first sign of impatience Selim said to his colleagues:
—Do you both feel, as I do, on the basis of these depositions—
Elie Madi erupted, laughing:
—Bloody sheets! Look, in the windows of Ashrafiyeh!
—Take him out again, yallah.
Elie gave a piercing laughter:
—Look at yourselves, what do you call it?
—Prisoner, rise.
—Fuck you, kel'b.
Giorgio shoved him outside.

XIV

Before long they were called back inside the office, and Giorgio gave Elie a playful kick in passing, which sent him to his knees before the desk.

Selim saw this and frowned. When the two had reassumed their place he spoke:
—Madi, you leave us no choice: the realities of our world have never implied a choice of destinies. Yes, if you will, our fate is a virgin, and her name is Mary. We do believe in her; we aren't ashamed of it . . . On the other hand we've had to protect our interests. We worked hard, our parents worked their lives long for these interests.

And they are an honor to us, to Lebanon. Large portions of our privilege, as you term it, have been destroyed; no doubt the enemy thinks this is his way to a better future, one which is communist, totalitarian . . . Now, Madi, concerning your actions. Your wayward acts have run counter to the security of your own people. In time of crisis you doubted—at best! It seems you even had an influence on the course of recent events. And we find this makes you a traitor to the Party. It wouldn't surprise me if you were a spy, with this foreign correspondent as contact. You have a weakness for the refugees; although they have sown discord across our land.

—Listen to the liar.

Elie muffled a giggle.

—Yes, said Sakr, listen. And you'd better shut up.

—I will, friend. How was the blond, a good lay?

Elie smirked. Giorgio turned and rapped him across the mouth with his gloved hand. It jerked Elie's face to one side: blood drooled on his chin.

—I'm nearly finished, said the Politburo official, pausing to reflect. These proceedings are all but concluded, but just a word more. The worst sin in wartime is to question an order. You've done that again and again. We're fighting for our lives here, our existence as a people, yet you went against us. Now you won't do it any longer; really, you'll say nothing further. You have said only too much, Elie Madi, already. Therefore may God have mercy on your soul, because we in all conscience cannot.

He ended in a brusque tone, seeming a bit emotional. Selim stood up resolutely, his chair scraping, and perhaps there was something tragic in his movements, as he cast a soulful glance at the pitiful prisoner.

Then he raised the water-pitcher in one hand before leaving; he tilted back his greying head and swallowed the jet of liquid for a few seconds.

Selim stepped in front of the desk and held the *jarra* out to Elie, whose reaction was to clutch it convulsively with his bound hands.

But something came over him; he leaned back to drink but then paused, stared at the others and met their gazes, slowly, one by one.

Abruptly he tossed down the pitcher which exploded, splattering across the floor.

Glass jumped and splintered at their feet; the precious liquid ran off, as Nazo and the urbane official lurched backward.

Hilarious, Elie stared at them in silence, challenging their gaze. But Giorgio bent forward and struck him hard with the gunbarrel, knocking him to his knees, bathing his face in a sort of pink halo.

From the floor Elie still faced them, no longer laughing.

XV

—It is done, thought Morgan, on her third drink, and it is done.

Three men entered Ydlibbi's nightclub, approaching the bar. One glanced over at Morgan, who might have been a whore on time for a tryst. After serving them, Camille Ydlibbi moved to the back end of his counter and the panel of switches. Suddenly a light singled out Morgan's table, her blond hair and blouse. It shot toward the rear, and the slide projections started up: the sun dipped its finger in a tall drink, beside a turquoise pool. Snow-capped Mt. Sannine. Landscaping, jasmine and honeysuckle, of A.U.B. A once elegant cafe society along Hamra.

Joyous images, but the effect was elegiac—*Khayseran* restaurant, looking out on a purple beach at sunset. Gay convives in a mist of arak; people congratulating themselves on being a species... I'm not one of them, she thought, exulting. It is done, the response to follow—the FROGs, MD-660s, Gabriel and the greatest show on earth. Man writes suicide at the end of his epic résumé.

She remembered, during a therapy session in Tel Aviv, throwing out hints of an assassination she carried off personally, two years earlier. She wanted to mystify the smug psychiatrist, Bergland, and make him pay with the currency that counts.

XVI

In the dull blinking light she watched another man enter— Gaudenti. He came in alone and took a table; not seeing her as his eyes adjusted, placing his elegant portmanteau on a chair alongside. They had crossed paths at the Commodore, these past few days, during which he seemed particularly busy. Both were waiting for the evacuation of foreign nationals; and for an instant Morgan devoured the rich, respectable industrialist with her eyes. —Is done, is done... Her heart beat with a voluptuous sense of vindication, of impending freedom. Getting away had not been as easy as she hoped; unlike other times it required patience, and she balked at the need for self-control, waiting for the U.S. Embassy to arrange things at Bain Militaire.

Morgan rose abruptly; she took her handbag and crossed the room.

—Mind if I join you?

Gaudenti stood graciously, arms spread wide as if to rearrange the world.

—So, you are leaving Lebanon?

The three men at the bar looked on as Morgan installed herself, and Gaudenti beckoned for drinks.

He tried to stimulate conversation, but she seemed distracted. She was musing over something; or else, he thought, on some tranquilizing drug?

—Anything wrong?

—No, it's just—she rose, glimpsing the door. Listen, I need to see someone, in the neighborhood.

—Are you sure? There's danger.

—I know. In an hour I'll be back, maybe a bit longer. I'm going to save my place with you, alright? We'll catch a cab back to the Commodore, and leave together. You don't mind waiting?

—Certainly not, said Gaudenti; but really I—

—Just sit here. Be a good boy now, buon fanciullo.

Morgan pursed her lips and smiled at him.

—It's bad out there. Shouldn't I accompany you?

—No need. Wait for me until eight, at the latest. Leave word with Ydlibbi if you have to go before I return. This is just an errand; I promised someone.

She took up her purse, turning away. Camille and the three men considered her, foreheads reflecting a sinister green, as she passed the bar with an insecure smile. No question about it, she was high on something.

XVII

Again Morgan met the gray powdery scene strewn with corpses. Now the guns were deafening, and she put a finger in each ear. In Burj a Dushka-500 pumped its steady flow of dum-dum bullets from three cartridges. Across the water smoke rose from Christian towns and villages north of the Casino. At dusk the sun shone a smoldering orange off windows in the mountains beyond Zalke and Jounieh Bay.

She hugged the wall, eyeing the horrendous bodies. They stank. Her heart pounded: I did it, I'm the one. Lingering a moment, as if needing a final push, she slipped in the doorway of *Port Egypt* and saw no sign of the receptionist, with her monumental nightgown, straps and pink bulge. Inside, the roar was muffled to a tam-tam. Further along there was a desk with a customer's bell, which she tapped. The interior glowed with the red shade of a kerosene lamp; there were two divans, a love seat of tufted green velvet and several armchairs. The tawdriness, the plaster smudged and fissured, close air scented with cheap perfume: such classic signs excited Morgan, on the verge of a long deliberated act.

She drew back, looking almost offended, as one of the women appeared. And then another: both of them huge as cathedrals, owing their shape to a similar system of flying buttresses. In the lamplight the first was seductive: her face smooth, her gaze a bay of shadow in purplish mascara, with a dash of eyeliner over swollen eyebrows. Morgan felt her deepest entrails on display at the massive awful sight of them, in the excitement of her last hours in Lebanon. A night of apocalypse was in the offing; but the Middle East might go up in flames before these valiant workers took a pause. Her desire mounted as she felt on the verge of some sacred rite, some relinquishment of will, for once. The drinks at Ydlibbi's had made her ready; still she felt reluctant to inspect too closely these objects of her profound affinity.

The first said, in Arabic:

—Your pleasure?

Morgan put a finger to her lips; and the two of them, mimicking her, grinned and did the same. She made a sign.

—Both at once?

She reached out, touching the first woman's negligee at the hip. She thought: here and now. She gave a small sigh, and by now her desire was visible, her lust.

—Where?

She glanced past them. But the first, putting index to palm, smiling:

—Two hundred.

Morgan took three bills from her purse. The women nodded gratefully, and she looked away. At any instant the illusion, most precious of all things, could be ruined.

They went through a door, and led her behind a curtain. A wide mattress was spread there. Now the perfume smelled overripe, like something rotting. Were there others behind the curtain? Did the low door open on a prospect of humanity in its most candid postures? Were sinners whipped up to a greater ecstasy, by Satan's baton?

She stared at the two women, who waited, unsure but game for anything at that price. She leaned forward and kissed the breast of the first; she began caressing her shoulders, long exaggerated curves. Morgan took a dimpled hand to her lips and kissed the gaudy rings, groaning as if something big in her were seeking release. She played with the soft hand like a doll, and gave it a slapping movement against her cheek; and the other understood, and slapped her. She cried out, a sort of whining protest; again the other slapped.

—Ah!

She slipped off her blouse and brassiere, bruising her breasts on the other's knees and kissing her fatty hand, which was rough and moist, trembling slightly.

—Harder.

The woman gave her cheek a glancing blow while Morgan struggled to free herself from the rest of her clothes.

—Take my hair. Like this—

The first did as told. She hurt Morgan, and yanked her face to her thighs, by the hair. Both prostitutes were on the verge of laughter, but excited as well, perhaps, exchanging glances. The first struck Morgan who whimpered, stung with pleasure, outraged and breathlessly relieved, as if a big growth of pain in her were being massaged, soothed. She pleaded for more, her voice atremble.

—Please! . . . no!

It was like life in a seclusion ward. One woman stooped, gathering up her nightgown, unveiling her legs. She exposed her undulous flesh and its shadows seemed to drift outward, enveloping Morgan. Her pubic hair was perfumed and tipped with henna.

Brutally, getting in the spirit now, she pulled Morgan's blond head closer, tilting it back:

—Tiftah!

Open! . . . A hard slap, whine of outrage. Now wider!

She was beneath her, given up to her, utterly free—without a choice anymore.

—Please . . . Like an infant sobbing, pleading—ah!

PART SEVEN

I

The rain had ceased its patter on the boarded windows. A gray twilight filtered through on the half dozen men bound hand and foot like bales of hay. Several moaned beneath their breathing like old Bedu women; one was gagged to prevent his incessant cries for water. Muffled sounds; gurgling, sucking moisture from the rope. A thin gray light seeped through the crevices. The early morning hours had been tense with sporadic firing, as Ashrafiyeh survived its fourth night of constant shelling.

—Xubz!

Giorgio peeped in:

—Ma fi.

No bread.

No water.

No cigarettes.

Sighs... Artillery raging up the coast north of Jbeil. At midmorning the blasts mingled with moaning of prisoners.

—Alla-ah.

Tanks, APCs filed along Rue Gouraud; the horizon grumbled, southward, with aviation. Enemy anti-aircraft would squall across the city if a squadron of jets shrieked over.

Later, a boy brought water. Giorgio chuckled as a few drops splashed in their faces, rather than taking time to let them drink, which was messy.

A gush of sunshine lit the boarded casements.

—Shemis.

Elie looked up: warmth, daylight flowed into their dungeon. The rain had stopped.

II

Giorgio's boots moved past the door.

Giddy with exhaustion, Elie Madi thought:

—I could still turn back . . . It isn't too late, they would take me—even after I dropped the pitcher? I've fought for them: if I volunteered for a suicide mission, and squared accounts? There's always time to be saved; by God maybe, but by men? If I said: Please, Abu Joseph, put me in the front, send me on a mission and I'll prove my loyalty. Eh, and Sakr would answer: Too late, scum. We're not in any great need of traitors today; you can't be saved. And besides, you said things about me for which there *is* no forgiveness. Now die without honor, unblessed and alone.

Elie had to move and change positions; he lay on his left hip which was numb, but a pain stabbed his lower back whenever he turned. The idea of Sakr revived his anger, but dimly; his revolt was weakening, his fear was changed to a physical sinking, and mood of defeat. Elie tried not to breathe, not to prolong the dry malodorous sense of himself going under . . . —Still, he thought, they are people, *my* people and they need to be protected. I could catch Giorgio's replacement when he comes by, and tell him that. Give me another chance. I realize my error. My thoughts, all my doubts on the justice of our cause: I see how little they really mean, to us . . . Because it's life that matters, our life together. Why sacrifice myself for some vague idea? Why lose out because of a few treacherous words? No, you must live, and accept the compromises . . . Know your limits: stay where God has placed you. Don't get too excited even about the killing, let alone lying; when this counts for so much less than the rest . . . We aren't gods, we are only people trying to make our way in life and survive. Some mean more to us than others; those others mean more to their own, than we ever could. Why? Because God said so. He dictated it: man is fallen, and that's the law. So why disturb His plan? Why think up new schemes for the universe, when it shows no interest in being tinkered with? It will snap back at you if you try! What is your still small voice, in a debate with eternity? Yes, it's right that you be punished for your pride, and presumptuous words during the court-martial.

Elie lay on the concrete and moaned with the others. A Syrian called on Allah beneath each breath as his peasant grandmother used to do over the village stove. During the long night they hadn't been aware of a Phalangist prisoner among them.

—Kel'b! snapped Giorgio, highly disgusted with guard duty.

III

—When the guard changes, I'll take my chance.

But the effort to turn himself seemed hopeless. He wouldn't know when Giorgio left; and then lose his last chance to explain—it would be too late. Does anyone care what I do? Does anything matter? Yes, survival. If I say alright, if I call in this guard, raising a commotion about the thirst and the bindings which are too tight, if I call out and tell him, when he comes, that I repent and beg for survival: then I do it for myself, and nobody else. Whether he kicks me or sets me free with his blessing, it is not for others, not my family, not Jessie. They told me what interests them; their way of seeing things is the right way, no doubt... What am I doing here? for whose sake am I squirming on the floor? For the Party? For honor? The people I thought closest to me, the ones I loved? Did they care?

Elie managed to turn back toward the door, rapping his neighbor on the shoulder as he rolled over.

—Must be noontime, said the other.

Their eyes met, haggard, insufferable.

—Later.

One whispered:

—I can't move my fingers. No life in them.

—Keep pressing and rubbing.

—It's too tight, he said, a quiver in his voice. I'm going to lose my hands.

Giorgio peered in at them. Now he wore the black hood, which meant somebody might not have to die. When he puffed his cigarette, smoke came out the eye-holes in rings.

Elie cleared his throat and said:

—Why not loosen his hands? Look, they're blue.

—Giving me orders?

—Have pity.

—Madi, they told me to lay off, or I'd make a nice hole in you and let some shit out.

—You're the shithead.

The others stared in disbelief, even more immobile than before. The man rubbing his hands came to a pause, as if wanting no part of this maniac, returning Giorgio's ominous gaze.

—Not much longer now, Madi. You're fucked.

A traitor Phalangist? Informer planted among them?

Elie's presence infected the room like the slop-bucket.

IV

He lay squinting up at the door; there were instants when he felt so eager to save himself, he could hardly contain it. He would put things right after all the confusion. In fact what had he done wrong? What could be proven? This time the guard was a militiaman doing his chore, no crazy mercenary like Giorgio.

Elie had the curious idea his wracking thirst was pointless, and an error. All this punishment to his body, like a nightmarish journey... In a minute order would be restored. Soon a ceasefire would take hold, and life would go on as before. In cleaning up Ashrafiyeh there would be a chance for his own rehabilitation; he might dedicate himself to helping the victims.

No wonder everyone had been shocked by his attitude: Maronites were no more privileged than other people, they carried life and death around inside them, like everyone else. Those who worked hardest, earned most: so why shouldn't they be on top of things. France was a great nation, its legacy counted in Lebanon. Leftists were utopian.

The moment had come, but he waited in vain for a word with Giorgio's replacement. The prisoners made little sounds, gestating the misery. Tied up, their bodies on fire, they required no watch. Yes, he could forgive, it was possible. In a way they were responsible for his situation, Jessica, his mother and father, the Party; but he was ready to forgive them, if they were wrong. Maybe no one was right or wrong. And what was the point of dying? Die for others? When you were dead there were no others.

The hostage on his right emitted a muddied stream of words, delirious. He mentioned mother, father, a village called Ghabasiya... He regurgitated his childhood in broken phrases, adding to the fear in the room.

Elie rolled back on his other side, facing away from the door. He too began retreating into his memories, which had a strange regressive poignancy.

At one point the new guard did pass by.

His footsteps went unheard beneath the din of guns.

V

In childhood—a world separated by war; but clear in his vision now, for the first time in years—he always got his way by tagging after his mother; he whined and begged, while she rolled her eyes as if nothing would ever surprise her again. He pestered her in the kitchen, spilling something on purpose.

She stood by him when he was young, since Elie got in trouble more than other boys. As he grew and matured she began to admire him, and took his side in family disputes against his father. Elie was outspoken, and it aggravated matters at times.

But there was one thing she could never abide, namely his nose-bleeds. These were Nile River affairs, with long gory clots. When the blood stopped he would sneeze, or vomit from all he had swallowed; and the jolt started it flowing again. And on into the night. His mother avoided him in those times; he went in his room and handled it alone.

And then the fear came, and more nausea; he felt like crying. He was alone with the red enemy; but after awhile he took himself in hand, squeezing the bridge of his nose very tightly, rubbing his forehead with a cold washcloth.

Elie's father arrived home from work in a sour mood. He was a history teacher in the Government High School, in Ashrafiyeh. He stemmed from Antelias. For fifteen years, before his father's death, the Madis lived in a spacious residence in Hazmieh with two cars, a housemaid, a high-ceiling'd living room where each year he helped decorate a Christmas tree taller than his friends'. There was a long mantel with a row of family portraits, a ticking clock.

At night Elie dreamed there were lions and tigers roaming through the house: they had rainbows in their sleek coats of fur. It stayed on the verge of nightmare, as the wild animals showed a subtle hostility, but never growled, gliding by in silence. He was alone to deal with them, and terribly afraid.

When Elie came home in the afternoon his mother leaned from the kitchen window:

—Careful of the ivy!

When his father came in there were disputes, especially in winter, since Elie played great matches with a toy balloon in the living room. He used the hearth at one end, its firescreen at the other for opposing goals. The mantelpiece was a highly partisan grandstand with its row of dour portraits, as he called out the players' names, goal-kicked, dove for headers and back-passed, collided with an opposing fullback on a breakaway. He made a free kick on goal, as cinders flew like confetti over the Persian carpet.

—I told you *never* to play in here.

Deep voice of disapproval. It worked in high school history classes, but this was different: Elie was no longer very intimidated. Besides, never was a long time off, and it didn't include tomorrow.

No doubt it was this "never" plus his mother's backing which kept Elie Madi a world-class daydreamer.

VI

During the events of 1958 he had been a child; the sight of U. S. troops on Lebanese soil had made him cheer. In years following, the turmoil didn't interest him much either; though his friends picked up the tools of war and joined in maneuvers with a gusto. Elie went his own way, unconsciously resisting the pressure to conform. Sports were a refuge, or he went beach-bumming at Aqua Marina. He read dime novels and went to a lot of movies. He found Jessica.

In the early '70s, in the aftermath of the October War there were strikes and street demonstrations: his participation became unavoidable. In those days life was a continuous debate.

At first he resented politics, disagreeing with everyone from instinct; it all seemed a kind of conspiracy. Life was being twisted or controlled in some ulterior way. He sensed this without expressing it amid the conformity of the times. Instead, he grumbled over something trivial... People didn't seem to like him really, or one another for that matter. They were interested in other things, money, social standing. But he always had a strong sense of himself; he wasn't afraid to disagree. He thought most people didn't really like themselves; they made a strong show to the contrary, but the truth came peeping out when they least expected.

Since the outbreak of civil war in '75 he had felt somehow like an exile. Despite himself he had fallen from objective life, as he called it; fallen from *things,* in some sense, things in themselves. The war was a sort of pantomime to him: you over there, me over here, now shoot. How clearly he saw it all: politics had risen up and overthrown life. You could die or be maimed for ever in the deafening pantomime; but go along with the others, or you were in trouble. Any attempt at serious discussion was a disaster. Even sports were infected by it all, and manipulated in Camille Chamoun Stadium.

He was sixteen years old before he saw one of the refugee camps at first hand. On a lark, one afternoon, he and a car load of friends drove through Mazlakh making childish remarks, and laughing. Many could still love Lebanon and sympathize, in their way, with her sorrows; but now, lying bound hand and foot on a cement floor, trembling with dehydration and cold: now he saw the truth in full. There was no more love to nourish the old illusions. In reality Lebanon was too narrow, in its heart, and too exhausted for hope. Who would ever call so much wrongness to account? The idea of order, amid so much injustice, was like a desert mirage. Cain came into his own and administered the earth, condemning everyone else to wander in sorrow. And death was the endless itinerary. You might seek to return home, to the place where the world seemed whole, and life was in fact a miracle. You might look for it over and over, in memories of childhood, in love for another person, in sleep. But you would be rejected, and shot back out again, into the conspiracy of politics. Hazmieh, Ein Rummaneh, Burj, Tel ez-Zaater: these were the places where his life had run off in the sand.

Since puberty Elie had been angry, hardly aware of this fact, much less understanding why. Unclear, in abeyance, the anger was yet so deep in him. In early summer of '75 he went across town, one night, to join in the war. Children's voices no longer counted, and the birds were chirping a different tune. In the eighteen months that followed he killed seven men in instances allowing confirmation; he saw them fall, he expended an insurance round, if they were exposed. Two were clearly civilians.

Fight one must. But when the real enemy was . . . within?

Suddenly, he cried out loud, stark in the babbling pathos of the War Council room. It caused his pitiful neighbor to lay quiet a moment. Now Elie would never turn back over: never plead with the guard for another hearing, never change his mind, this time, or repent!

Or forgive them . . .

Or forgive himself.

For an instant he erupted, gasping. He opened his eyes, gazing at a bright tracery round the casements—*kishick,* food . . . *Lebneh* and dark olives . . . As the light faded, once again, he thought of Jessica.

Haram! He had drawn his conclusions too late. Maybe it was always too late, for them.

He had done his fighting on the wrong (this one, at least, he knew) side . . .

Never!

VII

The long wait, the misery—hostage roulette. Being kept alive as human barter . . . Each heartbeat was a muffled drum; each breath a step away from hope; their little ploys, seeking a crumb of sympathy, all went to waste with the changing of the guards. But one after another, at mid-afternoon, the prisoners muttered and tried to impress this new guard with the fact of their humanity.

—I'm a foot soldier. I was drafted, my family's homestead is in the east of Syria, near Mari, on the Euphrates.

The guard looked in glumly.

—I've done nothing to anyone, said another, a Chi'ite. But I must suffer. *Ma'shalla!* I wish all men well, including Lebanese Christians who have been a light, and a beacon. I should have let my little ones cry, and not ventured out for food and paraffin in such a time. Will they ever see me again?

He spoke in a stoical tone, stating the facts. He was a man of the people wearing hand-me-downs, unmatching vest and jacket, soiled gray trousers with the cuffs ruffling over a pair of unlaced boots. But he gave the captive Phalangist a look—had Elie been planted among them?

In the doorway the guard shuffled; he was absorbed in thoughts of himself, girlfriend or family. An M-16 rested on his shoulder.

What time was it? What was the weather like outside?

Elsewhere such things still mattered; and people bobbed about on the surface of their lives, like bits of scree in the eternal drift.

VIII

They came for him: not Giorgio but another, a businesslike guard. Elie Madi bristled at sight of them. Gone were all his good intentions, when that one spat forcefully in his face, his eyes. The saliva ran down Elie's rigid, quivering cheek.

—When the potato goes bad, threatening the bushel, toss it out. Sakr.

The other Phalangist cut the rope on Madi's ankles.

—I should take you over to that slop-pail, said Sakr, and dunk your head. But there's no more time—for cowards.

Elie staggered to his feet, groping the first few steps. He didn't want to be blindfolded.

The two officers appeared hurried, preoccupied with other things. When they led the prisoner from the room, he glanced back at his cellmates a last time: bound hand and foot so they could hardly squirm, forming black mounds where the darkness, blending floor and walls, seemed to congeal. One was having a six-course meal from the odds and ends, a bit of paper, tobacco, lint, which he managed with great maneuvering to extract from his pocket.

—Make trouble and you'll be shot.

They pushed Elie through a side door, and he stood startled by the sky at dusk. There was an instant when he might have made a dash, perhaps; but instead he stood gazing at the silvery-blue shimmer of the hour . . . He looked off across Charles Helou, where the northern coastline seemed to be seeping smoke. In the far distance, on the slopes of Sannine, missile launchers resembled a match being struck. Early evening in Ashrafiyeh had an unearthly beauty amid the sheets of fume, dispersing upward.

They shoved him in front, and the ragged march was underway. Circling behind the War Council they moved off in the shadows. Abu Joseph pointed the way with a handgun while his assistant scanned the hostile distance. It was a grim struggle for Elie to walk, like climbing over thorns. But a leaden sinking sensation seemed to prod him along toward a quicker resolution. He was propelled forward by all the thwarted life inside him, and by the intriguing scent of evening.

—Cross here.

The Phalangist seized his arm. By now Elie's clothes were in tatters.

—Stoop, and run!

The assistant booted him forward; he fell on the asphalt of an eerie vacant Charles Helou. He groped and stood back up, expecting fire in this sniper zone. They kicked, shoved him onward. The wide avenue on its way toward Bourj Hammoud and Antelias, becoming the Tripoli Highway, stretched away in an utter vacuum—as if this, abhorred by nature, were the natural state of war.

There were isolated shots: here and there, snipers gleaned. For now the brunt of fighting was on Sinn Il-Fill side, and northward up the crescent shoreline.

In stretches they dragged him by the scruff of his neck, crouching down, both using him as a shield. With a final shove, and poke of their gunbarrels, they flung him from the road and down onto a path through Karantina stubblefield.

—Why waste time?

—Wait, said Abu Joseph, gesturing ahead.

The hood wrinkled grotesquely, like the carcass of a soul, when he shook his head no.

IX

Three dark silent figures: they moved on the border of wasteland, with the sky looming somber in front of them. Structures on the upper slopes, across the darkening water, had a roseate hue from the sun going down to their backs, behind the wide arc of the city. Along ridges northward the houses seemed aglow. Windows were lit up red in the mountain villages.

The surf was a shimmering blue along Karantina strand. The businesslike guard studied Elie's every movement; he followed his stumbling ragamuffin steps with a certain impatience, catering to his superior's whims. Abu Joseph crouched slightly as they moved past an expanse of gray, heavy-headed rushes.

They trekked away from the ramparts of the harbor. How many were buried under their footsteps, from Karantina? The two men and their captive tramped over a dumping ground strewn with garbage so skeletal it no longer interested the rats.

—Move, hurry up!

The guard murmured:

—This is pointless.

—Shut up.

Elie felt a great thirst, but his mind was clear; he was taken with the tragic argentine beauty of the earth, the mountains and sea. Thirst no longer mattered; he knew where he was going. The pain in his chest would pass in a moment: he knew where they were leading him, but the fact had begun to have an almost gladdening vortex effect. If there was no water, what did it matter? There was no more need of water, either. Here was a sea of it, waiting for him at the end of his journey. No grave, no coffin, but instead the sea. He was glad of that; he transferred his morbid hope, with each step on the prickly shale, to Sakr following along just behind. He only had to walk through this earthly paradise, and his thirst would be slaked forever; his yearning, his restless unquenchable need would soon be over.

—Start crossing, this way!

Elie felt no fear. Mostly he was grateful they let him go without a blindfold. It was easier for them; why drag him the entire way?

Now the sun was down. The gloaming beach lay before them, a hundred steps to the north; he heard the waves plashing over pebbles with a distant, reminiscent sound. He seemed almost to hear their particular note, each of them, as he trudged along. The music of earth came wafting across to him, and sang its astonished meaning. An arc of red neon on the Casino still hadn't been extinguished: it emerged in the gathering twilight at the foot of hostile towering mountains. Smoke rose and dispersed in the deepening sky over a crook of coastline. Detonations. Mt. Sannine bathed in crimson, presiding over the flux of twilight... Few lights twinkled in Zalke, in the low-lying towns and villages.

The guard stared blankly at Elie; he glimpsed Abu Joseph, sensing the personal vendetta.

—Keep moving.

—Across the sand?

—Down to the edge.

As they approached, their words seemed lost in the surf vying with the big echoing guns. Along the rim of Karantina a chill breeze went amid the grasses; there were whitecaps in profusion across a twilight sea.

The waves went level like an escalator on the flinty shallows, and the foam. Elie, wrists bound, his hands blue and without feeling, felt his boots sink into the sand. He breathed in the salt marine air, and thought of summer afternoons, the slow and careless pleasure of the Christian beaches. An adventure novel open on his chest, he began to daydream, he dozed off—was Jessie there?... Or his mother came to check on him, in his room. Why had he grown so quiet for a time? A friend was outside, calling him to play and head off on some boyish foray. He was twelve years old...

Abu Joseph gazed ahead for a suitable site; his hood resembled a black sail in the whipping breeze. With the butt end of his handgun he struck the prisoner on the shoulder:

—Down there, toward the water, *yallah!*

X

Suddenly, Elie was possessed by an immense clarity. Night was falling. Behind him, across the city, people huddled in the shelters and rode out the waves of shock. Up and down the coast whole sectors were being torn and shaken: so many had perished, and for what?

He trudged past a first high-tide line of seaweed, and the crunch of his boots on sand was now louder than all the detonations. Elie Madi limped toward the surf about ten yards further; he slid a few steps; the two hooded escorts followed closely, their gaze fixed on him, as if he wasn't quite at their mercy.

The oncoming night was intensely clear. It glittered, blue and silver. He felt it like a kind of exposed membrane, and had no fear anymore.

At the water's edge he stared at the surf a moment before turning around. He meant to face them, but sea and sky claimed all his attention. Here the salt tang, so fresh yet laced with a fresh drying seaweed, was like a welcome—as full of secrets as the layers of a man-o'-war jellyfish. He nudged the purple pebbles with his boots; doing that, being himself just a moment longer, escaping . . . he felt a deepest twinge of pleasure.

Sakr stood alongside, glaring darkly:

—Madi, always, since I first met you it was the same thing: self-centered, the egotist . . . You thought you knew better than anyone else; you wanted people to accept you, as you were, no matter what nonsense you came up with. Me you liked to criticize, behind my back. Sometimes a look from you was enough to make me detest your presence, and everything about you.

Elie listened, but he shrugged. There was no more time for chatter. Life had opened up suddenly, spread its arms and clutched him to its heart before parting. He could feel a pounding, pounding inside himself like a surf of joy. He glimpsed life's great meaning, its goodness. Now words were such a waste, but he said, in passing, staring at the whitecaps:

—And you wore a hood.

Sakr forced a laugh, gesturing:

—You would also, if you weren't so naive.

Elie had no reply; but he intended to prolong the moment, seeing things in their purest light:

—You needed to hate, he said, calmly. So you quit engineering and decided to play captain.

—Shut up.

—See? You never cared what anything meant.

Jessica, his parents, friends, they all loved one another so partially. They were unable to love people enough, so they played a pitiful game called "adulthood", like bad children sitting in a circle. No wonder for things in themselves! Everything contingent on something else! They went from room to room and whispered little debilitating secrets.

—Who is more realistic between us? Sakr gave him a prod with the handgun. Who is dreaming, Madi?

—This is your time. Others' will come.

—Maybe, but yours never will. Strange thing about the world, it sweeps away traitors like trash.

—And Hitler's nephews.

The guard listened to them, shuffling alongside. He was impatient for the festivities to end, and stood hefting the M-16, peering about; his black hood jutted up in the gathering darkness.

Intently, Elie absorbed the meaning of the landscape, and thought he might burst with the beauty of the scene. The language of life could be read by a child, and yet who took the trouble? Who ever risked?

His childhood lay before him like a panorama.

Getting a bus back from the beach. Jessie smelled like sand and sun-lotion. They were clean, together.

His older brother was singing a popular tune. Elie felt a spasm of love for him. He died.

There would be no more thirst, in a moment. No more pressure—never.

It was all so clear!

XI

The wide sea of kindness spread before him. He had a vision of humans paddling about in rowboats on the eternal sea. Elie felt an invincible force of forgiveness, of pity for himself.

Sakr said:

—In a minute you have to die. Say your prayers.

—What would it change?

Sakr reached forward and ripped, with his gloved hand, the silver chain and tiny crucifix from Elie's neck. He tossed them on the sand.

—Your foolishness might change, with a little more torture. You got off too easy.

—Wrong, Sakr, as always. I'm afraid of pain; but my real fear is to become like you, and not know it.

The other gave a start:

—So eager to die?

—No, I don't want to.

—Then why keep telling lies?

—You call them lies. I think—you can't help yourself.

—You should die a hundred times, Madi, once for every insult. I'll do with you like I did as-Sa'iqa—gouge out your eyes.

—I'm not strapped to a chair, bully. I won't let you.

The third Phalangist stared from one to the other.

Were they both crazy?

Sakr laughed:

—Supposing you ever hit on a word of truth, who would hear? Or care?

—Only you. And this one, whoever he is... You wear hoods.

Elie coughed, feebly. Now his eyes were blurred; he stared through his tears at the night and the sea. The surf broke with a steady hiss; it swirled up to his feet with rings of foam. No more thirst, in a moment. No more stinging in his wrists; or fear at the sight of his bloated lifeless hands.

He took a step forward. He was fairly menacing despite everything. It was Sakr who drew back and raised the gun.

—You see how people in the wrong are cowards? Did you hear me—I'm telling you a word of truth now. You're a lying coward, and it makes no difference how many people you killed at Dbayyeh, or in Burj on Black Saturday, or here in Karantina. You're wrong, Sakr! *all wr* ————*wrong*—

A shot rang out; but dull, puny on the open beach, in the wind and surf, after the years of cannons.

XII

The childish limp body lay at the edge, in its tattered fatigues. Arms thrown out, legs in a running position it seemed in a transfigured race toward the finish-line... But Abu Joseph shoved it over, and again, with his boot, down the pebbly sand. Blood flowed on the sandy forehead, as if pumped by Elie's brain. Night was coming on. In disgust the Phalangist captain nudged the body surfward.

—Scum is scum, he said. In the end, it matters only to itself.

The guard nodded:

—*Xallis:* let's go back.

—Another shithead dies; but dangerous, this one.

The other turned away.

—Eh, let's go.

Abu Joseph started backing off as well, but hesitantly, away from the water. His boots made a suction sound, like a drain.

The two strode up the shore a hundred meters; they glanced back once or twice at the place where darkness hardened, a little, around the body lolling on the rim of waves.

After a moment the two soldiers disappeared. They went running across the rutted bristling acres of Karantina, as if that was their intent all along.

A gull flew overhead. Its cry was sharp and clear, not too high above the surf.

Northward, the coast lay bathed in blue, limpid evening. To the right, and high overhead, a long line of mountains curved in the starlit sky over Lebanon.

Slowly, wave upon wave, Elie's body was giving way. The blood flowed copiously from his forehead and mingled with the sea. A wave came murmuring, caressing his curly hair, the first to enfold him.

The seagull dipped and fluttered past, reluctant to scavenge where there might still be life. Its call was a flute played by distance, aggressive yet plaintive. The sand slid away beneath him; another wave curled over, claiming Elie for the undertow.

In deeper now, limbs bobbing like a doll, already half covered... His eyes were open in the twilight, with a tiniest glint of starglow; seeming to blink, when a wave jarred him, an incendiary shell streaked above Ashrafiyeh.

Now the bird strutted alongside, on the rim of foam.
The coastline dissolved in a deep sequined blue.
Enfolding surf, its rhythmic hissing.

Later, when the tide turned, he would meet with the roaming sharks in Beirut harbor.

His hair streamed out like seaweed, gradually losing his last foothold. The glint in his eyes had glazed over, with the obsessive, questioning look of the dead. His limbs gave a sort of abandoned paddle, into the sea.

Elie Madi, giving way, on the strand bordering what once was Karantina campsite, before the tide turned...

XIII

Hana'a Chahrour was alone on the patio. She heard a child playing, and the distant rumble of guns, while a soft breeze stirred in the tamarisk leaves.

Nearby, singsong, the childish voice sounded strange. But suddenly it rasped with anger, like a hedgehog in a trap. There was most precocious talk of explosives, mine fields, barbed wire.

Oh, the voice seemed so alone, though childish and resounding in the clear night. It was Sheikha's son, Walid, or Abu Said as he called himself. He carried a long stick sometimes, and would hit you with it. This game he played, which Hana'a could hear from across the path at Sheikha's, was called "Border Raid".

At moments he slowed down. Then his voice subsided. There was a long caravan of camels; there was a well that tasted salty, and an enemy, not far off. Walid's thoughts began to wander; his play sort of spun on itself, like a top.

Hana'a needed badly to be with someone. She felt on the verge of breaking down completely; and also afraid, for some reason, of other people. Where was Dr. Kamel? Where was Sitt tonight? Hana'a would have liked to talk to a child, and get down on the floor and play awhile pathetically. She felt a longing for her old doll, Laila, the one that belonged to herself and her sister, Zeina, when they lived in Tel ez-Zaater and used to accompany Sitt Chahrour to Sylvie Helou's house in Ashrafiyeh.

She could go across the path to Sheikha's, but this meant the strain of conversation with a grownup. A slightest bit of pressure might bring on more sadness than she could even handle. She didn't want to start crying! She didn't want to hear her brothers' names... or Selman's, whom she had been in love with secretly. Nothing— not a word about what had happened, when the Camp fell. People took on a tragic look, which they couldn't hide, the instant they saw her.

Poor Sheikha was a Tel ez-Zaater widow, with three children to raise by herself. Sheikha's life was hardworking and lonely; she supplemented her pension with piece-work in the *Nejdeh* women's atelier.

Hana'a wished she could cross over to visit Sheikha, but something foreboding held her back.

XIV

The breeze stirred like a restless guest in leaves overhanging the patio, as among the sea of olive trees in orchards along the Chouf foothills. The night air had an algae smell; it was cool, but she wouldn't bother to fetch a pullover. She had something deep in her, which hurt terribly, like a dead baby perhaps; and it would hurt much worse if she weakened even for a second. In her thoughts she was back at the Camp: again she listened to the cries of families, clutching at one another as they went under together, tearing their hair when the men were led away in groups. Women wailed, with voices from beyond the grave. The road from the central mosque was strewn along its shoulders with swollen bodies beneath a cloud of flies.

They had taken her away too. They took Hana'a to a bare room with mattresses, cigarette butts on the floor, jagged loopholes in the walls. She remembered the exposed tubes and wires of a broken radio.

Delighted with their find, better than booty, they had raped her, Hana'a, who was just a girl and had hardly ever thought of being a woman, so demanding and fast was the life all around her. Three of them, rightists: they kept her there in the room with them, preferring this to looting the ramshackled huts of the Camp, or adding a few notches on their klashins since it was open season on refugees.

They tried to feed her, and gave her Coca-Cola to drink. They tossed her a wet towel where she lay traumatized and bleeding profusely on a mattress.

They partied, and kept after her through the long terrible afternoon, with incessant screams in the background. Later, one went out. When he returned they gave her champagne, and pâté from tins. When they finally left her alone, thinking her half-crazed by this time, drunk and helpless, she stumbled out into the darkness. From then on, each step she took led somewhere beyond memory, beyond war, hatred, Kataëb.

Toward nightfall several of the Camp defenders found her, including Selman who was still alive; and together with them she broke Phalangist lines, moving off in two groups toward Monteverdi Woods. Scrub country, dry hills and ravines, with burnt-out stretches. There were flashing lights among the treetrunks; there was shooting, it seemed, all over the earth, as the Phalangists came hunting after hundreds of Camp fighters who fled for their lives. For women and children there were observers, the Red Cross; but all males above fourteen had received orders to flee.

The woods were full of corpses, men and boys, also some Phalangists. Propped like Buddha against a tree, their eyes reflected the glimmer of firing. Crossing a road Hana'a saw a dead fighter run over and over by cars like a forest animal. On the other side they jumped back from a rigor-mortised rightist balanced with props on his two feet, M-16 in hand, like a scarecrow ambush.

During the second night they were in fact intercepted, at Monsourriyeh, and Selman leading them was shot in the chest. Before the Camp fell he had gone fifty days without seeing his mother, though she was just nearby in a shelter . . . Two more were wounded badly in a volley of grenades; and Hana'a, who had thought she couldn't walk anymore, helped drag one of them backwards, hour after hour, toward the lights of Alay.

When they came to a ridge, crouching, they could make out the friendly lights. On the third day, the survivors reached Baddieh, a Druze town, and were taken in and bathed.

XV

But awhile before Baddieh she had fallen silent, and would not utter a word to anyone. Her brothers were dead, Saleh, Ismail, Khaled, Ashraf, Ahmed, Mansur—all of them, and she felt a shame so intense it made her want to explode with hatred for all the living.

Above all, it was crucial not to cry. She might still avoid eternal dishonor if she never used *that* part of herself, in *that* way, again ... For days she had been using her utmost strength simply to suppress the tears.

But the hurt kept on, and worsened. The hardest part was trying to avoid Sitt Chahrour, and the older women, their eyes. She would fall down wailing and pounding her fists, gnashing her own flesh, if she wasn't very careful. She tried not to think anymore of her brothers, and sister Zeina. But she thought of them, ripping the scab off her soul, day after day.

Then Dr. Kamel asked her to keep house for him, and still assist in his pediatrics clinic. So she threw herself into the work with all her hobbled, hurting force, and desperate courage.

XVI

Her heart was beating violently. She was unable to stay here any longer, waiting for no one. She started slowly up the path, thinking she might visit Mayser, the mystery case.

The sky had grown lighter: a full moon lurked off beyond the ridges of the Chouf. When Hana'a walked, her body seemed to sway with the evening breeze like a brittle reed.

Behind her the little boy, Walid, warbled toward sleep after his day of stormy warlike play. Hana'a heard a fading murmur among the houses; she could sense all the loneliness in other people's voices. Artillery exchanges drifted down the coast; and she paused an instant, listening for planes.

Nearing the clinic she felt a deep aversion. Could she stand the sight, right now, of those suffering, blighted children? Still she went along, and entered; a nurse was seated at a desk in the first room, reading over an old newspaper.

The woman looked up, seeming glad for the company.

—Are you okay?

Hana'a wavered. She was unable to return the other's greeting. She passed by the desk like an apparition, and into the second room—saying nothing, as the other stared after her.

At once she felt nauseous. It was the usual overripe odor of sick children; she heard them swallow, teeth grinding, in the darkness. They breathed with difficulty, rustling their sheets a little, like things that burrow in the night when nobody is watching.

Mayser had survived. He was quiet for now: the elaborate ritual was in abeyance. On the next bed Marwan lay playing his violin— entire upper body still housed in the white cast, emitting a silent anguished kind of music. His spine was broken a week before the siege began, when the Camp UNRWA school was bombed. No Beirut hospital would accept him. So from day to day he lay there, a concerto for broken life.

The sight of him made Hana'a bend forward with a spasm, a first small convulsion. She tottered an instant, but then remembered a note she had to write Dr. Kamel, about Nadja's eyes.

Backing a few steps, as if driven off by the sight of them, Hana'a turned and went from the room.

The night nurse said:

—You're all alone down there. *Ben't,* I can imagine.

—Any new problems? Mayser?

—No change so far.

The nurse paused; she was caught between her newspaper and the distracted air about Hana'a. A child whimpered in one of the rooms:

—*Abba, ta'l Abba . . .*

Hana'a stood thinking: why is it all my fault? She hesitated on the threshold of the pediatrics clinic, and listened a moment longer to the small chorus—thin, toneless voices of children too stunned to utter much protest. Already, thanks to Dr. Kamel's initiative, this site was becoming a catch-all for the other camps, Wavell, Nahr Il-Bared; now the doctor rarely slept.

She lingered, trying to decide. Beyond the entry was a huge menacing emptiness. What have I done? she thought. What terrible thing did I do, for all this to happen to us? If I stay here any more, it will make me sick.

—Nabila, I am going.
—Salaamtik!

She glanced back at the desk and went outside.

XVII

There were less people along the main road, some Fedayeen with their wives, a few others. Mamdoueh's car came past, slowly, hugging the darkness with its parking lights.

Hana'a Chahrour turned down the path toward the empty house. Dr. Kamel was almost never there. She thought: I could do some cleaning, but in the dark? I'd be better off living in a pigsty, where I belong . . . She walked on, feeling sick. On the path she almost fell headlong.

She doubled over with nausea and panic, giving a deep groan. A cramp shot up from the pit of her stomach; it gripped her chest and caused her almost to fall. For an instant she nodded: this is my fault, yes, it must be mine. But she also glimpsed the truth, as well, and a vision of the world too bleak even to be considered.

Then she went to her knees. She gave a first strange sob in the silence, in the absence, there on the dirt path. She clutched at a root as the convulsions started. For a moment she seemed to vomit her tears, choking as the sobs wrenched her body, and she fell on one elbow. Hana'a slumped to her side and then levered up again; she groaned too weakly to be heard by anyone.

She coughed out her panic, and knocked her head forward on the damp ground; she bruised her forehead on the root she was holding for dear life. Her despair gathered force. Now the floodgate was opened, and her coughing, sobbing grew to a steady flow, like shockwaves ridden by those ruined children, in Dr. Kamel's clinic, between waking and sleeping nightmares.

Hana'a was beside herself. She cried out and whined:

—I'm sorry!

Pain wracked her body, propelling her a few feet down the path. The strangled cry repeated itself:

—I didn't mean to—please! . . .

For some minutes she lay weeping, apologizing. She called out to her dead mother, and to Sitt Chahrour:

—Immi, I didn't mean it! I won't, ever again! It is all my fault, *Immi* . . .

By now some people must have heard, but they had listened to grieving before. Fifty years' worth of women mourning their dead . . . And which among them didn't have her full cup? Besides, in the gloom of shelters the refugees were preparing, seeing to the necessary before another endless night of war, and restless waiting.

—Why? she groaned.

Her voice was guttural—an adult given over to incoherent cries, and infant babbling. A woman losing her mind.

For a moment the pangs subsided, as she slipped, the time of a blink, from consciousness. But then Hana'a doubled over, holding her side.

—Aaangh!

XVIII

Awhile later Sheikha appeared on the path. She had Walid on one arm, since he couldn't be left alone inside the house. Also, the strange voice had frightened him.

Sheikha spotted Hana'a Chahrour where she lay sprawled and gasping for air. Despite her own hard life, and loneliness, Sheikha had a way of smiling at things. There was an eagerness about her, as she took the girl by the shoulders and caressed her hair.

—Eh, it's alright! We'll be okay; it's not your fault at all.

—But why?

Hana'a hiccoughed and tried to catch her breath.

—Don't even think that! *Ya* Walid, you come back here.

The small boy was unimpressed by the sight of yet another wailing woman. This one's face was besmirched with dirt and spittle.

He began stumbling along the dark path toward Front headquarters, and the Fedayeen who were his friends.

—Walid, I'm warning you!

—My name is Abu Said.

Hana'a made more garbled pleading sounds, staring up through tears at Sheikha.

—You'll stay with us tonight. And no need to be afraid anymore, we're sisters. Also, it's good for you to cry this way . . . Walid!

—Abu Said!

His voice was further along the path.

—Yes, from now on you stay with us, when Dr. Kamel's away. It's alright. Go ahead, cry.

—My brothers are dead. Selman's dead . . . he was good to me!

Sheikha purred:

—I remember . . . for a year my older brother sold newspapers at the entrance to Summerland, and gave us the money. We needed it to live. Then he was killed, down in Burj one afternoon, by a sniper.

—Selman was kind! cried Hana'a, hiccoughing. Now who will take care of us?

—We will; we'll all help to do it.

—If only he wasn't so kind, said Hana'a, crying.

—You are too, said Sheikha.

—I loved him, she sobbed. And Ismail, who took care of Sitt so well, and all of them!

—Shh, I know, said Sheikha, caressing her. We all loved Selman, so much, though maybe not the same as you . . . We won't forget him. Even this will make us stronger.

She gestured. She could hear Walid who, afraid of the dark, had turned back a ways and started in playing. Now he muttered dramatically about a "border raid".

Hana'a was crying more steadily, her head on Sheikha's shoulder. They sat together on the path; they sat in the consoling shadows, as a sliver of moon emerged, lemon hued, over a distant ridge of the Chouf.

—This is good, Sheikha cooed. We'll just sit here a little while. Go on and cry.

XIX

A nervous crowd jammed the quay at Bain Militaire, extending back up into the parking lot. By the time Kim Ligury arrived, there were hundreds of people obviously weary of waiting, dusty with the impeded trample toward the landing craft. It was a jumpy herd. At any moment a few shots might cause a stampede for safety, with respected American colleagues tossed in the drink. Meanwhile people called to one another; flashlights darted and crisscrossed.

Their voices had the pathos of departure, but with a difference. Generally, the mood of this crowd was resentment, and subdued impatience. There were cats meeowing in perforated boxes; there were birdcages with a pitiful flutter against the wire. A spaniel puppy whined, its ears murdered by the weeks of artillery barrage.

A blustery businessman-type tried to move toward the lighter. He cried:

—I'm looking for my wife.

There were heaping mounds of boxes, radios and even television sets, along with other precious objects being rescued from the barbarous hordes. Conjecture was rife as to a quota or poundage the U. S. Navy might try to enforce. Away from the water two children lay on a bed of luggage; they were draped with coats against the night air of the Corniche. Their mother said:

—Why can't the United States Government do things right anymore?

Gangplanks were down. By the long jetty a pair of landing craft waited to receive the evacuees. But some snag was holding up the operation.

—Dear, said her husband, please be patient. It's probably some bureaucratic snafu.

He was bespectacled and tall, an academic. He strained for a glimpse of the embarcation point.

—Hundreds of marines offshore; but instead they trust these, these—

She pointed with her chin. *Fatah,* as the only group capable of providing ground security, had agreed after days of parleying.

—Bet your life, if it was Harry Truman!

Her voice had a raspy twang—a southern housewife, Ligury surmised, who had not exactly taken to Lebanon. No doubt her husband taught at A.U.B.

—Dear, the world has changed since then.

—Not it, we have: we lost our pluck.

Most folks were quiet, and increasingly tense. They stood exposed to chance and the manmade elements; they raised on tiptoes for a look beyond the crowd. In the distance there were explosions, a constant roar: what was happening in Jbeil? in Tripoli, and the northern plains?

Wild rumors had been circulating throughout the day. The UNIFIL zone in the South was ablaze with skirmishing. An Israeli joint-pincer maneuver, with heavy sea and air support, was closing once again on Tyre; while an Israeli offensive directed toward Zahle and the Bekaa came perilously near the "Red Line" and most explosive situation yet with Syria.

Fires, detonations from Beirut suburbs reflected on the underside of clouds. Offshore, the USS Spiegel-Grove awaited its passengers, as part of a 7-ship task force of the U. S. Sixth Fleet, including a thousand battle-ready marines. On an anti-aircraft carrier further out, there were F-16s on alert for a possible air strike.

The evacuees waited. They appeared quite irritable, frowning in an aura of pre-apocalypse.

XX

Kim Ligury made his way on the edge of the mixed crowd. A few grumbled, as he moved forward in the direction of the pier.

—There's a line, Mac—see it?

—I'm not evacuating. Press.

—Oh yeah? Or just pressed?

The few hundred anxious people converged dangerously some thirty yards from the first gangplank. There was a narrow luggage-obstructed aisle along the quay, above the tossing waters.

—Not leaving . . . journalist.

—Well, don't show yourself on that lighter.

He flashed his card in the teeming darkness.

He might board, nonetheless. But was she here? And if she asked him: are you coming? If her face lit up with the words, and she was waiting just for him?

Ligury stepped over baggage, nearing the boarding ramp. Someone with a hopelessly American accent said:

—Knock that in, and you'll go fish for it in Davy Jones' locker.

They were tired, fed up. This was hardly their thing, to stand waiting two hours in the flashing darkness. Over his shoulder he glimpsed a torchlight, flickering on the striated water. The tide was high, and luminescent waves washed all along the Corniche. He heard the soughing of a breakwater a hundred yards across the small harbor.

He listened for Morgan's velvet voice amid the murmuring throng. There were traders, business people and staff from the Western embassies. A fair number of Lebanese carried dual citizenship; this operation was exclusively for U. S. and European nationals.

Of course, there were boats available from Jounieh or Sidon, if the price was right. But impossible, at present, to go by motorized convoy to Damascus; it couldn't be arranged after numerous high-level attempts. No, this was the last train out of a Middle East on the verge.

Ligury grasped a piling. He raised on tiptoes, trying to scan the tense crowd edging its way still closer. He thought: If I see her, then what? Wade right in, fool. His heart thumped: Do I really know her? Who the hell *is* this woman I love? We played games, in silence, with one another's minds—or did we? And what am I doing here now? By telepathy she knew I would show up, all full of a tactless need, well-bred Britisher in nuanced desperation: she went as fast as possible in the opposite direction. Morgan decided to stay on the assumption I would leave. She chose participation in a holocaust, rather than the farce of caring for someone who cares ... A holocaust is concrete at least. You can relate to a plutonium bomb with relative ease; and the outcome is clear, that's a kind of advantage. But go head to head, sometime, with the humiliation of "true love". No, she's in this crowd somewhere, hardly the type to linger. Was she a creature of another species? What could be stranger than a relationship with someone who refused, ever, to divulge? Ha! Satan had put her on earth to deal with the still, small sincerity remaining in a few dupes, dangerous despite themselves, among the male sector.

XXI

A signal was given from somewhere. The crowd began nudging its way forward. There was a sigh of relief, as adults hefted their kids and luggage. Passports were checked. The first passengers took their belongings out along the concrete dock (in peacetime used for diving and sunbathing) to where a landing vessel slung forth its gangplank. Ligury posted himself at the checkpoint and waited; but a militiaman turned to him and said, quietly:

—You can't stand here.

—I'm press. See? no luggage.

He held up his hands, trying to look important, a man on a mission.

The commando, dark-skinned and wearing camouflage, met his eye and turned away.

Ligury watched them board: men in natty tropical suits or sportjackets, with expensive gear. Women in slacks, dressed voguishly with silk scarves, ascots; one actually wore riding attire. They confronted the unknown with their silken whimsical charms. A few wore sunglasses in the darkness, posing oblivious to the chaos.

But approaching the embarcation point, and Fatah guerrilla, they grew a bit less self-absorbed. Some were drunk, and kept up a slyly seductive chatter, nodding yes, responding to offhand questions. But there was a certain hostility, being exposed this way, and then made to state their final destination.

Most grew quietly eager. The jig was up in Lebanon. Time to depart, gentlemen; go and wait it out elsewhere.

A dour American sat with a Lebanese at the inspection table:

—U.S. citizen?

—Greek.

He checked her passport by penlight.

—Destination?

—Athens.

—Down the ramp.

Forms would be filled out in Cyprus. Also, this little service was in no sense gratis.

Ligury waited to one side. In fact he hoped not to see her; he wished she was staying, but if she did arrive, if she embarked he might well follow after. Never mind his gear back in the Hamra apartment. Never mind anything, last train to happiness.

Across the dark sea there was a single red light: the American ship awaited its evacuees. Even while dying, thought Ligury, Lebanon remained a "miracle". Arms traffiquants, contraband: her carcass bred millionaires like maggots. Fabulous real estate deals swung in absentia, "closings" for the burnt-out sectors. Oh, her stench was a fine perfume luring necrophiliacs. And the Lebanese pound still rallied, more or less, corseted and firm by day. Such an opulence of pudenda:—whoever was privy to them might explain the "miracle" of her economic curves.

A young woman exchanged banter with the two men checking passports. She eyed the Fatah comrade's klashin, giving a pert smile.

Ligury cast his gaze above the masses, off toward the smudged and gutted Holiday Inn towering over a shadowy Corniche.

XXII

He saw her: there. Morgan's towhead was unmistakable, as she engaged someone in conversation. It was an Italian businessman known to Ligury from Ydlibbi's nightclub. Too well-fed, with a quiet bonhomie.

Morgan's blond face stood out from the crowd even here. She had her coy smile, caryatid sneering at mortal humanity. Was it a mouse she just swallowed? For some reason she seemed quite contented with herself, and expansive.

Ligury's heart was ribald as he tried to catch her eye. The debonaire escort, Gaudenti, was balding with a tress of dark hair slightly roguish on his hale, suntanned forehead. He wore amber-rimmed glasses, suggestive of a mundane Weltanschauung. He appeared to guide Morgan along; though neither was able to move for the moment. His lust was obviously cultured, as with his free hand he gestured, and made some clever remark.

As they drew closer Ligury noticed a curious fleeting expression on Morgan's face. Was she high on something? She seemed to float in a kind of voluptuous inner realm. Her eyes were glazed.

Ligury felt a tension, and desire for her quite beyond the physical. But he also felt sympathy: imagining she was lost, in some sense, and hurting. Her escort added to the impression, portly, suavely opportunist.

By now they were a few steps away. Ligury endured an awkward moment while Morgan recognized him. She had a little-girl air about her, in a doll-like hazy wonder. Tilt her and she might blink.

The escort struck a noble pose: who is this wage earner? What gives him this right of intimacy?

—Hello.

Morgan nodded. She seemed rather amused, making the presentations.

—Gaudenti, amore, this is . . . What is your name?

Ligury nodded:

—I need a word with you. It won't take a minute.

—Not even a "minute"?

She chuckled. The ironic tone took him aback. He glimpsed behind at the embarcation point, the table a few feet further.

—But alone.

—Alone? I think that may be difficult.

She giggled. Gaudenti's features followed along after hers, but with the reserve of a man counting lucre.

Ligury hesitated.

—Then . . . I wanted to know if you were leaving. Also, to wish you well.

—Oh, she laughed at him. And to you, sir. Jolly good.

—Why not stay on awhile? You might catch a bit of the fun, even join in.

—What sort of "fun" do you mean?

—Fireworks in any case. But I mean (his voice fell) the struggle.

He gave a gesture: others were prodding, with their combined anonymity, to embark. Morgan realized this with a hint of impatience.

—What "struggle"?

—There are people here, suffering. I had friends in the Camp.

Ligury seemed full of something inexpressible, easy to ridicule. She studied him, wistfully sarcastic:

—I don't see anyone suffering. Vieux pote, en vois-tu?

She touched Gaudenti's silk-shirted paunch, and chortled.

Ligury nodded, insistent:

—The survivors . . . they could use a hand.

—Haven't *we* suffered, Chérie? said Gaudenti. Vivre est souffrir.

Ligury said, a note lower:

—I was even thinking . . . I might join them. Teach English in one of the camps—something—

—Good for you, she said. Eagle scout.

—But come with me, he blurted. If you knew the life there is, and how much they'd love you.

—Love me?

Morgan broke forth with a peal of laughter.

Heads turned. Someone asked, in a strident voice, why traffic was being held up.

—They would, said Ligury. And I would, I—

His voice broke off; and Morgan, on the verge of hilarity, raised an eyebrow.

They had inched together almost to the table. But she paused, squinting with mirth:

—What did he say?

She gave forth with the eerie laugh. Gaudenti beckoned:

—Viens, Chérie.

—No, wait. This could be important: I'm setting a record for proposals, offers of marriage from idealists you see. Is it official?

Kim Ligury bowed slightly:

—We all need help. I know it sounds absurd, but I love you.

She broke into a rich laughter, fairly beside herself, and by now they had an audience.

—"Absurd" he says! Ha! ha! It seems I'll never lack for help!

She bent over coughing. There were tears in her eyes. Only Gaudenti appeared unruffled, making an elaborate show of patience. He guided her carefully forward, but Morgan glanced back at Ligury; her voice rang out insanely.

Gaudenti said:

—Monsieur, it will suffice.

He turned her away. Ligury stared after them. But then Morgan dropped her passport on the table; she swung back toward him and hissed:

—You idiot, don't you understand yet?

The checkpoint paused in its activity, as people sized up the beautiful drunken woman. But she looked in Ligury's eyes another instant, with a sort of recognition:

—Some men never do learn.

And that was the funniest yet, to her. She stood there leering, hilarious; it seemed she wanted him to be the one who turned away.

He glanced toward the table, and his eyes met those of the Palestinian worriedly scanning the crowd; surveilling the bay of light round the passport desk. He spoke a few words in his walkie-talkie, while the AK in his other hand was like part of his body.

Ligury bowed to her, and began moving away. But Morgan gave another peal of laughter, quasi-hysterical.

All this time the general chatter had died down. The dense crowd was subdued, with a disapproving silence; though something of the big fear, and aspiration of escape, was expressed in the raving comportment of this female.

XXIII

The sound of her voice followed him, as he jostled his way through the ranks of Westerners. Where did she get that perfume? one which he had never smelled before, and it would be in his nostrils forever. Now the few hundred evacuees were past annoyance at being made to wait so long. A large man drawled in Ligury's face:
—Hold yeh hosses.

It was an A.U.B. professor from Arkansas, or someplace, alongside his stick of a wife and three kids. The journalist had met him at a party; and suspected that beside his degrees in agriculture, and prestigious publications, was a niche in the secret service.

Morgan's laughter echoed, ironic and silvery. Ligury felt like the morning after a family row—queasy, vaguely shameful. With a violence he groped his way, tripping, nearly sprawling on someone's baggage. They grumbled at him; though he posed no threat anymore to their position in line. A few tried to stand back and let him pass.

Then he was running up the dusty driveway of Bain Militaire. He made it to the sea-sprayed Corniche before bending forward with a cramp and vomiting. The flow of mucus and food poured from his lips like birdseed on a rainy pavement.

Ligury went to his knees in it, trying to catch his breath.
—Ya! said a militiaman guarding the entry. Ente mariid?

Kim shook his head solemnly; he got to his feet. Suddenly he felt calmer, and began wandering off by himself. Her mockery, the elegant sleaze of Gaudenti, nausea ... All faded, but there was still a dizziness, so he leaned over the railing and breathed in salt air. One by one the waves came sweeping over, sucking at rock shelves and mossy caves along the edge. Midnight approached. Wind and surf were on the rise. There was sempiternal shelling in the distance, as by starlight he watched the dark play of waves in caverns ten feet below. Kim paused by the railing and thought: So I'm staying on ... No more planes, no motored caravans; and xenophobia, a new wave of kidnappings sweeping the city, after the shock of assassination. Where's a lifeline? I could still go back; I could get on that lighter, except for her devil's laughter.

The night air and the waves had a settling effect on his nerves.

XXIV

He started walking. He passed A.U.B. tower, rounding a dangerous bend; and the tense darkness of downtown Beirut spread before him. To his right was the stark outline of Gefinor, straight ahead the Holiday Inn contours, huge gravestone for Lebanon. Now there were no lights in the mountains on the Christian side. Traffic had desisted on the Corniche where it curved into Minet Il-Hosn toward the burnt-out hulk of St. George Hotel. Phoenicia Street was a vacant strip without services, elegiac, abused in war as it had been in gaudy peacetime, long ago.

He was heading for Ydlibbi's which would probably be closed also, since most of its clientele was leaving the country. Where to? Was it necessary to take sides? Back with Mamdoueh, in the village, there would be people at least, and they related to one another with an unaccustomed force. Children like Walid, son of Sheikha, were blessed with hopefulness in some crazy way; though they had no country it was possible, thought Ligury, they deserved to inherit the earth... Better to be hit over the head with Walid's stick, than deal with this invincible loneliness, day after day. Better to go among the living, and share their hopeless cause: pay the price of their lacerated ideals. Where to? Ligury was rebounding from his fit of nausea. He felt light on his feet now, almost giddy.

But if the leaders like Mamdoueh asked too much of him? If they said: prove yourself, go here, go there, since you are British. Take this, find that out, be *our* spy... But if I join them it has to be for better or worse, no more liberalism, or hedging. History is an ocean river of blood, but which way does it flow? Sure there are small deceptive eddies, here and there—but how many worlds were crushed in order to produce the great Western nations? And now the martyred masses should be squeamish as to tactics. No, humanity will rid itself of Gaudenti's masters, but by fits and starts; a few steps forward, then one or two big ones back. The need to isolate and exploit is so deep in man.

Along Ahmad Chaouqi the tough Syrian checkpoint was on alert; but he ignored it and kept walking past, toward the deadly downtown sectors like a somnambulist on his ledge.

—Ente!! Ween raayih?

—You stop!

The two Syrian regulars shouted after him, but he stumbled away in a daze. Ligury's coatsleeve had been ripped when he pushed his way back through the crowd; so he resembled a vagrant tripping over his own cuffs. In view of the soldiers crouching behind their sandbags, he wandered out into no-man's-land with its checkerboard of sniper zone.

He was crossing into a disputed sector; the ground puffed up by his side with a first warning shot. But Ligury went on enraptured— O my country, do you murder and then lie about it? Do you extort your prodigious wealth off the sweating shoulders of others? Oh, I've known your greed, your willful ignorance of the real problems, and long campaign of slander.

XXV

He went tripping along Avenue des Francais into the dilapidated mouldy mausoleum of the souks. In the darkness he found Ydlibbi's locked up and closed; there were no more vermilion negligees in the doorway of Port Egypt. He waded nonchalantly among the shadows.—Do I go present myself to the victims? Here, I see the truth now, it will never stop. They will feed on all of us until we're rid of them.

And if the great *yes* were finally sung in a chorus, then what? If the eternal struggle were tipping our way, and our dispossessed millions were just one battered door away from the hoarders of sweet, abundant life? If they were exposed despite their media, and the lines were drawn with the clarity of a sword, and we all shouted together: Come out of there! and with your hands out of your pockets! And we stood there in our immense universality, pounding on that door; and the truth was our battering ram as we fought for the reclamation of kindness—stood besieging the computers! And now their epic résumés and entries in *Who's Whose* weren't worth the fine vellum they were printed on: not even worth a fig leaf. Ah, then, would they plead in a falsetto voice from their bunkers, where they held life hostage; would their finger be poised on the button of destiny, masturbating godhead as they cried:

—Not ours, suckers? Alright, not yours either.

And oh, my comrades, we would hear, in that instant, the awful laughter in the muezzins. Scheherazade would fall silent, all out of stories. Then a long promenade among the stars would begin for us... O the delirious laughter! O this light at the end of humanity's tunnel, flickering! And our love would flare up, so ultimate, a revelation even to Swiss bankers as to the meaning of our visit.

And that would be the Last Judgment. And our lives would be right there before us, comrades, along with the achievements of years and nations past. So that we might see, by the light of that global flicker, the mistake we made with our flying leaps to religious hierarchy; or with the wealth we prayed to so very faithfully; or the atrocious envy we felt daily toward our fellows. Oh, my sisters and brothers, then the halo round our sad faces, in that cosmic mirror, would be multiplied a trillion times.

And then the long struggle of the people, the high deeds of the enlightened would have led only to this; and only to this ignominy, nothing more. Clancy lowering the boom—and then nothing. Not Anaximandre's expiation; not one more spin of the wheel, for poor Pascal.

Ergo: nothing, THE END, written in stars. Indelible as cosmos. Inscribed for no one in particular, across the blackboard of human history. And the first real lesson would be learned, finally, perhaps.

XXVI

He stopped. The sliver of lemony moon reappeared, hovering above Cyprus. It blended with starlight on the ruins of souks, on corpses distended beneath a skeletal arcade.

He passed by Patriarch Hoyek, along toward Rue Allenby. He wanted to see Burj. The old-world colonnades dripped stone, jutting, bristling, gouged—they exuded the horror.

Junked autos cluttered the entrance to the Port area. He turned up Rue Foch. Fumes of a hundred fires trailed skyward, confluent with the big river of smoke from Dowra. There was nothing alive, no movement that he could see. The fighting had flown northward up the coast, except for snipers lurking in these deserted quarters, maybe a few gold miners with their dental instruments.

Ligury turned left on Rue Weygand, approaching the center. From step to step he nearly fell, haggard, wondering what to do with his life.

XXVII

Kim Ligury entered a shimmering Burj, like an ocean surf carved in stone. He glanced up at an ancient title on the Rivoli Theater marquee, faded, torn, announcing a final film before the romance of prewar Lebanon would itself close: LES DIVORCEES.

Charred casements, Spanish balconies spattered with graffitti, claw-marks of klashins... Once, in these genteel precincts, there was a grace borne of affluence, a nobility of fetishes. It was an Old South based on courteous relations; it was "modern Lebanon" with a hundred tragic flaws.

—Once upon a time, Ligury mused, in the barrel-vaulted ruins; once there were children in crinoline, and a chatter of merchants in perfumed sunlight. The ruler of such a contented land was known the world over, as from week to week the tall-masted ships strewed wealth along his shores. Day to day, the alien dockers lugged a fabulous treasure up to his palace on the verdant hill. *Ustaez* king deemed a glimpse of his train's shadow was reward and nourishment enough for their toilsome lives.

But one year he developed a mania for bathing in a swamp. His Local Heinous spent part of each day taking cure-baths in stagnant water which some claimed was a sewer. Advisers warned this was bad policy; it could hurt morale, and might even lead to selfatitis. Their words went unheeded, however, as the King's mania grew more acute. And then finally people began to murmur, a dangerous practice! What if someone lost respect? Soon they were muffling their laughter, and saying: our sacred King is just like us, maybe worse.

And then, lo! one extravagant afternoon the first gunshots echoed in the suburbs. And before long a bullet came rapping on the palace facade, like history's tax collector. And then, from the King's cure-swamp a monster emerged, dripping slime; it rose up and stalked the elegant land. Some hinted there was a family resemblance between the retributive monster and His Heinous.

Ligury felt a poke on the shoulder, as if someone coughed in his face.

He spun around; he nearly fell with the impact, and began chicken-walking back among the bluish shadows of the old Opera House. There was a sense of dread mingled with nausea, as he paused on his knees. He was stunned. He thought: the shot came from a sniper diagonally across, in the rubble of Place Debbas. But he never heard it.

Already his shirt and jacket were sticky with blood. He pressed the wound with a handkerchief, causing a sharp pain. His mind started to drift, and he surmised: Hm, my jacket is blue cord... Crouching behind a column he peeped out at Burj toward the Statue of Martyrs.

The square was a rapids—fragments of stone, reefs where the darkness seemed to take on contour, impeding the flow. These were the dead, absolute in their bodies, cluttering Burj and streets surrounding... They lay in doorways, or by the curb, twisted in strange poses. Suddenly Ligury seemed to feel them; they were fusing with the charred stone, as if deliquescent, gunked. The moon was rising, seeming to scythe a crop of stars as midnight approached. The journalist felt dizzy, and pressed harder on his shoulder. Blood had trickled from one's head, another's torso, forming a black pool like a shadow. In the lighter Morgan was laughing, a velvet peal, to the rhythm of waves plashing the bow; she was headed off toward another world, Cyrpus, peace and luxury items in the stores... Some lay charred by petrol, glazed and wrapped in their sinews, anatomical. Others were bloated, ballooning their olive drabs since the day before, or the day before that, Friday. Not unhappy, now, to be things, thought Ligury. They bequeathed their nightmares to the living... Am I dying, like them, down here in Burj?

There were hundreds of corpses, rightists, leftists. They had come sprinting forth in units of five; they had stormed east-west and fallen wildly, arms flung out in a last desperate gesture. Something went flitting in the far corner of the square, beneath the word HOOVER in high vertical letters on a building. A torch, a flicker of moonlight, out there alone. But it seemed to do a hurting dance, in the moon-mist, like a pathetic girl ... Ligury thought of Elie Madi, wondering where he was: what was Elie doing now, making love to Jessica? Celebrating the Camp victory? Fighting in Ein Rummaneh? In his mind's eye he saw the Phalangist clearly, but as someone lost, standing there in the sad tarnished light of his own smile. He remembered hauling the crazed girl, Sylvie Helou, to the hospital in Elie's jeep. Right, left: she lashed out at them, striking her captors. Kim Ligury squinted, staring out at Burj, but he saw nothing further; nothing white and ethereally fleeting, but only this deathscape, these phenomena of sleep, when the mind is submissive, and an infant crying resounds sadly through the limestone quarters... Only inert forms, in a glimmer of moon-shroud; some seemed to gesticulate, but the debate was all over. Remove me, cover my shame. See how it is, on the *other* side ... ?

XXVII

Ligury got to his feet. He saw they were everywhere; but none moved; no one tried to cross lines anymore. On a shard of cluster bomb he read the initials of its maker, like one shown him back in the village of refugees, by an Italian who had fought in Tyre. For some reason Ligury felt exultant; as if the searing pain might show him the way, and bring him home to himself, after years of divorce and exile. I could! he thought, and stood up in amazement. It's my choice! ... A silence spread over Burj, with no gunfire nearby. Burj, for all its leaping writhing ballet of death took on a silence that seemed universal. Later, the street-to-street fighting would flow back from the suburbs, into Bab Edriss; and then the AKs, the tanks would roar at one another again, routinely, in attendance of a far greater violence on its way northward. For the moment these corpses lay undisturbed, limbs askew, strewn there in the wake of an uncharted war—in the still vortex, in the silence that drowned out the guns.

XXIX

The pain made him wince. It broke in on his errant thoughts: I tried to give my life away; and to that person, *her,* like a willful child following its mother from room to room. Now I see she was right; the choices are limited... Some bastard shot me! No, it's good, I thank you: a bullet puts me in touch with myself. Sniper, you were sent to me, a messenger from reality... An alarm clock rings at last: time to wake up? time to die? Ligury's head was spinning. Strange ideas, images came flooding one after another. "I need to forget history awhile," said Dr. Kamel. "It is too devious, and heartbreaking; it is devil's work and may at last prevent one from believing in—what?"

He heard Kamel Rehanna's kindly voice, and thought: in the most violent dance many false steps are taken; no rhythm is guaranteed. *Marouf Saad is dead,* but who killed him? Who made the first massacre, in Ein Rummaneh? Who fomented this war if not the Kataëb, with its conspiring allies? Ah! you rightists, just look at you. All programmed for apocalypse, just wind me up, I'm a metronome of death. O finaglers for Freedom, trying to work out, in your benevolence, a final solution for love... I've got news for you, Mr. President, heaven is not a bunker.

Ligury took a step forward, but went to one knee, delirious... Now your big evil secret is inscribed on the horizon like a corporate ad. Now your Oedipus is exposed—blind so the rest of us might see, and conduct a species free to prosper at its own expense.

He got up and took another step forward: out from behind the dusty pillar, under the crumbling archway. Kim stood there in the frail moonlight: they invited me, he whispered to himself, in the village... He gazed across the tragic proscenium which was Burj; but remembered the doctor again, smiling, wise in his inevitable struggle, so open and questioning, affirming. He recalled Dr. Kamel and the girl, Hana'a: a tenderness that seemed to pass, with no words spoken, between them. Selman was gone now, a memory, but of the best, sustaining.

—Wait! Kim whispered, this isn't the way. (Then ducking back)—Be devious, but choose, join up, with the living!

Ligury turned, a hand to his bloody shoulder as if pledging allegiance. He stood outlined by the blond glimmer, amid delapidated stone. He was balding, burly, slightly ridiculous, like a bear despairing of honey. A stubble of beard framed Ligury's wan cheeks; but his eyes were rapturous, and trying to focus... He seemed hesitant before some drastic act, maybe his first! There were no steady lights, no voices, but only the seeping depths of smoke, gray-blue.

Now he laughed out loud, as his first reviving steps crackled over glass. This struggle of ours to survive, he confided to the ruins, it's good! It is just, as Dr. Kamel insists, to be a human being!

And Kim Ligury laughed heartily. Ha! He went stepping quickly through the bombed-out Opera House; he moved toward a band of light, and what seemed an opening:

—Ha!

Beirut—New York City
1978–1987